Erin's Children

Eileen O'Finlan

Print Isbns
Amazon Print 978-0-2286-1621-4
LSI Print 978-0-2286-1622-1
B&N Print 978-0-2286-1623-8

BWL Publishing Inc.

*Books we love to write ...
Authors around the world.*

http://bwlpublishing.ca

Copyright 2020 by Eileen O'Finlan
Cover art by Michelle Lee

D1495227

Dedication

For all immigrants, past, present, and future. You are what makes America great!

Acknowledgments

My sincere thanks go to the following:

Jude Pittman and the entire BWL Publishing, Inc. family for your guidance and support. I have learned so much about writing and publishing from you and am proud to be part of this group.

Eileen Charbonneau for her superlative editing. Eileen has been and continues to be a wonderful mentor. Eileen you always make my writing better.

Victoria Chatham who did an amazing job on the final edits.

Michelle Lee who's cover art always astounds me.

Betty Ann Harris, thanks for making me more visible on social media.

All the members of my writing group – Lee Baldarelli, Barbara Lamacchia, Pam Reponen, Cindy Shenette, Rebecca Southwick, S. M. Stevens, and Jane Willan. Extra thanks go to Cindy Shenette for taking me on a private walking tour of Worcester's historic Crown Hill neighborhood and Jane Willan for countless hours of writing together and bouncing ideas off each other.

Randy Bloom for opening his historic Crown Hill home to me for a private two-hour tour. Randy, I hope you enjoy the portrayal of your house as the Archer home in *Erin's Children*.

The staff of the Worcester Historical Museum, especially Wendy Essery, Holly Izard, and Lynn Soucy. The knowledge and helpfulness of this team was invaluable as were the resources made available to me by the museum. Thanks also to Robert Stacy, Salisbury Mansion Site Manager, for staying late to answer my questions about Worcester history after our tour of the mansion.

Lynne Zacek Bassett for her expert advice on 19th century fashions.

Everyone at Vision Advertising for helping me learn the ropes of marketing and branding. I am especially grateful to Laura DiBenedetto, Julia Becker Collins, Chris Corbett, and Chris Miller.

Father John Madden, Pastor of St. John's Church in Worcester for the copy of *To Preserve the Flame* which offered great insights into the history of St. John's.

The folks at Computer Central in Holden, Massachusetts who keep my laptop working.

My cousin, Patty Duffy, for making it possible for me to get away on a writing retreat. Without your help this book would probably still be a work in progress.

Friend and neighbor, Wendy Stafford, for all her help with everyday life stuff during some very difficult times. No one could ask for a better neighbor.

Katie Kelley for being both a beta reader and my NaNoWriMo "Stalwart Supporter." Katie, your unflagging encouragement keeps me going!

My sister, Cindy Kazanovicz (aka The Grammar, Punctuation, and Spelling Police), for proofreading.

Thanks to Lavinia the Chicken – hope you're feeling better sweetie!

As always, my greatest thanks go to my favorite research historian and one of my dearest friends ever, Tom Kelleher. Thank you, Tom, for patiently answering my many texts, emails, and phone calls (some far too late at night) about both the grand historical questions and the minutia. You continue to amaze me with the breadth of your historical knowledge!

A very special thanks to my mom, Barbara Charbonneau, who has always believed in and encouraged my writing. Thanks, Mom. You're the best!

Key for Pronunciation of Irish Names

Irish names are often pronounced differently than they appear to speakers of English. This key gives an alphabetical list of Irish characters in *Erin's Children* whose names might be unfamiliar to readers along with their pronunciations.

Aoife – Ee-fuh
Breccan – Breck-awn
Brigid - Bridge-id
Clodagh – Clō-dah
Darragh – Dar-ah
Eamon – Ay-mun
Nuala – Noo-ul-ah
Roisin – Roh-sheen
Saoirse – Seer-shah or Sur-shah
Siobhan – Shov-awn or Shoo-awn
Seamus – Shay-mus

Erin's Children also contains a few Irish words and phrases that may be unfamiliar. Here are their pronunciations and meanings:

A stór – Ah-store (treasure – used as an endearment meaning "my treasure" or "my love")
Bagarthach – Bah-gert (threatening or menacing)
Curragh – cur-uh (a light weight fishing boat)
Tigh 'n Alluis – sweat house – their use dates from the time of the ancient Celts

Part One

Chapter One

Worcester, Massachusetts 1848

"Jesus, Mary, and Joseph, do not be telling anyone you're married!"

Meg stared at Nuala, dumbfounded. "Why not?"

Nuala glanced around the crowded waiting room of the employment service. She leaned closer to Meg.

"Don't you know? All the help is single. A husband will never do."

"But that's why I came. It's why Father O'Malley married us just before I boarded the ship. So I could work and save money to bring Rory over as well as the rest of my family."

"You've got sisters, I'm supposing?" Nuala asked.

"Two," Meg answered. "Kathleen and Brigid."

"Bring them first. Does your Rory have sisters?"

Meg nodded. "Aisling and Loreena."

"They come next, after your own."

"But – "Meg began.

"Once you get a sister or two here, they'll help you with paying passage for the others so you can save more of your own money. Then you're ready to bring over yer man."

"But that could take years."

Nuala shrugged. "The men who are working are in the factories or on the railroads – making a pittance if they can get hired at all. You've seen the ads. 'No Irish Need Apply.' As a 'Bridget,'" she scrunched her nose at the derogatory term for an Irish maid, "you live with the family. You can't do that with a husband in tow. Secure your own future before bringing a husband into it."

Meg was staying at the Arcade, a large wooden structure built on the site of the old Arcade Malleable Iron Works in the eastern section of the city known as the Meadows. Its rooms were barren and squalid. The building overflowed with Irish families, every one of them poor. All she wanted was a roof over her head, enough food to keep from starving, and Rory by her side. If she had that, what difference did it make where they lived? In Ireland, they had no food, a cottage crowded with the remnants of the O'Connor and Quinn families, and no work. She'd come to America to keep them from starving. Beyond that, nothing mattered.

"I'm staying with the Lintons for now," Meg explained. "Mrs. Linton is the sister of the woman I came with. They're nice."

"As like as not, they are, but I'm saying you can do better," Nuala told her.

"The Arcade is already a site better than back home. It's grand to know there's a daily meal coming."

Nuala shook her head. "A year ago, I thought myself a lucky lass. Then I started working for Mrs. Perkins. Besides pay, I got room and board. I lived in a grander house than I ever imagined. I'd be with her still if she hadn't died. I worked hard, mind you. You'll find that out fast enough once you're hired. But you'll eat three meals a day. You'll have a room with a real bed, though it be in the attic. Granted your job will be to clean all the rooms, but still you'll live there, surrounded by luxuries. Mark my words, you won't stand the thought of going back to the Meadows after that. Your Rory won't be able to provide anything near what will be given you by your employer."

Meg could barely picture living in a home as Nuala described. She knew the hours Mr. Linton put in at the wire works. Now she realized he had little to show for it. The Lintons had children, too. Once Rory arrived, they'd have bairns soon enough. How would they feed them if Rory couldn't find work? His right hand was damaged from an accident. Would a factory hire him, being both Irish and maimed? She was staggered by the reality suddenly staring her in the face.

"Margaret O'Connor!" A woman's voice called from the doorway. Faces in the waiting room looked up.

"Is there a Margaret O'Connor here?" the voice called, irritation evident.

Hearing her maiden name, Meg was flooded with relief that she'd been a Quinn only a matter of months, mostly on a ship crossing the Atlantic. It hadn't stuck with her yet.

As she rose, Nuala grabbed her arm, pulling her back long enough to whisper, "Don't forget what I said. Keep your husband a secret."

"Do sit down. I'm Mrs. Harriet Cane," said the woman who'd called her into the room. "Let's get right to it. I've many people to see today."

Mrs. Cane's no-nonsense tone pulled Meg back to herself. She nodded.

"Well, Miss O'Connor, I see you've experience in mending, though not in keeping house."

Meg nodded again. Her heart hammered so that the blood pounded in her ears.

"You've a tongue in your head, girl?"

Meg started to nod again, then quickly blurted, "Yes, Ma'am," grateful she'd remembered Mrs. Linton's coaching to use the English 'Yes' rather than the Irish 'Aye.'

"Good. Then I'll thank you to use it."

"Yes, Ma'am."

Mrs. Cane eyed her up and down. Meg had been delighted with the plain, but clean dress Mrs. O'Sullivan's sister, Maureen Linton, loaned her for the interview. As Mrs. Cane's sharp eyes took her in, she wondered if it passed inspection.

"Do you think housekeeping is something you could learn?"

Meg didn't know. There wasn't much to it in her family's cottage in Ireland. One room, a table, and a few chairs, a cook fire with one fry pan, one cauldron, a kettle, a few utensils, and a dirt floor for bedding down hadn't called for much housekeeping. Meg, Kathleen, and their mam had taken in mending from the English ladies in town. She'd seen the back halls and kitchens of their fine houses, their maids in uniforms bustling about and knew there was much to keep them busy, but she had no idea what.

"My da always said I learn quickly," she finally answered.

"I see." Mrs. Cane pursed her lips. "Well, you'll have to do, but you'd better be as your...ahem...*da* claims. I can set you up with the Claprood family. They've never had a domestic before, so they'll have no one to compare you to. Meet me here tomorrow afternoon at one o'clock sharp. I'll take you to meet Mrs. Claprood. If she approves, you can begin right away." Mrs. Cane ushered Meg out of the office as she spoke.

Back in the waiting room, Meg headed straight for Nuala. She had many questions to ask and prayed her new acquaintance could answer them.

* * *

April 3, 1851
Worcester, Massachusetts

Three years Meg had worked for Emily Claprood. Having full access to a house with more than one room, and each room with such an assortment of furniture was daunting at first. All she'd wanted to do was wander from room to room marveling, sinking her feet into the carpets, gazing out the windows – aye, windows! – more than just the one in her cottage back home. In this house there were sometimes two or more windows in a single room! Long ones at that – nearly reaching floor to ceiling.

The Claproods must be amazingly wealthy she'd thought. Nuala set her straight.

"They're what's known as middling," she explained. "Not poor and not rich, but something in between. All of the middling sort would like to be rich, though, and so they put on airs, trying to imitate their betters as much as their

10

means allow. That's why they hire us. To show they've got money enough for a servant or two." Nuala's tone showed what she thought of their airs, but Meg's mind reeled at the idea of living in the Claproods' house and eating their food.

Nuala's prediction was correct. Once she'd gotten a taste of the Claproods' home, Meg couldn't dream of living in the squalid conditions at the Arcade.

This awareness caused her more than a modicum of guilt. Father O'Malley had put Meg together with Mrs. O'Sullivan and her daughter, Aoife, on the ship to America. The O'Sullivans had a destination planned. After their ship docked in Boston Harbor, they would take the railway to Worcester and stay with Maureen and Darien Linton. Meg supposed she'd be left in Boston to fend for herself.

"Are ye daft, lass?" Mrs. O'Sullivan exclaimed as they'd disembarked. "I made a promise to your mam afore we boarded that I'd care for you like you was my own and I mean to keep it. As you've no kin in this country, you'll come with us to my sister's."

"But she doesn't expect me. Won't she mind?"

"No. Maureen's a good heart. She'll take you in right along with us. You'll see."

Though they hadn't expected a third arrival on their doorstep, the Lintons greeted Meg as warmly as they did Mrs. O'Sullivan and Aiofe.

For her first two weeks in America, Meg lived in the Lintons' tiny rooms at the Arcade. Darien's salary from the wire works barely paid the rent. Maureen took in washing to feed their four children and with three more mouths, rations grew scarcer. Meg found live-in employment as quickly as possible to lessen the burden on these kind people.

Meg's employers supplied her with a uniform, so she returned the dress Maureen loaned her as well as sending the Lintons her first week's salary in hopes of repaying their generosity.

At first Meg felt like a queen in the Claprood home surrounded by such finery and assured of three hearty meals a day. After the starvation she'd endured, the con-

11

stant filth, disease, and death she'd left behind in her little town of Kelegeen, her good fortune seemed unreal. Often, she'd dreamt of beautiful rooms and tables laden with sumptuous food only to awaken upon the dirt floor, shivering in rags, and with a belly so empty the pain was constant. She now feared the Claproods and their fine home dissolve in the morning light.

Her reality was as confusing as it was reassuring. She rose well before dawn, dressed quickly in her dark attic room. Then she raced to load wood into the stove, a behemoth that soon became her sworn enemy. Never having laid eyes on such a contraption, she'd had to learn how to operate it. The Beast, as she'd dubbed it, seemed determined to keep the secrets of its inner workings to itself. Meg was grateful every day for the patience of Emily Claprood who taught her to use the stove and to make the dishes the family expected.

Once The Beast was fired up and coffee brewing, Meg set the table for breakfast. By the time she had the morning meal cooked, the Claprood family assembled at their places ready to be served.

Chester Claprood, co-owner of the Claprood – Pratt Iron Foundry, sat at the head with his wife, Emily, anchoring the other end. Between them were their children. There were two girls – Pamela, sixteen, Deborah, fourteen, and one son, nineteen-year-old Oliver. Meg was obliged to remain in the room throughout every meal, standing by the sideboard ready to be of service should any family member require something not immediately in front of them.

Once the family finished, Meg cleared the table, washed, dried, and put away the dishes. Alone in the kitchen, she hurried through her own breakfast. She then had to make the most of every minute to get her day's work completed before she could close down the house for the night and drop bone-weary into bed for the five hours of sleep, that usually felt like five minutes, before getting up to do it all over again.

Meg learned from Nuala how to parcel out her pay, sending so much home once a month to help her family, putting so much into the bank account Nuala helped her establish, and saving so much to spend on herself now and then. Meg balked at that at first. She had her room and board. What more did she need? She'd rather send the money to her family or put more in the bank to save for passage.

"'Tis a bad thing not to keep a bit back for your own use," Nuala had warned "You needn't spend it, but it's dangerous to be caught without a cent to your name."

Reluctantly, Meg gave in, keeping a small amount tucked into the little sack Father O'Malley gave her before leaving home. In it she'd carried all she owned. The sack contained her bedding for the ship, a cup, plate, and utensils, all a gift from her beloved parish priest, and her rosary. The only other item in it was her one prized possession, the comb Rory carved for her from a piece of driftwood. It was a sturdy thing, not so much as a single tine had snapped in all the years she'd owned it. Its beauty captivated her. Into the comb's thick wooden shaft Rory had worked a set of roses surrounding two intertwined hearts. Meg loved to trace them with her finger, to breathe in the fragrant scent of the wood, to reminisce over the moment Rory drew her away from the moondance, held it out to her, his usual self-assurance shaken as his voice cracked on the words, "I made this for you, Meg."

Meg could still see the comb lying in Rory's outstretched hand. Though only half visible in the moonlight, she sensed its beauty. She'd caressed its smooth wood, the curves and spirals his knife had deftly created.

"Ah, but it's lovely," she'd whispered.

"I'm glad you think so," he'd answered, his voice shaking just enough that Meg pulled her spellbound gaze from the comb to his face.

"I wanted to give you something special. It seemed the right thing to do at such a time."

Puzzled, Meg cocked her head to one side. "What do you mean, 'at such a time'?"

Rory kicked absently at a loose stone, ran a hand through his curly auburn hair. "Well, since now's the time I'm going to ask you to marry me, I thought –"

"Marry you?" Meg had gasped. "Are you just now asking me to marry you, Rory Quinn?" Meg's breath seemed almost to have disappeared, taking her words out to sea on the breeze.

"It appears that is what I'm doing," Rory responded. "I'd be pleased if you wouldn't leave me to wonder after your answer."

A fountain of excitement welled up in Meg. "Aye! Oh, aye, Rory! Indeed, I will marry you!"

Tears of joy pricked her eyes at that ecstatic moment seconds before Rory swept her up, whirling her in a circle.

Remembering that moment now, tears filled Meg's eyes again, but heartache and yearning mixed with remembered elation. How long ago had it been? It felt like another lifetime. Before the blight, before all the potatoes in Ireland rotted in the ground leaving cottier families like theirs destitute, starving, sickly, and in many cases, dead. That lethal hunger came before they could wed and begin a family. As the years of starvation crept on, as loved ones died and others wasted to mere shells in mind and body, it became apparent that something drastic had to be done or none of them would survive.

And so Meg sold her comb to pay the passage money for a ship to America. The comb and help from her dear friends, Father O'Malley, Doctor Martin Parker, and Mr. Breckett, the baker, gave her what she needed. After she'd set sail, she found that the package Dr. Parker thrust into her hands at the last minute contained the very comb she'd given him to sell, bless his soul.

Father O'Malley had married them the morning of her departure. Three years and an ocean lay between them, the comb her only tangible link to the life she'd left behind.

* * *

Meg climbed the stairs at the Foster Street station, grateful that her sister's train was arriving on a Thursday, the universal afternoon off for all domestics. Following Nuala's advice, Meg had bought a passage ticket for Kathleen. She'd written to Rory, explaining that Irish women had far better luck finding employment in America than Irish men and it would be best to send for Kathleen first. She could work – Meg had already procured a position for her – and together they could save more quickly for the next passage ticket.

Rory understood. He was not ready to leave yet anyway, what with being the only man to look after Meg's mother, her sister, Brigid, and his own sisters, Aisling and Loreena. Meg's father as well as both of Rory's parents and the rest of his siblings had all been victims of the Great Hunger.

I could not leave your mam and the lasses on their own, Rory wrote, *especially with Aisling and Brigid still in weakened conditions, though they do improve steadily thanks to the money you send. Loreena's the strongest. She is fourteen now, grown a bit since you last saw her. She's a blessing to your mam as she helped so with the nursing of Brigid and Aisling when they were still needing it. She's tried to put aside her hatred of sewing and let Kathleen teach her. The fancy work is beyond her, but Kathleen says she can stitch a straight seam or mend a tear as well as anyone. Now that Aisling has recovered enough to sew again, she's taken to helping for as long as her strength holds out. Your mam and Kathleen say Aisling's a talent for it like none other. Kathleen and Loreena walk into town to fetch the mending. They've new clients. Between your mam, Kathleen, Aisling, and Loreena they can make quick work of the heaviest load of mending. Your mam says Kathleen can be spared and they'll do fine.*

Rory hadn't said how Meg's mam felt about losing another daughter to America, but she could guess it was a mix of sadness and hope that formed itself into resignation.

15

Meg relied on Rory for all family news. While they were growing up, Father O'Malley had instructed the children of his parish in reading and writing in Irish, despite its being outlawed, along with their catechism. Meg and Rory were illiterate in English as her mam was in any language. Kathleen and Brendan had some schooling, too, and could write a good hand. But Brigid's studies came to an end with the blight.

At first Rory's letters were difficult to decipher. The accident that shattered his right hand forced him to use his left. His earliest correspondence had been short, consisting of cramped lettering she'd strained over. With time and practice his penmanship improved to the more legible scrawl she was now accustomed to.

A loud whistle jolted Meg from her reverie. She hurried toward the latest train's arrival. Pushing her way through the crowd, she carefully eyed each alighting passenger. Finally, a young woman in a shabby brown dress, hair caught up in a bun, and carrying a sack resembling the one Meg brought to America, stepped from the train. Her eyes searched the crowd.

"Kathleen!" Meg called. "Over here!"

Her sister caught sight of her amongst the throng. "Meg!" she cried.

Kathleen and Meg fell into each other's arms, oblivious to the jostling crowd.

Kathleen stepped back, holding Meg at arm's length. "I'd not have recognized you had you not called to me. Oh, Meg, you look grand!"

It hadn't dawned on Meg until that moment how much she must have changed. When she left Ireland, she'd been scrawny, hair dirty, scalp always itching. Her clothes were rags, her only shawl a tattered remnant. After three years of working for the Claprood's, living under their roof, eating three meals a day, she'd put on a healthy weight. Her long black hair was glossy again. Her tiny bedroom tucked under the Claproods' attic eaves even had a looking glass. She'd watched herself in that glass come back to life. Her body regained much of its strength, a good thing too, given

16

the long hours she labored. If only the bone-weariness would leave her. She knew the dark circles beneath her eyes marred her looks. At the end of each day when she finished her work a powerful wave of exhaustion engulfed her and she sometimes fell asleep atop her coverlet fully dressed.

"You look more than a mite better than last I saw you," Meg said.

Though still thin, Kathleen had put on weight. Her drawn-up hair regained some of its luster. Though exhaustion showed in the lines on her face, the sparkle in her blue eyes reminded Meg of the old days when they'd both been vibrantly engaged in the act of living, not merely surviving.

"It's the money you've been sending," Kathleen explained. "You saved us, Meg, just as you said you would. We could buy food. First enough to survive, then enough to get well. All of us are alive because of you."

Tears streamed down Kathleen's cheeks.

All Meg's work – the rising before sunup, cooking, cleaning, serving, polishing the silver until it gleamed, lugging baskets of wood for the stove that made her back ache, choking on clouds of dust from beating the rugs, the constant battle with soot from the coal burning fireplaces – all of it faded away as she watched the gratitude play across Kathleen's face. Her family was worth all of it and more.

Leaving the train station, arms around each other, they walked into the bright sunlight of downtown Worcester.

"Tell me of everyone at home." Meg heard the longing in her own voice.

"Who first?"

"Mam."

Kathleen cocked an eyebrow. "Not Rory?"

"I've got letters aplenty from Rory. I want to hear more than what he has space to write."

Kathleen smiled. "Mam is grand."

"Is she? Really? I've worried after her more than anyone."

"Aye!" Kathleen nodded. "Mam's come back to herself – commanding who'll do what and when."

17

"That's good to hear." Meg feared her mother had endured too many losses during the starving. But Deirdre O'Connor was a strong-willed woman, the strongest Meg had ever known. She believed more than ever now that nothing could defeat her mam.

"She misses you, Meg. And Brendan." A shadow of pain crossed Kathleen's face when she mentioned their brother, deported to Australia for theft. "But when she speaks of either of you, she says how much better off you are, how you're making new lives for yourselves. Doing her proud."

"Any word from Brendan?" Meg asked.

Kathleen shook her head. "Maybe they don't let convicts write home."

They didn't even know if his ship had made it to Australia or if he managed to live through his sentence of hard labor. She wondered if they'd ever know.

"How is Father O'Malley?" Meg asked.

"Well. He and Doctor Parker get on better than ever. Between the money you and others who've come to America have sent back and the work of Father O'Malley and Doctor Parker, Kelegeen's coming back to life."

An image of Meg's homeland rose in her mind – lush green pastures nestled amongst gently rolling hills beneath a blue sky and thatched roof cottages dotting the land like brown and white buttons. Homesickness engulfed her. She pushed it away with more questions.

"And our lasses? How do they fare?"

"Aisling's improved so much you'd hardly know her. She's grown taller and looks more like a woman than a lass. She tires easily, but that's the only lasting effect of her sickness. She's an amazing hand at sewing. You, Mam, and me, we're good, but Aisling is in a world of her own. I swear you could give that lass a piece of scrap cloth and in no time, she'd turn it into some fancy lady's ball gown."

"Even as a wee lass she had talent," Meg said, remembering the ten-year-old Aisling who'd loved to sew more than anything.

"Loreena's a different breed altogether," Kathleen continued.

"Aye. Rory's letters tell me," Meg said. "She and Brigid always hated sewing, but he says she's now taken it up."

"That she has. Loreena has changed most of all, I think. She was always sturdy. She withstood the Hunger better than most and recovered the quickest. She's not just a wee lass playing with the pigs anymore. She's grown tall, her hair is gold and grown to her waist. She appears older than our more delicate Aisling."

"I wonder if I'd recognize either of them," Meg said, thinking of Rory's sisters as she remembered them.

"It's not just her looks," Kathleen continued. "Loreena's got a strong-willed way about her. She's a bright lass, thinks things through, decides on something, and does it. She brooks no shenanigans from anyone." Kathleen giggled. "Most especially not from Kevin."

Meg stopped abruptly. "Kevin Dooley? What's he to do with Loreena? With any of us?" Meg felt heat rise in her chest and flame into her cheeks.

Kathleen sighed. "I thought Rory would have told you."

"Told me what?" Meg demanded.

"About the change in Kevin."

"I've heard nothing about Kevin Dooley at all. I'd prefer never to, but since he seems to have wormed his way amongst us again, I suppose I must."

"Kevin's not like he used to be."

Meg's eyes narrowed in response.

"Now, Meg," Kathleen's voice became stern. "I'm not moonstruck over that lad anymore, but it's the truth." Kathleen took a deep breath before continuing. "Not long before you left, Father O'Malley took Kevin in. He was in a bad way, if you remember. His da had run off. His mam and sisters went to the workhouse." Kathleen shuddered. "Kevin started driving a cart, carrying out the workhouse dead and burying them in the pits. The day he found his own mam and one of his sisters among the pile of corpses it about finished him. And that's when Father O'Malley took him in and began to work his magic on him."

"Magic?"

Kathleen nodded. "Folks say 'tis a miracle. Father O'Malley claims it's the grace of God working in ever mysterious ways. He had Kevin helping him around the church and spent many an hour talking with him. Later, after Doctor Parker got Kevin's sister, Liddy, out of the workhouse and settled with Dacey and Rose Kilpatrick, Father O'Malley brought Kevin to see her. Needing someone who could calm Liddy, her being so addled, the Kilpatricks took Kevin to live with them, too. They've treated Kevin and Liddy like their very own. Kevin finally got the father in Dacey he never had in his own rotten da. And you know what a good and gentle soul is Rose Kilpatrick. Well, all together it worked a wonder on the lad."

Kathleen jutted out her chin. "You'd take him for the old Kevin's long-lost saintly twin."

"Saintly?" Meg gasped.

"A powerful change has come over him. Ask Rory yourself. Mam lets him in the house. Called him a good-hearted lad once, she did."

Their mother had forbidden his name to be uttered in her presence. Meg would indeed ask Rory for an explanation in her next missive.

"And Brigid? How does she fare?" Meg's voice softened when speaking of her youngest sister.

Kathleen sighed. "'Tis sad, though Mam says we're not to think of it so."

"She's still locked within her own world?" Meg asked, her eyes filling with tears picturing her once vivacious sister.

"She's not as bad as you remember. She eats well enough now. She speaks at times, though not much. She smiles when Loreena puts a piglet in her lap. That's the one time when she seems most like her old self."

Meg remembered the young sprite whose greatest joy in life was playing with and caring for the pigs and piglets.

"But she's still silent more often than not, goes into those odd states where she seems to be in another world. She won't sew a single stitch. The very sight of the mending pile or the rest of us working at it makes her curl into a corner. It's sad to see, but what can we do? We must make our living."

Meg nodded. "Poor lass." It had been Brigid's carelessness in getting a stain on the clothing of their most inflexible customer that had cost them the mending work by which they'd earned enough to get by. The loss of customers sent the family into a devastating spiral of starvation.

"Can Loreena do nothing?" Meg asked.

"Loreena's the only one who can bring Brigid 'round when she gets into one of her states."

"It must be terrible hard on Mam."

"Mam has managed by believing that Brigid is fey. She claims the lass has inherited the 'gift,' that when she goes into those strange states, she's really gone beyond the veil and is communing with the other world. Who's to say," Kathleen shrugged. "Perhaps 'tis true."

Meg cocked an eyebrow as they continued their trek down Foster Street. "Do you believe it?" she asked.

"I don't know," Kathleen replied. "Mam has the 'sight' after all. She knows when something important is going to happen. Could be that Brigid has acquired some similar gift, could it not?"

"Possibly," Meg acquiesced. She'd seen too many of her mother's *feelings* as she called them, come to fruition to totally dismiss the idea.

"Mam says we should not feel sad," Kathleen explained. "She says Brigid's been blessed in a certain way. I don't know if that's true, but believing it brings Mam comfort, so we leave it be."

"And what about –" Meg began, but Kathleen interrupted her.

"Your turn, Meg. I'm in a strange land and you're the only soul I know. Please, tell me about this place, about the Lintons, and the family I'll be working for."

Meg felt selfish. Her sister was exhausted from travel and disoriented in a foreign land. She must help Kathleen settle into this new American life.

"Stop here," she said. She turned Kathleen to face the street. "The train station was on Foster Street, see? Now we're on Front Street. We'll keep heading east until we get to Pine Street. We are going to a section called the Meadows just beyond Washington Square. It's where the Lintons live, in a building called the Arcade. Take a good look around and mind where we've come from and where we're going."

Worcester was a city unlike any the O'Connor family knew in Ireland. There were people in all manner of dress from beggars sitting on street corners to financial barons striding purposefully to their lofty destinations. Horses and carriages mingled with pedestrians, kicking up clouds of dust from the unpaved road. Work crews dug through one section as they prepared to lay sewer pipes under Front Street. Railroad tracks scarred the streets. Buildings, larger than any back home loomed everywhere.

"What are those?" Kathleen asked, pointing to the tall structures atop many buildings spewing black into the sky.

"Smokestacks," Meg told her.

"Are they what makes it so hard to breathe?" Kathleen asked. Kathleen held the front of her shawl over her nose. After three years Meg had become accustomed to the acrid smoke.

"They are what make this city work. It's a factory town."

"Is all of Worcester like this?"

"No, just in the mill and factory sections. Up where I live and where you will live it won't be so thick. You'll only notice it if the wind blows just right."

"I will live near you?" Kathleen's voice held both excitement and trepidation.

"Aye. You'll be in a fine section of town. The house is grand, though not like the mansions on Main Street. You'll have lots to do. Busy from sunup to sundown. Our Thursday afternoons are free and Sunday mornings we have off for Mass. We go to Saint John's Church on Temple Street." Meg stopped, took her sister by the shoulders and looked directly into her eyes. "Don't be letting your employers talk you into going to their church. You're Catholic. Don't forget it."

Kathleen's brow furrowed. "How could I forget?"

"Some of these Yankees are itching to take the Catholic out of the Irish. Some refuse their help time off during Mass. 'Tis a disgrace."

Kathleen gasped. "Will my employers do that?"

"I don't think so. They're friends of the Claproods. The two gentlemen are in business together. That's how I found your position. The Pratts were in want of a maid at the time I could buy your passage. Mrs. Pratt was visiting Mrs. Claprood when she mentioned that she wanted help."

"What is she like? Mrs. Pratt, I mean."

Meg shrugged. "I only see her when she comes to call. I don't pay much mind to guests other than to take their wraps, bring their refreshments, and clean up after them when they leave."

"And they live near the Claproods?"

"Only a few streets over. But Kathleen, we'll be too busy for much visiting, except on Thursdays. And I'll come get you each Sunday to walk to church together."

They turned a corner, headed down an alley where a group of raggedly dressed children played. Grabbing Kathleen's hand, Meg maneuvered her through the horde. Together they climbed the rickety steps to a wooden door. "This is the Arcade," Meg said.

Inside and up a flight of stairs, Meg stopped and knocked at one of the many doors. Maureen Linton, opened the door, baby on her hip, smiled and bid them enter.

"Kathleen! Meg hasn't stopped talking about you since she knew you were coming," Maureen said, ushering them into the small room. She offered them each a chair and a cup of tea.

"You look weary, lass," Maureen said to Kathleen once she'd finished her tea.

"I am."

23

"Come." Maureen led Kathleen to a straw mattress in the corner of the room. "Lie down a while."

Maureen and Meg chatted while Kathleen slept. Two hours later, Meg shook Kathleen's shoulder. "I've got to get back to the Claproods before dark, but first I have a surprise for you." Then she turned to Maureen. "Ready?" she asked.

"It's perfect, Meg," she said surveying Kathleen then the calico dress draped over a chair. "You've a good eye."

"What's going on?" Kathleen asked.

"It's yours," Meg explained. "You don't want to meet the Pratts looking like you just got off the boat."

Kathleen blinked. "But I did."

Maureen handed her the dress and pointed across the room. "Go behind that curtain. There's a tub of fresh water, a rag, and a bit of soap. Scrub yourself good and dress in your sister's gift," she said.

When Kathleen returned from the curtained partition, Maureen exclaimed, "Ah, but you look a rare sight!"

"Do I?" Kathleen asked, smoothing the front of her skirt.

"I believe it will do nicely," Meg agreed.

"I've never had such a lovely dress. Is it really mine to keep?"

"Aye, but keep it clean for tomorrow. You'll sleep here tonight, and Mrs. Linton's Mary will walk you to the Pratts' home on Oxford Street tomorrow morning."

Meg hugged Kathleen. "Meg, it's been three years and I'm losing you again already."

"Not at all. I'm on Crown Street, a short walk away. Remember, I'll fetch you early Sunday morning for Mass. It's a walk but at least it's downhill. Going, that is."

Despite her smile, Meg felt the pain of sudden loss after so recently being reunited.

"Be your wonderful, sunny self tomorrow and you'll have the Pratts wondering what they ever did without you." She kissed Kathleen, then started the long trek home

Chapter Two

"I hope you're not lazy. You can't sleep all day and expect to keep a job." Kathleen peered up at Sophronia Pratt, a tall, broad-shouldered matron with a sour turn to her mouth.

A sideways peek out the kitchen window, told her it was barely past dawn.

"I'm sorry, Ma'am," she muttered.

"You must rouse yourself ahead of the family. It is your job to have our breakfast ready by the time we're up."

"Aye, Ma'am," Kathleen answered as she rolled up the straw mattress that Mrs. Pratt had given her the night before. Mrs. Pratt explained that they were preparing a section of the attic for her, but it was not yet ready. Meanwhile, she would sleep on the floor of the kitchen, storing the mattress in the cupboard.

"The word is 'yes'."

"Ma'am?"

"You said 'aye.' In this country, we say, 'yes.' You will learn to use proper English in this home."

"I'll do my best," Kathleen said.

"Let's get on with breakfast. You need to get the stove going first. I understand that you Irish girls are unfamiliar with their workings."

"'Tis true. I've never laid eyes upon such a grand contraption in all my days, though my sister, Meg, did tell me about it. She calls the one at the Claproods 'The Beast', she does," Kathleen said, marveling at the cast iron giant hulking against the wall.

"Does she indeed?"

Mrs. Pratt's features distorted into such a disapproving arrangement that Kathleen did not respond.

"I do hope *our* stove will be to *your* satisfaction," Mrs. Pratt said.

"I'm sure it will be. I'm eager to learn to use it."

"We'd best get started. Here, put this on," she said, handing an apron to Kathleen. "You should already be in uniform, but as you slept late we haven't time for you to change now. Watch closely," Mrs. Pratt said, opening the stove's heavy side door with one hand and grabbing a log from the nearby basket with the other. "Mind you, I expect you to be in uniform before you begin work every day."

"Aye, Ma'am," Kathleen whispered, suddenly wishing she could kick the rotund backside that faced her into the stove along with the wood.

Mrs. Pratt, still bent over the wood basket, twisted to face her. "What did you say, girl?"

"Oh, I meant yes, Ma'am."

"Remember."

Cooking had been something of a mystery to Kathleen in Ireland. She could boil an egg, mix up a bit of oatmeal, and on rare occasions, keep the flesh of a chicken or a fish in the fry pan over the fire until it was cooked. She'd learned a number of ways to fix potatoes. Until there were none. She'd also learned how to boil handfuls of grass, leaves, nettles, and, if they were lucky, a half-rotted turnip or two in the cauldron, pretending it to be soup. But in America, food was plentiful, the ways of preparing it complex.

When Mrs. Pratt showed her how to cook a breakfast, it was as if all her senses awakened at once. Slabs of meat sizzled in the huge cast iron fry pan, forming a pool of grease. When Kathleen moved closer to watch, the scent of the cooking pork slices overwhelmed her. She quickly wiped a speck of drool from her mouth, while thanking God that Mrs. Pratt was too intent on what she was doing to notice. Mrs. Pratt shoved the shrinking meat aside and cracked an egg, deftly dropping its contents alongside. She did this with several eggs and Kathleen watched in astonishment as the translucent substance spreading across the pan turned thick and white and the bright orange yolks stood up like the sunrise. After sprinkling the eggs with salt and pepper, Mrs. Pratt flipped them with a spatula. To Kathleen's surprise, the yolks did not break, but pushed upwards from underneath the whites as if trying to break through.

Once finished, the bacon and eggs were transferred to a creamy white platter and set on the kitchen table. Mrs. Pratt retrieved a loaf of bread from a cabinet. With a long, sharp knife she cut several slices. Kathleen was then charged with setting the dining room table with plates, utensils, and cups, each member of the family getting their own full setting. Once the family was assembled at their places, Kathleen carried in the platter of bacon and eggs, steam still rising from them.

"Stand over there." Mrs. Pratt pointed to a corner. "Be available throughout all meals to serve or fetch anything from the kitchen."

Kathleen stood silently in the corner, watching the family eat, listening to their idle chatter, while devouring the food with her eyes. Her stomach growled loudly more than once, causing the youngest child to giggle.

When the meal ended, Kathleen was told to remove the table settings, take the platter back to the kitchen, use what remained for her own breakfast, "eaten quickly, if you please," per order of Mrs. Pratt, "then wash the dishes."

Kathleen gathered up the table settings, managing to get them all back to the kitchen in two trips. Then she carried back the platter, a milk-white, oval dream come true. One egg jiggled beside stubs of cold bacon which slid around on the plate as she hurried into the kitchen.

Sitting at the table, she picked up a fork and broke into the white-topped yolk. Though nearly congealed, it still ran a bit. Kathleen devoured every bite, wiping up the liquefied parts with a slice of bread. The bacon crunched, the delectable taste of solidified fat causing her mouth to water. She barely noticed. Tears welled in her eyes. How could anything have such scent, such flavor? Could she really taste such grandeur every day? What a magical place, this America!

During her first month with the Pratts, Kathleen developed a love affair with the stove. Cooking became her favorite chore, the stove her best friend. It was a remarkable thing, an object that could render the most splendid fare.

If cooking was her joy, cleaning was her nemesis. Never before had she thought to care about such a thing as dust. Her family's one room cottage in Ireland had a dirt floor, one window, and a small hole in the roof to let smoke from the cook fire escape. Furniture was but a table, a few chairs, and a stool and that was before they had to chop them up to make a coffin for Rory's mam. Dusting was a task unknown.

Mrs. Pratt, however, had a powerful aversion to dust. She insisted that it be cleared of every surface in the house including all the trinkets on tabletops, pictures hanging on the walls, and every article one could lay eyes on. Dust became Kathleen's sworn enemy. Mrs. Pratt would run her white gloved finger over the tables, into the crevices of intricately carved furniture, even, Kathleen was appalled to learn, the mantels of the fireplaces where something worse than dust gathered - soot. What did the woman expect would congregate near a coal burning fireplace if not ashes and soot?

The floors, too, were a constant challenge. They were to be swept daily as were the stairs. Carpets were regularly taken outside, hung up and pummeled with a long handled, round-headed beater. Only after the dust burst forth in great choking clouds, could the offending carpet be allowed indoors.

There was also the washing, not only of dishes, but of clothing and bedding as well, followed by the ironing. Mrs. Pratt spoke of hiring a laundress. Kathleen sorely wished she would.

Chamber pots must be emptied and washed, silver polished until Kathleen could see her face in it. Each day of the week held its own list of duties. It was not long before she understood why Meg's letters home so often held apologies for not writing more frequently.

"Wait until the holidays," Meg told her during one of their free Thursdays. "First you'll be expected to turn the house upside down, sweeping, mopping, dusting, and, washing –"

"Don't we do all that now?" Kathleen asked.

"Aye, but not like you will when preparing for a holiday, especially the one they call Thanksgiving. God help you when November rolls around. You'll not sleep from then until January."

Kathleen's heart sank. "When will I find time to cook?"

Meg laughed. "Cook? At Thanksgiving? Why a feast the likes of which you can't imagine is the center of all the fuss."

Kathleen brightened. "Truly? What will I cook?"

"The main thing is a turkey – a right devil it is to do, too. You've to pluck and boil it first before you roast it."

"Like a chicken?" Kathleen interjected.

"Aye, like a monster of a chicken. I've seen bairns smaller than some of the birds they want gracing the center of their tables. Then there are the sweet potatoes, mashed potatoes, cranberries, apple and pumpkin pies, custards, and stewed prunes. It's a never-ending muddle of food at least three times as much of each as you'd make for an everyday meal."

Kathleen's eyes widened. "How can one family possibly eat so much?"

"Oh, but it's not just them. They bring in aunts, uncles, cousins, even grandparents if they've still got 'em. The house will be full to the rafters and you'll be expected to do for all of them as well as the rest of your work. If they've invited those who have wee ones, it's for sure they'll be underfoot making your work all the more difficult. And unless they live in Worcester, they'll stay for days or even weeks."

None of this sounded possible to Kathleen. "Ah, Meg, you're fooling me, now aren't you? There's no such thing as this Thanksgiving."

Meg sighed. "I'd not have believed it myself until I lived through the first one. You'll see. At least it's still several months off."

If it's true, Kathleen thought, it would be the price paid for the enjoyment of cooking such a tremendous meal. Best, what the Pratts and their guests did not eat would be hers to enjoy.

That night, Kathleen lay awake pondering Meg's words. How would one go about preparing all that food and having everything ready at once? She got up, lit a candle and carried it to the stove.

"Four fire holes on top," she whispered to herself. "One oven." She opened the oven door. *Is there enough room?* It didn't seem as though this one stove could manage all the food at once. Would she cook a few dishes at a time? But how to keep them warm while others were cooking? And how long would it take to cook a bird as large as Meg described? Then a thought struck her. The kitchen had a small fireplace, though it sat with the painted fire board in its center. Perhaps it was put to use at holiday time.

The next afternoon Mrs. Pratt entered the parlor where Kathleen dusted.

"Mrs. Pratt, I've a question," Kathleen began, straightening up from her work on the table legs.

"Yes?"

"My sister has told me about a holiday called Thanksgiving. Is it something you celebrate?"

Mrs. Pratt's back stiffened. "Why of course we celebrate Thanksgiving. Every good New England family does."

Kathleen smiled. "From what Meg said it sounds grand."

"I should think so. We celebrate the feast of our ancestors who brought civilization to this country. Until their arrival, this land was infested with savages."

"Savages?" Kathleen asked.

30

"Indeed. Indians. They ran amok in the country wearing next to nothing, symbols painted all over their faces and feathers in their hair. The stories I've heard, well…" a shiver passed through Mrs. Pratt. "That's nothing to speak of. The point is, our ancestors celebrated making it through their first year here by holding a great feast just after the harvest. So now we commemorate that day with our own feast."

"It must have been hard that first year," Kathleen mused. "How did they manage?"

"Well, the Indians did help," Mrs. Pratt conceded. "They showed how to plant and prepare corn, squash, and beans. I suppose other things as well." Mrs. Pratt dismissed the rest with a wave of her hand.

"I don't understand. If the Indians were such savages how did they all get on well enough to learn from them? And if they helped the immigrants why would they be thought of as frightful?"

"Immigrants?" Mrs. Pratt asked, wrinkles forming in the space between her eyebrows. "What immigrants?"

"Your ancestors. If they came to this country from another one that makes them immigrants. I learned that word from Meg. 'Tis what we are now."

Mrs. Pratt's eyes blazed. "My dear girl. You and your sister are indeed immigrants. My English ancestors, however, were settlers."

"What's the difference?" Kathleen asked.

Mrs. Pratt let go an exasperated sigh, then pulled herself up so straight it seemed to Kathleen she'd suddenly grown several inches. "The English settlers took this country from a wild, savage wasteland and made it into a Christian civilization. They did a great favor to the Indians by doing so. Had the savages adapted to our ways, listened to our teachings, and become Christians, their lives would have improved immeasurably. Instead, most clung to their ways. Sorry thing what happened, but no more than can be expected given their obstinance."

Kathleen was still confused, but she longed to know more about the cooking. "I was wondering about all the food for Thanksgiving. The stove doesn't seem big enough to handle all that Meg said would need. Will the kitchen fireplace be used as well? How is everything made ready at the same time?"

Mrs. Pratt held up her hand. "You needn't worry about it. First of all, it's months away, and secondly we go to my sister's home in Concord for Thanksgiving."

Chapter Three

Two weeks previous Meg and Nuala assisted Kathleen in opening a bank account. Now it was time to use some of that money to make herself as fine as any Yankee lady.

Kathleen, Meg realized, was much more tractable than she had been. Nuala practically had to drag her to the dry goods emporium. It wasn't until Meg saw the vivid blue silk that she'd quit complaining. The sight of it brought back a dream she'd often had during the starving time in Ireland – a dream where she was a grand lady, dressed in deep blue, standing before a table laden with food. That dream both haunted and sustained her. When the blue silk, the very color of the one in her dream, lay before her eyes it felt like a sign. Once she'd given in that far, she'd no heart to argue with Nuala over the bonnet, white gloves, and kid boots. A later trip reaped a matching cloak. She wore the ensemble now, sans the cloak, as she strode down Main Street with her sister and friend.

"You should get a fan, Meg," Nuala told her. "Ivory, perhaps. Something with blue printing to match."

"First we must outfit Kathleen." Meg said as they entered a dry goods emporium.

"Look!" Kathleen exclaimed, moving from one shelf to another, her hazel eyes growing wider with each discovery. "Imagine what Aisling could do," she said, holding up a bolt of lavender silk. "Could we send some to her, Meg?"

Aisling's growing skill with a needle was well known, but there were no patterns from which to make a dress worthy of the fabric.

"We're here for you, Kathleen," Meg instructed.

Kathleen took her time wandering the store. Finally, she settled on a yellow muslin patterned with dainty flower sprigs. She held it up. "This?"

"Perfect!" Nuala exclaimed. "The color goes well with your complexion and brings out your eyes."

"It makes your hair look even blonder," Meg noted. "Mam would approve." She turned to Nuala, "Mam always called Kathleen her Viking child."

"Now for the accessories." Nuala, all business, turned to the shelf upon which sat a row of bonnets. "Here, try this," she said handing Kathleen a cream-colored bonnet with green and yellow striped ribbons.

She put it on, holding the muslin fabric in front of her.

"Aye, then," Nuala declared. "You'll need gloves and shoes."

Once Kathleen was fitted out, Nuala insisted that Meg not leave without a fan.

"Honestly," Meg objected. "Why on earth?"

Nuala answered by picking up a white one, flipping it open to show the blue figures dancing within the folds. She held it before her face and batted her lashes.

Meg burst out laughing. "I hardly think I need a flirtation device. I am a married woman."

"Shhhh…" Nuala hushed, glancing around the store.

"What's going on?" Kathleen asked.

"Meg can't let on that she's married," Nuala whispered.

"I know about that. I mean the fan."

"A fan has a language, you see," Nuala explained. "The young Yankee ladies convey all sorts of messages by the way they hold and use their fans."

Kathleen looked to Meg.

"True," Meg confirmed. "It's ridiculous. If a person has something to say, they should say it. 'Tis why God gave us a voice." She took the fan from Nuala, snapped it shut, and replaced it on the shelf.

Kathleen sighed. "I wonder if I'll ever learn American ways."

"Here's a lesson," Nuala stated, as they left the store. "When you get back to the Pratts' keep your new clothing out of sight."

"Why?" asked Kathleen.

"Yankee ladies disapprove of us dressing like them," Meg informed her sister.

"Aye," said Nuala. "I heard a friend of my employer complaining that when she goes out on a Thursday, she's hard pressed to tell the real Yankee ladies from the Irish impostors. 'There should be a law against it,' she said."

The three young women wound their way along Main Street marveling at the opulent mansions lining the road, making the homes of their employers look humble by comparison. They had to pick their way carefully among the piles of crushed and cobble stones as workers edged them along the sides of the street. Teams of oxen pulled heavy equipment for the road crews, kicking up dust as they went.

"I wish Aiofe had come with us today." There was a sad note in Meg's voice.

"I can't understand why she went to the mill to work when she could as easily have done what we're doing," said Nuala.

"Aiofe?" asked Kathleen. "The girl you traveled to America with?"

"Aye," said Meg. "She and her mam, Mrs. O'Sullivan. Aoife's about your age. When the Lintons found a job for her mam in the Merrifield she wanted to go there, too. They tried to talk her into applying for a maid's position, but she said she couldn't think of living away from her mam."

Nuala shook her head. "Too bad. That stuffy factory."

Meg sighed. Her heart felt heavy when she thought of Aoife. A wisp of a thing she was – more like a bird than a lass with hair that might once have been a pretty light brown, now like dirty, tangled straw.

Nuala brightened. "On Sunday, after Mass," she said. "We'll ask her to walk with us. Then we can speak to her about changing jobs. It could be she's ready, but doesn't know how to go about it."

"We can try," Meg agreed. "I've been thinking of speaking to her mam to see if she's willing to persuade her."

"Why would anyone want to work in one of those places?" Kathleen mumbled as a breeze blew soot from the belching smokestacks.

"It's all some can get and better than nothing," Nuala explained. "Especially the men. They're lucky if the factories hire them. They don't like to take on Irish." Nuala brushed at the flakes of ash that clung to her blue and white striped skirt. "I'll have to give this a good cleaning," she said through gritted teeth. "As if I've time for that."

As they turned down another street, a gentleman tipped his hat to them, bringing a smile to Nuala's face. "That's why the Yankee ladies don't like us dressing this way," she told Kathleen.

"You love being mistaken for a Yankee," Meg observed, flashing a wry smile at Nuala.

"And you don't?" Nuala teased.

Meg's friendship with Nuala had made them as close as sisters. They looked enough alike that they were sometimes mistaken for siblings. Both were fair skinned with black hair, and vivid blue eyes. They differed most in size. Nuala's head came nearly even with Meg's shoulders. Meg's slender figure contrasted with Nuala's compact, solid build, appearing as though she could barrel through a brick wall. Nuala had a temper when riled and will to match. She was the first lass Meg had ever met who might be more headstrong than she herself.

Meg did not want her sister to feel left out. Kathleen, tall like Meg, but with blond hair and a softer visage, was also different in temperament. She had a quieter determination. Meg worried for her. Kathleen was no simpleton, but she was an innocent.

"I've a question," Kathleen spoke up. "You've said I should hide my new clothes from the Pratts, but where?"

"Haven't you a room of your own yet?" Nuala asked.

Kathleen shook her head. "I put my mattress in a cupboard in the morning. I suppose I could hide my finery there, but my bonnet will surely get crushed."

"And what of your attic room?" Meg asked.

"Last time I asked, Mrs. Pratt said it was too hot to be in the attic so it could wait until autumn."

"I see," said Meg.

"Is it hot in your attic room, Meg?"

"'Tis," Meg acquiesced, still rankled, her nascent suspicions of the Pratts deepening.

Chapter Four

"What are you doing, Kathleen?" Young Clara Pratt flopped into a kitchen chair, her arms flung out on the table before her.

"What does it look like *a stóre*?" Kathleen asked. Her hands were caked with flour as she kneaded a mound of soft dough.

"Mother says you're not to call me that." Clara stuck her chin in both hands. "She says you're calling me a store."

Kathleen smiled.

"She doesn't want you to speak Irish, only English and she wants you to call me Miss Clara."

"Aye, and what do you say?" Kathleen asked.

"Tell me again what it means."

"My treasure or my love," Kathleen answered. "In Irish it's a word for a beloved child."

A smile spread across Clara's face, still scrunched in the palms of her hands. "I like that."

"Me, too," Kathleen agreed. "So, Miss Clara, what are you after doing today?"

Clara shrugged. "I don't know. I'm bored."

"I can see that." Kathleen had grown fond of the twelve-year-old, the only daughter in the Pratt family. The two others were boys, Lemuel age eighteen, and Harvey, sixteen. Kathleen thought it a terrible burden for a lass to have no sisters. No wonder the poor child hardly knew what to do with herself.

"May I watch you?" Clara asked.

"Aye. Unless your mother –"

"Oh, she won't care." Clara's face brightened. She bolted upright in her chair. "Would you teach me to cook?"

Kathleen laughed. "I barely know how myself! I'm still learning from your mother. Sure it is she's taught you some cooking by now?"

"Some," Clara agreed. "But I want to learn more. Perhaps we can learn together. Wouldn't you like that?"

"I would, if your mother will allow it. Why don't you ask her?"

Clara thought a moment. "What if she says 'no'?"

"Well, it seems a mite more efficient to teach us both together and we know how much your mother prizes efficiency."

"That's true," Clara allowed, "but I'd like it better if it were just the two of us."

Kathleen watched as Clara's face took on a serious cast. "What deviltry are you up to, lass?"

Clara gave Kathleen a sly smile as she rose from the chair and went to the cupboard.

"Here," she announced. "We'll use this."

Clara laid a worn book on the table before her.

"What's this?" Kathleen asked.

"A book of receipts by Mrs. Lydia Maria Child. Mother uses it all the time. Hasn't she shown it to you?"

Kathleen shook her head.

"Which of the receipt books do you like best?"

"I don't use any books," Kathleen said.

"Why not? You could learn much more quickly than by waiting for mother to show you every step and trying to remember."

"Lass," Kathleen sighed. "I can't read English."

Clara's eyes widened. "Oh!" she said. "Goodness. I hadn't thought of that."

Clara picked up the book, carefully flipping its pages. "Here's one of my favorites," she said, "a receipt for rhubarb pie. And we've rhubarb aplenty." She sighed wistfully.

"I wish I could make it for you, *a stóre*," Kathleen said.

"What if I read the receipt aloud?"

39

"Read it to me now," Kathleen instructed. "That way I'll know if we've got all we need and how long it will take."

Clara resumed her seat across the table, read the receipt, then lifted her head. "What do you think, Kathleen? Might we make it today?"

In truth she didn't have time, but Clara looked so earnest she hadn't the heart to disappoint her.

"Are you willing to gather rhubarb, strip it, and cut the stalks into small bits as the receipt says?"

Clara jumped from her chair. "I'll start now," she said racing past Kathleen, grabbing a garden knife on her way to the side door.

"Child! Apron!" Kathleen called.

Clara spun around, grabbed an apron from a hook and set off.

Before long, Clara returned to the kitchen smeared with dirt, hair hanging lank where it had come loose from its ribbons, sweat gleaming on her face and neck, making damp spots on her dress, her arms loaded with rhubarb.

"Do you think this is enough?" she asked Kathleen. "I can cut more."

"'Tis more than enough. Put them down and wash them, else you'll have a rhubarb and dirt pie."

Clara unburdened herself of her precious bundle.

"Aye, you're a sight. Saints preserve us if your mam were to see you. Thank heaven it's her day to go visiting. She could be back at any time, though, so you'd better wash yourself before you tend to the rhubarb. Quick now! And fix up your hair, too."

"What if there isn't enough water left for washing the rhubarb?"

"We'll worry about that later. You might even put on a different dress and do change that apron."

Clara looked down at herself. "I'll change the apron, but my dress isn't dirty."

"No, but it is sweaty."

"Mother knows how hot it is. I want to get right to fixing the pie."

Kathleen sighed, wiping sweat from her forehead. "Are summers here always this hot?"

"Not usually this early. It's only June. Father says we're having an early summer. It could change, though," Clara explained as she washed from a bucket near the doorway. "Our weather is awfully mixed up in New England. You never know what we'll get. Tomorrow could be cold enough to freeze a Russian, then change again the next day." Pride in her fickle homeland rang through Clara's voice.

"Sounds a mite odd," said Kathleen.

Clara finished washing and retrieved another apron from the closet hook. She slopped clean water into the basin and scrubbed the dirt from the rhubarb stalks.

"The receipt said we need to boil these once they're cut and stripped," Clara said, peering into the water barrel. "Will we have enough?"

Kathleen checked the barrel. She'd been dipping the ladle into the cool water to quench her thirst all day. "Enough for the rhubarb, aye, but not enough for washing tonight's dishes," she said, wondering how she'd fit in another trip to the city pump.

"What are you making?" a male voice asked. They looked up to see Harvey, the second of the Pratt children, entering the kitchen.

"Rhubarb pie and I'm helping," Clara told him proudly.

Harvey's eyes widened. "I love rhubarb pie."

"Master Harvey, we're running short on water. Would you be so kind as to fetch more for us?" asked Kathleen.

"Lug water in this heat, Bridget?" Harvey asked, his tone light. Harvey, Kathleen had observed, had a penchant for teasing. "Positively cruel of you to ask!" He winked at his little sister.

Clara giggled then asked, "Why do you call Kathleen 'Bridget'?"

"All the Irish help are called Bridget."

"But her name is Kathleen."

41

Harvey shrugged, but gave Kathleen a smile as he headed for the water bucket.

"Aye, but you're a grand lad for helping, Master Harvey," said Kathleen. "There will be an extra-large slice of pie for you tonight."

Once Harvey left the kitchen, Clara asked, "Don't you mind that Harvey and Lemuel call you 'Bridget'?"

"Not so much. 'Tis my sister's name, after all," Kathleen answered. "Though you pronounce it a wee bit different."

"I thought your sister's name was Meg."

"I've another back in Ireland." Kathleen pictured her younger sister sitting by the hearth, a piglet in her lap.

"Do the Claproods call Meg 'Bridget' too?" Clara asked.

Kathleen gave a hearty laugh. "They did once, so she told me. But only once."

"What happened?" Clara looked up from her chopping.

"It was during her first week working for them. Their son, Oliver, said 'Bridget, fetch me a drink of water.' Meg remembered her friend Nuala telling her that they call all the Irish servants 'Bridget.' So she rounded on him and said, 'my name is Margaret Mary O'Connor. You may call me Margaret and nothing else.'"

Wide eyed, Clara asked, "Is that really true?"

"Well, I wasn't there, but I know my sister. I believe every word. And no one in that family has called her ought but Margaret since."

Clara grinned. "I like that story." Clara sat pensive for a moment, then asked, "Kathleen, what is it like to have sisters?"

"Oh, 'tis grand. I can't imagine not having my sisters. That's not to say we get along all the time, but on the whole, 'tis a blessing."

"Tell me about them, please?" Clara asked as she continued peeling and chopping stalk after stalk of rhubarb.

"Well, there's Meg, of course. She's older than me. Meg's like a rock in our family. She knows what she wants and always finds a way to get it. She's the one who thought up the idea of coming to America and sending back money so we could eat. Then, when she was able, she bought my passage ticket. Can you imagine a young lass like her getting on a ship and sailing across the sea to a place she'd never been, where she'd no idea what to expect or how to go about anything? But she did it. And now look. She found work right away, our family was able to eat enough to survive, she brought me here, and before you know it…" Kathleen caught herself before saying Meg would have Rory here with her.

"What?" Clara asked.

"Another family member will come here, I suppose," she mumbled.

"Who will it be? Your other sister?"

Kathleen sighed. "Brigid isn't well enough to make the voyage."

"She's ill?"

Kathleen pictured Brigid sitting mute by the cabin's peat fire, lost in another world. "Aye."

"What's she like?"

"She's a year older than you. And she's a darlin' lass." A giggle escaped Kathleen. "She hates sewing, but oh my does she love taking care of the pigs."

"Which do you like better, being an older or a young sister?"

"Ah, now that's hard to say. Meg and I are closer in age. We share secrets. Talk of things only girls our age would. Now with Brigid, it's different. I feel more a second mother to her. She'd come to me with her troubles. It would often be me she'd curl up next to when she had a nightmare. I can't choose which is better."

"You are so fortunate," Clara said, looking wistfully at her.

Kathleen smiled as she rolled out the dough for the pie. "Aye. The good Lord blessed me."

"What about brothers?" Clara continued. "Have you any of those?" Her tone was far less envious.

"One. His name is Brendan. He's younger than me, but not by much."

43

"Does he tease and scold you like Harvey and Lemuel do to me?"

"As the only lad in a family of lasses? He was smart enough not to bother us." Kathleen laughed.

"Do you think Meg will bring him over?"

The smile dwindled from Kathleen's face. "He's not in Ireland anymore." Her voice grew soft.

"Is he already in America?"

"No. Australia."

Clara was silent for a moment. "Isn't that where convicts are sent?" she asked, a timid note in her voice.

Kathleen nodded, keeping her eyes focused on the dough.

"What did he do?"

"Nothing!" Kathleen snapped. Her tone was sharper than she meant it to be and it startled Clara. "I'm sorry, lass. His conviction was unjust. It makes my blood boil to think of it."

"What happened?" Clara asked.

"He was arrested along with a group of older lads who were stealing sheep. He wasn't part of it. They didn't even know he was following them. He just wanted to see what they did. But he was thought to be amongst them when they were caught."

"Didn't he explain that to the judge?"

Kathleen snorted. "'Aye, for all the good it did him. The judge wasn't about to trust the word of an Irish lad even when the ones doing the stealing admitted he wasn't one of them. So off to Australia he went. Alone and only fifteen years old, at that."

"Fifteen?" Clara gasped. "That's even younger than Harvey. Can he ever return?"

"They gave him ten years of hard labor. I suppose he could come back when his time's up. Lord knows my mam is praying for it. But maybe it would be better for him to stay. There's not much to come back to in Ireland."

"Do you think you'll ever see him again?"

The pace of Kathleen's rolling pin slowed, her hands hardly touching the handles. Faces of so many she feared she would never see again – her mam, Brigid, Rory's sisters, her many friends and neighbors – swam before her eyes. Then there were those taken forever by the Hunger or its allies disease and accidents, her da, Rory's parents, and all the rest of his siblings. Without hearing the chair move or the footsteps come towards her, Kathleen realized that childish arms had wrapped around her waist and a face rested against her side.

"I'm so sorry, Kathleen. I just wanted to know about your family. I didn't mean to make you cry."

Kathleen hadn't felt the tears until now. She hugged the child close and whispered. "'Tis all right, *a stór*. It's not your fault. We all have our sorrows." She held Clara at arm's length, wiped her face with her apron and said, "We'd best get back to work. This pie won't bake itself."

Just as they began to simmer the rhubarb stalks on the stove, the kitchen door opened. Harvey and Lemuel entered, each with large buckets of water from the city pump.

"Look who I found on the way," Harvey announced, jutting his head toward his older brother. "It took a bit of doing, but I talked him into fetching more water." Harvey wore a self-satisfied expression.

Lemuel gave Kathleen a look that made her wish she were invisible. "Is it true you're offering extra pie for the water, Bridget?" He brushed up against Kathleen as he passed her. "I'd be mighty happy to sample an extra taste," he whispered.

Kathleen shuddered. Lemuel had unnerved her from the day they'd met. Harvey could be annoying at times, but she'd never felt threatened by him. The air about Lemuel exuded dominance and danger.

"You may have an extra bit of the rhubarb pie, Master Lemuel. I thank you for helping replenish the water." Her words were crisp, clipped.

"Why thank you, Your Highness," he said, bowing with a flourish.

"Go away, both of you," Clara ordered. "Can't you see we're busy?"

"I think I'll stay a while and watch," Harvey said, dropping into a kitchen chair.

"Fancy doing the work of kitchen wenches?" Lemuel teased.

"Nah," Harvey snorted. "But I do enjoy the results."

"Out! Now!" Clara screeched, stamping her foot.

Both boys laughed. Kathleen kept her head low, intent on the simmering rhubarb stalks.

"Come on, Harvey. Let's leave the women folk to their tasks." Lemuel grabbed his brother by the arm and hauled him up.

Relief flowed through Kathleen as the kitchen door swung shut behind them.

Kathleen took up her post in the corner of the dining room while the Pratt family consumed their meal. Clara struggled to maintain the proper decorum Mrs. Pratt expected at the family table. She had a grin on her face and a twinkle in her eyes as she scooped her dinner into her mouth, occasionally rocking from side to side.

"My dear, Clara," Mrs. Pratt admonished. "Please remember your manners and stop fidgeting."

"I'm sorry, Mother," she said, glancing at Kathleen and giving her a wink.

Good thing Mrs. Pratt didn't see that, thought Kathleen.

When the meal ended, Kathleen cleared the dinner plates. While she was in the kitchen she heard Mrs. Pratt's voice.

"What ails you, child? You haven't been able to sit still for one minute. Are you not well?"

"I'm very well, Mother," Clara answered. "I have a surprise for you."

"Cooked up something special this afternoon," Harvey interjected.

"Harvey!" Clara exclaimed. "It's my surprise."

Kathleen entered the dining room, setting the pie down on the sideboard next to the stack of dessert plates.

"It's a rhubarb pie and I helped bake it!" Clara's voice rose in excitement.

Mrs. Pratt stared at her wide eyed.

"That's the surprise, Mother," she explained, taking her tone to a more acceptable level. "We haven't had rhubarb pie in ever so long so I asked Kathleen to make it. I found Mrs. Child's receipt book and we did it together."

Mrs. Pratt stared at Clara, then at Kathleen, seemingly at a loss for words.

"Rhubarb pie. Why, I haven't had that in a coon's age." The deep voice came from the end of the table opposite Mrs. Pratt. Arthur, her husband, looked up at Kathleen, his mutton chop sideburns puffing out as he smiled broadly. "I've almost forgotten what it tastes like."

"May I slice a piece for you, sir?" Kathleen asked.

"Ladies, first," he answered, nodding towards his wife.

"Of course," said Kathleen. "A slice, Ma'am?"

"I suppose," she answered, smoothing the tablecloth before her.

Kathleen placed the dessert plate with the perfectly sliced piece of pie before her employer. She then served Mr. Pratt, followed by Lemuel and Harvey, to whom she kept her promise by making their slices larger than the others. Lastly, she placed a plate before Clara.

Kathleen awaited their reactions. Though the pie looked pretty enough and Clara had assured her it smelled heavenly, she'd never tasted rhubarb before and had no idea if what they'd created had turned out well or not.

"Now this," Mr. Pratt said after swallowing his first forkful, "is the best rhubarb pie I've ever tasted. You two ladies have done a remarkable job. Don't you agree, my dear?"

"It is very good, indeed," said Mrs. Pratt. "You've done well, Clara," she added.

Kathleen's heart soared as Clara beamed.

"Well, Harvey?" asked Clara. "What do you think?"

"First-rate!" he exclaimed. "What's your opinion, Lemuel?"

Lemuel, slowly finished the bite of pie in his mouth before commenting. He lowered his fork and leaned toward Clara. "Acceptable for a first try."

"Oh, come on, old boy," Harvey said. "Don't be such a prig."

"That's quite enough, gentlemen," Mrs. Pratt interjected. "It's just a pie. It hardly requires such extravagant commentary and name calling."

Once all had left the table, Kathleen cleared the plates, her stomach growling. She quickly made her own dinner from what remained in the serving dishes.

Finally, she sank her fork into the last wedge of pie, eager to try it. Before she could raise the fork to her mouth, Mrs. Pratt entered the kitchen.

Sighing heavily, the woman said, "My dear girl, one does not eat directly from the serving dish. It is terribly poor manners. We do not lack for plates in this house, so I would appreciate it greatly if you would make use of them."

"Yes, Ma'am," Kathleen answered. In her mind it made little sense to give herself yet another dish to wash when there was only one piece of pie left and no one in the kitchen to care from what she ate it, but by now she knew better than to question Mrs. Pratt's rules of etiquette, that being one of many new words she'd learned since she'd begun working for them.

"I had a talk with Clara," Mrs. Pratt continued. "She told of your afternoon. She was quite taken with the idea of the two of you learning to cook and bake together."

Kathleen swallowed hard, expecting a reprimand.

"Frankly, I am pleased at the idea. It's high time Clara went beyond the rudiments of cookery and you, of course, still need much tutelage in the art. However, I am overwhelmed by many social engagements." A look of smugness crept across her face. "I haven't time to oversee the training of both of you. Therefore, I believe the system the two of you have begun – Clara reading the receipts and working together to prepare meals – is a good one. You may continue."

Kathleen felt her body relax. "Thank you, Ma'am. I think we will both enjoy it. She's a darlin' lass – I mean girl, and –"

"I have not finished." Mrs. Pratt held up her hand. "Before this goes any further, you must understand some important rules."

Kathleen nodded.

"First, you will remember that you are the servant. You may be older, but you are not Clara's equal. You will call her 'Miss Clara' and not that awful 'store' name you've bestowed upon her."

Kathleen lowered her eyes.

"Secondly, I am deeply concerned that Clara not pick up any of your Irishisms." Mrs. Pratt's tone rose in volume as she continued. "You will make a concerted effort to remove the words 'aye', 'lass', ''tis', and any other utterances that are clearly not of English origin."

Kathleen felt her cheeks burn. She knew Mrs. Pratt did not approve of the way she spoke. She truly tried not to use the words that seemed so offensive to her employer, but they often slid out of her mouth before she realized it.

Mrs. Pratt continued, "Clara knows proper etiquette. Perhaps not fluently, but enough to be your tutor. You will learn acceptable behavior and manners from her. If ever any of your slovenly Irish ways begin to rub off on Clara, this experiment will come to an end. Is that perfectly clear?"

Kathleen felt anger rise, but only uttered, "Yes, Ma'am."

"Lastly and most importantly you will not ever, under any circumstances, discuss with my daughter the falsities of your Papist religion. That would be an egregious offense for which I will have no tolerance whatsoever." Mrs. Pratt's eyes bored through Kathleen, seeming to momentarily hold a flicker of hate. "Do you understand?" she asked.

"Yes, Ma'am," Kathleen whispered, struggling to keep her voice from shaking.

"Excellent. Then I hope this arrangement will be a great success for you both. Now then, I will let you get on with your work." Mrs. Pratt beamed in an almost friendly manner as though she hadn't heaped one insult after another upon Kathleen's head.

Kathleen dropped into the chair as Mrs. Pratt strode regally from the kitchen. She stared at the table. The sight of the pie now turned her stomach.

Chapter Five

"Come, Aoife. Let's take a different route today," Nuala said, tugging her arm as they descended the steps of Saint John's Church.

Aoife glanced at her mam.

"Aye, go. You should be spending more time with lasses your own age," Mrs. O'Sullivan urged before heading back to the Arcade with the Lintons.

"Where are we going?" Aoife asked as they reached the steep hill of Chatham Street.

"Crown Hill," Meg answered.

"Why?"

"There's nothing says you can't take a stroll on a Sunday," Nuala answered. "'Tis a lovely neighborhood. You'll enjoy it."

"Besides we don't get to see you except in church," Meg added.

"Tell us about your work." Kathleen said.

"I sew. Like my mam."

"Do you like it?" Nuala asked.

"They have machines that help the sewing go faster."

"What a marvel!" Kathleen exclaimed. "Meg, can you imagine? What would Aisling make of it?"

Irritated by the heat already causing her to sweat though it was still early in the morning, Meg glowered at Kathleen's enthusiasm. Making Aoife's job sound exciting was hardly what they'd had in mind.

Kathleen, oblivious to Meg's disapproval, continued. "What do you make?"

"We stitch the leather for boots and shoes."

"That's all?" Nuala asked. "Over and over?"

Aoife shrugged. "'Tis a job. I get paid. Mam and I have a roof over our heads, and we can buy our food."

"Wouldn't you like a little finery?" asked Meg, sweeping her hand across her skirt.

"For what?" Aoife asked. "I've no occasion for it."

"If you had a better job, you wouldn't have to live at the Arcade," Nuala ventured.

"I don't mind it much."

They continued to trudge the steep dirt roads leading into the Crown Hill section. As they went, the houses grew larger, more expensive. Construction was everywhere with new homes in various stages of completion all over the neighborhood. Cresting the hill, they reached their own neighborhood, or rather, that of their employers.

"Look," Nuala said, pointing out several new homes. "You could live in one of those."

Aoife stopped, staring at the temple-like structures with their columned porches and long windows. "They are lovely," she sighed.

"You'd be closer to us and we could spend more time together," said Kathleen.

"You'd eat better too," Meg added, noting how little weight Aoife had gained since arriving in America.

As they turned down Oxford Street, Nuala pointed. "That's where I live. And down the other end is Kathleen's place."

Aoife looked at the houses, then at Nuala. "You *work* there. Work hard, too, I'm thinking. You don't even have a full day off on Sunday. You've to go back to work before much longer, don't you?"

"That's true," Meg agreed. "But we do have every Thursday afternoon until Friday morning off. We don't pay rent and our food is free. It allows us to save money to send home to our families or purchase passage to bring someone over."

Aoife stared at the ground. "There's none of mine left in Ireland."

"Then you could save it for yourself and your mam," Nuala offered.

"Aoifa, you could do so much better," Kathleen urged.

Aoifa looked wistfully at the burgeoning neighborhood. "I could not live in such splendor and leave my mam at the Arcade. I daresay no one would let me bring her with me." She shook her head. "I will stay where I am and make the best of it."

"Can't your mam get a job as a maid?" Kathleen asked.

"Mam finds it hard to be on her feet. It's how the starving affected her. She's no strength in her legs. They ache something awful. At least she can sit at the sewing machine."

"So, that's it then?" Nuala asked. "A life not much better than what you came from? Is that what your mam wants for you?"

"No. She's always saying to find a job like yours, but I couldn't bring myself to leave her alone in a place like the Arcade."

"She'd have the Lintons and Mrs. Linton is her sister. They'd look after her, wouldn't they?" Meg asked.

"Of course, they would, but I'd feel guilty."

Nuala let out a sigh of exasperation.

"Well, that's not to say I'm without a plan," Aoife stated, her voice taking on a defensive tone.

"A plan?" Kathleen asked.

Aoife's face brightened. "There's a nice lad who lives a few doors down in the Arcade. His name's Ned MacBrody. I believe he's taken a fancy to me. I'm hoping we marry someday. We'll put our earnings together along with mam's and maybe find a better place."

"Where does this lad of yours work?" Nuala questioned.

"He's not got a job right now. So many places won't hire Irish. He'll get one, though, I'm sure of it. Then things will change. See if they don't."

The three glanced at each other.

"Aoife," Meg began, gently. "You can't count on that. Maybe he'll find work, maybe not. If he does, it won't be anything that pays much. Once you marry, you won't be able to work anymore. You know the Church is against it and most places won't hire married women. Too soon you'll be swelling up with your first babe and all the ones to follow after. With your husband maybe working, maybe not, and having more and more mouths to feed you'll end up in a worse condition than you're in now." As Meg described Aoife's likely future, she couldn't help but think of what would happen to her once Rory arrived.

"Would you like to see inside?" Nuala asked, indicating the home of the Dentons, where she lived.

"Would that be allowed?"

Nuala shrugged. "They're an old couple. Children all grown and gone. The Dentons aren't ones to mind me having a few friends over when I'm not working. Besides, they aren't home. They spend nearly all of Sunday at church."

They followed the brick walkway to the door in the back where the house turned a corner, making an ell. Nuala slipped her key in the lock letting them into the kitchen.

"Two stoves!" Kathleen exclaimed the moment she stepped through the door.

"Aye. Aren't I the lucky one?" Nuala said, rolling her eyes.

"I should say!" Kathleen marveled.

"Show Aoife the parlor," Meg suggested.

Nuala led them down a hall to a doorway opening into a large room. Aoife gasped. An upholstered sofa and several matching chairs in the center surrounded two round tables. The grouping sat before a marble fireplace, a large looking glass hanging above it. Next to the fireplace was a square ottoman with upholstery that matched the sofa and chairs. Next to that, tucked into a corner that seemed made for it, was a pianoforte. A chandelier with four frosted hurricane lamps and long shards of sparkling crystal hanging from the bottom dominated the room despite being off center in relation to the furniture. At the far side open pocket doors led to another room with a matching fireplace and chandelier. That room featured a large desk, a wide oval table, and a huge chest of drawers along with a sofa and set of chairs identical to those in the first parlor.

"Why would anyone need two parlors? And all these chairs?" Aoife questioned.

"Company," Nuala said. "Gatherings, parties, receiving of visitors. Whether they *need* all this or not," Nuala spread her arms wide, "doesn't matter."

"Aye," Meg agreed. "All the houses have room after room and enough furniture for an entire clan."

"It's glad I am of it, too," Nuala stated. "If it weren't so, I'd not have this job."

"What do you do here?" Aoife asked.

"Keep everything tidy." Nuala shrugged as if it were a trifling task. "And make the meals."

"But everything looks perfect."

"Thank you, kindly," Nuala said. "I'll take that as a compliment seeing as it's my work that keeps it that way. Now," she said, plopping down on the sofa and indicating for the others to join her, "wouldn't you like to live in a place like this?"

Meg sat next to Nuala and Kathleen pulled up one of the chairs, but Aoife remained standing.

"Make yourself comfortable, Aoife," Nuala told her. "Try that one." She pointed to a chair next to Kathleen's.

"I'm afraid. My clothes. They're not so clean as yours."

Nuala stood. "Look around the rest of the house, then."

"No. Please. Let's go." Aoife sounded frightened.

"What's wrong?" Kathleen asked.

"What if they come back and find us? Would they not have me arrested?"

Meg looked at Nuala. "Overwhelming our Aoife," she said softly.

"Aye," Nuala agreed. "Come. I'll show you out."

Once on the street, Aoife looked around. "I don't know how to get back."

They stood at the crest of one of Worcester's many hills overlooking the heart of the city. From their vantage point, the center appeared to lay in a deep valley. "That way," Nuala pointed.

"It's not as far as it looks," Meg said, noticing Aoife's concern.

"I'll walk you back," Nuala said. She glanced at the sky. "I've just enough time to take you home and get back before the day's work starts."

Meg turned to Kathleen as Nuala and Aoife set off. "We've still got a bit of time. Let's go to the Claproods. You've never been inside and I want to show you my room."

When they entered through the kitchen door, Kathleen gasped.

"What?" Meg asked.

"That!" Kathleen said, pointing to a stove twice the size of the Pratts'. "And that!" she exclaimed, turning towards a large cupboard with cooking implements behind the glass doors of its uppermost compartments. Beneath those doors was a large marble counter with drawers below it.

"Oh, Meg, you are blessed! I wish I had such wonders."

Meg crinkled her brow. "You're welcome to them."

"How can you say that? This kitchen is a dream come true."

"None of my dreams. What makes you so charmed by stoves and cupboards?"

Kathleen's hands flashed out at all the kitchen's apparatus. "They help us prepare meals we could never have dreamed of!"

Meg smiled at her sister's ecstasy. "Perhaps one day you'll be a cook in one of the mansions, a big step up."

"Do such jobs exist?"

"Aye, they do. The truly wealthy families have several servants, the cook being near the top."

Kathleen sighed. "That would be grand, indeed. I've a lot to learn, though. I wish I had equipment like this."

"You do have a lot to learn and not about cooking only. Let's climb up to my quarters." Meg said, her no-nonsense older sister tone taking over.

"Saints, but it's hot in here," Kathleen complained, entering Meg's attic room.

"And private." Meg opened the lone window to let in the morning breeze. In the three years she'd been in America, Meg did not remember a summer so hot as this one.

Kathleen flopped onto Meg's bed. Meg sat beside her.

"Why did we have to come up here to talk? No one's home."

"I wanted you to see my room." Meg regretted not opening her window early in the morning once the rain stopped. She'd wanted to impress on Kathleen the importance of having a private place of her own. The stifling heat would not help make her case.

Kathleen looked around the small space. "It's nice," she said, halfheartedly.

"No it isn't," Meg countered. "The roof angles down so that there's only a small amount of space to stand up straight and it's hot as a *tigh 'n alluis*."

"I see that."

"The point is," Meg continued, "it's mine. No one else comes in unless I invite them. After I finish working, I come here to be by myself. I write letters to Rory and read the ones he's sent to me. It's not fine like the family's bed chambers, but it's a place I can be alone."

"Mr. Claprood owns the whole house, Meg, including the attic. Any of them can come in whenever they've a mind to."

"Aye, but they don't. I doubt they would."

"I'd not blame them," Kathleen muttered, wiping the sweat from her forehead.

Meg grimaced. "You're still sleeping in the Pratt's kitchen."

"What of it?"

"You should have a space of your own. They promised to fix up an attic room when you first arrived in April."

"If it feels like this, I'm grateful they haven't. I like the kitchen."

"Fine," Meg conceded, "but I worry if they don't keep their word to you on one thing they may not on others. You haven't been here long so you don't know how things work. Irish servants have the upper hand. You must make it work for you."

"How so?"

"All these middling Yankees are desperate to have a servant. It makes them feel like they're moving towards being on the same ground as those rich Yanks on Main Street. There's plenty of us coming in, but still not enough that they've got their pick. The truth is, 'tis us that's got our pick of them. They just don't want you to know it." Meg leaned towards her sister as she warmed to her subject. "I was lucky. I got a good family on my first try. Mrs. Claprood is kind and even does some of the work herself. She makes her daughters help, too. She thinks it's important for them to know how a house should be run."

"I don't think Mrs. Pratt cares about that. She's more interested in making her calls than teaching Clara to run a household."

"Mrs. Pratt is ambitious for a higher station," Meg stated. "She probably thinks that because her husband half owns that foundry they'll be rich one day. She wants to be ready for it."

"Why should that matter to me?"

"It means she's selfish. I hope you don't ever want a room for yourself or a better stove, or a raise in your pay. If it's not to her benefit, you won't get it."

"You could be right. She's talked of hiring a laundress since I started, but nothing's come of it. I wish she would as that's a task I dread. But otherwise, I don't care much what she sets her mind to. I do my job. I get paid. I eat whatever's left over –"

"What do you mean?" Meg asked, cutting her off.

"After each meal, whatever hasn't been eaten by the family is mine."

"Their leftover scraps?" Anger ripped through Meg's chest like fire.

"Isn't that how it works?"

"I eat after the family is finished, aye, but I have my own food, not their leavings. I'm not the family dog and neither are you!"

"There's never been a time when there wasn't something left for me." A plaintive note quivered in Kathleen's voice.

"What happens on the day they don't leave anything? Are you supposed to go without?"

"I don't want to complain or make demands. I just got here. I'm doing well enough. I need to leave it be the way it is for now."

"You sound like Aoife."

Now Kathleen looked indignant. "Am I sitting at a sewing machine stitching boot leather all day and going home to the Arcade?"

She'd pushed too far. Meg put a consoling hand on her sister's shoulder. "There are things you need to watch out for."

"Like what?"

"At Nuala's first job the people she worked for wanted her to become a Protestant. They wouldn't give her any time off on a Sunday morning unless she used it to go to their church. She refused. Got up well before dawn every Sunday so she could walk to Saint John's for the six o'clock Mass and be back before the family was up. She had to sleep the whole time they were at church or she wouldn't make it through her workday."

Kathleen shook her head. "Mrs. Pratt forbid me to speak a word to Miss Clara about my faith."

Meg thought a moment. "Do the Pratts speak often of their own religion?"

"Mrs. Pratt seems the most religious of them. She teaches Clara. I suppose she taught it to her sons as well, though I don't see much that's religious about them."

"Do the Pratt gentlemen bother you?" Meg asked.

Kathleen's fingers toyed with the coverlet. "Mr. Pratt's rarely home. He's kindly enough when I do see him. Harvey can be bothersome, but he means no harm."

Kathleen didn't continue. "And Lemuel?" Meg prompted.

Kathleen bent close to Meg whispering as though she feared the walls would hear. "I don't like him, Meg. He scares me."

Meg froze, immediately afraid for Kathleen. "What's he done?"

"Nothing, really. It's the way he looks at me. He comes too close. And it's not what he says, but the way he says it. It feels..." Kathleen searched for the right word. "*Bagarthach.*"

Menacing.

"Stay away from him as much as you can," Meg instructed.

A noise from below caught their attention, announcing the Claproods return home.

"I'd better go," Kathleen said. "The Pratts will be back from church, too. They'll not like it if I'm late."

The sisters scurried down the back staircase to the kitchen door. Just before Kathleen left, Meg grabbed her arm. "From now on," she said, "when you cook a meal make a little extra and hold it back. Mrs. Pratt needn't know. That way it's sure you'll get enough to eat."

Kathleen smiled and nodded. "Aye," she said, racing out the door.

Meg rubbed her arms as she watched her sister hurry away. Lemuel Pratt was thick with the Claproods' son, Oliver. Both stood to inherit their fathers' share of the Claprood-Pratt Iron Foundry. They'd recently begun to learn the business. Lemuel had been in the Claprood home on numerous occasions. Though he'd paid no mind to her, Meg never liked him. She prayed Kathleen would be able to keep her distance.

Chapter Six

"When does the heat end?" Kathleen asked, interrupting Clara's reading of the latest receipt. Their arrangement was working beautifully. They'd started with the easiest receipts, working their way to more complicated dishes over the summer. Kathleen purchased some paper, a nib pen and ink, and wrote the receipts in Irish to create her own receipt book.

Now that it was mid-August Clara spoke of the coming harvest, naming vegetables the likes of which Kathleen had never heard. Though they could purchase most of what they needed, they did keep a small vegetable garden. Clara explained to Kathleen the custom of pickling and preserving food to last throughout the cold months.

Cold seemed welcome to Kathleen at the moment. July had been blistering. August was proving even worse. Sweat made her uniform cling to her before her morning chores were finished. By afternoon the weight of it dragged on her. She'd taken to soaking it in sudsy water each night and hanging it near the stove, hoping it would be dry by morning. Mrs. Pratt made multiple clothing changes throughout the day. As the wash pile grew, Kathleen dreaded Tuesdays and Wednesdays, her days for washing and ironing, more than ever. She'd reminded Mrs. Pratt of her intention to hire a laundress and received, "Oh, yes, I must look into that," for a reply.

"It should start to cool down by the end of this month," Clara told her. "September is usually lovely. In October it gets chilly but the leaves are splendid."

"I wish it was October now," Kathleen said, mopping her forehead with a towel. "Read that last part to me again, please."

The weather made everyone lethargic. Mrs. Pratt napped a good part of the day. Harvey went off with friends most days. Lemuel, thankfully, was at the foundry with his father. After returning home they'd have dinner then retire to Mr. Pratt's study to discuss business until they went to bed. The heat had at least made keeping her distance from Lemuel easy for Kathleen. Other than Clara, no one wanted to be in the kitchen. Even Kathleen embraced the chance to escape the grueling heat of the stove when she could.

Upon placing their latest concoction into the oven, Kathleen told Clara she was going to the city pump for more water. "I should be back long before that's ready to come out, but you keep an eye on the time just in case," she instructed.

Stepping outside brought only the mildest respite. Though the stove made the kitchen hotter than the out-doors, the humidity was like walking into a mist. The tin cup Kathleen had thrown into the water bucket rattled as she walked. Her attention was captured by the deep cerule-an sky dotted with puffy, billowing clouds. *'Tis glorious*, she thought. It must be magnificent to be in heaven among the ever-changing celestial canvas. Was her da peeking out at her right now from behind one of those puffy clouds? What of Rory's mam and da? They were up there, too. She smiled at the picture of the many souls lost in the Hunger now hopping from cloud to cloud, dancing a jig, swirls of white puffs flitting about their legs. Then, unbidden, her mind conjured up Rory's younger brother, Aiden. Her smile faded and her gaze dropped to the rutted dirt road.

Aiden had been near her own age and in love with her. She'd loved Aiden, too, but as one loves a brother. Neither he nor anyone in either family could understand why she couldn't return his ardent feelings. But she'd had eyes only for Kevin Dooley, a miscreant in those days. He was the lad who'd made her heart race just by smiling in her direction. Meg despised him. Their mam barely allowed his name uttered in their home. He'd been Aiden's best friend and so was tolerated by the Quinns until that horrible, stormy day when Kevin's *curragh* overturned in the crashing waters drowning Aiden. Rory had tried to save his brother, but heartless waves pulled Aiden under as they threw the *curragh* in the air, slamming it down on Rory's hand, ruining forever his ability to make the intricate carvings that he'd been selling to hold their starving at bay.

Kathleen's infatuation with Kevin ended in the moment she saw him abandon Aiden to save himself, refusing to go back as they watched Rory struggle. Much later she learned that he believed Rory had saved Aiden. Kevin was shocked and deeply saddened when he realized his best friend was dead. The words he'd bellowed as Aiden's body lay lifeless had never left her. "I told him we shouldn't go out, but he wanted to become an expert fisherman to win the hand of his dear, sweet Kathleen."

Kathleen had forgiven Kevin for his part in Aiden's death. But she'd never been able to forgive herself.

The following day, Kathleen was alone with her thoughts again as she labored through the laundry. Meg had stopped by after sundown the day before to tell her she'd received a letter from Rory and was eager to share it. He'd had word of their brother.

"Tell me," Kathleen had begged.

"Come to the Dentons' on Thursday as soon as you can. We'll meet in Nuala's room. It's not as hot in there. I'll read it to you then."

Kathleen wanted to protest, but the exhaustion evident in Meg's face as well as her own fatigue suffered her to consent. Now, up to her elbows in wash water, sun beating on her aching back, she wished she'd insisted Meg tell her what Rory had written. Curiosity assailed her as she spent the day plunging one grimy article of clothing, one bed sheet, one table linen after another into a pail of boiled rainwater mixed with sal soda, hard soap, and spirits of turpentine. For half an hour she stirred them with a long stick as though making a fabric stew. Then she'd take all out and rinse them one at a time in three pails of rainwater, the last of which included bluing for the sheets and white clothes.

It was late afternoon when she finished the washing. Still having a meal to prepare, Kathleen gathered all the clean laundry into the kitchen and set the irons on the stove to heat. If there was ever a day she could have used Clara's help it was today, but Mrs. Pratt had taken her daughter to the dry goods store to replace the clothing Clara was constantly outgrowing.

Kathleen lined up three kitchen chairs, laying the press board atop them. Once the flatiron was hot enough to press but not to burn, she began working on the clothing, replacing the iron on the stove when it cooled and picking up the second iron to substitute. A third, smaller, oval iron came into use on the more delicate articles. Once finished with the clothing she could start on the sheets and table linens. These took the larger, heavier flatirons. Over the months of weekly ironing along with all her other chores, Kathleen's arms had grown strong. She no longer struggled with the irons, but was able to lift and slide them with ease. She'd also mastered the intricate dance of heating the various irons on the stove, knowing when to replace one and pick up another.

Now her thoughts turned to supper. How much time did she have before it needed to be ready? How long would it take to prepare? She settled on red flannel hash, despite that it was considered a breakfast food. She had the ingredients – left over corned beef, boiled potatoes, and beets. It was quick and easy to cut up and fry in the skillet.

The kitchen was stacked with ironed clothing and linens awaiting their turn. Leaving the irons on the stove, she quickly carried the clothes upstairs, depositing them in their owners' wardrobes, then raced back. She laid a clean sheet over the press board, tested an iron – too hot – set it aside and retrieved the remnants of the noontime meal along with a large skillet. By the time she'd brought a handful of beets up from the root cellar, the iron was at the right temperature. Leaving the food on the table, she set to ironing the bed sheet. Once done, she folded it neatly, setting it on the kitchen bench, then reached into the basket, pulled out another sheet, snapped it smartly and smoothed one section over the press board. Her first iron had cooled, but the others were too hot. Returning it to the stove, she lifted another and set it to cool while she took up the washing and chopping of the beets.

In her frenzied activity she never heard the front door open, so the creaking of the kitchen door took her by surprise. She expected to see Clara back from her shopping trip. Now she could set Clara to work dicing the meat and potatoes while she returned to the laundry.

But the looming presence of Lemuel filled the modicum of free space just inside the kitchen door.

"What's this?" he asked, a smirk playing about his lips. "Barricaded yourself in?"

"Master Lemuel, I didn't expect you home so early."

"Keep track of my comings and goings, do you?" He tilted his head to the side.

"I thought you might be Clara."

He laughed. "Hardly." His face became unreadable, his next words spoken neither harshly nor kindly. "You have not answered my question. I asked what this mess is all about."

Kathleen looked around. The kitchen was in disarray, but no more than on any other wash day. Had he never seen it so when his mother had done the homemaking? "I've to finish the ironing, but I don't want supper to be late, so I'm trying to do both at once," she explained.

"Hardly seems efficient." His eyes roved disapprovingly about the room.

"It will all come out right and be cleaned up proper by the end of the day, Master Lemuel," she stated.

"I'm sure." His tone was dismissive. Forgetting the mess he'd just complained of Lemuel advanced towards Kathleen. As he approached, his eyes bore into her. A shiver ran up her spine as if his very look could graze and bruise her skin.

"Is there something I can help you with, Master Lemuel?" Kathleen asked.

"Indeed there is." His words oozed like slime.

"What would that be?"

"My father has meetings until suppertime. Meetings I've no need to attend. So I'm home early. I simply came in for drink of water." He looked about the kitchen. "You've barred the way."

"I'll fetch you some," Kathleen said, hurrying to fill a cup and hand it to him.

Lemuel's hand brushed hers as he took it from her. As he raised the cup to his lips, Kathleen turned toward the table. Lemuel's hand gripped her upper arm and pulled her back. He drained the cup before letting go of her.

"More," he said handing the cup back.

Kathleen's hands shook as she refilled the cup. This time she did not turn away. She'd wait rather than be grabbed again.

Lemuel took a sip, lowered the cup and stared at her. "What are you doing just standing there, Bridget? I thought you had work to do."

"Waiting to see if you wished another refilling," she answered.

"Good. I like a servant who knows her place."

"Will that be all, then?" she asked, ignoring his snide remark.

Lemuel took his time draining the cup of water before answering. "For now," he said, handing the cup to her. Before Kathleen could turn away, he pinched her chin between his thumb and forefinger, tilting her head so she'd no choice but to look him in the face. "When I want something from you, Bridget, you'll know it."

His tone unnerved Kathleen, making her stomach feel as though she'd swallowed one of the irons.

"The iron!" she gasped.

Lemuel, momentarily taken aback by her outburst, let go. Kathleen scrambled to the stove, throwing on an oven mitt and grabbing a heavy flatiron. Now she had the table, the press board, and the stove between them. The hot iron pressed against the damp linen sizzled. A haze of steam rose.

Lemuel cocked his head, one side of his mouth turned up in a triumphant half-smile.

"You can barricade yourself in if you want, little lass," he said, the word 'lass' sounding like the hiss of a snake, "but I will always be able to break through."

Kathleen's anger overtook her fear. She held the sizzling iron aloft, its flat bottom facing him. "Master Lemuel," she said, her tone dignified and strong, "I've much work to do and little time to do it in. I should like to get on with it."

Lemuel glowered, his face turning dark as a thunder cloud. The kitchen door creaked loudly behind him. Clara bounced into the room, pushing past her brother to announce, "Kathleen, wait until you see the fabric for my new clothes. It's lovely."

Kathleen's legs felt as though their bones had disintegrated, so filled with relief was she.

"I'd love to, Miss Clara," she said. "Show them while I'm working, if you please."

The anger on Lemuel's face disappeared to be replaced by a false smile. "I'll leave you to your fashion parade," he said and stalked out of the kitchen.

A breeze wafting through the window awoke Kathleen just before sunrise the following morning. It was earlier than she usually rose. She lay on the straw mattress, luxuriating in the feel of gently dancing air currents playing across her skin. Gazing up through the window, she watched light beginning to illuminate long, thin clouds stretching far across the sky, the mild wind pushing them along. She had not completed all the ironing yesterday. Clara's interruption, though welcomed in the moment, had set her back. After she'd cleaned up and fed herself, she was too weary to resume ironing. Instead, she rinsed out her uniform, hung it to dry and went to bed. Before changing into a clean shift for the night, she placed a chair against the closed kitchen door for privacy. Last night she'd considered leaving it there until morning. No one had ever entered the kitchen after her work hours. But Lemuel's behavior unnerved her. Barricading herself for the night seemed a good idea. Still, what if Mrs. Pratt had need of her? She would be furious if she could not get into her own kitchen. Reluctantly, Kathleen returned the chair to its rightful place before crawling onto her mattress.

As dawn broke fully, she forced herself up. She always felt a slight ache in her arms on Wednesday mornings, but this morning they were more sore than usual. The front of her right arm just below her shoulder throbbed as she reached for her uniform. Remembering Lemuel's tight grip, she examined her arm. Purple bruises ringed her skin. She would speak to Mrs. Pratt of Lemuel's behavior. Meanwhile, she had much to do before the family arose expecting breakfast on the table.

As Kathleen worked through the day, her thoughts were fixed on the news Meg had of Brendan. Her brother had been deported to Australia four years ago. No one knew what happened to him from the moment his ship sailed. All they could do was pray he'd made it there safely, that he was being fed and housed, and that the work wasn't too much for him. Whenever Kathleen thought of Brendan, she pictured him hale and happy. No matter he was labeled a convict and set to hard labor. There was no shortage of food in Australia that Kathleen knew of. As long as he could eat, he would survive, please God. Someday, as her da had hoped, maybe he'd even make a good life for himself. She could hardly wait to hear Meg read Rory's letter.

Just before noontime, Kathleen sent Clara to pull some carrots for dinner. Clara had been gone but a moment when she returned to the kitchen empty-handed.

"Kathleen, you must come see this."

"What is it?" she asked, following the girl outdoors.

"Look." Clara pointed skyward.

Puffy white clouds filled the deep blue sky. The wind, a mild breeze in the morning, had turned blustery, seeming to push the clouds together, piling them one atop the other like giant mounds of whipped cream. Clara pointed at one particular cloud. It was the strangest shape Kathleen had ever seen. A bank of white stretching near the horizon formed its base. From the center rose a thick column, the whiteness of it mixing with the sky, turning the column's center a translucent dark blue. The cloud's top was round and flat, whiter than the column and turned under at the edges. Viewing it gave Kathleen the feeling of staring up at the underside of one of Mrs. Pratt's round tea tables.

"Have you ever seen a cloud like that before?" Clara asked.

Kathleen shook her head. "No. 'Tis a curiosity and no mistake."

"Maybe it's a table for the angels," Clara suggested.

The wind picked up suddenly, whipping their skirts around them.

"We'd best get the carrots quickly," Kathleen said. "I fear it's going to storm."

"Maybe it will break the awful heat," said Clara. "It's felt cooler since the breeze began this morning."

"Indeed it has," Kathleen agreed, helping Clara pull carrots from the kitchen garden.

All afternoon and into the evening the wind got stronger. Gusts came more often. Kathleen couldn't help but peek outside every now and then. The odd cloud stayed a while, but eventually rearranged itself to appear like the other mounds of white fluff. She wondered how long before the rain began, hoping for a good soaking and full rain barrels.

In mid-afternoon, Kathleen stepped outside to dump the wash water from the dinner dishes. The sky was still a deep blue, still dotted with massive creamy clouds, but something had changed. The air had quieted. Not the slightest zephyr disturbed the atmosphere. Kathleen stood motionless, barely daring to breathe. No birds sang, no small animals rustled amongst the garden leaves. Not one sound reached her ears. *Aye, a storm's on the way*, she thought, *but for certain it's taking it's time getting here.*

"Mrs. Pratt, may I speak with you in private?" Kathleen asked that evening as she cleared away the supper dishes, arresting her mistress before she could leave the dining room.

The sky had grown overcast as the day wore on. The wind, which had returned with greater vigor, now rattled the windows, echoing the rattling of Kathleen's nerves as she prepared to speak to her mistress about Lemuel.

"What is it?" asked Mrs. Pratt as the two women stood alone in the kitchen.

Kathleen had rehearsed the words in her head all day. Now faced with Mrs. Pratt's sober and self-assured countenance, she wasn't sure how to begin. An image of her mam filled her mind. Her mam would brook none of Lemuel's nonsense. The hope that Mrs. Pratt would feel the same allowed her to plunge ahead.

"Something happened here yesterday while you were out shopping with Clara. I thought at first to say nothing of it, but after I saw the results this morning I felt I'd better tell you."

Mrs. Pratt looked quizzical. "You broke something." It was a statement, not even a question. "What? It will come out of your pay."

Kathleen straightened her back. "No, Ma'am. I've not broken a thing."

"Oh. Well, then what is it?"

"Yesterday, while I was ironing and cooking dinner, Master Lemuel came into the kitchen for a drink of water. I fetched a cup and handed it to him."

Mrs. Pratt's bored expression never wavered.

"Once I handed him the cup, I turned to go back to my work."

"And?" Mrs. Pratt was losing patience.

"And that's when Master Lemuel grabbed me."

"Grabbed you? What do you mean?" Her eyes narrowed.

"My arm. Here." Kathleen rubbed her bicep.

"Is that all?" Mrs. Pratt asked.

Kathleen gritted her teeth. "When I woke this morning, my arm was bruised. It's been aching all day."

"I'm sorry for that, Kathleen," Mrs. Pratt said, though her expression had not changed to one of sympathy. She turned to leave.

Indignant, Kathleen continued, "My mam would never allow my brother to touch a lass, much less harm her even if the lass be no more than a simple servant." A gust of wind slammed the shutters on the windows.

Mrs. Pratt jumped.

"Well," she said, turning towards Kathleen. "I have raised my sons to be gentlemen. I will speak with Lemuel."

With that she turned her back on Kathleen and left the room.

In the wee hours of Thursday morning, the sound of roaring waves awakened Kathleen. "Aiden," she cried out, sitting bolt upright on the mattress. Pressing the palms of her hands into her eyes she realized she'd been dreaming of that horrible day that claimed the life of Rory's brother. She waited, willing her heart to stop racing, the blood to stop pounding in her ears. The roaring began again. How? She was awake now. Then she realized. It was the howling of a gale force wind. A dense splattering hit the window above her. The rain had finally come. In the darkness she could not see it, but she heard it on the windowpane. She hoped it would end before it was time to leave for the Dentons. For days she'd been waiting to hear the news of her brother. If she could not get through the storm she'd have to wait until Sunday after Mass.

Kathleen lay back down, but her sleep was fitful, interrupted by wind and rain pelting the window and sides of the house. It was difficult to tell when dawn arrived. The sun strained to break through the low-hanging clouds. Only glimpses of grayish light told her it was time to rise.

She quickly donned her uniform, stoked the fire in the stove, set the table for breakfast, swept the first floor rooms, gathered up the mending Mrs. Pratt had left outside the kitchen door for her last night and set it in her basket for later, then returned to the kitchen to prepare breakfast. Her eyes strayed constantly towards the windows as she worked, willing a break in the weather that never came.

Once she'd cleaned up from the morning meal, Kathleen changed from her uniform to the calico dress Meg had presented to her on the day she'd arrived in Worcester. She was determined to go to the Dentons no matter the weather, but she'd surely not wear her fancier clothing. As she finished changing, the rain and wind slowed. The sun fought its way through the clouds.

Kathleen left by the kitchen door, hoping to make it to the Denton home before another squall broke. As she headed down Oxford Street, she wondered if she should go first to the Claproods in case Meg assumed this weather would keep her home.

Indecisive, she stood halfway down the street. Wind gathered up her skirts, lifting them so high she had to grab hold to keep her legs from being exposed. Dark clouds swallowed up the sun. Rain that moments before had tapered to a trickle plunged down as if a cloud had been rent asunder over her head. The Denton home was steps away, the Claprood home on another street. Kathleen headed towards the Dentons. Though only three houses away now, she could barely see it through the sheets of rain. The wind made her grab hold of wrought iron fences, streetlamps, and hitching posts to stay upright.

Reaching the Denton house, she pounded on the kitchen door. She could not hear the sound of her own knocking. She waited, pounded again, waited some more. Moving to the window, she knocked as hard as she dared on the glass. The door burst open and Nuala pulled her in.

"Are ye daft, lass?" Nuala admonished.

"Aye," she answered, gasping for breath. "Has Meg come?"

Chapter Seven

"Meg's here," Nuala said. "Made it just before the last squall." She scurried to the pantry. Returning with towels, she handed one to Kathleen who rubbed her face and hair with it. The other she draped over Kathleen's shoulders. "Take off your shoes and leave them by the door. Where's your bonnet? Did you lose it on the way?"

"I didn't wear it. I knew it would get ruined."

Nuala looked aghast, then shrugged. "You'll have to borrow one of mine when you leave. You can't be seen outside without a bonnet. As far as the Yankees are concerned you might as well be walking about town in your undergarments."

Kathleen had only a moment to consider yet another Yankee oddity before Nuala whipped the soaked towel from her shoulders, throwing it in a corner by the stove. Nuala hurried her up the back staircase to the third floor and into her bedchamber at the far end of the hallway where Meg was poring over Rory's letter.

"Tell me of Brendan," Kathleen burst out the moment she saw her sister.

Meg rose. "Kathleen, you're soaked to the skin," she said.

"There will be no reading until we get you dried off," Nuala stated as she commenced stripping off Kathleen's clothes.

"I can undress myself," Kathleen said, brushing away Nuala's hand. "What am I to wear?" she asked as the sodden clothing landed with a *thwap* on the floor.

"Nothing of mine will fit you," Nuala observed. She looked about the room. "I know," she said, opening the chest at the foot of her bed. "Wrap yourself in this." She pulled out a woolen blanket.

Nuala gathered up the wet clothes. "I'll hang these by the stove. With luck they'll be dry by the time you go home."

Kathleen sat on Nuala's bed feeling ill at ease being naked beneath the blanket. She glanced at the bedchamber door. "The Denton's won't come in?" she asked Meg.

"We're in Nuala's room and on our own time," Meg answered. "You must insist on getting out of that kitchen."

Kathleen glanced at the papers in Meg's lap. "Two sheets?"

Meg nodded, lifted the pages. "Rory shared lots of news."

"All about Brendan?"

"Not all," Meg said. "There's other news as well."

Kathleen peered eagerly at Rory's letter straining to see in the dim light. The storm continued to rage outside Nuala's window. Only one candle burned in the room. Meg brought it close to where she and Kathleen sat on the bed.

"Hold this so I can see to read," Meg said.

Kathleen reached out a bare arm from beneath the blanket.

"What's that?" Meg asked. "Bruises? How did you get them?"

Kathleen sighed. "Lemuel," she said.

Megs eyes narrowed. "What happened?"

"I fetched him a cup of water and when I turned away he grabbed my arm to keep me from leaving. Seems he wanted a second drink," Kathleen said, not completely successful in keeping the anger from her voice.

"You need to find another place."

"It's not that bad, Meg. And I've not been there long. I can't leave yet." Kathleen thought of her desire to block the kitchen door with the chair last night. But she'd grown so fond of Clara, she hated to leave her.

"Did you speak to Mrs. Pratt?"

"Aye. She said she would talk to Lemuel."

"Mmm," Meg muttered. "You must make it clear that if anything of the sort happens again you will leave immediately."

"Where would I go?"

"To the Lintons at first. They'll get word to me. I'll set you up with the agency or ask Father Gilbert to help you find a new placement. Promise me."

"Aye," she agreed, hoping Mrs. Pratt would convince Lemuel to leave her be.

"That storm is beyond any I've ever seen," Nuala said, flinging open the door. "I brought more candles. Like night it is outside. Look."

Nothing was visible beyond the window pane.

"It's worse," Kathleen marveled. The window glass rattled.

"I stuck my head out the door," Nuala said. "The trees are bending over, looking about to snap."

She set the extra candles into holders and lit them.

"I wonder how long it will last," Meg said.

Nuala shrugged. "Mrs. Denton says it's likely to be bad for some time and you aren't to venture out into anything as wild as this."

A bolt of lightening flashed, cutting through the curtain of rain and momentarily lighting up Nuala's bedchamber. Within seconds two sharp cracks pierced the air followed by an ear-splitting explosion of thunder. In the candlelight, Kathleen noticed a broad grin on Nuala's face.

"You enjoy a storm, do you?" she asked.

"Aye. Right exciting, it is," said Nuala. "Now, Meg, onto your letter."

With Kathleen and Nuala holding candles on either side of her, Meg unfolded the pages.

My dearest Megeen,

I've so much to tell you. How I wish paper wasn't so dear. First and most importantly, there's been news of Brendan. It seems he's written before, but this was the first letter to make it through to us. He wonders why no one writes back. He doesn't say it, but I think he fears we're all

dead. Don't worry, Meg, I wrote to him even before I start-
ed this letter now that I know where to send it. He says he
works hard. He's learning about planting and harvesting
all manner of crops. Gets to eat some of what he plants as
well. He's caring for sheep and cattle, too. He's got meat to
eat fairly regular. He's put on weight, feels strong and
healthy. He's doing well, just as we all hoped. Here's the
best news – he says in one more year he can earn a ticket of
leave. With that he'll be allowed to seek paying employment
within his district. He won't be able to leave the district
without permission or board a ship, but he will be able to
earn money, buy property, and even marry if he's a mind to.
He has to stay out of trouble, attend muster and church ser-
vices in order to have his ticket renewed each year. He as-
sures us he'll go to their services to honor the requirements
of the ticket, but he will never leave the faith. He plans to
save every bit until his sentence is up. If he has enough he'll
buy passage home. If not, he'll keep a paying job until he
earns it. Either way, he's coming home. He's got six years
yet on his sentence, but having a goal to work towards
keeps him going. In one year half his sentence will have
been served and then he can apply for a conditional pardon
which would remove all restrictions except for leaving the
colony.

    You can only imagine how your mam reacted when she
heard the news. Nearly fainted, she did. Even Brigid
seemed to understand. I swear she smiled, Meg. Your
mam's got a new vigor. She's certain now she'll live long
enough to see her only son walk through the door. I've told
him that in my letter as it will help him when time seems to
drag. I know you and Kathleen will be as delighted as we
are that all's going well for Brendan and for your mam's
newfound hope. Perhaps it's just the thing that will bring
Brigid 'round at last.

"Oh, Meg!" Kathleen exclaimed. "God be praised! 'Tis
the most blessed good news!" Kathleen gripped the blanket
tightly around herself as she rocked back and forth, unable
to contain her joy. "Brendan's alive. He's well. He's coming

home! Mam will see him again." Her happiness spilled over in a torrent to rival the rain.

Meg threw her arms around Kathleen. Nuala grabbed Kathleen's candle as the sisters hugged and cried until a crash of thunder jolted them apart.

Nuala moved to the window. "Listen," she said. The wind roared. "Have you ever heard it such?"

Meg and Kathleen joined her at the window.

"I can't see anything," Meg said. "The rain is blinding."

The glass in the window pane rattled hard enough to make them all jump back, afraid it might break.

"Are we safe?" Kathleen asked.

"If the window breaks, this room will be soaked," Nuala said, her tone more annoyed than frightened.

They all turned at a knock on the door. Kathleen scooted behind Meg, wrapping the blanket tightly around herself. "You said they would not come here," she hissed into Meg's ear.

Nuala opened the door to Mrs. Denton. The woman held a light linen dress. "Your friend's clothing will take a long time to dry. Perhaps this old frock of mine would do," she said, handing the dress to Nuala.

"Thank you, Mrs. Denton."

"Of course, dear. We can't have the poor girl unclothed. It's not proper."

"We've wrapped her in a blanket, but this will be much better."

Peeking over Meg's shoulder, Kathleen saw a woman of perhaps sixty, white hair piled atop her head, black shawl around her shoulders despite the dense humidity. Her puffy cheeks reminded Kathleen of heaps of dough, her mouth a cherry in the middle.

"Thank you, Ma'am," she called from behind Meg. "'Tis most kind of you."

"Not at all, dear," Mrs. Denton called back, modestly averting her eyes from Kathleen.

77

"Mrs. Denton, this storm is horrendous. The worst I've ever seen," said Nuala. "My window is rattling so hard I fear the pane may break."

"Come downstairs," said Mrs. Denton. "I don't want any of you cut by flying glass."

"We will once Kathleen has dressed," Nuala told her, then closed the door after Mrs. Denton departed.

"Help me, Meg," Nuala urged while Kathleen put on the dress. Together they draped the discarded blanket over the curtain rod then dragged a chest to the windowsill to hold the bottom of it in place.

"Do you think that will do any good?" Kathleen asked, smoothing out the skirts of the dress. It was almost a perfect fit.

"It may not keep it from breaking, but at least it will prevent glass shards from sailing about the room," said Nuala.

Another blast of thunder was followed by a gust that shook the pane again.

"Let's go," Nuala said.

"The letter!" said Kathleen, picking it up from the floor. "I want to hear the rest."

They settled in the kitchen. Kathleen watched her dress drip little rivulets onto the floor.

"The rest of the letter, please," Nuala urged as she set out three teacups and put water on to boil. Kathleen forgot her dress, her attention riveted to Meg's voice.

Aisling's improved immensely since last I wrote. Loreena showed Aisling's work to a customer who knows a widowed seamstress looking for an assistant. The woman agreed to take on Aisling as a sort of apprentice. Aisling goes three times a week to the woman's shop to learn the trade. We thought at first the walk into town would be too much, but instead it's done her a world of good. She learns quickly, pleases her mistress, and gets a meal when she's there. The seamstress, Mrs. Fairfax, sometimes sends her home with food. Mrs. Fairfax says Aisling's gifted in the sewing arts and will offer her a paid position once she's learned enough to be a true assistant. Aisling about glows with joy.

"Can you believe it, Meg?" Kathleen exclaimed. "I always knew Aisling's sewing was something special. Now she's going to prove it."

"It seems so," Meg agreed. "Perhaps she'll have a shop of her own one day."

"Wouldn't that be something!" Kathleen glanced at her soaked dress, no longer caring if it was ruined forever. To hear such news from home was worth it.

Nuala poured tea into each cup. "That's sounding to be the best letter anyone ever got," she said, smiling. "Makes me wish I knew the rest of your family."

It dawned on Kathleen that Nuala never spoke of her own family. "Do you hear much from yours?" she asked.

Nuala's smile faded. "They're gone," she stated.

"Is there no one at all?" Kathleen asked.

Nuala shook her head. "Mam and Da died from the Hunger. Fever took both my brothers. I came to America, saved all my earnings, and bought passage for my sister. Her ship was wrecked on the way. There were no survivors." Kathleen barely caught the last words, unsure if it was because Nuala's voice had dropped or because the wind had begun a high-pitched whine.

"I'm so sorry," she said.

Nuala gave a slight nod, then said, "Meg, go on with your letter."

Meg continued, though she almost had to yell to be heard over the wind.

Doctor Parker is teaching me all about horses. He's got me mucking out Lily's stall, brushing and feeding her. He's teaching me what to look for regarding her health and all manner of her care. I'm getting better with my left hand and can use the right enough now that I've no problem doing the work. He pays me for it even though he's still teaching me. I'd never have thought to work with horses, but I find I like it. Of course, Lily's the only horse I've ever worked with and she's a sweet animal. I don't know how I'd fare with another especially if it didn't have Lily's angelic disposition. Doctor Parker believes I have a knack for it. He thinks I should prepare myself for a job as a groom. When I finally join you in America, if I could find such work, I could do better than in a factory. Would you look into it for me, please, Meg, and tell me what prospects I might have? I've no doubt Doctor Parker will give me a good reference.

"What do you think, Meg?" Kathleen asked. "Are there such jobs?"

Meg looked at Nuala. "I don't know. Do you?"

"There is the livery stable on Exchange Street that rents horses. The Dentons have rented from them. They must have grooms," said Nuala.

Meg looked back to Kathleen. "That's true. The Claproods rent from them, too. Not many people here own horses so they have to rent."

"Rory could get a job there, couldn't he?" Kathleen asked.

"That depends on whether or not they hire Irish," Nuala stated.

Kathleen groaned. "It's so unfair. What have we ever done to be so hated?"

"Kept our Catholic faith," Meg answered. "And we'll continue to no matter what they say or do to us."

Kathleen looked down at her lap. "They're not all bad," she said, fingering the fabric of the borrowed dress.

"True," said Meg. "There are some good-hearted English souls. Just not enough."

"Sounds as though this Doctor Parker is one of them," Nuala observed.

"Oh, he is," Kathleen said, warming to the subject. "We met him at the Gale Day fair when both Mam and I got hurt. He took care of us, gave us a ride home, and has been our friend ever since. He even became friends with our priest, Father O'Malley. The two of them go to all the parish families caring for everyone as best they can."

"And what of his horse, Lily?" Nuala asked.

Meg and Kathleen laughed. "You'd love Lily," Meg told her. "A grand horse, she is. Tall, pure white, and as gentle a beast as ever lived. Doctor Parker treats her like a queen. He must trust Rory immensely if he's letting him care for his Lily!"

"What else does he say?" Kathleen asked, indicating the second sheet of paper.

Meg continued reading.

Father O'Malley asks me to send his blessings to you and Kathleen. He prays for you both daily. He seems well enough, though he moves a bit more slowly than he used to. He has pain in his fingers often, especially when the weather is poor, but otherwise he's the same as always.

Loreena continues to grow like a weed. She gets prettier every day. I daresay the lads will take note of her before long. I'll have to practice my older brother glare for when they start coming 'round. Brigid eats better. She's with us more often. We pray her mind will come back fully one day. Perhaps when she sees Brendan, but that's six years yet.

In your last letter you asked me what I think about Kevin. I know it's hard for you to believe being so far away and not seeing the great change in him, but what Kathleen's told you is true. Father O'Malley has made a new man of him. He lives with the Kilpatricks, helping them with everything. His sister, Liddy, being far more addled than Brigid, lives there, too. They care for her like she was their own, but Kevin is the only one who can calm her when she becomes agitated. As you might remember, Mr. Kilpatrick always had the best crops of anyone, until, like the rest of us, he had none. He's teaching Kevin all he knows about potato farming as well as caring for the landlord's other crops. Kevin's becoming a right good hand at it. Once a lazy lout, he's now in the field sunup to sundown working to shame the devil. He's respectful, too. No more of his arrogant bluster. Even your mam allows he's changed. She didn't trust him at first, but he's made steady progress. He's proved himself a new man and finally won her over.

"Whatever his shortcomings, it sounds as though he's mastered them," Nuala observed.

"I'll admit, it's hard for me to imagine," said Meg. "But if Rory believes he's sincerely changed, then perhaps 'tis true. I don't think Kevin could fool Rory. Father O'Malley is a miracle- worker. That's all I have to say."

"Is there any more in the letter?" Kathleen asked.

"Only this."

The potatoes we planted in the spring have fared better than expected. We lost much of the crop, but for the first time in years there were some we could save. That's a good sign for next year. Perhaps this disaster will finally end. With the money you and Kathleen send we are managing better than before the starving began. You have the ever-lasting gratitude of us all.

I hope I can come to you soon, Meg. I miss you more than I can say. I long for us to be together. If only there was someone who could care for your mam and the lasses, I'd be there in the blink of an eye. I pray every day that God will create a way for us.

With all my love, ever yours,
Rory

"I do wish Rory could come soon," Kathleen said. "You must miss him something awful, Meg."

Meg nodded, tears glistening in her eyes.

A monstrous crack made them all jump.

"This storm seems to have no end. Are they like this often?" asked Kathleen.

"No," Nuala answered. "We get thunderstorms throughout the summer, but nothing like this." Even she appeared apprehensive.

The kitchen door opened and Mrs. Denton stepped in. "Ah, you came down."

Nuala rose and the others followed suit.

"Mrs. Denton, please meet my friend, Meg's sister, Kathleen O'Connor. Kathleen works for the Pratts."

Meg and Kathleen bobbed curtsies towards Mrs. Denton. "Pleased to meet you, Ma'am," said Kathleen, grateful for a proper introduction. "Thank you again for the loan of the dress."

"You are quite welcome. It appears to fit you well."

"It does at that, Ma'am." Kathleen smiled.

"Is there something I can do for you, Mrs. Denton?" Nuala inquired.

"No, dear. I only came to check that you'd come down where its safer."

Kathleen was nearly in love with this woman. Why couldn't Mrs. Pratt be like her?

"We were just talking about how long this storm is lasting," said Nuala. "I've never known a thunderstorm to be so violent or go on for so long."

"This is no ordinary thunderstorm," said Mrs. Denton. "This is a hurricane."

"A what?" asked Kathleen.

"A hurricane. It's a mighty storm that forms in the ocean. Usually they stay there, but when they come upon land they can cause tremendous damage. Hurricanes are very dangerous."

"Have you experienced one before?" asked Nuala.

"I haven't, but my husband has. Girls, please sit," she said, helping herself to a cup of tea and joining them at the table. "Mr. Denton, in his younger years, served aboard a merchantman. Oh, the stories he can tell." She dipped her head, saying in a conspiratorial tone, "but don't get him going or he'll never stop."

They all laughed, though nervously, as the wind beat against the house.

"He told me this morning that we were in for a hurricane. These storms popped up often in the West Indies. They originate in tropical areas, it seems. He never thought to see one again. It's very unusual for a hurricane to travel this far up the coast."

"Did he say what we should expect?" Meg asked. "Will it get much worse?"

"How long will it last?" Kathleen added.

"It could get worse and it could last well into tomorrow."

"Tomorrow!" Kathleen exclaimed. "But Meg and I have to be on duty early in the morning."

"I daresay your employers won't expect you out in such weather. Besides, I refuse to let either of you leave this house until it's safe."

A sense of foreboding crept over Kathleen. Mrs. Claprood would understand if Meg returned late, but she wasn't so sure about Mrs. Pratt.

"My mistress won't like my being away beyond my allotted time," Kathleen said.

"Hmmm..." Mrs. Denton drummed her fingers on the table. "Sophronia Pratt?"

"Aye." In her uneasiness, the dreaded word escaped Kathleen.

Mrs. Denton took no notice. She pursed her lips. "A bit sour, that one."

Kathleen suppressed a giggle.

"Listen," said Nuala. "It seems to be slowing." Indeed the wind had died down somewhat, the rain still coming down hard, but not the pelting torrent it had been moments ago. "Perhaps it's nearly over."

"Excuse me," said Mrs. Denton, rising from the table. "I'm going to consult Mr. Denton. He will know what this means."

"Nuala, you are so fortunate," Kathleen told her. "If only Mrs. Pratt were half as nice as Mrs. Denton."

"I am and I know it," Nuala agreed. "I doubt even Mrs. Claprood would sit in the kitchen for tea and a chat with the likes of us, and she's kind. What do you say to that, Meg?"

"Mrs. Claprood is a good mistress. I've no complaints. I'm not sure if she'd be as willing to mix with us in the way of Mrs. Denton, though."

"I only wish the Dentons were younger," said Nuala. "I wouldn't mind staying with them my whole life, but given their ages, that's surely not destined to be."

"Do you want to be a maid your whole life?" asked Kathleen. "Don't you ever think of marrying?"

"Marrying? Jesus, Mary, and Joseph! Why would I want to do that? I've got a good job, fair pay, decent food, and a roof over my head. I can afford the same fashions as the Yankee ladies. Why would I throw all that away to be shackled to a man who'll earn less than I can? So he can set me up in a place like the Arcade? Besides popping out bairns every other year? No thank ye! I like this life. I plan to keep it."

Kathleen noticed a strange look pass over Meg's face. Was she worried that her life would change for the worse once Rory arrived?

"Father Gibson says it's a woman's duty to marry and raise children. That it's what the Lord wants," Kathleen said. They'd heard this from the pulpit many times.

"Father Gibson isn't the one who'll be stuck in the Arcade with a pack of hungry, screaming bairns. He's one to talk!"

"The Church as a whole expects it of us," Meg said, quietly.

"Find me a man who can give me a house like this one and hire a maid for me and I'll marry him," said Nuala. "Do you think Father Gibson would be willing to play matchmaker?"

Meg broke out in a hearty laugh. "Now that would be something I'd love to see."

"He's not much like Father O'Malley, is he?" asked Kathleen.

"Noticed that, have you?" said Meg, rolling her eyes.

"For the life of me, I can't understand why he was sent here," said Nuala. "A priest from England, of all places, sent to serve a parish filled with poor Irish. The man looks down his nose at us. I don't know your Father O'Malley, but from all you've told me, it's a priest the likes of him we need here, not some pretentious Brit."

Kathleen gasped. "He is a priest. You needn't be disrespectful."

"Aye," said Nuala. "May God forgive me." She appeared anything but remorseful.

Mrs. Denton returned to the kitchen along with a man who could only be her husband. Mr. Denton reminded Kathleen of Mr. Pratt with his bushy mutton chop sideburns and twinkling eyes, except that Mr. Denton's whiskers were pure white whereas Mr. Pratt's were just beginning to gray and Mr. Denton had more crinkles around his eyes. Mrs. Denton introduced him to Meg and Kathleen.

"Ladies, glad to have you safe with us in this wretched storm."

Ladies. Kathleen's eyebrows lifted in surprise. No one had ever called them ladies, especially not an employer.

"I understand my dear wife has told you about my sailing days." Mr. Denton stationed himself in the center of the kitchen, legs wide as though standing on the deck of a rolling ship. His eyes danced as he spoke.

"The storms we saw in those days make this one look like a sun shower. That's not to say it couldn't do some damage. We'll learn of the havoc it's wreaked once it passes. The most important thing to remember is never underestimate a hurricane. They're a wicked sort of beast, never to be trusted."

"It seems to be slowing down," Nuala said. "Listen. The wind has almost stopped."

"And look," said Meg pointing towards the kitchen window. "It's light outside."

"It must be over," said Mrs. Denton, breathing a sigh of relief. "Should we go outside and assess the damage?"

"We'll go out," said Mr. Denton. "But stay close to the house and be ready to run back in at a moment's notice."

The women looked at one another. Surely the gentleman was having fun with them.

The street was a mess. Masses of leaves were strewn everywhere. Trees were bent, exhausted limbs hung limp. Fences and sides of houses were covered in mud as if a giant hand had scooped it from the road and flung it about the neighborhood.

"Such a shambles," said Mrs. Denton.

"Better than torn sails, timbers reduced to splinters, and a deck hip-deep in water," said Mr. Denton, looking around. "This here's been but a faint gale." His tone was light, almost genial. "But I daresay it's not over."

"Whatever do you mean?" asked Mrs. Denton. "The sun is shining. There's not so much as a breeze."

Stepping off the porch, Kathleen's feet sank into the spongy earth. The scent of wet grass and dirt permeated the still air. "'Tis a wonder it should be so calm after such a fierce storm," she said, then, with a glance at Mr. Denton, added, "Sir, I've never seen a worse one."

"You're not done seeing it, my girl," he told her. "We're in the eye. That's why it's so calm now."

"The eye?" asked Nuala.

"The very center of the storm," he explained. "That's where it's perfectly calm. The storm itself spins around the eye. But you'll see. Once the eye passes, we'll be in for it again only this time the wind will blow from the opposite direction."

Several neighbors had ventured outside. Most ambled about their property wearing dumbfounded expressions.

"Go back in!" Mr. Denton called to them. "It's not over."

Their countenances changed to disbelief. Many shook their heads.

"The neighbors think I'm rather mad," Mr. Denton confided to the assembled group near his own doorstep. "More's the pity for them. In this case, at least."

"Eccentric might be a kinder word," said Mrs. Denton, offering her husband a gentle smile.

"If the storm is going to come back, perhaps it's best if Kathleen and I leave now," said Meg. "We're not far. We should be able to make it home before it starts again."

Kathleen thought of spending the rest of the day trapped in the Pratt house. Her heart sank. For the first time she wished she did have a room of her own, even if it was just a corner of the attic.

"I'll not hear of it," said Mr. Denton. "There's no telling what you may run into on the way home. The streets are mud pits. The storm could start again at any moment. Mrs. Denton and I would worry ourselves sick over your safety. I insist you both remain until the storm is over. Then I will walk each of you to your employers' homes."

"I agree," said Mrs. Denton.

Kathleen felt tears well in her eyes. Not since she'd left her family in Ireland had she felt so cared for, and from a Yankee couple who barely knew her, no less.

"You are both so kind," she said. She would have hugged them, but Mrs. Pratt's stern lessons in propriety held her back.

"Indeed you are," Meg agreed. "Thank you so much."

"Not at all," said Mr. Denton. "What kind of people would we be if we left you to fend for yourselves in a dangerous time?"

A light breeze broke the stillness. Dark clouds scudded across the sky, devouring the sun. A drop of rain hit the porch railing, another the tip of Kathleen's nose. The breeze became a gust, rain pattered down in quick staccato beats.

"Back inside, quickly!" Mr. Denton ordered.

They piled into the kitchen just making it before a new deluge descended.

That night was the first time in Kathleen's life that she'd ever slept in a bed. The storm had not let up. Working together, the women prepared supper then all ate at the dining room table. Later, Mrs. Denton insisted on the use of a guestroom for Meg and Kathleen.

Kathleen had made up the beds in the Pratt home. Often she'd wanted to lie upon one just to see what it was like, but she hadn't dared. As she climbed into bed beside Meg, she thought how strange it was to lie above the floor. Despite the heat, she scooted close to Meg wanting to be away from the edge in case she should roll over and fall out.

"What an odd day this has been," Meg said. She blew out the candle, plunging the room into darkness.

"Aye. Are you worried about getting home in time to begin work?" Kathleen asked.

"Not much. We'll leave as soon as the weather allows, but even if we're late we can hardly be faulted. Mrs. Claprood knows where I am. She'll expect me to stay if I could not get back through the storm."

"The Pratts don't know where I am. I wonder what they'll think."

"When you return, pay attention to whether they've worried or not. That should tell you something."

"It's hard to fathom all the Dentons have done for us. It's as if we're family."

"They are unusual," Meg agreed. "Nuala is blessed to work for them."

For a moment the only sounds were the raging wind and the pelting of rain against the house. Kathleen's thoughts wandered through the day's events. The letter from Rory bringing an abundance of welcome news and the generosity and acceptance of them by the Dentons as near equals made her mind whirl.

"Meg, have you ever thought you'd sit at a grand dining table and eat with people the likes of the Dentons?"

"I've imagined it, but not believed it," Meg admitted.

"And this," Kathleen continued. "To sleep in a chamber meant for guests. In a real bed." From the moment she'd stretched out, Kathleen felt as though she was floating on a cloud. "I never want to get up."

Meg chuckled. "I've a bed, but my mattress is straw." Meg sighed. "I could get used to this."

Wind blasted. A muffled crash came from somewhere in the house. Both sat upright.

"What was that?" Kathleen asked.

"Something must have broken."

Within moments footsteps hurried down the hallway stopping at their door. There was a quick knock and the door opened to reveal Nuala, candle in hand.

"Move over, please," she said, climbing into the bed, squeezing Kathleen into the middle. "That dratted wind finally broke my window."

It was well after sunrise before Mr. Denton declared it safe for Meg and Kathleen to leave. True to his word, he walked each to their respective employers. Mrs. Denton insisted Kathleen keep the dress. The trio picked their way down the street, stepping over broken limbs and trying not to slip on wet leaves and slimy mud.

"Good Lord, would you look at that!" Mr. Denton pointed. A pitchfork stuck straight into the side of a house, tines fully embedded in the clapboard. "What fool left that outside?" He shook his head. "Don't know enough to take care of their own tools," he grumbled. "And they think I'm addled."

They reached the Pratt home first.

"I can't thank you enough for all your kindness, Mr. Denton," Kathleen said, preparing to head round the back to the kitchen entrance.

"You already have. The two of you have not ceased thanking us all morning," he said, blue eyes twinkling.

"You can't imagine our lives, Sir," Meg said. "The way you and Mrs. Denton have treated us has been like a dream."

Mr. Denton frowned. "Shouldn't be so," he said. "All should be treated well."

Suddenly, Mr. Denton didn't remind Kathleen so much of Mr. Pratt as he did of Doctor Parker. "I'm so happy to have met you, Mr. Denton," she said. "Thank you again for walking me home. I'd best get in and get to work." She resisted the urge to kiss the man's cheek and settled for a handshake.

Around back, leaves and vegetables from the kitchen garden littered her path. She sighed at the thought of cleaning the mess. She'd have Clara help her salvage any they could. She climbed the stairs to the kitchen door and stepped inside. Standing in the kitchen, hands on her hips, Mrs. Pratt glared at Kathleen the moment she opened the door. Her employer's eyes raked her from head to toe, noting the damp calico dress slung over her arm.

"Where on God's green earth have you been?"

Chapter Eight

Meg hadn't stopped thinking about Rory's letter since she first read it. The thought that Rory might join her before long both thrilled and frightened her. She missed him dreadfully, ached to be with him, yearned to finally settle down to create the home and family they'd dreamed of for so long. But what kind of home would it be? The fact that Doctor Parker was training Rory to be a groom, she hoped, meant he could do better than factory work. Yet how much call was there for such a position? There was the livery stable. Where else? The only families she knew of who owned horses were the very wealthy – the ones on Nobility Hill or moving from there to Elm Street. Surely they had the grooms they needed.

Meg snapped the sheet in the air before laying it over the bed in the master bedchamber. She tried not to think of Nuala's assertions about marriage.

I wish we'd known, Meg thought, smoothing the sheet. *I'd not have married first. I'd have waited and brought Rory over and we could both work and save until we had enough to live decent.*

A dart of guilt stabbed her. Was she being unfaithful for not wanting to return to a life of poverty despite it being with Rory? If only she could talk to her mam, but as her mam was illiterate, she could not read any letter nor write back. There was Father O'Malley, but she felt the need to speak face-to-face with another woman. Kind Mrs. Claprood was not the one. Meg would never make her marriage known to the Claproods. Another pang of guilt stung her. She'd been living a lie for going on four years. Not only were the Claproods ignorant of her marital state, but she

91

hadn't told Rory the full truth. He'd no idea that she kept their marriage a secret. She didn't want him to think she saw having a husband as a burden, afraid he'd be hurt or worry that she wouldn't want him to come.

Finishing in the master bedchamber, Meg moved on to that of the daughters. *There is Mrs. Linton*, she thought, *or Mrs. O'Sullivan.* Both had been motherly towards her and they knew her reasons for keeping her marital state a secret.

Meg's thoughts continued to churn as she went about her duties. Mrs. Linton had a husband and children. They lived at the Arcade. She'd understand Meg's turmoil. Or would she? Such a kind and gentle soul, she didn't seem to mind her hard life. She adored her husband and children. She might think Meg was selfish. *Am I?*

Mrs. O'Sullivan, then. A widow with a daughter both trying to support themselves in a factory. They would never leave the Arcade if they continued as they were. She wished they could have talked Aoife into finding a position as a domestic.

As she pushed the dust mop, having moved down to the first floor. She thought, *I will speak with Mrs. O'Sullivan about convincing Aoife to change jobs. The conversation can move naturally to my dilemma.* As soon as the thought came to her, she grew angry with herself. Premeditating the turn of a conversation that was supposed to help Aoife to her own benefit?

"Margaret Mary O'Connor Quinn, you should be ashamed of yourself!" she said aloud, banging the mop head on the floor sending a cloud of dust into the air.

Meg jumped as the front door opened.

"We can bring them in, can't we?" Deborah, the youngest of the Claprood girls asked as she and her sister entered the front hall.

"I suppose we can try, but they're in a terrible state. I'm not sure it would do any good," answered Pamela. "I'm distraught over their loss. I put my heart into those flowers. That awful storm ruined all my hard work."

Meg had noticed the wreck of the flower garden when she'd returned home the day after the hurricane.

Pamela Claprood had a passion for horticulture. Both girls were given to spending their free time pouring over botany books, copying pictures of flowers with their colored pencils, memorizing their Latin and common names, and quizzing each other. Their fondest pastime, though, was engaging in what they called the language of flowers. Each flower symbolized something – an emotion or ideal. To send certain flowers to someone was to send that person not simply a gift, but a message. Even the way flowers were held meant something specific. The Claprood girls were quite taken with this craze, but Pamela was so enamored she'd immersed herself in gardening and the art of floral arrangement. Though Meg acknowledged the girl had a talent for both, she could not understand the obsession. Not that she didn't like flowers. She thought them lovely. It was the veiled meanings she found ludicrous, akin to the language of fans. All this fuss with hidden meanings seemed frivolous.

"Margaret, could we enlist your help?" Pamela asked, entering the parlor.

"Yes, Miss."

"My poor flowers have been devastated by the storm. We'd like to salvage whatever we can."

"What would you like me to do?" Meg asked.

"Help with preparing a section of the back parlor. The part that gets the most sun. We'll set up a conservatory there, if Mother will allow it. I've always wanted a conservatory," Pamela continued, warming to her idea. "I could grow flowers all year, continue those I have now and start new from seed in the winter. Then I'll transplant them to my garden in their season." Pamela's pretty face beamed. "Perhaps the storm was a propitious event, after all."

Pamela headed towards the back parlor. "Oh, do let's get started right away," she called. "We'll need to move furniture to make room for the plants. I'll ask Father to purchase the necessary materials."

"What about your Mother, Miss?" Meg called after her. "You'd best get her permission."

Deborah, who had followed the conversation from the parlor doorway, now skipped along after her older sister to the back parlor. "Mother will agree, I'm sure," she said. "Let's plan!"

Meg rolled her eyes. "Plan all you like, but I'll not move one stick of furniture until your mother agrees," she said, returning to her dust mopping.

The Claprood girls chattered excitedly the rest of the afternoon. Meg watched them as she dusted in the back parlor. They'd gathered all their botany books, sketch pads, and pencils. Setting them out on a table, Pamela drew an outline of the room, indicating where she thought to put her various plants.

"Let's add a terrarium," Deborah said, leaning over Pamela's shoulder. "And cloches."

Meg glanced at the well-crafted drawing. She couldn't help but think of herself and Kathleen at the same age. Pamela, sixteen, and Deborah, fourteen, were worlds away from Meg and her own sister at those ages. They wouldn't have known what to do with a sketch pad had they owned one. Books were unheard of in their tiny cottage. Botany, a word Meg had learned since coming to work for the Claproods, was known to them only in the rudimentary way of all Ireland's peasants – as knowledge passed on through generations of working and foraging the land, providing what they could to stay alive. Even in the good times, when potatoes were plentiful, nothing was ever taken for granted.

Meg had always appreciated the beauty of nature, but to purposefully grow a thing for the sake of its beauty alone would have entered no one's head.

How different her life would have been had she been born here. She watched the lithe figures of the two girls as they flitted about the parlor checking their locations, adding and subtracting from their diagram.

Pamela moved about the room with stately grace, her light brown hair pinned atop her head. Deceptively delicate looking hands with long tapered fingers adroitly removed objects from shelves as her large doe eyes confidently ascertained if a space was the correct size for her needs.

Deborah, the blue-eyed, curly-haired, wheat blond sprite followed behind at a bouncier pace, her exuberance impossible to conceal when a new adventure emerged in her life.

Finishing her work in the back parlor, Meg headed for the kitchen to begin the afternoon meal. Passing through the dining room, she caught a glimpse of herself in the mirror above the fireplace. In Kelegeen she'd been thought a beauty. Long, glossy black hair, striking blue eyes set in a face with a finely honed bone structure, a robust figure strong as a bull, she was like a warrior woman of ancient days. Comely to look upon, built for work and breeding, she was the envy of many a lass in her village.

America, though, had a different vision of the ideal woman. Delicate, dainty, graceful – these were not words that described Meg. Staring at her reflection she was overcome by the feeling that she did not fit here. An odd sensation crept up her body – a feeling of not knowing who she was anymore. Was it possible to become someone else? Could she lose the person she once was and, more importantly, did she want to?

Meg stood at the sideboard while the Claproods ate.

"Please, may we do it?" Pamela asked, while Deborah turned pleading eyes on their mother.

Mrs. Claprood looked to her husband. "That room doesn't get much use. What do you think, Chester?"

The heads of both girls swiveled toward their father seated at the other end of the table.

"I suppose," he said with a heavy sigh. "Get Margaret there to help you." He waved a hand in Meg's direction.

"Thank you, Father," Pamela said while Deborah clapped her hands in delight. "We'll need several pots, a terrarium, some cloches –"

"Get whatever you like, my dear," he interrupted, "only don't break the bank. At the moment, we've more important things to concern us," he nodded toward his son.

"Was the foundry damaged by the storm?"asked Mrs. Claprood, a note of concern in her voice.

"Some broken windows, but those are easily repaired. Oliver's already spoken with the glazier. We were fortunate, though. That blasted wind took the roof right off of the school house over at Quinsigamond Village."

"Chester, language!" Mrs. Claprood admonished.

"Sorry, my dear." Mr. Claprood had the decency to appear ashamed for the sake of his wife and daughters over the 'blasted' that had escaped him, while Oliver suppressed a grin.

"The entire roof?" Deborah asked.

"The whole thing," Oliver answered.

"Did you see it?" asked Pamela.

"I did. It looks as though a giant knife sliced it from one end to the other. The roof itself is a jumbled mess on the ground along with a great deal of debris, mostly whatever had been in the upper level of the schoolhouse."

"I hope no one was harmed," said Mrs. Claprood.

"None that I've heard of," Oliver answered. "But I'm glad I'm not responsible for cleaning that mess."

"We've enough mess of our own to clean up," said Mr. Claprood, "Our premises is a shambles. Have you looked outside?"

"We have, Father," said Pamela. "The disaster of my garden is what gave me the idea for the conservatory."

"Well then, I suppose part of your plan is to clean that up?"

"Indeed. We will bring what we can salvage inside. I suppose we must discard the rest." Pamela sounded truly dejected over the loss of her flowers.

Despite her usual exhaustion, Meg had difficulty sleeping that night.

"I still love Rory. I know I do," she whispered to the darkness of her attic room. *But do I love the life I'm living now even more?* The question came often in recent days. She slammed a fist down on the mattress beside her. She hated that question.

Chapter Nine

The hurricane cleared away the oppressive heat and humidity. The remainder of the summer was beautiful. Warm days eased into cool evenings. Kathleen enjoyed the delicious weather, finding reasons to get outside. The combination of balmy temperature and being out from under Mrs. Pratt's scrutiny became intoxicating. Since Mrs. Pratt's irate greeting following the hurricane, the gulf that already existed between them widened. It should have been obvious she could not return earlier given the weather. Yet Mrs. Pratt was furious. "We had no knowledge of your whereabouts," she'd accused, as if Kathleen had sneaked off. "We could have used your help here. Whatever were you thinking going abroad in such abominable weather?"

When Kathleen explained, Mrs. Pratt's only response was to call her an empty-headed fool.

"From now on I insist you inform me of where you will be whenever you leave this house, day off or not."

At first, Kathleen dared to hope that this was simply Mrs. Pratt's way of saying she'd been worried, but as time progressed, she sensed a growing distrust. Perhaps it had to do with her accusation of Lemuel. Whatever fueled it, Mrs. Pratt constantly wanted to know where she was and insisted on a detailed report of her workday.

Mrs. Pratt visited her friends every Tuesday. She would take her calling cards and stride along the nearby streets with an air that all must be anxiously awaiting her. Kathleen relished Tuesdays.

"I'd like to ask you something *a stór*," Kathleen said to Clara one Tuesday in late September as they carried vegetables to the root cellar, "but I'll only ask if you promise not to mention it to anyone."

"I promise," Clara said, eagerness showing in her face.

"Only agree if you can honestly make the promise."

"I believe I can," Clara stated.

Kathleen hadn't wanted to bring Clara into this, but she could not understand what was happening and there was no one else she could ask.

"Have you heard your mam say that she's unhappy with my work?"

Clara's eyes widened. "No. I've never heard her say anything of the sort."

Kathleen nodded her head. That, at least, was a relief.

"Why do you ask? Has Mother said so to you?"

"No, but she seems different of late. Like she doesn't trust me. I can't imagine why."

Unburdened of the load of vegetables, they emerged from the root cellar. "My mother is rather a taskmaster, though I'd be pleased for you not to tell her I said so."

Kathleen smiled at the seriousness of the young girl's tone.

"Not a word from me," she agreed. "Aye, she's always been a strict mistress. I've come to expect that. But something has changed since that storm when I couldn't get home until the next morning. It couldn't be helped. 'Tis unreasonable to blame me, as if I could control the weather."

Clara's face contorted as though the concentration pained her.

"What is it, *a stór?*" Kathleen asked.

"Kathleen, what does the word 'diabolical' mean?"

Kathleen's stomach flipped. "Did your mother call me that?" she asked, her voice barely above a whisper.

"No, but Lemuel did. Well, he didn't exactly call *you* diabolical. He said all Papists are diabolical. He said other things about Papists that I didn't understand. I remember that word, though, because something about it sounds frightening. He told Mother we should be very careful having a Papist under our roof."

"Did he now?"

Clara nodded. "Catholics are called Papists because you follow the pope and want him to take over the world, Lemuel says. Is it true?"

Kathleen knelt between the rows of vegetables, caring nothing for the dirt on her uniform. Eye to eye with Clara, she said, "Many people think this, but it is not true. Aye, the pope is the head of the Catholic Church, sort of like the way your father and Mr. Claprood are the heads of that iron foundry they own. Or like your Mr. Millard Fillmore is the head of the United States. You have respect for the president of your country, don't you?"

"Yes, of course."

"Catholics have respect for the leader of our church, but we don't expect him to take over the world any more than you expect Mr. Fillmore to."

"Are you certain? Lemuel seemed awfully sure."

"Did he tell you this himself?"

Clara glanced sideways. "Well, no. He was speaking with Mother. I overheard."

"I see. What else did he say?"

"That Papists –"

"Please say Catholics," Kathleen interrupted. "Papist is an insult."

"Oh! I'm sorry. I didn't know."

"That's all right, *a stor*. I know you didn't. Go on."

"Well, he said you are pagans who worship Mary as a goddess and those saints are your little gods. Other things he said, too, but I didn't understand them."

Kathleen sighed deeply. "Miss Clara, I am going to explain something to you and I hope you will understand and remember it."

Clara focused all her attention on Kathleen.

"Catholics do not worship Mary, or as we call her, Our Lady or the Blessed Mother. We hold her in high esteem because she is the mother of our Lord, but we know she was as human as any of the rest of us. God chose her to be the mother of His son. Doesn't that seem reason to treat her with great respect?"

Intense concentration showed on Clara's face. "If God thought so highly of her, I suppose we should as well."

"There now. You understand. As for the saints, we don't worship them either. They are our friends in heaven. They help us by praying for us. We learn about their lives, about the ways in which they loved and served Our Lord. They show us how a good Christian life is lived."

"But you pray to them, don't you? And to Mary? Reverend Hunt says we should pray to God alone, or Jesus, of course, but he is God so it's the same. Why do you pray to all these saints when you can simply pray to the Lord?"

"We do pray to the Lord. We pray to Our Lady and the saints as well, but when we do we are asking them to intercede for us."

"Intercede?"

"It means they bring our prayers to the Lord."

"Why can't you just ask the Lord?"

"We can and we do." Kathleen thought for a moment. "Clara, has anyone ever asked you to pray for them?"

"Yes. When my friend, Anne, was terribly sick her mother asked us all to pray for her."

"Couldn't Anne's mother have prayed to the Lord herself?"

"I'm certain she did."

"But she asked others to pray for Anne, too."

Clara nodded.

"It's the same. Anne's mother asked others to pray because the more prayers, the better. Why shouldn't we ask the saints, the holy ones already standing before the throne of God, to pray for us?"

Clara appeared to be deeply considering these new ideas. "I can see your point, though I doubt Mother or Lemuel would agree."

"You needn't mention it to either. In fact, it's best if you don't. Your mother told me before we started cooking together that she did not want me to discuss my religion with you. I've obeyed that instruction until now. Oh, Clara, you're such a good girl I can't stand the thought of your head being filled with..." she wanted to say *filthy lies*, but

100

thought better of it... "mistaken notions. Well, it's more than I can bear."

"Why do you suppose Lemuel believes all that if it isn't true? He's well educated."

"Educated in some things, but in the Catholic faith, his knowledge is lacking."

Clara smiled. "I love you, Kathleen. I would not want to think you were doing anything that would harm your soul."

"Oh, lass, you are a love." Kathleen threw her arms around the child, hugging her tight. "Well, that's enough catechism for one day," she said. "Let's start on dinner."

Kathleen was more wary than ever of Lemuel. He seemed to watch her as closely as his mother now.

On an evening in early October, Kathleen was involved in her mending in a corner of the family parlor, when she became aware of male voices in the next room. At first, she could only hear the rumble of conversation. It was Mr. Pratt and Lemuel speaking of business, a matter in which she had no interest. It was only when the voices rose that she could not help but overhear.

"I'll not have it!"

"I've said nothing that isn't true." Lemuel sounded defensive.

"Be that as it may, you've upset your mother with your wild accusations. You will stop."

Kathleen began to gather her mending to move to another room, as the conversation had obviously changed from business to personal matters. As she rose from the chair, Lemuel's next words arrested her.

"That Papist bitch is infecting our home and family. If Mother insists on having help, I don't see why she couldn't hire a good Protestant girl."

"It's nigh impossible to find any but the Irish. No Yankee girl would lower herself to such a position."

Dear God, do all here but Clara hate me? Kathleen wondered. Tears came unbidden to her eyes, but she forced them back. She would never allow them to wound her so.

"We've seen no behavior to suggest that our Bridget is untrustworthy. I insist you stop filling your mother's mind with worrisome nonsense that this girl is part of a conspiracy or that she's teaching pagan ways to Clara, or that she's the devil's mistress, or whatever the deuce else you've been telling your mother."

Kathleen gasped, then quickly covered her mouth. Gathering her mending in her arms, she hurried towards the kitchen.

Their conversation remained in her head. *The devil's mistress.* And what sort of conspiracy could he have meant? One to take over their home? To convert Clara? To help the pope take over the world? Kathleen laughed out loud at that last one. *If Mrs. Pratt believes a word of this, she's the empty-headed fool,* thought Kathleen. She was but trying to do an honest job to help support her family back home. How could Lemuel be so vindictive? He was the one who had hurt her. *Don't think on it now,* she told herself. *Tomorrow is Thursday.* She would seek the advice of Meg and Nuala.

* * *

"Aye, but these Yanks can try one's patience to its very end," Nuala said after Kathleen explained all that had happened. The three of them strolled through the shops underneath City Hall. "My last mistress had a mind to 'lead me in the right path' so as to save my wretched Papist soul. She tried to force me to attend her benighted church, insisted I discard my rosary, and renounce any and all allegiance to the Catholic Church and to the pope."

"What did you do?" Kathleen asked.

Nuala squared her shoulders, jutted out her jaw in a way that must have been reminiscent of the stance she'd taken with her employer. "I told her she'd have better luck convincing a mule to put on a tam and dance a jig than she would of me doing any such things."

"And she didn't fire you?" Kathleen was astonished.

"No. She was an old widow living alone. I was the only help she had. She was sickly often, too. I spent more time nursing than cleaning and cooking. Stayed with her 'til the day she died, but I never once gave in to any of her demands. I'm sure she died thinking she'd go straight to heaven and I'll be bound for hell. The Dentons either don't believe my soul's in jeopardy or don't care. Either way, I'm grateful."

"What about you, Meg?" asked Kathleen. "Do the Clap-roods say anything about your religion?"

Meg shook her head. "Not to my face. If they don't like Catholics, they keep it to themselves. I hope it stays that way. I like my place, but I'd leave if I were forced to choose between their church and mine."

"What will you do?" Nuala asked Kathleen.

"I have to work and it's better than what Aoife does. I don't want to live at the Arcade. I'll have to make the best of it."

"What if they try to force you to go to their church?" Meg asked, her eyes blazing.

"I *would* live in the Arcade and sew boots and shoes rather than surrender my faith."

"It's not fair that you have to put up with this, all because Lemuel is such a scoundrel," said Nuala. "But if you do decide to leave, you'll get a position with another family. The Yanks are looking for help all over the city. Think about it, Kathleen. Despite his father telling him to stop, I've a feeling Lemuel's not the type to take orders from anyone, even his own da."

"I'd hate to leave Clara," Kathleen lamented. "I'd miss her terribly. She thinks of me as her sister."

"Aye, but you're not her sister," Meg interjected. "As much as she wishes you were, her mother will never allow that type of connection."

"But it's already begun," Kathleen insisted.

"That may be a reason to leave sooner rather than later," said Nuala. "The closer she grows to you the harder it will be on both of you. Meg's right. Mrs. Pratt may refuse to allow you near Clara much longer by the sounds of things."

Kathleen felt as though a stone had settled in her stomach. She loved Clara and had already lost her own younger sister. Brigid would never leave Ireland. Kathleen was not likely to return. She'd never stop missing Brigid, but Clara helped to fill that empty place in Kathleen's heart. For Clara's sake, she would stay with the Pratts as long as they would keep her.

"Did you notice who was sitting with Aoife at Mass last Sunday?" Meg asked.

"You mean the young man?" Nuala asked with a knowing smile.

"I do."

"That was Ned, I suppose," said Kathleen. "The one she's sweet on."

"Aye," said Meg. "Mrs. O'Sullivan told me they're courting now that he's found a job at the wire works."

"I hope she's not thinking of marrying him," Nuala stated. "He can't be making much. She won't get out of the Arcade that way."

"I don't see why she can't keep working," said Kathleen. "With both salaries, maybe they could live somewhere better."

"And what will they do when the bairns come?" Nuala questioned. "Do you expect Aoife to bring them with her? Can't you see her now, running leather pieces through the sewing machine while nursing a wee one? She'd need to grow an extra arm."

Kathleen sighed. "Still, it's most unfair." She looked at her sister. "What will you do when Rory comes, Meg?"

Meg shifted her gaze. "I don't know," she said, then pointed to a shop. "Let's try over there."

"Aoife appears happy right now. She was grinning ear to ear looking at Ned last Sunday," Kathleen said, a wistful sigh escaping.

"She'll have a far different look when they're married with more mouths to feed and not enough money for food," said Nuala. "And if he doesn't work quickly or well enough, or gets sick he'll be out the door. His Yank boss won't care that he's got a family to feed. There are others waiting to take his place. I don't understand why Aoife won't listen to sense and find a placement like we've done."

"Perhaps she's in love with him," Kathleen offered.

Nuala laughed. "Love! That won't last once times get harder for her than they are already."

Meg was leaning over a table appearing to study the bolts of cloth laid out on it. Kathleen noticed Meg stiffen at Nuala's words.

"Aren't these lovely," Meg said, turning towards the others. "I wonder how Aisling's coming with her seamstress training. I wish I could send her some of this, but I don't know what she'd need and the money must be spent for food and rent first. I suppose Rory might tell me if Aisling could use some cloth and, if so, what kind. Ah, perhaps the price for shipping it would be too dear?"

Meg's rambling was so unlike her. Her hand trembled as it smoothed the bolt of cloth.

"Beautiful," Nuala agreed. "Now I could use something warm," she continued. "It's already much colder than usual at this time of year."

"Does it get very cold in the winter?" Kathleen asked.

"Aye, but it does. Much colder than back home," Nuala told her. "You'll want warm clothing for the coming months."

"It snows here, too," Meg added. "Plenty."

The thought of snow made Kathleen shiver. "As much as we had at home?"

"More," Meg said. "The winters here are fierce. Snow can pile up as high as your knees or higher."

Kathleen remembered the snowstorms during the starving time in Ireland. In a land that rarely saw snow, that horrid winter it covered the ground ankle deep like a cold, white blanket and brought on the greatest suffering she'd ever known. "How do you stand it?"

Meg shrugged. "The fireplaces are going all day. Your work keeps you moving and that helps you stay warm. The stove makes the kitchen hot in all weather. I can't bear the heat of The Beast in the summer, but in the winter it's a mite more welcome."

Kathleen tried to picture the landscape covered in knee-deep snow. "How do people get about with it so deep?"

"The City packs down the snow on the roads with oxen and horses," Nuala told her. "Then folks can walk on it well enough or drive their sleighs. The Yanks love it so much they hold sleighing parties. When the ponds freeze over they skate on them."

"Skate?" asked Kathleen.

"They strap a sort of contraption with a blade on it to the bottom of their boots and go gliding across the ice on them," Meg explained. "It's quite a sight. They make a party of it, skating together until they're frozen to the bone. Then they come inside and make a row while they're drinking hot chocolate."

Nuala laughed. "First an old widow and now the Dentons. There are no skating or sleighing parties for me to clean up after." She turned to Kathleen. "It's the young people who partake in those frolics."

"The Claprood girls love their winter escapades," said Meg. "They take turns hosting, but when it's at their house I spend half the day making hot chocolate and mopping up wet floors from all the melting snow they drag in."

"Don't forget the sleds," said Nuala. "Flat wooden things on runners they can pull with a long rope. They use them as much for coasting down the hills as they do for carrying things. They make a sport of the whole season, they do."

Kathleen felt as though she moved to a new land every few months. This autumn she'd seen leaves change from green to a multitude of colors. They did so in Ireland, but not with the vibrancy she saw here. Apples seemed about to take over her life. Apple pies, apple cobbler, apple turnovers, apple cider. "After the first hard frost, Bridget," Harvey had told her. "That's when the apples become tart. We'll get loads. You and Clara can make so many confections with them." Harvey, at least, didn't seem to have any problem with the growing friendship between Clara and Kathleen.

"It'll be dark before long," Meg said as they left the market stalls below City Hall. The air had a crispness to it despite the smoke-belching factories. As they walked toward home, it become sharper, with a tang more noticeable as they left the manufacturing area. It was a good smell, not clean and pure like that of spring, but something that made Kathleen think of food; food in abundance. She and Clara had already laid away more vegetables in the root cellar than Kathleen had eaten in any one year of her life. They had preserved and pickled what seemed an endless supply. Such processes were new to Kathleen, but she loved the tart scent of pickling spices and vinegar. Looking over the jars of preserved fruits and vegetables in the evening just before going to bed gave her a feeling of security. If only she could feel accepted by the Pratt family.

"I wish they'd hurry up and finish these roads," Nuala grumbled as they picked their way through partially paved streets. As the light began to fade, workers gathered their tools, set equipment aside, and led the draft animals away. "It seems they've been working on them for as long as I've been here."

"Aye," Meg agreed, "Paving roads takes a long time."

Meg drew her cape tightly about herself. "It is colder than usual for this time of year. I wonder if this means the winter will be especially harsh."

"Lord, I hope not," said Nuala.

Kathleen was shivering. She would need her coming pay to purchase a warmer cloak.

As they climbed the steep hills towards home, they heard the sounds of hammers and saws. More homes were being built in their neighborhood.

"We must work on Aoife," Nuala stated. "It's for sure the owners will be hiring help once they're settled in."

"She doesn't seem agreeable," Kathleen said. "We can't force her. Meg, what does Mrs. O'Sullivan think of Ned?"

"I gather she thinks him a nice enough lad, but I don't believe she wants Aoife to marry him."

"Why not?"

"She knows what Aoife's life will be like raising a family on one man's factory pay. She sees it every day with her sister's family."

"But the Lintons seem happy, don't they?"

"Happy with one another, aye, though I doubt with their situation. Right now they're but a step or two above what we all came from. And a step or two down is as possible as drawing their next breath. I can't live that way again!"

Meg bolted toward the Claprood home.

"Meg, wait!" Nuala called, starting after her.

Kathleen took Nuala's arm. "Let me."

Nuala nodded. "I'll see you both Sunday."

Kathleen caught up with Meg at the kitchen door. She placed her hand over her sister's. "Meg, look at me."

Meg hung her head.

Kathleen wrapped her sister in her arms. "This is awful for you."

A great sob escaped Meg. "It never stops. Not for us."

The two sank to the step, holding onto each other. "All we're asking is to survive without constant torment."

Kathleen, in the unfamiliar position of comforter to her older sister, was not quite sure what to say. *Oh, Lord, give me the right words*, she prayed.

"Meg, why haven't you written the truth to Rory?" she asked.

Meg pulled away, wiped her eyes. "I'm afraid."

"Of what?"

"Of something Father O'Malley told Rory and me before I left."

"What was it?"

Meg swallowed hard. "Our marriage was never consummated what with me boarding the ship right after the ceremony.

Father O'Malley said if we found no way for Rory to make it here, the marriage could be annulled. The Church would grant it under such circumstances."

"Do you want that, Meg?" Kathleen whispered.

"What I want is Rory here with a good paying job."

Meg looked up at the lovely white house looming above her. "I'd be happy in a home half this size with but a portion of what they have, yet that seems out of reach. I'm afraid if I write Rory, he'll think I don't want him, that I want the life I have now instead. Though he said he would never ask for an annulment, I'm afraid he won't come if he thinks he'll make my life worse. I couldn't bear that."

Kathleen took Meg's tear-streaked face in her hands. "All through the Hunger you were the one who insisted we would survive. You were the one who found a way to come here, earn a living, and send back money so we could eat and pay the rent. You were the one who brought me here. You've always been the strongest of us. You cannot let this country with its damn Yankee Brits change that! You will find a way to have the life you want here in America with Rory and as many bairns as the Lord sees fit to give you. A good life. A happy one. Oh, Meg, you've earned it."

"People don't always get what they deserve," Meg said. "This country has changed me. Once I could live on a handful of potatoes, spend my days doing mending work in a tiny cottage with a dirt floor and one window. But now..."

"You've turned soft? Is that what you're telling me?"

"I'm afraid I have." Meg put her head in her hands.

Kathleen stood with her hands on her hips, feet firmly planted. Meg's stance.

"Margaret Mary O'Connor Quinn," she summoned.

Meg lifted her head.

"You rise every morning before the sun. You light the stove fire, set the table, bring up the scuttle from the cellar, polish the stove, shake out the door mats, sweep the steps, and shine the brass before a single member of that family is awake. Once they do arise, you stand ready to jump at their slightest command. You don't stop for a minute. You don't go to bed until after they do because you just might be needed for something so long as one of them is awake. By your own bedtime you're so tired you can hardly move. And I know you. I know you don't let yourself rest before you've knelt down and prayed. I've fallen asleep pray-

108

ing myself more than once. And the next morning you get up and do it all over again. Sure you get Thursday afternoons to yourself and Sunday mornings for Mass, but otherwise you're at their beck and call every minute. You've been doing it for going on four years now so that you could take care of our family across the ocean. Two families, counting what's left of Rory's. And you've done a brilliant job of it. Soft are you, now? Soft in the head, perhaps!

"Get up from that step. Go into that house, eat a good meal and go to bed. And beginning tomorrow, figure a way to make having Rory, a decent home, and a family more than a dream. You've already done more than we could imagine, Meg. You can do this, too."

Seeing Meg so close to broken unlocked something inside Kathleen. A spark deep within her soul had ignited. Meg, the family's stalwart warrior, needed help. Because of Meg she was here instead of sitting on a dirt floor in Ireland, wearing rags. Or, more likely, laying in the churchyard. She would never forget what her sister's courage had accomplished. She would fight for Meg with all she had.

Slowly, Meg rose, looking at Kathleen with a kind of awe.

"You will do it," Kathleen said, her voice now quieter. "I will help you." She embraced her sister tightly before heading off into the darkness toward the Pratt home.

Chapter Ten

"Do they think to tell me how to run my own business?"

Meg had never seen Mr. Claprood in such a foul mood.

Oliver had come home with news that several state and local politicians were lobbying for the ten- hour workday to curry votes from complaining factory workers.

"It's not a law yet. It won't be. Too many Whigs still in power," Oliver stated.

The Claprood gentlemen were in the parlor. Meg, tidying up the back parlor, turned conservatory, hung on every word. Kathleen's admonishment had roused her spirit. She understood little of their conversations when they spoke of business or politics, but she listened, tucked things away in her mind, hoping somewhere there was a nugget or two that could help her.

Laborers were pushing for greater rights, most especially fewer hours in the workday. If conditions improved, Rory might not do so poorly as a factory worker if he did not find employment as a groom. She also hoped, for Aoife's sake, that Ned's situation would get better.

"They've passed the Secret Ballot Law just this year. We've no longer any way to know how our workers vote," Mr. Claprood complained. "It's a step towards passing the ten-hour workday."

"It is, of course," Oliver agreed. "It removes our leverage, but it hardly guarantees the passage of a bill."

"Would it be so awful?" asked Mrs. Claprood who had just entered the parlor. "Wouldn't your workers do a better job if they were happier?"

"My dear, you don't understand. One must get the most one can from the workforce."

"Chester, that's exactly my point. If I had to work so many hours that I had no time for my family I would resent my employer, especially if he seemed to be purposely preventing me from home and hearth. Yet if he looked to my well-being and

110

that of my dear ones, I would be willing to offer him the very best of my service. And my utter loyalty. Would that not make up for a few hours?"

Mr. Claprood sighed. "My dear Emily, you've a soft heart. So appropriate for a wife and mother, which is why you are exceptional in those spheres. A man's duty is to support his wife and children. Why would a good man want to reduce his work hours? Hours which decide his pay. The little extra time he'd have with family wouldn't be of much service to them if it lessens their food and other necessities of life."

"Then simply pay your workers more," Mrs. Claprood stated. "Surely, they earn it."

Meg felt the smile stretch across her face upon hearing Mrs. Claprood's words. The conservatory was growing dim despite the large windows. It was time to begin preparing the evening meal.

"Mother, we are in competition with other foundries," Oliver explained. "We must have a greater output than all the others else we'll be done in by them. Our workers must put in the hours necessary for us to remain competitive."

"But don't you think –"

Mrs. Claprood was interrupted by Deborah's excited cry as she burst into the room. "It's snowing!"

Meg, about to leave the conservatory turned back. Pulling aside the window curtain, she could see in the waning light the soft fluttering of white flakes.

So soon, she thought. *It's not yet November.*

"It can't be," said Mrs. Claprood.

"Look!" cried Deborah.

Meg entered the parlor to find them all staring out the window.

"It has been unusually cold," Oliver stated. "I suppose we're in for an early winter."

"This won't stay long," Mr. Claprood assured them. "It's a peculiarity, nothing more."

He was wrong. Winter arrived early. A killing frost hit before farmers could harvest all their crops. By mid-November, the snow had come to stay.

* * *

"Do you think we'll have enough for Thanksgiving?" Deborah asked.

Pamela, distracted by her efforts to coax an ivy vine up one of the marble pillars that anchored each end of the conservatory's window seat, asked, "Enough what?"

"Food, of course," Deborah chided. "When Mother said we should be frugal about food this winter, I couldn't sleep thinking it might ruin Thanksgiving."

Meg stopped polishing lamps. She walked to the open pocket doors separating the parlor from the conservatory. Both Claprood girls had their backs to her.

"It's only vegetables. We'll still have meat and bread," Pamela said, climbing atop the window seat for a better perch while winding the ivy vine. "Help me with this, would you?"

Deborah handed the trailing vine up to her sister. "I do wish we'd bought more cranberries. Cranberry sauce is my favorite. I love it with turkey."

"There will be enough sauce for you," Pamela assured her.

"You know Mother. It would be rude of me to have the sauce all to myself."

"Then you'll go without. There, I think we've got it," Pamela said, stepping away to examine her work. "Does it look like an embellished Greek pillar?"

"Let's check the book's illustration."

As they approached a large open book on the table in the center of the room the girls finally caught sight of Meg.

"Margaret, is something wrong?" Pamela asked. "You are just standing there."

Meg squared her shoulders. "Is there anything you need of me?" was all she could think to say.

"No. We are fine on our own," Pamela told her.

Meg hurried away, but before she was out of the parlor she heard Deborah ask, "What do you suppose that was about?"

"I've no idea," Pamela replied.

Meg headed straight to the root cellar. In the dim light she could make out shelves of beets, carrots, potatoes, squash, cabbages, parsnips, onions, radishes, pumpkins, apples, and pears. A massive table held slabs of meat layered in salt, pepper, and brown sugar. Dried fish hung on the walls. A large basket of eggs sat by her feet. There were two great wheels of cheese and a large tub of butter. Barrels of flour and corn meal stood against the wall. Upstairs the cupboards held jars of jams, pickled foods, and spices. Dried herbs hung from the kitchen ceiling. Her family in Ireland, even with the money she'd been sending for years, would look upon this as a bounty sent from God Himself. An anger she hadn't felt since before coming to America welled up inside her. Turning to climb the stairs she noticed a small container of cranberries. The overwhelming compulsion never to waste a morsel of food was the only thing that kept her from dumping them on the floor and stomping them to a pulpy mess.

"Margaret, there you are," said Emily Claprood as Meg returned to the kitchen. "Mrs. Pratt has come to call. We'll be taking tea in my room. Please bring it up along with some bread and jam."

"Of course, Ma'am." Meg put on the kettle. She smeared strawberry jam across a few slices of bread. Meg did not mind that the Claproods were conserving food. What bothered her was the air of self-pity, as though one less helping of mashed potatoes was a tremendous sacrifice.

When the tea was ready, Meg carried it upstairs to Mrs. Claprood's bedchamber, setting the tray on a table near where the two ladies sat.

"I don't know what to do with our Bridget for Thanksgiving," Mrs. Pratt said to Mrs. Claprood as Meg poured.

"Won't you take her with you? Surely your family in Concord could use the extra help?"

"I don't think so, Emily. They've two. Bringing ours along would mean they'd have to find a place for her to sleep and they'd have to feed her, as well."

Meg took a step back from the tea table awaiting further instruction.

"That will be all, Margaret. Thank you," said Mrs. Claprood.

Meg bobbed a curtsy and left the room. She did not go far. It was her sister of whom they were speaking. She could not simply walk away.

"I dislike the thought of the girl unsupervised for several days."

"Surely she knows her routine well enough."

"It's a matter of trust."

Meg's cheeks burned.

"You don't trust her?" There was concern in Mrs. Claprood's voice.

"It's possible she would do her work faithfully. Perhaps even likely. She's not one to slack off, I will give her that much."

"What's the problem?"

"Must I say it outright?"

"I'm afraid you'll have to. I'd trust our Margaret without reservation."

A twinge of guilt at eavesdropping assaulted Meg, but she shoved it aside at Mrs. Pratt's next words.

"Emily. They are both Papists."

"Oh, Sophronia, I've never held a person's religion against them."

"I have warned you not to be so gullible. Lemuel's well-versed in such things."

"Indeed," said, Mrs. Claprood, disapproval in her voice barely evident, but there.

"Emily, they are all involved in the plot."

"For the pope to take over the world?" she asked.

"Of course."

"I cannot fathom what part two serving maids could play."

"I'm sure it's a humble one, but every Papist has a hand in it. My son has convinced me of that."

Meg heard a sigh escape Mrs. Claprood.

"Kathleen could help us here while you're gone."

Meg had to clasp a hand over her mouth so her excited gasp would not be heard.

"Stay with you?"

"Yes. We will have my brother's family again this year. I'm sure Margaret would be delighted to have her sister's help with her extra duties."

"If you're sure it's not an imposition."

"You leave the day before Thanksgiving? Send Kathleen over then. She can stay until you return."

"Emily, you are a dear friend."

Meg nearly danced down the hallway. She could hardly wait for Kathleen to hear the news. They'd be under the same roof for days! Her anger at Mrs. Pratt's bigotry changed to delight.

The Claprood girls caught her singing while dusting the furniture later that afternoon.

"You're feeling better, Margaret?" Pamela asked.

"I am, thank you." She beamed at the girl who returned her smile.

"I'm glad of that. We were afraid you were ill."

114

"You are a darlin' lass to worry after me."

How she wished Kathleen had a family as kind as the Clap-roods. At least there was Clara. Thank God for her.

Meg's workload increased as Thanksgiving approached. After Oliver and Mr. Claprood moved the heavy furniture, it fell to her along with Mrs. Claprood and the two girls to do a thorough housecleaning. Grateful for their help, Meg was glad that Mrs. Claprood trained her daughters to accept caring for one's home as a normal part of family life. Still, Meg had more to do. Beating every rug in the cold November air until not a speck of dust or dirt remained. Preparation of bedchambers for their guests. Assist Mrs. Claprood with preparing the menu for the great feast along with the other meals she'd prepare for the Claproods and Mrs. Claprood's brother and his family.

Thanksgiving brought Meg's monumental confrontation with The Beast. Not that she didn't have a daily row with it, but this particular holiday was especially trying. So many dishes prepared at once, the constant stoking of the stove and the struggle to keep the heat regulated properly nearly drove her mad. Several dishes made days in advance only increased her daily culinary duties.

But this year her spirits remained high because each day brought Kathleen's arrival closer. Meg wondered at her own childlike excitement. It wasn't as if she didn't see her sister regularly. But they would be pulling together for a common purpose, able to converse as they worked, and, if exhaustion didn't completely overtake them, talk in the privacy of Meg's attic room afterwards. Kathleen, with her growing talent for cookery, might even be able to tame The Beast.

That night, Meg lay in bed thinking of home. She still felt like an outsider in America. She desperately missed the tiny cottage with its dirt floor, one window, and sparse furnishings. How strange since she was living in splendor now. No, it was not the cottage itself she missed. It was her family, her memories, the love contained within its walls.

Chapter Eleven

Wednesday, November 25, 1851 dawned clear and cold. A good deal of snow had fallen within the last few days leaving the land blanketed. Kathleen squinted against the sun's glint on the snow. She'd slept little the night before. The mystery of this American holiday was about to unfold and joy of all joys, she would spend it with Meg! Not only the day, but a whole week while the Pratts remained in Concord!

This morning she'd had her first look at a sleigh. The Pratts hired one to take them to the train station. Peering out the window, Kathleen's mouth dropped open at the sight of the long, oddly shaped conveyance pulled by two steaming horses. A merry sound came from the myriad tiny bells covering the horses' harnesses as the sleigh magically glided across the packed snow.

"It's here!" Clara called from the front entry. The family quickly gathered, their baggage waiting by the door.

"Kathleen!" called Mrs. Pratt. "We are ready to leave."

Kathleen pulled herself away from the parlor window and joined the family in the front hall.

"I wish you were coming with us," Clara said.

"We've discussed this," said Mrs. Pratt, her face hard as marble.

Clara appeared close to tears.

"You'll not mind a bit once you've got your cousins round you, Miss Clara." Kathleen could not hide her cheerfulness.

"Do not forget yourself," Mrs. Pratt warned one last time. "You are to serve the Claproods, not to have a high time with your sister. I will obtain a full account from Mrs. Claprood upon my return."

"I will give my very best effort, Mrs. Pratt," Kathleen promised. She wondered, though, if an excellent report would be more of a disappointment to her employer.

As the family made their way to the sleigh, the driver jumped down to assist them with their baggage. It was the first time Kathleen had ever seen anyone with skin the color of coffee. She'd heard about Negroes, as the Pratts referred to them, but she hadn't realized there were any in Worcester. From the talk, she imagined them all to be in a place called the South, where they were held as slaves. Yet here stood a man who must be a Negro. None of the Pratts seemed to find his presence unusual. He intrigued her as much as did the sleigh. Like the conveyance, he moved with grace and fluidity. Once all were settled, he leaped to the front, gathering the reins. Just before he snapped them, Mrs. Pratt called to Kathleen.

"Stop gawking. The Claproods are waiting for you."

She shouldered her sack and began her trek to the Claproods'.

Kathleen had barely rapped at the kitchen door when Meg threw it open with a flourish. She pulled Kathleen into a tight hug. "I can hardly believe we have seven whole days together!"

Kathleen was almost as excited about using the larger, roomier stove as she was about the time she'd spend with Meg.

"Clara has read out many receipts from her mother's books and I've copied them down," she said, pulling her homemade book from her bag.

Meg flipped through the pages. "How handy. May I copy some? It's a struggle memorizing receipts. So many ingredients. I can't keep them all in my head."

"Of course. Now, where do we start?"

Meg looked about the cluttered kitchen. "The pies are made. They've been packed into a blanket chest upstairs. The north facing chamber has been closed off for the winter, so we keep them there. They'll stay frozen until needed. I suppose we'll have to bring enough down tonight so they can thaw in time. I wish you'd been able to come weeks ago for the pie making, scores of them, all sorts – apple, pumpkin, mince meat, chicken, and Marlborough pudding pie. I thought it would never end.

Kathleen smiled. "Clara and I have made a quantity of those as well. She tells me they'll keep in the upstairs chamber all winter."

"The rooms stay so cold everything freezes. Our blanket chests are full. Did you think you'd ever see such an amount of food?" Meg asked.

"Sometimes I think I'm dreaming and I'll wake up at home starving."

"I have those dreams, too," Meg marveled. "Well, we'd better get started."

The day flew by as Meg and Kathleen did a final cleaning of the house before the Claproods' guests arrived. Mrs. Claprood's brother, Peter Amberson along with his wife, Martha, and five children were expected late that afternoon. Everything must be in place when they appeared, and an evening meal prepared for all. Mr. and Mrs. Amberson would occupy the spare bedchamber on the second floor while the children, who ranged in ages from six to seventeen, would sleep in the larger section of the attic opposite Meg's quarters.

Mrs. Claprood, Pamela, and Deborah assisted, though the two girls were so distracted by anticipation   they were of little help. Pamela, especially keen to show off the conservatory to her cousins, frequently crept away to rearrange plants, move terrariums, and fiddle with the ivy vines. Deborah, whenever she realized her sister was missing, followed after, not to bring her back, but to join her. Mrs. Claprood finally gave up trying to corral her daughters. She, Meg, and Kathleen worked like a whirlwind until she realized that her brother and his family were due within the hour.

"I must change my clothes before they arrive and drag Pamela and Deborah away from their plants to do the same," she told Meg and Kathleen. "You girls carry on from here."

Kathleen poked a thawing chicken pie with a fork. "It's still frozen in the middle," she said.

"It will unfreeze in the oven, won't it?" Meg asked.

"Aye, but we'll have to get the heat just right and keep it regulated, else you'll have burnt edges and a soggy middle."

"I've no head for that."

Kathleen laughed. "Let me try." Kathleen began loading fuel into the oven, testing again and again until the heat was as she wanted it before sliding the pie inside. They worked side-by-side at the table and the stove, chopping, stirring, and mixing, all the while keeping up a constant chatter. Unexpected emotion overtook Kathleen while peeling vegetables. Other than preparing potatoes their work back home was nothing like this. But they'd often sat at the table with their mam and Brigid as they worked on the mending they took in from the wealthy British town ladies. Kathleen lifted her apron to stem the flow of tears.

Meg, dropped her paring knife.

"I'm sorry," Kathleen whispered. "Working together reminds me of home. I miss Mam and Brigid, Meg. We'll never see them again."

Meg took Kathleen in her arms. "At least we have each other. I felt so alone before you came."

When Meg returned to her chair, Kathleen asked, "Do you ever regret it?"

Meg took a deep breath. "No, but I wish I could bring them all here. I know that's just a dream. Brigid could never endure the journey. Though Aisling apparently is much improved, I'm afraid it would be a terrible detriment to her health. I've no doubt Loreena could make it, though I'm not sure she'd leave Brigid. And Mam would never leave a single one of them behind, especially not now that she's awaiting Brendan's return. Rory is the only one I'm sure of, but even he won't leave until he knows the others will be cared for."

"Are you reconciled to Rory's coming?" Kathleen asked.

Meg sighed, picked up her knife. "I still feel torn, but I took to heart what you said about finding a way to make it work. I hear the things said by Mister Claprood and Master Oliver. Workers are pushing for a ten-hour workday and insisting upon better conditions. I pray that by the time Rory comes, the work for Irish men will have improved. At the present, praying is all I can do."

A commotion coming from the front hall signaled the Claproods welcoming their relatives.

"I never heard the knocker," Meg said, rising from her chair. "The girls must have been watching for their sleigh."

Kathleen grabbed her arm. "What do we do?"

"Stand out of the way, take their coats, don't speak unless spoken to, and once they've gone into the parlor we'll put their wraps away, then take their baggage to their rooms."

The sisters hastened to the front hallway stopping just outside the family circle of a swarm of hugs and kisses. A cold blast of air whipped through the hallway as the sleigh driver deposited the last pieces of luggage just inside the door. Kathleen glanced at him. Like the Pratts' driver, he too, was dark skinned. At Meg's nudge, Kathleen returned her attention to the coats, hats, gloves, and muffs being piled into her arms. Children's wet boots were kicked off and left by the door. The adults and oldest children formed a little knot around which the younger children circled, all as oblivious to Meg and Kathleen as their elders.

"Meg, bring tea to the parlor," Mrs. Claprood called over her shoulder.

"Right away, Ma'am," Meg answered.

"Come with us," Pamela said to Alice and Elizabeth. "We've set up a conservatory and can't wait to show you."

"Where is Oliver?" asked Benjamin, the eldest of the Amberson children.

"He's at the foundry with Father," Deborah explained.

Benjamin frowned.

"Come with us to the conservatory," Pamela invited.

Benjamin shrugged and joined the young ladies as they trouped off together while the two littlest ones, Nancy and Ethan, followed their parents into the parlor.

Back in the kitchen, Meg handed Kathleen a mop to wipe up the slush in the entryway while she started tea.

While mopping, Kathleen glanced into the parlor. Mrs. Claprood's brother, Peter Amberson, stood by the fireplace. Meg had said he was a lawyer in Boston. Certainly his clothing displayed success. His wife, Martha, a plump, cheerful lady sat upon the settee with their two youngest propped beside her. Mrs. Claprood occupied a richly upholstered chair. The guests, appearing only slightly worn from their travel, eased into pleasantries with Mrs. Claprood. From the next room, girlish voices exclaimed. Benjamin wandered into the parlor and stood opposite his father near the fireplace.

When Kathleen returned to the kitchen, Meg was scurrying about setting cups, saucers, and spoons on a large silver tray. Last she added the silver teapot, fragrant steam puffing from its spout.

"Please take the luggage upstairs while I serve," she told Kathleen. "You may use the front staircase if you can do it quietly."

Kathleen started up the stairs with the baggage, but when the weight caused her to bump into the treads she retreated, resigned to lugging it through the kitchen and up the back staircase.

"Benjamin, make yourself useful, son, and assist that young lady," said Mr. Amberson.

The younger Mr. Amberson appeared at her side, taking the bag from her hand.

"Thank you, sir," she said, surprised.

120

Benjamin shrugged. "Not at all," he said, though he avoided looking at her. "I suppose my parents will be in their accustomed room?"

"I believe so," Kathleen answered. "I don't usually work here. My sister Meg does. I'm helping for the week."

A quick nod, then Benjamin hefted his parents' luggage up the stairs. Kathleen grabbed the smaller bags and followed. She left him at the threshold of the spare chamber and continued to the third floor. The end of the attic where the nieces and nephews would be sleeping was much larger and better appointed than was Meg's. There were two large beds, a chest of drawers, a dressing table, a washstand, and four chairs. The long chamber still had space enough for easy movement. Kathleen dropped the baggage at the foot of one bed. She looked wistfully at the darkening room. It was larger than her family's cottage back home. Were Yankees aware of their abundance? They seemed to take so much for granted.

"Mrs. Claprood's family appear a nice enough lot," Kathleen stated as she and Meg cleaned up from the day's final meal.

"Aye. They must have had a good mam and da, I'd say. Wish there were more like them in this country."

"I thought Benjamin rude at first, but it might be he's just a shy lad," said Kathleen. "He perked up once Master Oliver came home. Idolizes his older cousin, he does, there's no doubt." Kathleen laughed at the memory of watching the young man at table mimicking the manners of his cousin. Benjamin had become as animated in the presence of Oliver as the young ladies were about their conservatory.

After the last dish was put away, Meg announced that final preparations for tomorrow would now commence. A multitude of pies were brought from the north chamber and set out all about the room. They lined up all manner of vegetables on the kitchen table and set out pots and pans. The sisters loaded wood and coal into hods. Stacks of plates, cups, and cutlery were set aside for the swift setting of the morning's table.

As they climbed the back staircase, Meg told Kathleen, "I'll rise extra early in the morning so I can get to the market first thing to pick up a fresh turkey and some chickens. While I'm gone, you can see to the morning duties, same here as at the Pratts. I'll be back before it's time to start breakfast."

121

Meg slid the bed warmer filled with hot coals between the icy sheets before they changed and slipped into the small bed. Nestling close together they settled in for the night. Before drifting off, Kathleen remembered something.

"Meg?" she asked. "Are all the men who drive sleighs Negroes?"

"The livery employs a few."

"I saw two. First when one came to pick up the Pratts and then the man who brought the Ambersons here."

"Uh-huh," Meg said.

"Have you ever spoken with them?" Kathleen asked. "What are they like?"

Silence answered Kathleen. Meg had already fallen asleep.

Chapter Twelve

Up well before the sun, Meg and Kathleen discussed the day's plans as they dressed.

"Fill the largest pot and have it boiling with water when I return," Meg instructed before heading out. Still worn from yesterday's work, Kathleen felt more asleep than awake. Chipping away the thin layer of ice that had formed in Meg's basin, she splashed a handful of cold water on her face.

"Oh!" she cried as the frigid wetness stung her skin, sending a shiver through her body. More awake, she descended the stairs to start the day's work.

Meg returned toting a large sack, then heaved it onto the table. Kathleen stood dumbfounded as Meg pulled the largest bird she'd ever seen from the sack.

"That's a turkey?" Kathleen asked. It dwarfed the two chickens Meg laid next to it.

"Aye. And we'd best get started. Hand me that knife, please."

Dawn had barely broken by the time they dipped the turkey and chickens into boiling water to loosen the feathers and commenced plucking.

"They'll be up soon and wanting breakfast. I'll keep working on this if you'll cook. You needn't make much. They're having a feast later so don't over stuff them this morning."

Kathleen couldn't help laughing. Meg sounded as though she was speaking of the turkey and chickens rather than of the Claproods and Ambersons.

Once the families were fed and breakfast cleaned up, an entire day of meal preparation began. They had the house to themselves as the families attended morning church services.

Kathleen was in her glory. She presided over the stove. Never having roasted a turkey she acquiesced to Meg though she did check her receipt book, making a few modifications to Meg's

123

instructions, assuming Lydia Maria Child knew more about the subject. Meg did not seem to mind, in fact, was grateful for Kathleen's skill. Before long they fell into a comfortable rhythm, but the pace was exhausting.

Late in the morning, having returned from church, Mrs. Claprood came to check on them. "You are doing wonderfully," she praised them, looking over the table "but you could undoubtedly use some help." Mrs. Claprood tied on an apron and immediately pitched in.

Kathleen was floored. Though Mrs. Pratt sometimes assisted in the kitchen, especially when they expected guests, she always behaved as though it was an imposition.

"I thought I would find you in here, Emily," said Martha Amberson, poking her head in the doorway. "Which of you is Margaret?"

"I am," said Meg as she worked.

"Emily speaks quite highly of you."

"Thank you, Ma'am," said Meg, a smile twitching on her lips.

"Then you must be Margaret's sister, Kathleen."

"Aye. I mean, yes," said Kathleen.

"How fortunate you were able to help your sister. I'm sure she appreciates it." The woman's smile appeared genuine, giving Kathleen pause.

"We all appreciate it," said Mrs. Claprood, handing an apron to her sister-in-law.

"What might I do, Margaret?" Mrs. Amberson asked, accepting the apron as though fully expecting it.

Both ladies looked to Meg. *Were they really asking Meg for instructions?* Kathleen could hardly take it in.

"Kathleen's in charge," Meg told them.

"Head cook, we are yours to command," said Mrs. Claprood. The jovial note and expectant expressions on the faces of the ladies both pleased and perplexed Kathleen. Not sure what were appropriate tasks to assign to the lady of the house and her guest, she decided to give them the most needed task at the moment. They could simply decline if displeased.

"The potatoes need peeling." Kathleen said, her voice tentative.

"Potatoes it is," said Mrs. Claprood and the two ladies set to it enthusiastically.

Before long they were joined in the kitchen by Pamela, Deborah, Alice, and Elizabeth.

"It smells heavenly in here!" Deborah exclaimed, drawing in a deep breath.

Kathleen smiled. The the yeasty scent of baking bread and the fruity aroma of hot apples simmering in their spices filled the kitchen.

The girls readily took directions from Kathleen as had their mothers. They even appeared to enjoy the camaraderie of working together, chattering away while they peeled, boiled, baked, and turned the turkey roasting on the spit, droplets of fat sizzling as they hit the sides of the tin kitchen.

This was different from what Kathleen had expected. She had assumed that all Yankee ladies let their servant do the work, only helping when necessary and then grudgingly. As she oversaw a kitchen full of women, she wondered who the unusual ones were, this family or Mrs. Pratt. If this warmth and joy were the norm, it was no wonder Clara felt so lonely and isolated. *If only that poor lass had a sister or two,* she thought, not for the first time.

With so many helping hands, the hardest of the work was completed by mid-afternoon. At that point, it was mostly a matter of allowing the birds to finish roasting, making sure the pies were heated through, mashing the potatoes, and finally, transferring everything to its appropriate serving dish.

"Well," Mrs. Claprood announced. "It's time we changed our clothes and readied ourselves for the feast."

The ladies deposited their aprons in a pile before heading out of the kitchen, the younger ones jabbering non-stop as they went.

"Let's set the table," Meg instructed, returning to her leadership role.

In the dining room, Meg snapped over the table a pristine white cloth. Together they brought in the best china and cutlery, creating twelve perfect place settings. Opening the glass door of the built-in corner cupboard, Meg removed the serving dishes reserved for special occasions. By turns they took the glossy blue and white vessels to the kitchen to be filled with the day's copious fare. Numerous trips were made between kitchen and dining room. Every inch of table and sideboard was filled with food with still more to come.

"Help me carry the tea table from the parlor," said Meg.

125

Setting it in a corner of the dining room, they quickly covered it with an assortment of pies.

Back in the kitchen, Meg placed the largest platter Kathleen had ever seen on the table. Together they carefully moved the turkey from the spit to the platter. Meg placed a large fork and carving knife next to it before plating the two roasted chickens on smaller platters. The chickens were set on the dining room table, but the turkey waited to make its grand entrance after all assembled.

Taking a final look at the magnificent spread, Meg announced, "We're ready. Wait here." She left the room, returning a moment later. "They're coming," she told Kathleen.

They stood silently by the sideboard as the Claproods and Ambersons found places at the table. Once all were settled, Mrs. Claprood nodded towards Meg who gently tugged Kathleen towards the kitchen.

"You bring the knife and fork," Meg said indicating the bone-handled carving set. "When we get to the dining room, I will place the tray before Mrs. Claprood. You lay the carving set beside the tray. Then we step away and wait by the sideboard."

Grunting softly, Meg lifted the platter. Kathleen followed her to the dining room. Meg stopped before entering. Repositioning the platter, she hoisted it above her head, carrying it in an attitude of triumph.

Appreciative exclamations greeted its arrival. Deftly, Meg lowered the platter and set it before Mrs. Claprood who sat opposite her husband at the end of the long table. As instructed, Kathleen placed the carving set, their handles crossed one over the other, next to the platter.

Serene, smiling faces ringed the table. Kathleen watched in fascination as their eyes took in the feast before them.

Mr. Claprood cleared his throat. "Let us give thanks to our Lord," he said.

At once all at table bowed their heads as Mr. Claprood spoke a prayer in which he thanked God for their many blessings including the food set before them. He ended by giving thanks for "the hands that prepared this food and that assist us daily in many tasks." When all answered "Amen," Kathleen, without thinking, raised her hand to make the Sign of the Cross, but Meg quickly pushed her hand down and shook her head.

Mrs. Claprood stood to carve the turkey. Plates were passed. Meg and Kathleen came forward to serve the many side dishes.

They were kept busy refilling plates and glasses, occasionally going to the kitchen to fetch one item or another. When not serving, they stood quietly by the sideboard.

Conversation moved smoothly from compliments on the food to the early onset of winter and what it might mean for the coming months.

"I apologize for the lack of cranberry sauce. The early frost prevented an abundant harvest. The markets hardly had any and we have but a precious few on hand," said Mrs. Claprood.

"Quite all right," her brother assured her. "We'll manage without it."

"I do miss the cranberry sauce," Deborah complained.

"I'm sorry, dear," Mrs. Claprood consoled.

"Of course, you're right, Emily," Mrs. Amberson agreed. "Though, they are a staple of Thanksgiving. It's a pity they were in short supply."

Kathleen caught the grinding motion of her sister's jaw.

A thoughtful look crossed Mrs. Claprood's face. "Margaret?" she summoned, motioning discreetly towards Meg.

Meg moved to Mrs. Claprood's chair. She bent forward as the woman whispered. Meg nodded. Kathleen saw her sister's face turn dark as a thundercloud. Meg stopped next to Kathleen long enough to whisper, "You'll have to serve on your own for a while. I'm to make cranberry sauce." The last word came out in a hiss. Frightened, Kathleen glanced around, but the diners chattered on.

"Tell me, Chester, do you worry about the passage of a ten-hour workday?" asked Mr. Amberson.

"Indeed. It's a strike at the authority of business owners."

"*If* it passes," Oliver added. "And I doubt it will."

"What makes you so sure, young man?" asked Mr. Amberson.

"Massachusetts has always been under the tight control of the Whigs. They staunchly uphold the rights of business owners. I know there's talk, but– "

"It may be more than talk," his uncle cut him off.

"How so?" asked Mr. Claprood.

"That fellow, Henry Wilson, was all over the commonwealth last year talking to anyone who would listen. He's got the whole state's workers riled up over their perceived rights. That coalition with the Free Soilers and Democrats are attracting followers."

127

"Do you think those radical upstarts are viable as a party?" asked Mr. Claprood. "Surely, they can't stand long against the Whigs."

"I would be inclined to agree were it not for the fact that they swept the 1850 elections with majorities in both houses. Now they've got their own George Boutwell as Governor, Benjamin Banks as Speaker of the House, and Wilson, himself, as President of the Senate. What do you call that if not a takeover?"

"An aberration?" Oliver offered.

"Perhaps," said Mr. Amberson, sounding unconvinced. "But if they can build on the start they've already made, they could well rival the Whigs at some point."

Mr. Claprood's face soured. "That secret ballot law won't help us. Factories are booming. How can anyone think of cutting back work hours now? We're growing this country. Just look at the increase in rail travel. Then there's the aqueduct bringing water into all parts of Worcester. Only a matter of time before water can be piped into individual homes. It's ludicrous to even consider shortening the workday. How would things get done?"

"Could we really have water piped into our house?" Deborah asked. "How would it work?"

"Something like the city pump, I imagine," Oliver offered. "Only the pump would be indoors. In the kitchen, I expect and emptying into a sink."

"It sounds miraculous! Pamela, think how much easier it would be to water all your plants."

"Those plants are all you girls think about," Mrs. Claprood teased.

"Enormous amount of work to lay the pipes, set the fixtures. How would it get done in only ten hours a day, I ask you?" said Mr. Claprood, addressing Mr. Amberson.

"You've no argument from me, Chester. I'm simply stating the possibility. This coalition may be a flash in the pan, or it may turn out to have teeth. It would be worthwhile to stay abreast."

"Lemuel heard Mr. Wilson speak when he came to Worcester," said Oliver.

Kathleen started at the mention of Lemuel's name.

"Lemuel?" asked Mr. Amberson.

"My partner's son," Mr. Claprood explained.

"I see. What was his impression of the man, Oliver?"

"He admired him, though not about shortening work hours. He's against that."

"What did he find admirable?"

"It was his concern about the influx of immigrants. He worries they will take over the country. Says America should be run by Americans, not immigrants. Especially Catholics."

Mrs. Claprood cleared her throat. Kathleen felt the heat rise in her face as a few glances from the table were thrown her way.

"Mr. Wilson spoke about ending slavery, as well," Oliver continued.

"Oh? Is he for abolition?" asked Mrs. Claprood.

"No, but he is anti-slavery."

"And your friend, Lemuel? Where does he stand?" asked Mrs. Amberson.

"Lemuel is strongly opposed to the peculiar institution. He wants what he refers to as a 'pure America'. Free them and send them all back to Africa or anywhere that isn't here," answered Oliver.

"That's hardly a wise solution," Mrs. Claprood stated.

"Why not, Aunt Emily?" asked Alice. "Wouldn't they be happier? They'd be free and back where they came from."

"My dear child, it has been illegal to import slaves since 1807. Most slaves have been here since birth as have their parents. They've no more notion of Africa than you or I."

"But they would be free, Mother. That's what's right, isn't it?" asked Pamela.

"Of course, they should be free. Slavery is an abomination before God."

"Mother, all set free at once? What would they do? Where would they go?" asked Oliver.

"You can't believe slavery should continue?" Mrs. Claprood looked incredulously at her son.

"No, but so many freed all at once would bring an influx north looking for jobs. We'd be overrun."

"There's also the problem of apprenticeship if such were to happen," said Mr. Amberson.

"What do you mean, dear?" asked his wife.

"Think of it. Unskilled men of their breed come looking for work. Likely many would want to learn a trade which means they'd have to take an apprenticeship."

"Which in turn means they'd live with the master and his family for the duration of their apprenticeship," Mr. Claprood continued. "With his wife. And daughters. That would hardly be appropriate."

Though Mrs. Amberson's back was to her, Kathleen noticed a shiver pass through the woman's body. "Certainly, that would never do."

"That's why Lemuel favors shipping them all out," said Oliver.

"Does he wish to ship back all the immigrants as well?" Benjamin asked.

"Lemuel would remove every non-English person from American soil if he could. He's rather shortsighted in that regard, if you ask me." Oliver laughed. "Without the immigrants who would do the work?"

Kathleen fought to keep her tears in check. Might she and Meg and all the others be returned to Ireland? Could all their dreams come to an end? *Damn those Brits and their American heirs!* Lost in her thoughts, she jumped when Meg appeared beside her carrying a tray with twelve tiny dishes each containing no more than a spoonful of cranberry sauce, the berries glistening like rubies in pools of thick, fruity pulp.

"Here it is!" Mrs. Claprood announced, as the tart aroma wafted into the room.

"Oh, Mother!" Deborah exclaimed.

"There's only a tiny bit for each of us," she explained as Meg and Kathleen set a dish by each person's plate.

"It's hot," Meg said. "There wasn't time for it to cool."

"We appreciate your making it for us." Mrs. Claprood patted Meg's hand as she set the dish beside her plate.

Kathleen's thoughts tumbled about in her head. She could not understand the mix of kindness, compliments, and praise with sentiments of bigotry and superiority. It was so confusing. At least with the Pratts she knew exactly where she stood.

The entrance of the cranberry sauce brought with it a transition in conversation, turning it to more personal matters. Were the children doing well in school? They were. Did Benjamin plan to follow his father in the practice of law? He did. Who was marrying during this holiday season? The daughter of Emily and Peter's eldest sister in Ohio would wed tomorrow and Mr. Claprood's sister's son in Maine would do the same three days hence.

The sun had nearly set by the time Kathleen began serving the final course. Meg lit the lamps and several candles, first in the dining room then in the parlor, conservatory, and study, the places to which she knew various family members would disperse once the meal was over.

After the table, sideboard, and tea table were cleared of all their dishes, Meg and Kathleen retired to the kitchen. Meg placed two settings of the everyday plates and cutlery on the one clear space at the end of the kitchen table. The two then helped themselves to as much of the Thanksgiving fare as they desired.

"It's always like this," Meg said. "By the time it's over I should be hungry, but I'm almost too tired to eat."

Kathleen looked at the food heaped on Meg's plate.

"I said, almost." Meg grinned.

For a moment the only sounds were of the sisters savoring the rich fare. Kathleen had placed enough of the food back into the still warm oven while they cleared dishes and place settings. Once ready to eat, the food had been warmed again.

"I would never have thought of it," Meg commended her. "For the past three years I've eaten my Thanksgiving dinner cold. I never realized how good it tastes."

Kathleen gave a wan smile.

"Tired?" Meg asked, digging into her mashed potatoes and gravy.

"Aye. There's something else, too."

"What?" asked Meg.

"There were things said when you were out of the room. Troublesome things."

Kathleen related all she'd overheard.

"I've heard much of that talk before. Mrs. Claprood has become quite taken with the Abolitionist Movement. Mr. Claprood broods over the possibility of a ten hour workday. Heaven forbid workers should do anything with their time but serve their employers. Perhaps if they paid them enough to live on they would be better workers? There will be none of that nonsense!"

Kathleen was quiet for a moment.

"Meg, why did the Pratts hire me if they hate Irish Catholics so?"

"Aye, now that was Mrs. Pratt's doing and no mistake. Mrs. Claprood has me and she couldn't stand her husband's partner's wife coming up in the world faster than herself. Irish help the only option? She had to accept it."

Kathleen sighed heavily.

"I'm sorry," Meg said. "I didn't know then how awful they'd be. I'd never have set you up with them if I'd known."

"Oh, Meg, I'm grateful to have a job and to be here. The Pratts are difficult, except for Clara, but I have food and a roof over my head. They've never cheated me of my pay so I have enough to save, buy a few things for myself, and send the rest home. You can't imagine how thankful I am. And then there's Clara. I truly do love the dear lass."

"She has you. She's lucky for that."

"I do my best, but her mother has turned so against me I wonder how much longer she'll allow Clara to spend time with me."

"Mrs. Pratt longs to be seen in society. She's not content and wants more. As long as she has you to keep Clara out from under foot, I'd wager she'll not interfere."

"That, too, makes me sad for Clara. Her own mam seeing her as an obstacle."

"They're a different lot here. For all their abundance they can't seem to get enough. It strikes me as a sort of madness."

"Do you pity them?"

Meg put down her fork, stared off across the room. "I feel like slapping some sense into them. But at times, I suppose I do."

Chapter Thirteen

"Come spend the afternoon with us," Mrs. Linton invited Meg and Kathleen after Sunday Mass. Since they'd worked through their normal day off, Thanksgiving being on a Thursday, Mrs. Claprood had given them all of Sunday.

"My sister and Aoife are coming for dinner. We'd love for you to join us, as well."

Meg and Kathleen exchanged glances. They knew how little the Lintons had and how many mouths to feed. Mrs. Linton caught the look. "Don't worry. Darien received extra pay for Thanksgiving. We got a chicken, some potatoes, and vegetables. I've made a stew. We've enough left. You can help us finish it."

Meg knew well that Mrs. Linton was making their windfall last as long as possible. She'd rather it was used to feed their own family, but they would appear rude and superior if they refused.

"We'd be happy to join you," she said.

"Good. Aoife has some news to share with you. She's quite excited."

"What news?" Kathleen asked.

"It's for Aoife to tell."

Mr. Linton joined them on the church steps. A shadow of concern on his face.

"Is something wrong?" asked Mrs. Linton.

"Father Boyce has heard things. I'll tell you on the way home."

They were soon joined by Aoife and Mrs. O'Sullivan along with Ned and his uncle, Owen MacBrody, with whom he roomed at the Arcade.

"Mrs. Linton tells us you have news, Aoife," Kathleen said.

"I do indeed." A wide smile spread across her face. She gazed up at Ned who took her hand in his. "Now that Ned has a job, we've decided to marry."

"So soon?" The words were out of Meg's mouth before she realized it.

133

"What's there to wait for?"

Meg felt herself blush. "I'm sorry. Congratulations to you both." For Aoife's sake she was glad Nuala had gone straight back to the Denton's after Mass claiming a headache. Heaven only knew what she would have said.

"When is the wedding?" Kathleen asked.

"We've just mentioned it to Father Boyce. The banns must be posted first, of course." Aoife cast an adoring look at Ned.

"I'm glad Father Boyce has come to Saint John's," said Mrs. O'Sullivan. "Perhaps I shouldn't say it, but I prefer him to Father Gilbert and I'm happy that Aoife will be married by an Irish priest." There were murmurs of agreement.

"Your job is going well, then, Ned?" Meg asked as they walked towards the Arcade.

"Well enough. It was good of Mr. Linton to help me."

"A spot opened up," Mr. Linton explained. "I put in a word for Ned."

"You said Father Boyce has heard some news?" Mrs. Linton reminded her husband.

Mr. Linton sighed deeply. "The ten hour workday faces powerful opposition from the Whigs."

"That's hardly news," said Owen MacBrody.

"True," Mr. Linton conceded. "I had hoped that the secret ballot would allow us to vote without worrying about our jobs. The trouble is that the same politicians who are pushing for the ten hour bill are also the ones who'd rid the country of Catholics. Father Boyce says they're just trying to get workers to vote for them. Once they're in, we'll be out."

"Are those politicians in something called a coalition?" Kathleen asked.

"Aye. What have you heard?" asked Mr. Linton.

Kathleen related the conversation of the Claproods and Ambersons during Thanksgiving dinner.

"I came to this country to escape the meanness of the Brits," Mr. Linton declared. "I'll not be chased out of it by their American cousins."

"Will it come to that?" asked Meg.

"I pray not, but there's much talk."

"Transplanted Brits," Owen interjected. "Sniffing the salt air from the other side of the sea."

When they reached the Arcade, Meg and Kathleen pitched in with preparing the meal. The food left over at the Claprood home undoubtedly surpassed what the Lintons had from the start. Meg silently vowed to eat slowly, doing her best to appear as though she had plenty.

Afterward, the women sequestered themselves in one corner, while the men moved to the other side. It reminded Meg of cottage life back home. She fell easily into the way of it.

The women talked of Aoife's wedding. Mrs. Linton and Aoife's mother would make her wedding dress.

"Meg, you've been closer to me than anyone since we left Ireland. I would love for you to be my maid of honor. Would you?" Aoife asked.

"I'd be pleased to," said Meg, though a knot formed in her stomach.

Aoife threw her arms around her. "Thank you so much. I know you're worried that I'm making a mistake, but Ned and I will make it work. You'll see."

Despite her skepticism, Meg could not help but smile at Aoife's beaming countenance.

"Where will you live after you've married?" Kathleen asked.

"That's not yet decided. I might move in with Ned and his uncle or Ned might move in with me and Mam. It's all so new. We've many details to resolve."

"Take your time with it, darlin'," said Mrs. O'Sullivan. "I know you're full of excitement, but you'll be better off having everything set straight before you set foot on the path of marriage."

Mrs. Linton pulled back the thin curtain to glance outside. "Ach! The time gets away from us when we set to talking. You lasses ought to head back. You'll not want to be walking the streets after dark. I'll send my husband with you."

"May I ask you something, Mr. Linton?" Meg said on the way home.

"Aye."

"Do you approve of Aoife and Ned marrying?"

Mr. Linton pursed his lips.

"Aoife, having no da anymore, and me being her uncle, Ned came to me to ask for her hand. I wasn't for it. Not that I've anything against the lad. But I know the hardship of trying to raise a family on the little money they pay us."

"But you gave permission anyway?"

"Aye. I've watched the lad work. He's dependable, a quick learner, does a good job. He should be able to keep the position so long as they let any of us stay. And he does seem to love Aoife and means to do his best by her. The lass wants a husband and children. It's not for me to deny her."

"Do you regret marrying?" Meg couldn't help asking.

"That I do not," he said, a grin spreading over his face. "Of course, Maureen and I came here already wed, though the bairns hadn't come yet. I love her with all my heart and will until the day they nail my coffin shut. As for the wee ones, they own me heart. I wouldn't give up a one for all the money in the world."

Meg smiled.

"And what of you, lass? When is that husband of yours going to show himself on this side of the shore?"

"He won't leave until he's sure all back home are cared for."

"How will you feel about leaving your position?"

Meg swallowed hard.

Mr. Linton chuckled. "You're of two minds. I don't blame you. Maureen and I can imagine how you must feel."

"You've discussed it?"

"We worry about you, given your situation. It's only natural that you feel torn."

The sun had set by the time they reached the Claprood home. A soft, inviting glow emanated from the candles and lamps. They thanked Mr. Linton, then let themselves in the kitchen door.

Exhausted from the past several days, they decided to retire early. As they readied themselves for bed, Meg said to Kathleen, "You were quiet on the way home."

"Your talk with Mr. Linton was important. I didn't want to interfere."

"What do you think of Aoife marrying?" Meg asked as they slipped into bed.

"I worry for her, but they seem so in love. If they can keep that feeling through whatever hardships they face, then perhaps they can be as happy as the Lintons."

"I hope so," Meg whispered. "But it might be very hard."

They awoke to a world of white. The Claprood girls, giddy with excitement, begged their father to rent a horse and sleigh for an impromptu sleighing party. Overcome by holiday cheer, he agreed. He and Oliver were taking Peter and Benjamin to the foundry. On the way they would stop at the livery service and send back a sleigh. Delighted, the girls gathered blankets and tin foot warmers, setting them by the fireplace.

"Margaret, you'll have hot chocolate ready when we return, won't you?" Pamela asked.

"Certainly, Miss."

As though suddenly gripped with inspiration, Deborah exclaimed, "Marzipan! I haven't had marzipan in ever so long. Would you make some for us, please?"

"I don't know how," Meg answered.

Deborah's face fell. "It's only ground almonds, sugar, and egg whites. Surely you can make it?"

Meg looked to Kathleen.

"I'll check my book," Kathleen said.

"If not marzipan, taffy would do nicely," Alice offered.

"Oh!" cried Deborah. "That's even better. We'll have a taffy pull when we return!"

"Best ask your mother first," Meg said. "She's determined to be frugal with the food this winter."

"She can't deny us such a treat during Thanksgiving week. And not while we have company."

Mrs. Claprood and Mrs. Amberson entered the parlor. "Did we hear talk of a taffy pull?" asked Mrs. Claprood.

"May we, Mother?" asked Deborah.

"I give you leave to enjoy yourselves as you wish as long as you help Margaret and Kathleen to clean up afterward. Is that clear?"

Mrs. Claprood staggered under the simultaneous hugs of four excited girls.

"Emily you've become a heroine in a single stroke," Mrs. Amberson announced, laughing at her sister-in-law lost in the gaggle of girls. "Now, if you young ladies would do something for me?" she asked.

"What is it, Aunt Martha?" asked Pamela.

"Nancy and Ethan need to be kept occupied. Please include them in your adventures."

"In the sleigh?" Pamela asked.

"You may bring them back if they become chilled and continue on. They're no longer babies. They're feelings are hurt when left out."

The jingling of the horse's harness could be heard in the yard.

"The sleigh is here!" called Deborah.

Girls dispersed in all directions, grabbing the pile of blankets, filling the foot warmers with hot coals from the fireplace. Mrs. Amberson bundled Nancy and Ethan head to toe. Meg and Kathleen handed coats, hats, and muffs to the girls then followed them out to the sleigh. The driver this time had fair skin, red hair, and a smattering of freckles.

Once Meg and Kathleen had all the blankets tucked securely around them with skirts draped over the foot warmers to hold in the heat, they stepped down from the sleigh.

"Do drive carefully," Mrs. Claprood instructed the driver.

"Aye, Ma'am. I'm as careful as they come. You'll have 'em all back safe and sound and merry as larks. Not a thing I can do about frozen noses, though. That the lasses will have to see to themselves."

Meg nearly burst when she heard him. It was all she could do to keep from asking how much his job paid. At least she could tell Rory the livery service hired Irish.

"Did you hear?" she asked Kathleen as they returned to the house.

"Could hardly miss, could I?"

"The livery might hire Rory. It must pay better than the factory, don't you think?"

"I wouldn't know. Might you ask Mr. Claprood?"

Meg thought a moment. "Not without arousing suspicion. Maybe I could come to it in a roundabout way."

They closed themselves into the kitchen. Meg pulled out several copper pots, a loaf of sugar along with the nippers, molasses, a block of baker's chocolate, and a large tub of butter. "It will be a while before they tire of sleighing, but we'd might as well have everything ready. We'll need to wash all those aprons before they come in to pull the taffy. Could you start heating the water? We've all the table linens to do, as well."

"Aye," said Kathleen. Setting a large kettle on the stove, she filled it with water to bring to a boil.

Within an hour, the kitchen door burst open.

"They're cold and want to come in," said Alice, depositing Nancy and Ethan just inside the door. "We're going to ride a while longer."

Nancy and Ethan scurried across the room.

"Stop!" Meg commanded. "Boots, please."

The children removed their boots, handed them to Meg, then hurried from the room. Meg shook her head. "Look at this floor. I'll be glad when the extra company is gone."

"Does that include me?"

Meg playfully nudged her sister. "Truth to tell, I wish for your company all the time."

"This week's been the most we've been together since before you left home."

"Only one more full day," said Meg. "I hope the Pratts arrive late on Wednesday and the Ambersons leave early. We might get a few hours of quiet before they send for you."

"Aye, but the day after that is Thursday. What shall we do?"

"I've been too busy and too tired to think that far ahead." Meg laughed. "No doubt Nuala will have some ideas."

"How much does it cost to rent a sleigh? It looks right jolly, gliding over the snow."

"I'll ask Mr. Claprood, but it's probably more than we can afford."

"Maybe you could find out about the drivers' pay without making him suspicious."

Meg tilted her head to the side. "You, sister, have a right good head on your shoulders."

Kathleen scraped the baker's chocolate into fine pieces while Meg finished the ironing, then placed all the scrapings into boiling water and milk, taking care not to let it scorch. Meg breathed deeply as she folded the last of the table linens. "I do love the smell of chocolate," she said, "though I'm not fond of the taste."

"I like it," said Kathleen, "after I've added enough sugar."

The rich aroma of melting chocolate and warm milk soon filled the kitchen. The girls arrived home as Kathleen was whisking the mixture into a froth. Coats, hats, muffs, and boots were quickly discarded. They gathered at the table, their eyes aglow, cheeks and noses bright red, huge smiles on their faces.

"How was the ride?" Kathleen asked, pouring the hot chocolate into china cups.

"Glorious!" Deborah gushed, spooning sugar into her drink.

139

"Sleighing is one of my favorite things," said Alice.

"I like it to," said Elizabeth, "but skating is my favorite. I can't wait until the ponds are safely frozen."

While the girls prattled on about clothing, school, boys, and the meaning of flowers, Meg buttered a heavy saucepan. Kathleen took over, constantly stirring the molasses, butter, water, sugar, and corn syrup. She had to keep the temperature just right so the mixture wouldn't scorch. It was a painstaking process. Meg wondered at Kathleen's ability to take so readily to the complexities of cooking. She felt always at odds with The Beast.

"Most of us aren't known for our cooking," Meg commented as she watched Kathleen. "The newspapers print cartoons ridiculing the culinary mishaps of the Irish. Truth is, we're used to open hearth peat fires. You are unusual among us!"

"It's getting close," Kathleen said. "I'll need a large buttered baking pan."

"I can manage that," said Meg, greasing the pan while Kathleen concentrated on keeping a gentle boil over the surface of the mixture.

Once ready, Kathleen carefully poured her concoction into the pan. "It will have to sit a while to cool," she said, setting the baking pan away from the stove.

"Mmmm...that smells delicious!" Pamela exclaimed.

"Don't touch it yet," Kathleen instructed.

"How did you learn so much about cooking, Kathleen?" asked Elizabeth. "Mother says all anyone in Ireland eats are potatoes."

"Your mother is right. Potatoes were all we had until we didn't even have them. I took to cooking after I got here."

"It's akin to Miss Pamela and her flowers," said Meg. "You love growing them so you learn all about them. Spend all the time you can in the garden and now the conservatory."

"That's true," agreed Pamela. "I wish I could spend every minute studying and growing them."

"What takes your fancy so?" asked Kathleen.

"Well, they're lovely, of course," said Pamela, "and many of them smell heavenly. But it's more than that. They hold meaning. You can have a conversation with flowers and never speak a word. They inhabit a world of their own. And I find it a miracle that something so beautiful comes from a small seed buried in soil."

Pamela continued to wax eloquent until the taffy mixture had cooled enough to handle. It was at that moment the gentlemen returned from their tour of the foundry. The scents of hot chocolate and taffy lured Oliver and Benjamin into the kitchen with Nancy and Ethan right behind.

"You've come in good time," Deborah announced. "We're ready to pull!"

Kathleen placed the baking pan on the table while Meg set the crock of butter beside it. Once everyone had thoroughly buttered their hands, they lifted the thickened mixture, each grabbing hold of a section. Meg and Kathleen watched as the young people stretched and pulled the taffy, then folded it in on itself to stretch and pull again. Laughter filled the room as they set themselves up in teams to see who could stretch it furthest. The combination of slippery butter and sticky molasses mixture made for plenty of adventures and a few mishaps.

"Don't you want to pull, too?" Alice asked Meg and Kathleen.

The sisters looked at each other. The thought had not crossed their minds.

"Try." Pamela encouraged them.

Kathleen's wistful expression decided it for Meg. She held out the crock of butter to her sister who eagerly greased her hands. She and Kathleen each held an end of the taffy and began pulling. To Meg's surprise, the odd mixture of slippery and sticky along with the sweet aroma appealed. She and Kathleen were soon laughing along with the others. For a few moments she felt part of the family. When their stretch of taffy broke, the end snapping back to curl around Meg's hands, she and Kathleen dissolved in gales of laughter.

When they'd worked it long enough, the taffy turned light in color and became too difficult to pull. Then they braided the strands, cut them into small pieces, and wrapped them in oiled parchment paper. Meg produced a glass canister for storage.

Remembering Mrs. Claprood's instructions, the girls helped clean up before heading off to other adventures.

Meg dropped into a chair once she and Kathleen were alone. "I don't remember the last time I've laughed like that. My face hurts," she said, rubbing the hinges of her jaw.

"Mine too, but it felt good, didn't it?"

"Aye. I wasn't looking forward to the extra work, but now I'm glad for it."

141

"I wonder what they'd think back home."

"They'd not believe it!"

"Brigid would have loved it. And Loreena."

"The mess they'd make!" Meg chuckled.

"Aye, but the joy they'd have!"

Silence engulfed them, both suddenly lost in thoughts of loved ones far away.

"Darlin' Brigid," whispered Meg. "I wonder if she'll ever be right in the head again."

Kathleen sniffled. "I pray so. It's not fair a lass so full of life should be locked forever in a silent world. I can't imagine where her mind has taken her. I hope it's not a bad place.

Their last full day brought a sweet surprise, a letter from Rory. Meg kept it in her pocket. They hurried through their chores, especially cleaning up after the day's last meal. The Ambersons were to leave first thing in the morning so the families made an early night of it. Once they were settled Meg and Kathleen took a last walk through the house, then scurried up to Meg's room.

They climbed into bed, sitting side-by-side with the covers pulled up to their necks. With hands shaking as much from excitement as from the cold attic, Meg opened the letter. Kathleen held a chamber candle close as Meg read.

My darling Meg,

We fare well here, thanks to you and Kathleen. Aisling continues so well at learning the seamstress trade that Mrs. Fairfax decided to take her in. She lives with the lady now, gets regular meals, and a real bed to sleep in. She earns her keep by helping with the household chores, maybe like what you and Kathleen do. We miss our Aisling, but we see her at Mass and she spends Sunday afternoon with us before returning. You'd not recognize her. She's still thin, but has filled out some, her hair has thickened. No more bald patches. It's pretty and golden in the sunshine. She has a liveliness to her I've never seen, even before the blight. When I think of how close she was to death for so long, I can barely take in the change. We thank God every day.

Loreena is spirited as ever. She continues to help your mam with the mending, but longs for something more satisfying to do. During the harvest, she got Brigid to come along with us to dig potatoes. Most of them were good, saints be praised. It seemed to bring Brigid 'round a bit. For a while she was more like her old self. Maybe she thought she was back in the days before the starving. Whatever it was, we were glad to see it. Loreena was not about to let an improvement like that go without making the most of it. She brought the piglets in and the two of them played with them like they did when they were wee. Brigid even laughed a few times. Your mam was in tears, so happy was she to see this sudden change for the better. I wish I could say it lasted and that all's right with Brigid again, but it's not so. She continues to go back to her own world. Her 'times away,' as your mam calls them. We pray that one day she'll come back to us permanently.

Overcome with emotion, Meg stopped reading.

Kathleen, whose head had been resting on Meg's shoulder, sat upright. "We just spoke of her last night, hoping she'd be right again. Oh, Meg this is the best news! God has answered our prayers."

Meg pictured Brigid digging up healthy potatoes, playing with the piglets, and laughing. She gazed toward the ceiling to hold back the tears. When she felt in control of herself, she continued.

There is some sad news to tell. Kevin Dooley's sister, Liddy, has passed from this world. You know she was in a far worse state than Brigid. She was taken by a fever in late September. The Kilpatrick's buried her with their own kin seeing as how hers had been buried in the pits. She'd been living with them ever since Doctor Parker rescued her from the workhouse, so they felt it only right she should be laid to rest with their own.

Kevin stays on with the Kilpatrick's, helping with everything he can. He comes here often, too. Like Loreena, he's restless, talks about going to America. Loreena wants to go, too, but your mam says she's too young. Besides, with Aisling gone and Brigid still not fully herself, there wouldn't be anyone to help your mam. Loreena speak s of you and Kathleen often. When I read your letters aloud, I can see how much she aches to be with you.

Your mam is well. She still counts the days (years) until Brendan can come home. I've written, telling him how the thought of his return keeps her going. Still I fear he might stay if his life in Australia goes well. I want what's best, but your mam couldn't take never seeing him again.

I continue working with Doctor Parker. I take full care of Lily now. I've learned to ride and to drive the phaeton. I take Doctor Parker on his rounds throughout Kelegeen. Have you found out anything about a position for me as a groom? My damaged hand is not a hindrance. Lily has the perfect disposition. I need some experience with horses of other temperaments. Doctor Parker says he will see if some of his friends will let me care for their horses now.

Father O'Malley asks that I send you his blessings and tell you he prays for you and Kathleen daily. He is quite well. I like driving the phaeton when I've Father O'Malley and Doctor Parker together. They keep up a constant banter that amuses me like nothing else.

Meg, I won't leave here until I know your family and what's left of mine are safe and tended to. That day will come before too much longer. So much here has turned for the better. We will be starting a new life with a home and family of our own in America before we know it.

I love you with all my heart, Megeen.
Rory

Meg carefully folded the letter and placed it on the stand by her bed. They put out the candle and scooted down under the covers, snuggling close for warmth.

"Much good news," said Kathleen, her voice dreamy. "Except for Liddy, of course, poor mite. You miss Rory awfully."

"Aye. I miss them all, but Rory especially. I must find out how much the livery drivers get paid. I wonder if it could be enough." For the first time, Meg allowed herself a glimmer of hope for the future.

"What do you think of Kevin and Loreena wanting to come to America?" asked Kathleen.

"Loreena's only thirteen. But when she's older, I think she should, if Mam can spare her. She'd be happier here."

"And Kevin?"

"He's got no skills that would be of use here. Maybe labor in a factory. We know how little that pays."

Kathleen sighed. "He's worked so hard to turn his life around, I'd hate to see him come here with high hopes only to find things worse than what he's left behind."

"I'll explain more to Rory about the work situation. He'll make sure Kevin's aware of it."

"What of Brigid? What if she came with Loreena?"

Meg thought for a moment. "I don't know. If Brigid continues to *go away*, even if only occasionally, it would not go well for her in any job."

"But if that stops?"

"Mam would worry something awful about her. Besides, someone needs to stay with Mam. She'll never come here. Not while she's waiting for Brendan to return."

"You're right," Kathleen sounded dejected, but resigned.

"All we can do is wait," Meg said with a yawn. "And pray."

"I believe prayers, ours and Father O'Malley's, are what is making things better."

"I believe it, too," said Meg. "So, let's pray that the livery service pays well enough and that a spot opens for Rory."

"Would it be selfish, Meg, to pray for me to find another job? After being here this week, I can hardly stand the thought of going back."

"Why would that be selfish?"

"Because I'm grateful to have a job. And because of Clara."

"You love Clara, but you are not responsible for her. You should look for another placement. But remember one thing. With the Pratts you know what to expect. Another family could be better or worse. You won't know until you've been there a while."

"Do you think I could do worse than Lemuel and Mrs. Pratt?

"I hope not, but there's no telling. I wish the Claproods would want a cook. Then perhaps they'd hire you and we'd work together always."

"I would love that," said Kathleen.

"Learn all you can about cooking. Find yourself a place that needs one and you could spend all your time doing it."

Kathleen was silent. Meg thought she had fallen asleep, until she whispered, "'tis strange in this country, isn't it?"

"What do you mean?"

"We have an honest chance at a life we never imagined. Yet we're as hated here as we were back home."

"Aye, 'tis true," said Meg.

Chapter Fourteen

Late January 1852

Lemuel was in a particularly jovial mood. The ten hour bill had finally reached the House Floor, but the coalition had been unsuccessful in securing its passage. The vote was one hundred and seventeen to forty-eight.

Kathleen, setting the table in the dining room could hear the two men discussing it in the parlor.

"I've heard much talk," said Lemuel. "The Free Soilers are thinking of creating an Act that would send all these damned immigrants back to their own countries. What if they unite the coalition further? Isn't a ten hour workday an acceptable price to pay for ensuring America remains in the hands of Americans?"

Kathleen felt her throat tighten. She kept her back to the door between the dining room and parlor, while moving as quietly as she could.

"There is the Pauper Removal Act, son. Though it won't send them all back. It only addresses immigrants living in almshouses and insane asylums."

"For now." Lemuel sounded smug. "It's the first step. Once we get that far – "

"We?" questioned Mr. Pratt. "Have you joined the Free Soilers?"

"Let's say I'm taking a strong interest in their ideas."

Lord Jesus, no! It was bad enough that Lemuel agreed with these hateful people, but would he now officially join their ranks? And what of this Pauper Removal Act? It was the first Kathleen had heard of it. The Irish made up the greatest concentration of paupers, many of them living in the almshouse and now worse; being shipped back to the excruciating poverty of Ireland.

Kathleen returned to the kitchen to finish preparing the meal. While working on a loaf cake with lemon icing, she mulled over what she'd heard. Flour, eggs, molasses, currants, raisins, cloves, nutmeg, saleratus, and butter went into the mixing bowl. With the large bowl held in the crook of her arm, she used the wooden spoon to beat the components into a batter.

"You seem determined to pummel that to death."

Kathleen jumped. She hadn't heard Lemuel enter the kitchen.

"Just in a hurry," she replied, wishing she could dump the contents of the bowl on his head.

"Hurry and you're likely to make a mistake."

"Quit badgering Bridget," said Harvey sauntering into the kitchen.

"This has nothing to do with you," Lemuel said.

"The deuce it hasn't! Most Bridgets are terrible cooks. We've got ourselves a first-rate one. Don't vex her so much she leaves us. Go away and let Bridget do her work."

"I don't take orders from you." Lemuel smirked.

"You'll take them from Father. He sent me to fetch you. Mr. Claprood has arrived."

"Damn!" The corners of Lemuel's mouth twitched. He glared at Kathleen before storming out of the kitchen.

"Thank you, Master Harvey," said Kathleen. She placed the mixing bowl on the table, her hands shaking, whether more from anger or fear she wasn't certain.

Harvey noticed. "Don't let that rogue trouble you. Full of himself, now more than ever since Father's brought him into the business. What are you making?"

"A loaf cake with lemon icing."

"I adore lemon icing."

Harvey seated himself at the table. Making allies in this household had become of grave importance, Kathleen realized. She determined to befriend him.

"Will you also go into business with your father and brother, Master Harvey?"

He shrugged. "I suppose. Not sure I want to, though. It's Lemuel that Father thinks has the head for it. I'd only become Lemuel's lackey."

"What will you do for employment?"

His eyes lit. "I'd like to become a jeweler."

"Truly? Why is that?"

"I've always been fond of gems, the way they shimmer when they catch the light. I'd get to travel, too. I'd go to exotic places to purchase jewels, wouldn't I?"

"What does your Father think of your plans?"

"Oh, I haven't mentioned it to him, nor to my mother."

"Why not? Won't you need to apprentice yourself before long?"

Harvey drew a deep breath. "I don't think they'll agree. Father assumes I'll work at the foundry."

"But he doesn't know you have another interest. He's got Lemuel. Must he have you as well?"

Harvey gave a derisive laugh. "Father and Lemuel both see things one way. Nothing else tolerated. Two peas in a pod."

"I never thought of them as being alike. Your father's always been pleasant to me."

"I suppose that means Lemuel is not pleasant to you."

Kathleen bit her lip.

"Take no more notice of him than you would of a pesky fly. That's what I do."

Kathleen removed the roast from the oven, adjusted the fuel, waiting for the temperature to be right before putting in the loaf pan.

"You can do that more easily. I'm just the help."

"I suppose, but I still think you shouldn't let him antagonize you."

Obviously, Harvey did not grasp her situation.

"So Lemuel and your father think alike then?"

"They don't always agree, but they both have strong opinions. My father's always been the friendlier of the two. And he's softened with age. Lemuel, though, is in the thick of thinking himself right on every front. And friendly is not a word many would use to describe him."

"He is to others the same as he is to me, then?"

"Oh, he'd never give offense to ones such as the Salisburys or the Lincolns. With those of his own age and social standing? He is quite sociable if they are in agreement and rather a bully if they aren't. To those of a lower status, he's positively obnoxious. It's all posturing, though, Bridget. He's harmless."

Harvey could afford to see Lemuel as a mere annoyance. She could not. If she was to make a true ally of Harvey, she would have to proceed cautiously. He and Lemuel were, after all, brothers.

"Is there is a problem at the foundry?" Kathleen asked.

"Not that I know of. Why?"

"It seems odd that Mr. Claprood should arrive unexpectedly at this time of day."

Recognition dawned in his face. "Oh! Mr. Claprood isn't here at all. I told Lemuel that to get him out of the kitchen." Harvey laughed.

"Won't he be angry?"

"Probably. I don't care."

You may not, thought Kathleen, *but I will if he decides to take it out on me.*

Kathleen couldn't help but compare the two brothers while waiting upon them at dinner. Lemuel was tall with fair skin, light brown, almost blond hair, and icy blue eyes. His passion for rowing kept him lean and strong. He favored his father in his looks. Harvey, however, came barely to Lemuel's shoulders. He had dark hair, a shock of which seemed always to be falling into his brown eyes. Harvey did not partake in athletic endeavors. He preferred quieter, more cerebral pursuits. Clara, she thought, was somewhere between the two brothers in looks, though in personality she was completely different. Kathleen didn't see much of either parent in Clara's character and wondered who in the family she favored.

At the end of the meal, Kathleen brought out the loaf cake.

"Now there's an appropriate treat to celebrate the demise of the ten hour bill and the heralding of the Pauper Removal Act," said Lemuel, looking smug.

"What is the Pauper Removal Act?" asked Clara.

"A brilliant idea, that when passed into law will gather up all the immigrants who live in the almshouses and insane asylums and send them back to the country they came from," Lemuel explained. "The state saves money by not having to pay for their upkeep anymore."

Kathleen noticed the pensive look on Clara's face. "How unkind. Reverend Hunt says we're to love our neighbors as ourselves. Aren't we supposed to care for those in need? Isn't that what Jesus taught?"

Kathleen returned the remaining cake to the sideboard. She smiled broadly at Clara's words. Truly that child was the best of the Pratt family.

149

"Of course a good Christian cares for those in need," said Mrs. Pratt. Kathleen waited for the word "but" to follow. She was sure it would have had Mr. Pratt not interrupted.

"To a point," he said. "We must be practical. We can't allow so much of our hard-earned money to be spent on foreigners who come here looking for a handout. Take the almshouse right here in Worcester. The vast majority of inmates are from Ireland."

Kathleen busied herself arranging things on the sideboard.

"Say, Bridget," Lemuel called. "Any friends or relatives of yours there?"

"Not a soul," Kathleen stated loudly.

"Lemuel, kindly stop conversing with the help during meals," said Mrs. Pratt.

"As you wish, Mother," Lemuel conceded.

Kathleen stiffened her back and turned once again to face them, hands folded, eyes straight ahead.

"But still," Clara continued. "Why should someone be denied assistance simply because they've come from another country?"

"It's not just that, Clara," said Mr. Pratt. "Remember these newcomers are Romans."

"You mean Catholics?" asked Clara.

"Yes. Romans, Papists. Almost pagans. We've no obligation towards them. They're not true Christians."

"But Father, the Good Samaritan wasn't of the same faith as the man who'd been robbed, but that didn't stop him. Jesus praised the Samaritan for what he did. He showed by that parable that we are all neighbors to one another. I think this Pauper Removal Act is wrong and we should not be celebrating it." Clara pushed away her plate of half-eaten cake.

"Clara Pratt, how dare you contradict your father!" Mrs. Pratt exclaimed. "You will leave this table at once. To your room. I do not wish to see you again until morning."

Clara sighed. "Yes, Mother." She stood to leave, but Mrs. Pratt stopped her. "Before you go, apologize to your father."

Poor lass, thought Kathleen as she watched Clara fight back tears.

The girl walked to where her father was seated. She looked him in the eye. "Father, I am very sorry. I did not mean to be disrespectful." With that, she left the room.

"I don't know what has gotten into that child," said Mrs. Pratt.

"I do," said Lemuel, giving Kathleen a pointed look.

Kathleen felt her jaw tighten. She prayed Mrs. Pratt would not forbid Clara to work alongside her. Kathleen's love for her had soared.

As Kathleen was cleaning up from the meal, Mrs. Pratt entered the kitchen.

"I would like an accounting of your interactions with Clara," she stated.

"Interactions?"

"Yes. What precisely are the two of you doing together?"

"Before the snows came, we tended the garden, harvested, filled the root cellar, and preserved some foods. As you know, we also cook together."

"And you talk while you do all this?"

"It would be difficult to do it in silence, Ma'am." Kathleen knew she sounded impertinent, but she could not help it. Her anger rose.

"What do you talk about?"

"Miss Clara tells me about her day at school, her friends, her favorite books. We speak of the weather, food, the seasons. Normal conversations."

"Hmmm..." Mrs. Pratt's eyes narrowed. "Where, then, is she picking up the nonsense she spouted tonight at the dinner table?"

"I believe she learned it in church, Ma'am."

For once Mrs. Pratt was at a loss for words. Kathleen fought hard to keep from smirking.

"I feel I must remind you that you are not to speak of your Catholic religion nor use any of your Irishisms in front of her."

"I have not forgotten."

"See to it you never do."

Kathleen glared at the woman's back as she strode from the kitchen.

Bitch! The word jumped so quickly into Kathleen's mind it took her by surprise. It also appalled her. Never had such language been a part of her thoughts. She determined to go to confession before Mass on Sunday. She could not allow this family to change her, to make her anything like them.

Chapter Fifteen

Saturday, February 7, 1852 dawned cold and raw after a freezing rain the day before. By early afternoon, the sun had melted some of the ice, leaving behind slush and slippery patches on the roads and walkways. By the time Meg arrived at Saint John's she was nearly frozen. She'd worn her best dress despite the dismal weather. It was Aoife and Ned's wedding day.

"You look beautiful," Meg said as she joined Aoife and her mother.

Mrs. O'Sullivan and Mrs. Linton had done a remarkable job of creating a lovely gown for Aoife. With her hair piled atop her head it was difficult to notice how dry and brittle it was. Meg couldn't refuse Aoife's request to be her maid of honor, but now that the day had come she found she didn't like being a party to what she feared would be a life of misery for her friend.

After last minute adjustments to Aoife's gown, they were ready to begin. The only guests were the Lintons, Ned's uncle, Nuala, and Kathleen.

The bride and groom stood before Father Boyce just outside the sanctuary with Meg beside Aoife and Ned's uncle Owen, acting as his best man, beside him. Ned, too, was dressed in what must have been his best clothes. They weren't fashionable, but they were clean.

Father Boyce turned to Ned. "Wilt thou take Aoife Mary O'Sullivan, here present, for thy lawful wife, according to the rite of our holy Mother the Church?"

Ned answered, "I will."

The priest then turned to Aoife. "Wilt thou take Edward Michael MacBrody, here present, for thy lawful husband, according to the rite of our holy Mother the Church?"

Aoife answered, "I will."

Meg was surprised by the tears welling in her eyes as Aoife and Ned joined hands. The words returned her to the day she married Rory. As Ned spoke after the priest, it was Rory's voice she heard in her head.

"I, Edward Michael MacBrody, take thee, Aoife Mary O'Sullivan, for my lawful wife, to have and to hold, from this day forward, for better, for worse, for richer, for poorer, in sickness and in health, until death do us part."

As Aoife spoke her vows, Meg was transported back to Ireland, to the little church of Saint Mary's in Kelegeen with her beloved Father O'Malley presiding. Until this moment, she had not realized what a blur her own wedding day had been. The moment her ceremony ended, she'd left the church for the ship taking her to America. Her thoughts were more on the trepidation of the coming voyage and long separation from home and family than they were on an event she'd long desired.

"I join you together in marriage, in the Name of the Father, and of the Son, and of the Holy Ghost. Amen." Father Boyce made the sign of the cross over the couple. "*Ego conjugo vos in matrimonium, in nomine Patris, et Filii, et Spiritus Sancti, Amen.*" He repeated in Latin, before sprinkling them with holy water.

After blessing the bride's ring, he gave it to Ned who placed it on Aoife's finger saying, "With this ring, I thee wed and I plight unto thee my troth."

Meg had removed her own wedding ring immediately upon finding out that she must keep her marriage a secret. She felt the ghost of the band around her finger.

Again, the priest blessed the couple with the Sign of the Cross. He prayed over them ending with "Look down with favor , O Lord, we beseech Thee, upon these Thy servants, and graciously protect this, Thine ordinance, whereby Thou hast provided for the propagation of mankind; that they who are joined together by Thy authority may be preserved by Thy help; through Christ our Lord. Amen."

Tears spilled down Meg's face. Was God protecting her marriage to Rory? Were they, now separated nearly four years, truly married? Would they ever be together, bring children into the world, live out the sacrament? The sacrifice Meg had made felt too much to bear.

As the ceremony ended, Meg turned to Aoife. "Congratulations. I am so very happy for you," she said, her voice sounding strangled to her own ears.

153

"Ah, Meg!" Father Boyce observed. "You're more joyful in sentiment than the bride herself! Dry your tears, lass!"

As they walked from the church, Meg let her mind turn to thoughts of the life Aoife likely had ahead of her. Two good people, obviously in love with each other who simply wanted to spend their lives together and raise a family should be able to do so without being plunged into grinding poverty. It was terribly unfair. Which was worse, she wondered – living in squalor with the person you love more than anyone in the world or living in comfort without him?

The Lintons' held a small party in honor of the new couple. The Claproods and Dentons happily gave Meg and Nuala the day off to celebrate their friends' wedding. Kathleen had to beg Mrs. Pratt who grudgingly agreed on the condition that she rise extra early the next morning and stay up as late as necessary to complete the tasks she missed today.

They spent the afternoon eating, singing, laughing, and wishing the young couple well. A spread of bread, butter, jam, cheese, a few slices of beef, and a prettily decorated cake covered the small table – a paltry fare compared to the meals Meg prepared daily for the Claprood family. But Aoife's eyes widened at the sight. *Perhaps if this seems a bounty to her, she'll never know any different and she will be happy*, Meg thought. She hoped so for Aoife's sake.

"'Tis done now," Nuala said, as the three walked home together. "I hope she doesn't live to regret it."

"Perhaps it won't be as bad as we fear," Kathleen said. "Ned's job seems steady enough. Aoife could take in mending or washing. Hard, but still not as bad as back home. And they'll have each other. Couldn't we stop wishing them ill?"

"I'm not wishing them ill," Nuala stated. "I being practical."

"At least Ned won't take to drink," Meg said. "Aoife says he took the pledge."

"Well, that's something," Nuala conceded.

"What pledge?" Kathleen asked.

"A few years back, Father Theobald Mathew came here speaking about giving up the drink for good," Nuala explained. "Abstinence, he called it. He challenged the men to take a pledge promising never to drink liquor of any sort as long as they live. About four hundred or so took it. Before long they'd started the Father Mathew Total Abstinence Society. It's still going strong."

"I'm glad Ned took the pledge, then," said Kathleen. "At least that's one thing Aoife needn't worry about."

"Aye, if he keeps it. When things are going well it's not so hard, but when things turn bad..." Nuala shrugged.

"Heaven knows there are enough Taverns in the Meadows to tempt a saint," said Meg. "It would be easy enough to entice a despondent man."

Kathleen stopped, bringing the others up short. "We should speak no more of this. Today is their wedding day. Only God knows the future. Let's rejoice with them and stop this wretched talk!"

Meg felt sheepish. "You're right, Miss Romantic Heart," she said.

"Aye," agreed Nuala. "But I'll never marry."

"Never? What will happen when you're too old to work?" asked Kathleen.

"As I've no one to send money home to I've been putting most of my pay in my savings account. That should give me a tidy sum by the time I'm old."

"Where will you live?" asked Meg.

"A boarding house, I suppose. But a nice one. Or maybe I'll be able to rent a small place. Or even buy a house."

"Buy a house?" Kathleen asked. "Could you?"

"Perhaps that's merely a dream. But I will live somewhere nice – a respectable, clean, comfortable place. See if I don't."

Sitting on her bed that evening, Meg held the comb Rory had made for her. Touching it always made her feel closer to him. As she stroked the carved hearts and roses she did something she had not done since leaving the ship that brought her to America. She spoke to Siobhan.

Siobhan was something between a ghost and an angel. Before she left, Father O'Malley had told her about when he'd been a young man, long before he became a priest. He was in love with Siobhan and planned to marry her, but that never came to pass as she was murdered by a British soldier. Even after all those years, he still felt her presence. He believed she watched over him, prayed for him before the throne of God. As Meg was about to leave on a perilous voyage to an unfamiliar land where she knew no one and had no idea of what lay ahead, he asked Siobhan to go with her, to be her guardian. Meg was sure she'd felt Siobhan's presence on the ship. When they encountered storms or when sickness broke out among many of the passengers, Meg spoke to Siobhan, begging her prayers. Always, she was delivered safely. Now she turned to her again. She needed a different kind of help this time. She hoped Siobhan was still with her.

"Siobhan," she whispered in the darkened room. "Please pray for me. Please ask God to guide me. Rory is my husband. I love him with all my heart, but..." Here she stopped as tears welled up in her eyes. "I don't want to feel this way. I've been spoiled by my new life. Please, help me."

* * *

"Mother, must we really have so much less?" Deborah asked at dinner the next day.

"The markets are in short supply. Besides, it's a good opportunity to remember others who are less fortunate. You are grateful for what you have, aren't you?"

"Yes." Deborah sounded dejected. "I just don't see how our eating less will help anyone else."

"Deborah," Pamela scoffed. "You act as though you're being starved. I've never seen anyone who loved vegetables as well as you. It's as if you'd fade away without them."

"It doesn't hurt to be forced into a small sacrifice now and then. I'm sure it's good for the soul," said Mrs. Claprood.

"I hope next winter doesn't come early." Deborah complained. "Sometimes I feel as though I am starving."

Mrs. Claprood sighed.

"Don't badger your mother, Deborah," said Mr. Claprood. "We've no control over the weather."

Meg stood in the corner of the dining room silently listening. The food currently on their plates was more than her own family had had for months at a time.

The meal over, Meg cleared the table. Her hands shook with barely controlled rage. "Spoiled, cossetted, ingrates," she muttered under her breath. Meg stalked off to the kitchen with her load of dishes. "Starving! You hardly know the meaning of the word." She kicked the door open.

Later that evening, Mrs. Claprood called for her. She sat alone in the soft glow of the parlor lamp.

"Margaret, I'd like to speak with you about something. Please sit." She patted the spot next to her on the sofa.

156

Meg approached with some trepidation. Mrs. Claprood had never before called her for a private talk.

"I must confess something to you."

"Ma'am?"

"After dinner, when you were clearing the table, I heard what you said under your breath. You appeared very angry."

A wave of panic flashed through her. Would she be fired for her rude words?

"I'm sorry, Mrs. Claprood. I meant no harm. I was just...I mean it was just that..." How could she explain herself without adding more insult?

Mrs. Claprood gently laid her hand over Meg's. "It was we who were being insensitive. We've all heard about the famine in Ireland. We know you came from a more difficult situation than anything we're experiencing."

Meg wasn't sure what to say so merely nodded.

"I wonder, Margaret, would you tell me what it was like? I want to understand."

There was sincerity in Mrs. Claprood's soft brown eyes. Meg liked this woman who seemed always concerned with the welfare of others. Yet this was a wound she'd rather not touch.

"It was very bad," she said. "Once the potatoes were gone, there was nothing to eat. We had no money to buy food. We sold what little we owned and took in mending work trying to feed us all."

"How many?"

"At first, six – my mam, and da, my sisters Kathleen and Brigid, and my brother Brendan and me."

"What do you mean 'at first'?"

"We took in Rory's family after they were evicted because they couldn't pay their rent."

"Rory? Who is that?"

Meg felt herself blush. She'd mentioned him without even thinking. "Rory Quinn. The Quinns were our closest neighbors."

"Was he the father of the family?"

"No. He was my...friend. We grew up together. When the constable and his men came to evict them, they tore their house down to be sure they couldn't sneak back in. Rory's mam was still inside. They pulled the house down on top of her and she died."

Mrs. Claprood gasped. "Didn't anyone tell them she was in there?"

157

"Aye, they knew. She was refusing to leave so they knocked it down anyway. My da and Mr. Quinn went in to rescue her, but it was too late."

The sight of Anna Quinn's mangled corpse was a memory Meg had long ago pushed from her mind. Its return brought a shudder.

Mrs. Claprood tightened her hold on Meg's hand. "How barbaric." She whispered, but there was righteous anger in her voice. "So the rest of the Quinn family came to live with you?"

"Aye. It was illegal to help anyone who had been evicted, but winter was close and they'd been our friends all our lives. My mam and da took the risk."

"God bless them for it. I suppose your house was small. Not many rooms for such a large group of people."

"Ma'am, our house *was* just one room and smaller than this one," Meg said, gesturing at the spacious parlor.

"Oh." The word was barely audible. Then she asked, "Where would they have gone if your parents hadn't taken them in?"

"They'd have likely built a *scalpeen* somewhere. That's what most who were evicted did."

"What is that?"

"A three-sided shelter made of whatever scraps can be found. If there's nothing to make one, then they'd dig a hole in the side of a hill or in the ground and live there. Those are called scalps."

"My Lord. How many came to live with your family?"

"At first, it was Rory, his da, and his six brothers and sisters. But the youngest ones all took fever soon enough and died. So there was just Rory and his sisters Aisling and Loreena along with their da. Later, Mr. Quinn died while on the Public Works."

"A government work program?"

"Aye, building roads and bridges that went nowhere. The money paid was so little it barely made a difference. Mr. Quinn died breaking rocks. His heart gave out." As Meg talked, it felt as though a knot deep inside her was beginning to unravel.

"How horrible! Did your father work there, too?"

"Aye, as did Rory and my brother, Brendan. But they all quit after Rory's da died."

"So you survived solely on the money you made from mending? That couldn't have been much."

"Before the Quinns were evicted, Rory made beautiful carvings – animal shaped toys for children, pretty boxes for the ladies. He sold them in town. That helped until the accident. His brother, Aiden, was fishing with a friend. It was a stormy winter day, but they had to try. Their *curragh* – oh, that's what we call our fishing boats – capsized in the rough waters. Rory, Kathleen, and I were nearby. Rory ran in to rescue them, but the wind was so wild it just threw the boat around. Rory's right hand was smashed against a rock. Aiden drowned." Meg stopped. Having that horrible day replay itself in her head was too much.

"And Aiden's friend?"

"He made it to shore."

"How badly was Rory injured?"

"After a while it improved some, but he was never able to carve again."

"So then it was just the mending work that brought in the money?"

"Aye."

"Was your work steady?"

Meg shook her head. "There were times we'd have none at all."

The look on Mrs. Claprood's face was so pained, Meg found it odd that telling her story should make her feel bad for the one hearing it.

"How did you survive? What *did* you eat?"

Meg would have preferred not to answer. She straightened her spine, set her jaw, and looked Mrs. Claprood in the eye.

"We foraged. We were lucky if we found a turnip now and then. We pulled bark off trees. Nettles from the graveyards. Sometimes we ate grass. Mam made a soup of anything we could get. Mostly it was a handful of whatever we could scrounge floating in a kettle. More often than not, we simply went without."

Mrs. Claprood's expression changed from pity to shock, but Meg was not to be deterred. Something inside spurred her on. "There were many who had nothing at all. They died slow, agonizing deaths. Some from illness, others from starvation."

"Was there no public assistance? No poorhouse as we have in Worcester?"

"The workhouse, we called ours, but only the most desperate would go there. Once you entered, it was sure you'd leave as one of the bodies piled into a wagon that carted away the dead.

159

Those bodies were dumped together in huge ditches – a place we called the Pits. There are hundreds buried there."

Mrs. Claprood stared at Meg open-mouthed. "What you must think of us!" she said.

Meg was taken aback. "Ma'am?" she asked.

"After all you've endured. Our complaining about smaller than usual portions. Speaking of it as a sacrifice. No wonder you were upset. Oh, Margaret, I am so very sorry."

Meg was stunned, not sure how to respond. "That is what made me angry. I know what it feels like to starve. I know what it means to watch people I loved turn into skeletons before my eyes. I woke every morning wondering who would die that day. Wondering when the time would come for me."

Mrs. Claprood stared at her, aghast. Meg suddenly worried she'd gone too far. She quickly changed course. "But you had no knowledge of my hardships, nothing to compare to starving. I'm so grateful to be here, to have this job. I send money home to help my family. They've been able to buy food and pay the rent because of your family. I saved enough to pay for Kathleen's passage. I'll always be grateful to you for taking me on."

"I'm glad we've an instrument of assistance, Margaret. We are so happy with your service. You must forgive us our thoughtlessness. It is as you said. We simply have nothing with which to compare. Dear Lord, what you've been through! You are a remarkable young woman, Margaret, exceptional."

"But I'm not," said Meg. "Nuala is here as is my sister, Kathleen. Hundreds of Irish lasses all over America are in service. We've had to or we'd all be dead. I'm no different than the rest."

"I'm pleased we had this talk, Margaret. I understand better now. Thank you."

"Of course, Ma'am," Meg said. She hadn't felt she'd had much choice in the matter, but now that she'd said her piece a tension within her released. Among the Yankee ladies, she knew Mrs. Claprood was the one who was exceptional. Most employers would never concern themselves with the lives of their servants. Certainly she could not picture Mrs. Pratt having a similar conversation with Kathleen, though Mrs. Denton might.

On the following evening Meg sat mending in the parlor. "May I ask you something, Mr. Claprood,"she said as he passed her on his way to the study.

"Certainly, Margaret."

"How much does it cost to hire a sleigh for a few hours?"

A broad grin brightened his face. "Thinking of going for a ride?"

"My sister Kathleen and my friend, Nuala, thought it might be pleasant for us on one of our Thursdays. The misses Claprood seem to greatly enjoy it."

"Quite true," he chuckled. "Let's see, now, you'll have to rent the sleigh and horses, plus pay for the driver. The total for, say two hours, should come to about a dollar and a half."

Among the three of them they could surely come up with that amount.

"Thank you, sir."

"Were you thinking of going this week? Now that it's February you'll want to do it soon."

"If the weather allows."

"If Thursday's weather is conducive, I'll stop by the livery on my way to the foundry and send the sleigh over. How would that be?"

"That would be wonderful! Thank you." Meg was delighted to have caught Mr. Claprood in a generous mood.

His expression turned serious. "I think however, it might be better to have the sleigh sent to the Pratt or Denton home. If my girls see it, they'll want one sent for them, too." The twinkle returned to his eyes. "Where shall it be?"

"To the Denton's, please," said Meg. Better not to bring any unnecessary attention before the Pratt family. "I'll gather the money from Kathleen and Nuala and bring it to you."

"Nonsense. It's my treat."

Meg was dumbfounded. "We couldn't, sir. It's too much. With all three of us contributing, we can pay. It's most generous of you, though, and I do thank you for the offer."

"Margaret," he said, his voice softening. "Save your money for your family in Ireland. The amount is far more to the three of you than it is to me. You girls work hard enough to have earned two hours of amusement. I'm happy to provide it."

Meg thought if she continued to protest he might see it as an insult.

"Mr. Claprood, you are so very kind. I cannot thank you enough."

His smile was like that of an indulgent father. "It's only a sleigh ride. Think nothing of it." With that he left her for his study.

Meg returned to her mending while continuing to mull over what had just taken place. It wasn't that Mr. Claprood was miserly. He was quite generous with his wife and children as well as towards guests, but she was a servant. He had never been cruel, but neither had he taken much notice of her. She couldn't help but wonder at his sudden benevolence. Had Mrs. Claprood conveyed their conversation to him? To others? She did not want the suffering and poverty of her past aired for public consumption, nor did she wish to become the object of anyone's pity.

* * *

With a fresh fall of snow the night before, Thursday was a perfect day for a sleigh ride. They gathered in the Dentons' front hall eagerly awaiting the sleigh. They had expected to wait in the kitchen, but Mrs. Denton brought them out to the entryway. "Why hide yourselves? The driver will come to the front door for you."

"I can hardly believe we're doing this," Kathleen said as they clustered, watching out the window. "If Mrs. Pratt knew, I'd never hear the end of it."

"What did you tell her?" asked Nuala.

"Only that I was coming here and spending the afternoon with you and Meg. It's not a lie. I'm weary of relating my every move to her."

Mrs. Denton appeared in the hall with an armload of blankets. "You'll want these to keep you warm. Once that sleigh gets going, the wind will feel like a whip if you're not covered properly."

"Thank you, Mrs. Denton," said Nuala.

"Think nothing of it. Now let me get you each a foot warmer with hot coals. Be sure to cover them with your skirts to hold in the heat."

"I'll get them," said Nuala, handing the blankets to Meg and Kathleen.

"Certainly not. This is your day off." Mrs. Denton hurried away.

"Nuala, wherever did you find her?" Meg asked. "There can't be another maid in all of Worcester with a mistress who waits on her!"

Nuala grinned. "She's a motherly woman. You should have seen her when her children were here for Thanksgiving. She couldn't do enough for them. And the grandchildren – how she spoiled them! She's not happy if she's not doting on someone. Most of the time I'm the only one she has. I can't say I mind. She's a love who I wouldn't trade for the world. But make no mistake, I do my work. Do it well, too. I earn my pay and keep."

Mrs. Denton returned with three tin foot warmers just as the jingling of sleigh bells sounded. Blankets and foot warmers in hand, the three bounded out the door. Two large chestnut horses trotted up the street, stopping in front of the house. The sleigh driver was the same Irishman who had taken the Claprood girls and their cousins for a ride.

"Where to?" he asked, jumping down to assist them into the sleigh.

"Anywhere you like," Nuala told him. "We're out for enjoyment. It doesn't matter where we go."

A flicker of recognition showed on his face as Nuala spoke, her brogue giving her away. "You lasses are the helps?"

"Aye," said Nuala, "but today we're your passengers."

Looking at Meg, he furrowed his brow. "Didn't I see you at the Claproods'?"

"You did. I work for them."

A broad grin spread across his face. "This is a grand thing indeed!"

"What do you mean?" Kathleen asked.

"'Tis the first time I've driven Irish lasses. It's always Yanks that hire me. We're every bit as good as they are even if they don't know it, aye? One day we'll be as successful as them. Then you'll ride in sleighs and carriages anytime you want."

They all giggled at the thought. Meg wondered if it could really be possible.

"What's your name?" Nuala asked.

"Seamus O'Herilhy, at your service, m'ladies," he said, with a sweeping bow that from most people would have seemed mocking, but from their countryman held an air of genuine respect.

"Pleased to make your acquaintance, Seamus O'Herilhy," Nuala responded. "I'm Nuala O'Flaherty, and these are my friends, Meg and Kathleen O'Connor."

"A pleasure it is," he said with a smile before climbing onto the driver's box. With a snap of the whip, the horses were in motion.

For the next two hours they traversed the hills and valleys of Worcester. It was obvious that Seamus knew the city well. They headed northwest to the Tatnuck section. Filled with meadows, pastures, and farmland, Tatnuck appeared like a fairyland. Last night's snowfall covered the landscape like a pristine white cape with a million glistening diamonds. Only where farmers had gone about their chores was the seamless white garment rent by plodding footprints.

Wind whipped their faces as the sleigh sped along, the horses picking up speed in the open fields. Meg gazed wide-eyed at the world of white domed by a clear blue sky. The easy glide of the runners with their accompanying whoosh made her grin so hard it hurt. She'd never before felt such exhilaration.

Nuala nudged her. "Aye, but this is exciting!" she exclaimed.

Meg nodded, the bracing air stealing her breath. She glanced at Kathleen. She, too, was grinning as she peered first one direction then another. The big draft horses kicked up sprays of snow as they advanced, their bells resounding in the brisk air. The sleigh slowed as they crested a hill, then sped up again as it raced down the other side. The friends screamed with delight, falling into a fit of laughter upon reaching the bottom.

Seamus slowed the horses to a moderate pace as he turned them away from the Tatnuck section and headed east. "Shall we have a look at the new houses on Elm Street?" he called.

They agreed and set off. Seamus pointed out the newly built homes, all of them much larger than those owned by their employers.

"I'd wager they have more than one girl to help," Nuala said.

"Oh, aye," Seamus called back. "Most have a staff. It's the rich folks from Nob Hill. Main Street is becoming more commercial, so they're moving themselves up here."

"What will happen to the houses on Nobility Hill?" Kathleen asked.

"'Tis odd, what they're doing with them," Seamus answered. "They're taking them down, reusing their parts. All those new houses in your area – they've got parts of the Nob Hill houses inside them."

"What? How is that possible?" Nuala asked.

"They move whole sections of a house then build the newer parts around them."

"I don't believe a word of it," Nuala argued.

Seamus laughed. "Lass, I see it all winter when I'm driving. They use a team of oxen to pull the sections. It's easier to pull a heavy load like that over the snow, you see."

"If the Nob Hill people are moving to Elm Street, why are the house sections going to Crown Hill?" Meg asked.

"The folks on Crown Hill buy the sections from them. Those Nob Hill folks are rich enough to build from scratch. It's less expensive for your Crown Hill people to buy an already made section. One thing's for sure, Yankees pride themselves on not letting anything go to waste. They've made an art of it."

"I'd like to see it," Kathleen said.

"I'll drive you over the routes they take," said Seamus. "If we're lucky we might spot one."

They rode through the newly developing Elm Street neighborhood then continued east towards Nobility Hill. "See there!" Seamus pointed ahead as they neared Main Street. "What did I tell you?"

All three stared, incredulous, as a team of oxen lumbered up the road pulling what could only be a parlor room behind them.

"God be blessed in His angels and His saints," Nuala murmured. "My own eyes tell me the truth of it."

Meg couldn't help but admire the resourcefulness of New England Yankees.

"This is a land of miracles," said Kathleen.

The two hours came to an end much too soon. Seamus brought the sleigh to a halt before the Dentons' front door then hopped down to help them out.

"I hope you ladies enjoyed the ride," he said.

"It was grand, thank you." said Meg. "You did a marvelous job. I hope they pay you well for your services," she added, hoping to get some idea of what a driver earned.

"Well enough," he said. "A mite better than common laborers, at any rate. Here, let me carry those." He gathered up the blankets so that the foot warmers were all they had to carry to the door.

"We need to go around back," Nuala told him as he headed for the front of the house.

"Of course, my mistake," he said. "I'm not used to driving the help."

They rounded the ell of the house towards the kitchen door.

"Do you get to do much driving?" Nuala asked.

"Not as much as I'd like. I'm always glad to be recommended."

"I thought they only rented horses and conveyances. Does the livery service employ many drivers?" Meg asked.

"I'm the only driver working for the livery. There's a couple of fellas from the hostelry who hire out as drivers, usually, when I can't do it."

"Are they Negroes?" asked Kathleen.

"Aye. Oscar and Jim. They seem decent enough sorts, what little I know of them."

"Are they...I mean did they..." Kathleen wasn't sure how to phrase her question.

"Are they runaways?" Seamus finished for her.

Kathleen nodded.

"No. They're both free men."

"You like your job?" asked Meg, trying to turn the conversation back to the information she needed to gather.

"Oh, aye. Most of the time. I like horses. Don't mind cleaning up after them. I enjoy being outside, though, so I'm happiest when I get to drive. Can't imagine how those poor lads stand it all day cooped up in those factories. That's not for me. 'Course it's not always pleasant. Sometimes I get caught in a storm. Been soaked through more than once, but nothing's perfect, is it?"

"How did you come to have this job?" Meg asked.

"I've been working for the livery service since I got here. Mostly I muck out stalls, feed, and groom the horses, hitch and unhitch them, and the like. I took care of the landlord's horses back home. Drove them sometimes, too. At the livery, they could see I knew what I was about when I went to inquire after a job. I might see about getting a job as a freight driver, soon. It's steadier work and they make more money."

Meg tucked this information away in her mind for her next letter to Rory.

"Thank you for the ride," Nuala said, opening the kitchen door. "If we're able to do it again, we'll ask for you."

"It will be my pleasure," he said. As he handed her the blankets. "Could I ask you something?"

"Aye."

"There's a dance at the church Saturday night. Would you like to go?"

Nuala appeared to think it over. "I like to dance. Aye. I'll go," she said.

"I'll come round to fetch you." Seamus tipped his hat. "A good day to you, ladies," he said, smiling.

Once inside, Kathleen sniffed the air. "Do I smell chocolate?"

"Aye," said Nuala. "Look." She pointed to the table where three steaming cups had been set out. "Mrs. Denton! She must have poured when she saw the sleigh drive up."

Nuala stacked the blanket and set the foot warmers near the stove before taking a seat at the table. Meg wrapped her cold hands around the mug. She bent over the cup, breathing in the fragrant aroma as the steam warmed her face.

"You made quite an impression, Nuala," said Kathleen.

Nuala shrugged.

"Taken by his good looks, were you?" asked Meg.

"He's attractive enough."

"Looks a bit like Rory, don't you think, Meg?" Kathleen asked.

"Well, they've both got red hair."

"Is your Rory a handsome devil, then?" asked Nuala.

Meg smiled over her hot chocolate. "Aye. That he is."

"So you think Seamus is handsome?" Kathleen teased.

Nuala blushed, licked her lips after taking a sip. "And did you get all the information you wanted?" she asked Meg, ignoring Kathleen's question.

Meg lifted her eyebrows. "What is a freight driver?"

Before Nuala could answer, the kitchen door opened. "How was your ride?" asked Mrs. Denton.

"Wondrous!" exclaimed Nuala. "We had a grand time. I especially loved when he drove fast in the field."

"And down the hills," Kathleen added. "I've never had such sport."

"Now I understand why the Claprood girls enjoy sleighing so much," said Meg.

167

"I'm so glad you had a good time," said Mrs. Denton.

"Thank you for making the hot chocolate for us," said Nuala.

"I wanted to surprise you." Pouring a cup for herself, Mrs. Denton took up a seat at the table.

"Mrs. Denton, what is a freight driver?" Nuala asked.

"He's the person behind a team of horses that carries large loads of goods. Why do you ask?"

There was silence as the three looked at one another.

"Just that the driver mentioned the job," Nuala explained. "We wondered what he meant."

"Was he a good driver?"

"Very good," Nuala answered. "Quite amiable. We liked him very much."

"Aye, and he liked Nuala," Meg said under her breath with a sly glance at Kathleen.

Nuala scowled at them over her cup.

"Give me his name," said Mrs. Denton. "We'll be sure to recommend him."

Later in the day, Meg and Kathleen helped Nuala cook the evening meal, stayed to eat and clean up before leaving for home. As they walked from the house Kathleen said, "I wish I worked for the Dentons." Her voice was so wistful it made Meg's heart ache.

"Is it no better at all?" Meg asked.

"The best I can say is it's no worse."

Chapter Sixteen

Kathleen's attempts to please her employers and stay clear of Lemuel continued to prove a struggle. Lemuel gloated when a fire broke out at the Jesuit run College of the Holy Cross in July, destroying nearly the whole building, joking that he wished he'd started it himself. But his disposition turned surly when early in 1853 John Knowlton took office as Mayor of Worcester.

"Fool! Idiot! Imbecile!" Lemuel ranted on hearing of the new mayor's statement that he believed immigrants had a right to their beliefs, and that Worcester's public schools, which strove to impart moral and religious structure, had no business forcing Protestant beliefs on Catholic students. "What next? Will he invite the pope himself to head the school committee?" Lemuel spouted.

Kathleen inwardly reveled in Lemuel's discomfiture, though his fury made her nervous.

Clara, now fourteen, spent more time with friends. Kathleen was happy the girl was no longer so lonely. Yet, she missed her company. One rainy afternoon in June, Clara surprised Kathleen by appearing in the kitchen.

"Change in plans?" Kathleen asked.

"Can't walk in the rain."

"You and your friends have umbrellas?"

"Yes, but that's for when one *must* walk in the rain. Why do it if it's not necessary? We'll go another day."

Kathleen smiled. "What do you propose for the afternoon, then?"

"It's been ever so long since we've worked together. I rather miss it."

"So do I," said Kathleen. She set Clara to shelling peas, while she peeled potatoes.

"I brought you something," said Clara, a sly smile playing about her lips.

"Oh?"

Clara reached into the deep pocket of her dress. "This," she said, holding out a book. "It's very popular. It was published a year ago, yet everyone still talks about it. I thought it might assist you in reading English." Clara had been secretly instructing Kathleen in reading and writing English since they began working together.

Kathleen wiped her hands on her apron. Taking hold of the book, she read the cover. *Uncle Tom's Cabin; or, Life Among the Lowly.*

"Thank you *a stór*. Why has it got everyone talking?"

"It tells about the slaves in the south. How badly they're treated and how they should all be set free."

"Haven't folks been arguing over that for some time?" Kathleen asked.

"Yes, but this book has caused a stir. It appeals to feelings, you see."

Kathleen considered the look of earnestness on Clara's face. The child seemed determined to grow up all at once.

"I see. Do you take a side on that subject?"

"Indeed I do. I can't believe our Lord wishes for anyone to be held in slavery."

"Do your friends agree?"

"They do." Clara let out a huge sigh.

Kathleen cocked her head. "What's wrong?"

"I do so wish my family felt the same way. Mother and Father don't take a strong position on the subject. Father says he wishes any further states admitted to the Union would be free states."

"That's something."

"But Mrs. Claprood has joined an abolitionist society. I wish mother would join, too. She won't. She worries that it might adversely affect her social standing. I don't see how that's more important than undoing a great evil."

"Does she mind you having such a strong opinion?"

Clara laughed. "Oh, she might if she knew. I keep my thoughts to myself around Mother. I do talk about it with my friends, though."

"What of your brothers? Have they an opinion on it?"

"Harvey is for ending slavery, though I don't believe his feelings are so strong that he would join the Abolitionist Movement. And, of course, Lemuel has an opinion on everything." She rolled her eyes.

Kathleen couldn't contain her laughter. "And what is his opinion?"

"Lemuel thinks all the slaves should be shipped out of the country, back to Africa or anywhere else. Just so long as they're not here."

Kathleen was hardly surprised.

Clara lowered her voice. "He bothers you, doesn't he, Kathleen?"

"What do you mean?"

"I've seen how he treats you."

Kathleen shrugged. She had no wish to bring Clara into her difficulties with Lemuel.

Clara set the peas aside, her expression more serious.

"What's wrong *a stór*?" Kathleen asked, pausing in her own work to give Clara her full attention.

"Is it a terrible sin not to like one's brother?" Tears welled in Clara's eyes.

"Oh, child."

"Lemuel has always been a trial, but lately he's worse than ever. Everything he says is so hateful. He has awful rows with Father. He ought to be respectful. They were in the study last evening arguing about a convention. I could hear them from the parlor! Lemuel told Father he was ignorant and stormed out of the room. I never saw Father look so stricken. I felt awful for him. How could Lemuel treat him so?" Clara put her head in her hands.

Kathleen rubbed Clara's back. "There now. It's just a phase. Your brother is feeling his own importance. He's not as mature as he thinks he is, but someday he'll learn. This will pass." Kathleen wished she could believe her own words.

After her talk with Clara, Kathleen couldn't help but notice the coldness growing between Lemuel and Mr. Claprood. They still went together to the foundry every day, but there was no more jovial talk between them. Conversations at mealtimes were stilted. Arguments between the two were no longer always kept behind closed doors.

The convention Clara had mentioned was a gathering of delegates at the statehouse on Beacon Hill that lasted from May through August. As reports of the goings on at the convention made their way to Worcester, there were moments of solidarity among the Pratts and times of terrible division. Lemuel and his father were in accord over the news that prohibitions against the use of funds for sectarian schools had been proposed. They claimed it was properly based on the separation of church and state. Kathleen heard at Saint John's that it was meant as a way to bar funding for Catholic schools. The ten hour workday was never addressed and industrial workers were never acknowledged as a separate class, much to the delight of both gentlemen.

However, when neither the Democrats nor the Free Soilers wanted immigrants to be counted as citizens or have the right to be represented in Massachusetts, the division between father and son erupted. Mr. Pratt, still adhering to his allegiance to the floundering Whigs, agreed with that party's idea of dividing the state into representative districts based on population. Since most immigrants were city dwellers, this would give the Whigs more representatives.

"Can't you see the Whig party is a sinking ship?" Lemuel railed. "Why do you insist on going under with them?"

The conversation had started at the dinner table. Though Mrs. Pratt had managed to quash it, it resumed more heatedly once the meal was over. Lemuel and Mr. Pratt remained at the table, oblivious to all around them as Kathleen cleared the dishes.

"You underestimate the Whigs, my boy. They're prosperous and money talks. Stick with them and you'll remain on the winning side."

"Balderdash! Everything comes to an end eventually. That time is at hand. It should have been plain enough when Franklin Pierce beat Winfield Scott for President. Farmers and small-town people want a new government framework that gives them a greater voice. They're sick of the Boston Brahmins."

Mr. Pratt waved his hand in dismissal. "They can want it until the cows come home. It doesn't mean they'll get it."

"They're gaining power, Father. There are many who are willing to give the coalition a chance. Why oppose it? Undercutting the power of Boston would mean shifting the seat of state government to Worcester! Don't you see what that means? The voting majority is now in the eastern part of the state. Moving the seat of government to Worcester would shift the power to here, the more heavily agricultural areas."

"A delusion is all that is."

"If anyone's delusional, it's you and your antiquated cronies. You've already allowed this country to become overrun with foreigners. This is America! It belongs to us and should be run by us!" Lemuel pounded the table with his fist. "You want to divide up the state so that the Whigs can be assured of the immigrant vote? You should be trying to get them out of here! What right have they to vote, anyway?"

Kathleen, clearing the sideboard, turned her head for a furtive glimpse. Mr. Pratt's face had turned so purple she feared he'd have apoplexy.

"How dare you speak to me that way?" Mr. Pratt's tone was low, threatening.

"I speak my mind," Lemuel said.

"You may take your mind, your mouth, and the rest of you from my dinner table."

Lemuel stood, threw his napkin onto the table. "I shall do better. I shall take myself from this house!" He stormed from the room. Within seconds the slam of the front door made Kathleen jump, followed by a flood of relief that he was gone.

She could not stay clear of Lemuel forever. One summer day while she was cleaning the parlor, father and son were again at odds. The proposition to move the seat of state government to Worcester had been soundly defeated, the coalition and Free Soil party in ruins.

"Well, what do you think of your coalition now?" Mr. Pratt gloated.

Lemuel slammed the fireplace mantel. "It's the fault of the damn Paddies. They formed a block against the coalition. If not for them, Worcester would be the capital of Massachusetts. How dare they interfere with American government?" Lemuel paced with angry strides across the floor.

Kathleen looked for a way to leave the room unnoticed.

"That accursed bishop in Boston – what's his name?" Lemuel snapped his fingers. "Fitz-something."

"Fitzpatrick, I believe," said Mr. Pratt.

"Damned Paddy priest. He's the one who got the whole lot of them to vote as a block. The imbeciles blindly follow whatever they're told by their clergy. Those people are ruled by the priests who are ruled by the bishops who are ruled by the pope. A massive conspiracy to destroy America."

"That's a bit dramatic, don't you think?" asked Mr. Pratt. "The defeat of that proposition was due to a strongly united Whig vote," said Mr. Pratt, drawing himself up, smugness rising

173

from his toes to his bushy eyebrows. The look only served to anger Lemuel more.

"If that's true, you've no idea what sort of damage your beloved Whig party has caused. Listen to this." Lemuel grabbed a newspaper from the parlor table. "It is from a Mr. R. H. Dance, Junior, a Free Soiler who wants to loosen the grip of the Whigs."

Standing in the center of the room, Lemuel snapped the paper open and began to read.

"We are in a peculiar state of things such as the world never saw from the days of Noah to the present time. There's a tide of immigration setting into this country and especially into the Atlantic cities. It is a transient population and an alien population. It counts in the census. Now I ask whether in this state of things that is the kind of numbers to which the principle of political equality in basing political representation is to apply. I apprehend not."

He threw down the paper. "I apprehend not, as well."

Before Mr. Pratt could respond, Mrs. Pratt entered the room.

"Goodness, I can hear the two of you all the way upstairs."

Catching sight of Kathleen, she glared at her. "What are you doing in here?" she asked.

"Dusting," Kathleen answered, holding up her cloth.

Mrs. Pratt's face turned stony. "You are relieved from your duties in this room. Find something to do elsewhere."

Kathleen was only too happy to remove herself. As she passed the front staircase, she noticed Clara huddled at the top of the stairs. Feeling eyes boring into her back, Kathleen turned to see Mrs. Pratt from the parlor doorway. She changed course, hurried to the kitchen, ran up the back staircase and, quickly traversing the long hallway, came up behind Clara. Kneeling next to her, she asked, "Are you all right *a stór?*"

"They're at it again," said Clara.

The girl's hands were balled into tight fists and she was gnawing on a knuckle.

Kathleen sighed. "Don't trouble yourself, Miss Clara. Men love to argue over politics. With different opinions, the sparks fly."

"Father and Lemuel hate each other."

Kathleen smoothed the girl's light brown hair. "For all we know they might be enjoying themselves."

Clara looked at her quizzically.

"Men are strange creatures, *a stór*. Rather than listen to the two of them blather on, why don't you come help me in the kitchen?"

When Kathleen was cleaning up from the evening meal, Mrs. Pratt entered the kitchen.

"I would like a word with you."

"Yes, Ma'am?"

"I don't know what you expect to accomplish by eavesdropping on family conversations, but I demand that behavior end immediately."

"Ma'am?" Kathleen was bewildered.

"Why did you stay in the parlor when Mr. Pratt and Lemuel were having a ...discussion?"

"I was dusting there alone. They came in. I was not eavesdropping. I was trying to finish my work."

Mrs. Pratt sniffed. "You should have excused yourself immediately."

How was Kathleen to explain to this woman that she would have loved nothing more than to have fled from the parlor, but feared crossing Lemuel's path?

"I'm sorry," she said instead. "I did not want to leave the dusting half-finished."

"By now, I would have thought you'd know when to absent yourself. It's true what Lemuel says. You Irish are a stupid lot. I shouldn't have to tell you this, but whatever is said or done by anyone in this family is no business of anyone outside this home. You are not to repeat anything you've seen or heard to anyone. Is that perfectly clear?"

"Of course, Ma'am."

"That includes your sister and your Irish friends."

A sense of injustice took hold of Kathleen. "I assure you, Mrs. Pratt, there is no one I know who has the slightest interest in anything your family says or does." Snapping the dish towel in her hands, she turned back to her work.

"Well, then...very well," said Mrs. Pratt. She gave Kathleen a sidelong glance before leaving the kitchen.

A smile played about Kathleen's mouth as she completed her work.

175

Not long after, Lemuel began spending most of his free time away from the house, especially in the evenings. He claimed he had joined a lodge. Whenever asked what he did at the lodge, he gave evasive answers. His parents seemed concerned. Kathleen was happy to see less of him. His mood changed. He no longer raged about the house. Instead he seemed fixated on something he nurtured within himself. Kathleen was certain it was something sinister.

Chapter Seventeen

Kathleen had lied to Mrs. Pratt. She told Meg everything she'd heard. Neither sister considered it gossip, but self-preservation. Kathleen felt more and more threatened by Lemuel. When Lemuel began making evening visits to Oliver, Meg made it her business to hear what was said between them. When they closed themselves into the study one night, Meg busied herself in the next room, staying as close to the door as possible.

"I've mentioned your name at meetings. You should come to the next one," Lemuel told Oliver. "Why does my father insist on hanging onto the Whig party? They're nearly finished. Anyone can see that," Lemuel complained.

"My father still considers himself a Whig," said Oliver. "They're older, set in their ways. I suppose it's hard to change."

"And you, Oliver? Where do you stand?"

"On which issue?"

"Start with the immigrants."

Meg crept closer to the door.

"Of course. Your favorite subject. I'm not as bothered by them as you."

"We're being overrun by them, especially those Papist Paddies. Soon it won't be the president who runs this country, but the pope."

Oliver laughed. "Lemuel, you sound like a nervous old woman. How could a bunch of ignorant laborers take over the country?"

Meg bristled at Oliver's description of her people.

"The foreign men can vote! They side with the Democrats, which throws everything out of balance. You can't believe they should have American citizenship."

"I don't believe a person should be denied citizenship indefinitely, but the amount of time one lives here before he can become a citizen should be lengthened. Also, immigrants should have to work steadily, contribute to our society and economy for a certain period to show that they're worthy of being an American citizen. If one does that, then I've no quarrel with it."

How generous of you, Meg thought. *As though an Irish man could get and keep a job when you Yanks keep posting No Irish Need Apply signs.*

"Well, that is one of the things our lodge proposes," said Oliver. "To increase the waiting period for citizenship."

"Really? Not to ship them all back at once?" Oliver laughed, as if the fate of America's immigrants was a merely a source of amusement.

"We'll work towards that. Meanwhile, we can at least prevent them from skewing the vote in their favor."

"How long should they wait to become Americans?" asked Oliver.

"Twenty-one years."

"That's a bit extreme."

"Not to me. Now let's talk about slavery."

"My mother's become a regular abolitionist."

"Women involving themselves in anything but housework, cooking, and raising children seems rather vulgar, does it not?"

Silence on the other side of the door. Then Oliver spoke.

"My mother is vulgar?"

"No, of course not," Lemuel stammered. "She's a fine lady. The finest. One of the rare examples of a lady who can balance the domestic sphere with...umm...other pursuits."

Meg smiled, arms folded across her chest, relishing the image of a squirming Lemuel attempting to wiggle out of the hole he'd dug for himself as he continued.

"But *most* women are not so adept at doing so and maintaining their feminine dignity."

"Indeed," said Oliver, his tone implying that he half accepted Lemuel's explanation. "As to your question, I agree with Mother that slavery should be abolished. It's a moral injustice as well as a sin."

"Yet another point of agreement with our lodge!" Lemuel stated.

"Oh? They see slavery as immoral and sinful?"

"Each man has his own reasons for wanting to end it. What's important is that it is abolished."

"And once freed, you'd have them packed on ships and sent to Africa?" The slightly mocking tone returned to Oliver's voice.

"They can go to the moon for all I care, along with the Irish."

"Mother would be distraught to lose Margaret. I daresay your own mother would not want to lose Margaret's sister."

Meg's heart hammered in her chest.

"What she wishes is that her help was not an Irish Papist bitch."

Meg gritted her teeth.

"No self-respecting American girl would take on their work. The choice is between an Irish girl or none. Is yours so bad? Our Margaret's work appears acceptable."

Acceptable? Meg expected better from Oliver.

"It's her attitude. The girl acts above her station. She thinks herself too good for me." Meg heard the fury enter Lemuel's voice.

"Ah-ha! That's your problem? If you want a slut, you'd better look elsewhere. It's a rare Bridget who'll give it away."

"How dare they not know their place?"

Oliver laughed. "They hold their virtue in high esteem. Can't fault them for that, can you?"

"She thinks she's a grand lady, dressing in finery on her days off. Our Bridget needs to have her reality drilled into her, the sooner the better."

Meg caught her breath.

"Your Bridget's a fine cook. That's unusual. Can't you appreciate that?" There was laughter in Oliver's voice. Was it all such a joke?

"Some things are more important than food."

"Like your cock?"

Meg blushed. Did men always speak this way with one another? What then made them consider themselves gentlemen?

"Like the pure race of this country." Lemuel sounded exasperated. "She's a minion of the pope. They all are."

"You, my friend, are far too consumed with thoughts of a house maid."

"My energy is perfectly focused through my membership in the lodge. Would you at least come to Tuesday's meeting?"

Oliver sighed. "I suppose it wouldn't do any harm."

"Good! I'll come by to fetch you."

Fearing they might exit the study, Meg hastened from the parlor. Lantern in hand, she left the house and made her way to the Pratt's. She pounded on the kitchen door. When Kathleen opened it, Meg grabbed her wrist and pulled her outside.

"What is it?" Kathleen asked. "Has something happened?"

"Not yet." Meg relayed all she'd heard.

Kathleen's face paled. "What should I do?"

"Gather your things. You'll not stay here another minute."

"But where can I go?"

"To the Lintons' for now. Stay with them until you find another placement."

"They have so little. I couldn't ask it of them. Besides, I don't want to walk to the Meadows after dark."

"I'll go with you."

"Then you'd have to walk back on your own. No."

"But you're in danger."

Kathleen folded her arms. "Lemuel and his father are not on good terms. Lemuel stays away a good deal. He might have been preening before Oliver. I'll be careful."

Meg reluctantly left with a pledge from Kathleen that if she felt at all in danger she would leave immediately.

* * *

"What will you do?" Nuala asked Kathleen as the three walked down Union Street on Thursday.

"Look for another position, though I don't know how to go about it. Lemuel hasn't bothered me recently."

"Not at all?" Meg inquired.

"Nothing more than usual," Kathleen confessed.

"You should go to the Lintons'" Nuala agreed with Meg. "What is this?" An entire section of Union Street was dug up making it nearly impassable. A crew of laborers was setting a large pipe into the ground.

"Is there a speck in this city that isn't having something done to it?" Nuala complained as she gathered her skirts.

"Could we not visit the shops today?" Kathleen asked. "I might be without a job for a bit."

Nuala shrugged. "Fine with me."

The three turned back up Union Street. "What shall we do?" asked Meg.

"Let's visit Aoife," Kathleen suggested.

"Good," said Meg. "While there we can talk to Mrs. Linton about taking you in should you need to flee that house."

180

"Meg."

"There were plenty of us in one tiny room back home! You've got money saved. You'd be helping them, when you think of it."

"I suppose," Kathleen said as they turned down Manchester Street.

"That's settled, then," said Nuala. "Now let's talk about something else. Ever since we took that sleigh ride, I've been thinking we're missing out on more merriment."

"What do you propose?" asked Meg.

"I did have a good time at the dance."

"With Seamus," said Meg. "You're going to see more of him, then?"

Nuala sighed. "Don't get ideas. It was for the dancing I accepted his invitation."

"The original reason, aye. I've seen you two looking at each other during Mass." Meg said.

"Is a romance brewing?" Kathleen asked. "I thought you said you'd never marry."

"Marry! 'Tis a long way from dancing to marrying. I've not changed my mind about that. But it doesn't mean I needn't enjoy myself."

"Does Seamus know you're not for marrying?" Kathleen asked. "He might have other ideas."

Nuala rolled her eyes. "You're making more of it than what's there."

"It has been more than the one dance," Meg observed. "It appears you two are courting."

Nuala shrugged. "He invites me to do things I enjoy. Why should I decline?"

"No reason," said Meg. "But you might be honest. He likely thinks you feel more for him than you do. 'Tis only fair he knows there's no hope before he gets up the courage to ask for your hand."

Nuala looked uncomfortable.

"Unless of course, you feel more for him than you're letting on," Meg added. She had a growing feeling that Nuala was more smitten than she'd admit.

They reached the Arcade.

"I wonder how Aoife keeps busy these days," Nuala said, as she knocked at Aoife's door.

Ned had moved into the rooms rented by Aoife and Mrs. O'Sullivan after the wedding. Another of Ned's cousins was expected to arrive from Ireland soon. He would live with Ned's uncle.

Aoife greeted them, ushering them into the small apartment. "Make yourselves at home," she said, smiling. "I don't get much company. I'll make tea."

There was a slight crack near the top of the teacup Aoife handed to Meg.

"What brings you by?" Aoife asked.

"Union Street all torn up. It was too difficult to make our way to the shops, so we decided to call on you instead," Nuala explained.

"I'm glad you thought of me."

Meg looked around the small room. There was a smattering of plain furniture. Plaster peeled from the walls.

"How is Ned?" Kathleen asked.

"Very well, thank you."

"And your mother?" asked Meg.

"She's well also, though she had a terrible cold. She dared not take a day off work. That's probably why it lasted so long."

Aoife's face took on a greenish hue. Setting down her teacup, she put a hand on her belly. "Excuse me," she whispered before running from the room. The sound of retching could be heard in the room's tiny alcove.

The three looked at one another. Meg went immediately to Aoife. "Bring a damp cloth," she called behind her.

When Aoife could manage, they helped her back to the room. "Where do you sleep?" Meg asked.

"There," said Aoife pointing to a mattress behind a pulled back curtain.

Meg led her there, helping her to lie down.

Nuala bathed her face with the wet rag.

"It will pass soon. It doesn't usually last long." Aoife breathed deeply then pushed herself up to sit upon the straw mattress. "I'm fine now."

Meg helped her to her feet. They resumed their seats. Aoife picked up her teacup about to renew the conversation as if nothing had occurred.

"How often does that happen?" Kathleen asked.

"Several times a day. I hope it won't last the whole nine months. Mam and Aunt Maureen say it's different for everyone."

182

"Does Ned know?" Nuala asked.

"Aye. It would be hard to keep it from him."

A bang sounded on the door, followed by it bursting open and two of the youngest Linton children running into the room.

"Aoife!" they called, climbing at once into her lap. "Mam said to come here while she gets her work done," one of the little urchins explained. "Mam's been washing all day. She said she'd tripped over us once too often."

"Did she now?" Aoife's tone was gentle as she cuddled the children, a boy of five and a girl of three, on her lap. "Be good. You see I have company."

The children looked up at Meg, Kathleen, and Nuala.

"They came to your wedding!" the boy proclaimed.

"That's right," Aoife said. "Meg and her sister Kathleen, and our friend, Nuala."

"I'm Eamon," said the boy.

The girl hid her face in Aoife's dress. "This is Roisin," Aoife told them. "She's shy, but only at first. Give her a moment and she'll be talking your ear off."

The children's faces were clean, but their clothes were worn and tattered and their hair needed washing. Meg couldn't help but contrast them with the children in the Crown Hill neighborhood. When she and Rory had children, which ones would they more resemble? Seeing the scruffy children in Aoife's lap, knowing that her friend would give birth in this squalid room on a straw mattress she was suddenly filled with indignation. She would do whatever it took to ensure a good paying job for Rory so that their bairns could have decent clothes and she the time to bathe them.

After their visit, the three headed back to Crown Hill.

"I know of an amusement for us," Meg offered. "There are the church fairs."

"They're always looking for people to bake," said Kathleen. "I could – "

"Oh, Mrs. Pratt would love her stove used for the purpose of benefiting the Catholic Church," Meg joked.

"Seamus promised to take me boating on Lake Quinsigamond," said Nuala.

Meg and Kathleen exchanged glances, smiling broadly.

"What about the church picnic?" Meg asked. "It's coming up soon. We've never gone."

"On a Saturday afternoon?" Kathleen asked. "How would we get the time off?"

"Perhaps we could switch Saturday for Thursday on the week of the picnic," Nuala suggested.

Kathleen looked at her under hooded eyelids. "Mrs. Pratt," she stated, flatly.

Nuala frowned. "Kathleen, you must find another position."

Chapter Eighteen

Kathleen missed the church picnic that summer. Meg and Nuala were allowed to switch days so they attended. Kathleen went alone to visit Aoife the following Thursday while Meg and Nuala worked to make up for their Saturday off.

Aoife's belly was just beginning to swell and her morning sickness was tapering off.

"Aunt Maureen knows so much about raising wee ones. I'll feel more prepared when my own makes an appearance," she said, patting her belly.

"Are you afraid?" asked Kathleen.

"Aye," Aoife confided. "I'm not sure which I fear more, giving birth or raising a bairn."

"I've seen you with your aunt's. You'll do well."

"You're a love to say so. For now I pray this babe will be healthy and that I don't die. A child needs a mother."

"Don't dwell on that," Kathleen advised. "We'll all pray for your safe delivery."

"Sometimes I walk to Saint John's to pray. I feel calmer when I leave the church."

"Do you like being married?" Kathleen asked. "Is it all you'd hoped?"

Aoife was quiet for a moment and Kathleen wondered if she shouldn't have asked.

"I love Ned," Aoife began. "He's a good man. A good husband. He works hard, never misses a day. He never drinks. He does his best for us always."

"You are happy?"

"I suppose."

"Aoife. Is anything amiss?"

"Not yet. But I worry now that wee ones are starting to come. What if we can't keep them fed?"

"The Lintons manage."

"Aye. I'm being silly. Aunt Maureen says being with child can make a woman feel and think all sorts of things. It will pass." She waved a dismissive hand, but her face still showed concern.

Kathleen returned to the Pratt home late in the day. Lemuel was too wrapped up in learning the foundry business and attending lodge meetings to pay her much mind. For that she was grateful.

"You're back early," said Mrs. Pratt. She and Clara were sewing together in the parlor. "Don't you eat with your sister and friend on Thursdays?"

"They worked today."

"Oh."

Mrs. Pratt's interest waned. She went back to her sewing, but Clara's curiosity remained. "Why did they work?" she asked.

"They swapped today in exchange for having last Saturday off so they could go to the church picnic," Kathleen explained.

"I love church picnics!" Clara exclaimed. "Why didn't you go?"

Mrs. Pratt gave her daughter a sharp look. "You well know that Saturday is a workday for Kathleen."

"But Mrs. Claprood and Mrs. Denton allowed Meg and Nuala to switch days. Wouldn't you have done the same, Mother?"

"I should say not! And who is Meg?"

"Kathleen's sister."

"You mean Margaret?"

"Yes. Kathleen calls her Meg. Didn't you know that?"

"I did not."

Mrs. Pratt muttered under her breath, but Kathleen caught the words, "Too familiar with the Bridgets."

"Mother, why didn't you allow Kathleen to switch days?"

"Because I do not approve of turning the routine of this household on its head so that one may frolic at a pagan festival."

Kathleen shoved her hands behind her back as they formed themselves into fists. She gave Clara a look, willing her to drop the subject. Clara caught it, returning her gaze to the sewing in her lap.

"Come," ordered Mrs. Pratt, rising from her chair. "Since you're back, you can make yourself useful. I will show you what I had planned for supper."

* * *

"Why don't you simply tell your father you want to become a jeweler?" Kathleen asked Harvey one crisp October afternoon. His father had decided it was time Harvey began learning the foundry business. Having recently taken to unburdening himself on Kathleen's sympathetic ear, he sat in the kitchen pouring out his frustration to her.

"Given his current dissatisfaction with Lemuel? I'm loathe to take Lemuel's place, though my brother won't believe me. He seems to think I've wormed my way into Father's good graces." Harvey blew out a hiss of air. "As if that were possible. Father's always favored Lemuel. He's simply using me as a threat to get Lemuel back in line."

"Don't you think you're being unfair to assume your father won't want you to find a career you like? You've not told him. How's he to know?"

"You don't understand how it works, Bridget. To my father it is a point of pride that his sons follow in his footsteps."

"Isn't Lemuel going into the foundry business enough?"

"It's enough for Lemuel. And for me. Not for my father."

Clara entered the kitchen at that moment, eager to help Kathleen bake pies. Harvey took it as his cue to leave.

"Kathleen, do you know what Father means by dark lantern politics?" she asked as they rolled out the dough.

"I don't. Why?"

"Father told Lemuel that he hoped he wasn't involved in any. The words sound sinister. Lemuel wouldn't be involved in something villainous, would he?"

Kathleen's first thought was that he most likely would. "You know Lemuel and your father disagree about politics. It's probably the opposite of whatever your father favors."

"It sounds fiendish, though, doesn't it? Dark lantern. Carried about by demons."

Kathleen laughed. "Your imagination is getting the best of you."

That night Kathleen dreamed of Lemuel chasing her through a tunnel with a lantern giving off an eerie, red glow. She awoke in a cold sweat. Sitting up, she glanced toward the door between the kitchen and dining room. Since Meg had brought the news of her overheard conversation, Kathleen had dropped any qualms about barring the entry. Every night she dragged the heavy kitchen table across the floor, pushing it against the door. Now, though certain she was alone, she couldn't shake the feeling that she was being watched. A sense of foreboding kept her awake. She finally drifted off again a short time before she was due to rise and awoke to sunlight streaming across her face.

Realizing how late it was, she sprang from her mattress, threw on her uniform, and quickly dragged the table back. She heard stirring on the second floor. They were awake, but none had come downstairs. She made a mad dash for the cellar, bringing up coal and firewood to stoke the kitchen stove then raced to all the downstairs rooms, putting coal in fireplace baskets.

Kathleen passed the front staircase as Mrs. Pratt descended.

"What is all this?" the woman demanded. The family's discord had made her more irritable than ever. "Why are you scurrying about with the coal hod? Is breakfast on the table?"

"I'm terribly sorry Mrs. Pratt," said Kathleen. "I awoke late."

"Be prepared to wait," she heard Mrs. Pratt call up the stairs as she hurried away.

"Wait?" came Mr. Pratt's voice from above. He must be on his way down the stairs.

"The house is cold and she's just starting the breakfast."

Kathleen was in the kitchen before she could hear Mr. Pratt's response. This was not going to be a pleasant day.

The kitchen door opened, admitting Clara dressed for school. "I'll help," she said, grabbing an apron.

"Thank you, *a stór*," said Kathleen just as Mrs. Pratt entered the room.

"What did you call Clara?" she demanded, her tone livid, her face like stone.

"I'm sorry, Ma'am."

"Clara, remove that apron and leave this room now."

"But mother, I was going to help get breakfast, else we'll all be late."

"You'll be late whether you help or not. Go!" she ordered.

Kathleen's heart pounded in her chest. Her hands shook as she set pots and pans on the stove. Mrs. Pratt donned the apron Clara left behind. "I suppose I will have to assist you if anyone in this family is going to get anywhere on time." She picked up a loaf of bread and began slicing.

"Thank you, Ma'am. I'm terribly sorry," Kathleen said.

"I don't want to hear a word from you. Is that understood?"

Kathleen nodded.

Rushed, the breakfast was meager, but with Mrs. Pratt's help, Kathleen managed to get it onto platters and into the dining room with a minimum of wasted time. She took up her place by the sideboard.

"What are you standing there for?" Mrs. Pratt demanded.

"Ma'am?" Kathleen was perplexed.

"You're behind on your duties. We'll manage to serve ourselves this morning. Go about your business. And don't forget to clear the table when we've finished."

"Yes, Ma'am." Kathleen gladly removed herself.

She went about her morning chores, while taking note of when they all left the dining room, at which point she returned to clear the dishes. A large blob of strawberry jam was smeared on the white tablecloth at Lemuel's place. She doubted it had gotten there by accident. By the time Kathleen cleared the dining room, replaced the tablecloth, and put the soiled one with the rest of the laundry, Mrs. Pratt had joined her in the kitchen.

Kathleen, up to her elbows in dishwater, wiped them off and stood to face her employer.

Mrs. Pratt drew her considerable girth up to full height. "You can plainly see how quickly things go awry when the household's schedule is not strictly followed."

"Yes, Ma'am."

"I trust this will not happen again."

"I'll try my very best to make sure it doesn't," Kathleen answered.

"Trying is not enough. I want your assurance."

"It's made for a difficult morning for me as well." Anger and frustration edged Kathleen's voice. "I'd not do it deliberately. I will do my best to never let it happen again."

Kathleen had barely finished speaking when Mrs. Pratt struck her cheek with a resounding slap.

"How dare you speak to me like that, you little chit? Remember your place!"

Tears stung Kathleen's eyes. She thought of grabbing her belongings and heading out the door. Only her determination to stand her ground held her in place.

"I've told you it was unintentional. I've said I am sorry. I've worked as quickly as I could to make up the time. I would promise it won't happen again, if I could make such a promise. I can't, however, because I won't make a promise I'm not positive I can keep." Kathleen could not stop there. "And you will never lay a hand on me again or you can find another 'Bridget'." She spat out the final word.

"Yes, I certainly can," Mrs. Pratt proclaimed, recovering from her shock. The smug look that crossed her face disappeared with Kathleen's next words.

"She won't be able to cook. Not like me."

Mrs. Pratt shut her mouth with a pop.

Now it was as if Kathleen's tongue had a mind of its own. "I've worked here for more than two years. I've done all that's been asked of me. Not once have you thought to increase my pay. You've never given me the attic room you promised. I don't remember so much as kind word from you." The threat of tears, tears she refused to shed before this woman, was the only thing that brought her to an end. She forced her voice to a normal tone. "Now, if you'll excuse me, I've a great deal of work to do."

Kathleen turned her back on Mrs. Pratt. Thrusting her hands into the hot water, she resumed the dish washing. She half expected Mrs. Pratt to accost her. Instead she heard the woman's footsteps retreat as she left the kitchen.

All day Kathleen's emotions swung between anger and fear. She knew this could not be at an end. If she was dismissed, she'd have no choice but to go to the Lintons, though she disliked the idea of imposing on them. Worse, she hated the realization that part of her reason for not wanting to go there was that she'd grown used to the comforts of a Yankee home. Despite Mrs. Linton's best efforts, their rooms at the Arcade were small, crowded, and dingy. The noise from their brood was always at a high pitch. *Still*, Kathleen told herself, *they're a cheerful lot*. She would use her savings to pay for her keep. It would help them, but it would also cut into what she could send home.

Kathleen scrubbed at the jelly stain on the tablecloth. There was always the chance that standing up to Mrs. Pratt had made the woman realize how unfair she'd been. Maybe things would change for the better. A bitter laugh accompanied that thought. Not likely.

When Clara arrived home from school, she came upon Kathleen dusting the parlor. Clara gasped when she saw her.

"What's wrong?" Kathleen asked.

"Your face."

Kathleen went to the looking glass above the fireplace. A red hand print was stamped across her cheek. Anger flared again.

"Did Mother do that?"

Before Kathleen could answer, Mrs. Pratt, who had been calling on friends, returned. Seeing the two of them, she immediately called Clara to her. "Alone, Clara," she said, taking the girl by the hand and leading her from the room.

Kathleen was preparing the meal when Mrs. Pratt entered the kitchen for the first time since their altercation.

"I've explained to Clara that I no longer believe it prudent for the two of you to work together. You are to have no contact with Clara other than as it pertains to your duties." This was delivered in an even tone before she left the room.

It made perfect sense. Kathleen had used her ability to cook to stop Mrs. Pratt from firing her. Now Mrs. Pratt was using Clara to punish her just as Mr. Pratt used Harvey to strike out at Lemuel.

Kathleen was not sure if she felt worse for herself or for Clara. Clara spent more time with friends now. She was not so lonely as she'd been when Kathleen began working for the Pratts. Still, this family had a deviousness that Clara lacked. Kathleen worried for the girl, prayed she would never become like them.

Kathleen checked the mirror shortly before dinnertime. Though faded, the red hand print was still visible for all the family to see. She would hold her head high refusing to let them think she'd been cowed.

Throughout the meal, Lemuel glanced her way, a smirk playing about his lips. When the meal ended, Lemuel lingered at the table after the others had left. He grabbed Kathleen's arm when she tried to remove his plate.

"Were you not finished, Master Lemuel?" she asked, keeping her voice cool.

"I'm quite finished. I think, perhaps you are as well, Bridget."

"Me?"

He laughed, though it was more of a snort. "I can see that Mother had, shall we say, words, with you after the rest of us left this morning." He reached up, stroked the back of his index finger across her cheek.

Kathleen snapped her head back.

"Come now, Bridget," he wheedled. "I'm Mother's favorite. I can set things right between the two of you. Get you back in

191

her good graces. How about a little something for me?" The smile he flashed turned her stomach.

"I believe your mother and I have settled things, thank you." The ice in her voice froze his smile into a leer.

"Watch yourself, Bridget. Your presence here is barely tolerated."

Her presence in their home or in the nation? Either way, his words caused the fury she'd felt towards Mrs. Pratt this morning to return. "My name is Kathleen," she said through gritted teeth. "I'll not answer to anything else."

Chapter Nineteen

It was now 1854. Six years had passed since Meg arrived in America. Six years since she'd seen Rory, her mam, or anyone in her family but Kathleen. She'd continued to ask for Siobhan's prayers, wondered if they were heard. Six years she had lived in a dual world of drudgery and luxury. She was now twenty-six. How much longer must she wait?

Normally, Meg fell exhausted into bed at the end of her workday, but on those magical days when a letter from Rory arrived, she was infused with renewed energy once she reached the privacy of her attic room. Now she sat on the edge of her bed, carefully unfolding the thin paper, holding it close to the candle-light.

My dearest Meg,

I have the most amazing news. You remember Blackburn, that horrid man who was agent for our landlord. He died about a month ago. Good riddance, I say, may God forgive me. It seems Sir Alfred Stokes decided he couldn't do without an agent to manage his properties in Ireland so for once he came himself from England to see about a replacement. Once we heard he was in Kelegeen, it about threw us all into a tangle. Too many of us living where we're not supposed to be through no fault of our own, but we figured he'd see it otherwise. Not knowing what to do we turned to Father O'Malley. He said we needed to give Stokes the full story of all that had happened and why. He thought it was finally the hearing we should have received from him had Blackburn not interfered. I was reluctant, never trusting a Brit other than Doctor Parker and certainly not the one who thinks he owns our land. Father O'Malley finally convinced me that intricate fabrications would only give him more of a grievance against us. He got Doctor Parker to help. That's what sold me on the idea. So I went with Doctor Parker to meet Sir Alfred. I let the good doctor do most of the talking. He's a way about

193

him, as you know. Sir Alfred proved susceptible to his charm. Once he'd told the whole story of how my da and yours tried to send him a letter asking for a change in terms, a letter that never reached him due to Blackburn's seizing it and how Blackburn stole our pig so we couldn't pay the rent then had us evicted and our house torn down killing my mam in the process just as winter was setting in and how you and I were to marry but couldn't because of the starving, but we saw ourselves as good as family anyway so your da and mam took us in, then most of us died anyway. Well, it nearly had the old man in tears. Doctor Parker laid it on thick. You'd have thought him an Irishman.

Bless him, it worked. By the time he'd finished the man was ready to do anything to right the wrongs against us. He has offered to pay the passage for the whole lot of us to America, if you can believe it.

Doctor Parker explained that Aisling and Brigid might not last the journey and that your mam would not leave when she knows your brother will be coming home. That left Loreena and me. I can't go as there's no one to care for the others. The idea was dropped for now, though he claims it remains an open offer should our situation change. We didn't tell Loreena. She'd have been grieved as she wants so much to go, but your mam can't spare her now with Aisling living in town with her mistress. Mrs. Fairfax has found Aisling to be such a gifted seamstress she wanted her with her at all times. Aisling's flourishing, I can tell you. There's no need for her to leave Ireland. At least she's one we needn't worry about.

Doctor Parker told Sir Alfred how he's been training me as a groom. Sir Alfred offered me a job in the stable on his land in Kelegeen. That I readily accepted. Meg, do you see what grand news this is? It's four horses he has. I will get the experience I need. When I finally come to America it will be with recommendations from both Doctor Parker and Sir Alfred Stokes. That should make finding work easier, don't you agree?

If only I could see a way clear to coming without leaving your mam and the lasses to fend for themselves. Your mam tells me to go, that they can manage. It may be they can, but I'd feel I was abandoning them. If I left and anything happened I wouldn't forgive myself and I fear you wouldn't forgive me, either. Three more years before Brendan is allowed to return. It seems an eternity. At least my new position will make it easier when I do come.

194

Your mam, Brigid, and Loreena send their love. Brigid con-
tinues to improve. That's another reason we didn't tell Loreena
about the offer of passage. We fear how Brigid would fare if she
lost her.
With all the love in my heart, ever yours,
Rory

Three more years? "God, give me patience," Meg prayed. "Thank you, Siobhan," she added, realizing now that Siobhan's prayers on her behalf had been heard.

Meg's work the next afternoon was interrupted when Oliver and Mr. Claprood burst through the front door. Meg, who was polishing the light fixtures in the parlor, noticed at once their stricken expressions.

"What's happened?" asked Pamela. She and Deborah had been in the conservatory, but hurried to the front hall upon the arrival of their father and brother.

"Fire," Oliver panted.

"Where?" asked Pamela.

"The Merrifield buildings," Oliver said. "It's raging all over that section of Union and Exchange Streets."

Alerted by the commotion, Mrs. Claprood appeared on the stairs. "A fire?" she asked.

"Yes, dear. It's a mess in the city. Everyone was ordered out of the way. The place is crawling with fire engines," explained Mr. Claprood.

Meg joined them in the front hall.

"Has anyone been hurt?" Mrs. Claprood asked.

"It's such chaos, who can tell?"

"Where did it start, Father?" asked Pamela.

"Are the shops gone?" Deborah appeared ready to faint.

"Not all when we left, but the fire is spreading rapidly. I've never seen anything like it."

"What caused it?" asked Mrs. Claprood.

"Seems an overheated sewing machine started the blaze. You know the shop where they make parts for boots and shoes?

"No!" Meg screamed before she could stop herself.

"Margaret?" Mrs. Claprood hurried down the last few stairs.

The room seemed to spin and Meg grasped the edge of the hall table to keep from falling.

Mrs. Claprood guided Meg to a nearby chair.

"My friend, Aoife's mother, Mrs. O'Sullivan works there. She sews the leather pieces for shoes and boots."

"Oh dear!" said Mrs. Claprood, who had knelt beside Meg's chair and now looked up at her husband.

Mr. Claprood stepped closer. "I've not heard of any injuries. It's likely everyone got out."

"May I go there?" she implored Mrs. Claprood. "I need to know if Aoife's mother made it out safely."

"I'm sorry, Margaret," said Mr. Claprood, "That whole section is shut down to all but the fire department."

In the distance they heard the clanging of fire bells. She thought of Aoife and her new baby. At least she'd have her Aunt Maureen. They could comfort each other. Another thought struck her. What of Mr. Linton, Ned, and his uncle Owen? Wasn't the wire factory close to the Merrifield complex? Were they in danger too?

Meg sagged in the chair, feeling helpless.

"Isn't there anything we can do?" asked Deborah.

"Only let the firemen do their jobs," said Mr. Claprood.

"Thank God for the aqueduct," Oliver put in. "They've hooked up to at least three, maybe four hydrants. I hope they don't drain the supply before the fire is out."

"Might we help with those?" asked Pamela, pointing to the fire buckets hanging on the wall near the door.

"Buckets, my dear, have become obsolete. They'd do little good with a fire this size," Mr. Claprood explained. "Besides, the last thing the fire department wants is a crowd getting in their way. No. I'm afraid all we can do is wait."

Neighbors came and went bringing news as the day progressed. According to Mr. Pratt who'd stopped by to consult with Mr. Claprood about the likelihood of the fire spreading as far as the foundry, the firemen were still going at it hammer and tongs hours later. There were reports of injuries, but thankfully no deaths.

Meg tried to keep her thoughts occupied on her work, but her distracted mind kept conjuring images of Mrs. O'Sullivan trapped, of Aoife and Maureen pacing, wondering when they would have word. Her hands shaking, she decided to leave off cleaning anything breakable.

Mr. Pratt's appearance at the Claprood home reminded Meg that Kathleen must be just as worried as she was. Nuala, too. She wished she could be with them now. Mrs. Claprood might let her go to Kathleen, but Mrs. Pratt would never allow Kathleen company, even that of her sister, on a workday. Going to Nuala without Kathleen seemed a betrayal of her sister, so she determined to stay put.

For sixteen hours Worcester's volunteer firemen battled the flames. It was the following day, Thursday, before the fire was finally out. As soon as her morning chores were completed, she put on shabby clothes, knowing she would not be spending this day off surveying the many shops. She went immediately to the Pratt house for Kathleen. Together they met Nuala who was awaiting them outside the Denton home. Grim faced, the three headed for the Meadows.

As they neared the Merrifield complex, people from their neighborhood mixed with others from the wealthiest areas of the city, still others from the Meadows and Green Island. The difference in clothing, posture, and bearing appeared odd as the citizens of Worcester surveyed the wreckage.

As they neared the periphery of the crowd, voices hoarse from exhaustion called out, "Stay back. We're working here." The firemen were combing through the rubble, making sure nothing still smoldered.

"I can't stand to look at this," Kathleen said.

"Aye. Let's get to Aoife," Meg answered.

The three trod carefully, avoiding shattered glass, fallen timber frames, charred hunks of buildings. Ashes covered their clothing, dirtied their faces.

When they reached the Arcade, they climbed the stairs to be met at the door by Mrs. Linton.

"I saw you in the street," she said, ushering them into the room. Her face was pale, her eyes tired.

"Mrs. O'Sullivan?" Meg inquired.

"Praise be to God, she made it out safely," said Mrs. Linton. "She's taken a terrible fright, though. The fire started just one row from her. A sewing machine began smoking. In seconds flames were bursting from it. There was a moment of terrible panic when the woman who'd been at that machine had her skirt catch fire. Others pushed her to

197

the floor to smother the flames. She's only some minor burns on her legs but the poor woman was out of her wits. Had to be carried from the building."

"They all got out safely?" Kathleen asked.

Mrs. Linton nodded. "All stayed calm, moving quickly out of the building."

"Where is Mrs. O'Sullivan now?" Meg asked.

"Resting. Her nerves are bad."

"Is Aoife with her?" Nuala asked.

"Aye. Go see them if you like."

Mrs. Linton walked with them down the dingy hallway, knocked on the door, then turned the knob letting herself in.

"It's me come with Meg, Kathleen, and Nuala," she announced as they entered the threadbare room.

Mrs. O'Sullivan lay on the bed in a corner of the room. Her hands covered her face. It was impossible to tell if she was asleep or awake.

Aoife met them just inside the room, baby in her arms.

"Mam tries to sleep, but keeps waking up always with a start, sometimes a shriek. I can't imagine what it must have been like in that building."

"Is she awake now?" Meg asked.

Aoife glanced over her shoulder at her mother's still form. The baby began to fuss. At the sound of the child's cry, Mrs. O'Sullivan's body twitched and she looked up.

"We've visitors, Mam. Come to see that you're all right."

Mrs. O'Sullivan sat up. The others moved towards her gathering on the bed, the floor, a nearby chair. Aoife propped the baby on her mother's lap. Mrs. O'Sullivan wrapped the whimpering babe in her arms, rocking back and forth, the motion seeming to comfort them both.

Maureen Linton draped her arm over her sister's shoulders. "You're safe," she cooed.

Mrs. O'Sullivan looked up. "Safe?" she asked. "I've no job!"

Chapter Twenty

"Arthur, we simply must move our plots." Kathleen, who was polishing the lamps in the dining room, could easily overhear the conversation between Mr. and Mrs. Pratt. They'd been arguing all Sunday afternoon about their cemetery plots. Like many others in Worcester, they had purchased plots in Raccoon Plain. Now that the City had taken up the latest craze of creating burying grounds that resembled fancy parks, Mrs. Pratt insisted that eternity in Raccoon Plain was not appropriate. She wanted to be buried in the new Hope Cemetery with its glorious lawns, shady tree-lined avenues, and exquisite statuary.

"I don't see what difference it makes," said Mr. Pratt.

Mrs. Pratt let out a loud huff. "Everyone of quality is going to be buried in Hope Cemetery. I'll never rest easy if we're stuck in Raccoon Plain. Even the name sounds common."

"Do you think all the dead will be gathering for high tea underground?" Kathleen could hear the exasperation in Mr. Pratt's voice. She focused hard on her polishing to keep from laughing out loud.

"Arthur," Mrs. Pratt's voice took on the tone of one speaking to a dull child. "You simply do not understand. If you depart this life ahead of me all our friends must follow the hearse to Raccoon Plain? I'll be mortified. So would you if the situation were reversed."

"What are we to do with the plots in Raccoon Plain?"

"Sell them, I suppose."

"It's not as though we'll be able to enjoy our time in Hope Cemetery, you understand?"

"Oh, Arthur, please! It's a beautiful site. People spend afternoons strolling the avenues and families have picnics on the grounds. Really, Arthur, this is as much for my family and friends as it is for me. I want a lovely, comfortable place for you all to visit me when I'm gone from the world."

"Truly? All for our benefit?" Mr. Pratt asked.

Kathleen quickly buried her face in the sleeve of her uniform to muffle a laugh.

"Why, of course, dear. And there's another thing one must consider. When the heavenly trumpet sounds and the dead are raised, do you really wish to have the Lord see you've been mired in some ungodly pit in Raccoon Plain?"

"Are you aware, my dear, that Hope Cemetery has set aside a number of free plots for those who can't afford a burial anywhere?"

"I've heard," Mrs. Pratt's voice turned frosty. "Those are on the outskirts. They'll not be near our kind." Her tone changed to one of begging, "Oh, please Arthur, you must exchange our plots for ones in Hope Cemetery. I'll be so embarrassed if you don't that I think...well, I think I'll be forced to live forever just to avoid being humiliated by my final resting place."

"Well, we can't have that."

Kathleen wondered if Mr. Pratt meant he couldn't have Mrs. Pratt humiliated or living forever. She knew which one she'd choose.

"Good. Now that that's settled, what have you heard about the new hotel going up on Main Street? What's it to be called?"

"The Bay State House Hotel," Mr. Pratt said. "They've moved a wing of the original eastward to make use of it as a carriage house. Good Yankee thrift, I say. Nothing lost. No sense in throwing out what's perfectly serviceable."

"The Bay State House Hotel," Mrs. Pratt said, letting the name roll luxuriously off her tongue. "I understand it's going to be quite elegant. Worcester is coming up in the world. Truly, Arthur, we must come up with it."

Finished with the polishing, Kathleen left the dining room, heading for her next tasks on the second floor. She was halfway up the back staircase when she heard the shuffling of feet above her. She stopped, listening intently. The servants' staircase led to the end of the house furthest from the chambers in which family slept. It was rare for anyone to come here. The staircase, enclosed on all sides, held no light despite being midday. Kathleen's candle flickered as Lemuel stood at the top of the stairs, blocking her path.

"Master Lemuel, you gave me a start," she said, hoping he'd let her pass without a fuss.

"My apologies, Bridget," he said, though the smirk belied his words.

Noting that he, too, held a candle, Kathleen realized he'd planned this encounter. Her pounding heart caused her ears to throb.

He said nothing for a long moment, nor did he move, so Kathleen asked, "Might I pass, please?"

"Of course," he said.

Relieved, she ascended, but he stepped directly in front of her.

"First, I've a question," he said.

Kathleen looked up. A sardonic grin creased his face, which, in the flickering of both candles appeared malevolent.

Kathleen swallowed hard. "Yes?"

"How was Mass this morning?"

"Fine."

"What did you do there?"

"Sir?"

"I'm curious. I wonder if what I've heard is true." His tone, though like honey, she knew was laden with poison.

"I've no idea what you've heard, Master Lemuel. We pray at Mass. We worship our Lord Jesus. If you please, I've work to do." She made to move up the stairs, but Lemuel continued to block her.

"What of your nuns and priests? I have heard the most vile things of them."

Indignation rose within Kathleen. "Whomever is telling such tales should be ashamed."

"But it's the nuns themselves."

Kathleen grew impatient with Lemuel's nonsense. "I must get on with my work."

"Don't believe me? I've read it in a book called *Awful Disclosures of Maria Monk or, The Hidden Secrets of a Nun's Life in a Convent Exposed*. The author was a nun in Canada. Haven't you heard of her?"

"I have not."

Lemuel gave a contemptuous snort. "Certainly, your bishops wouldn't want such awful truths revealed to the faithful souls."

Kathleen felt her face burning with anger. "Master Lemuel, please let me pass. I've much work to do." She attempted to sidestep him, but he glided in front of her.

"Don't you want to know what your priests are doing?"

"I *want* to get my work done!"

"Can't bear to hear it, poor thing." Condescension dripped from his voice. "Still, I think you ought to know. According to the book, written by a nun about her own ex-

202

periences you must remember, there was a secret tunnel that connected the convent to the seminary next door. The priests would come at night and have their way with the nuns. If any got with child, the baby would be baptized by the priest, then immediately strangled by its good Father, and buried under the convent basement. The author herself, ran away with her baby rather than have the poor thing suffer such an awful fate."

Kathleen's words poured forth in a furious hiss. "That is the most disgusting, loathsome lie I've ever heard."

Lemuel nodded in feigned empathy. "Disgusting and loathsome it is. Lie? I doubt it very much." A terrifying fire suddenly lit in his eyes. "Your so-called church is nothing more than the Whore of Babylon foretold in the Scriptures. Mark my words, you Papists will not take over this country. You'll be rooted out, expelled. All of you. By whatever means necessary."

He reached out, placed his index finger under Kathleen's chin, tipping her face towards him. "Perhaps you, such a dedicated, faithful follower, are a willing pawn in the Church's schemes. Hmmm?"

Kathleen felt sick.

"Lemuel! Lemuel, where are you?" The call from Mr. Pratt sounded from the top of the main staircase. Footsteps echoed down the hall.

"Coming, Father," Lemuel called. He gave Kathleen one last, chilling look. "We're not through, you and I," he said before joining his father.

Kathleen dropped down on the stairs, shaking.

Chapter Twenty-One

Meg went about her chores ruminating on what Kathleen related of her recent encounter with Lemuel. She feared for her sister, yet understood Kathleen's reluctance to leave the Pratts for the Lintons. The Merrifield fire had put five hundred people out of work. Everyone was scrounging for jobs, making them scarce. Ned was feeling the pressure of providing for Aoife, their baby, and now his mother-in-law as Mrs. O'Sullivan had yet to find new employment. Meg wished she could speak with Mrs. Claprood about it, but with Mr. Claprood and Mr. Pratt being business partners and Oliver and Lemuel going off together every Tuesday evening to their lodge meetings, she didn't dare.

The tinkling of a bell summoned Meg to the front parlor.

"Yes, Ma'am?"

"Margaret, please bring more tea," Mrs. Claprood instructed. The parlor was filled with guests, all members of the local anti-slavery society.

When Meg returned with a steaming teapot, she found Mrs. Claprood standing before the assembled ladies holding a banner on which had been sewn the palm of a hand with two squiggly lines on it.

"As we agreed at our last meeting, this shall be our emblem. The banner shall be displayed at all meetings as a reminder of the gravity of our cause."

Mrs. Claprood hung the banner from a hook in the wall amid enthusiastic applause.

"Well done, Emily! You've captured the essence of Mr. Whittier's poem perfectly," said one of the women who had risen from her chair, a hand over her heart.

"Thank you, Josephine. Now let us continue with our business. Caroline, I believe you wished to speak on giving up cotton and other products that come from the labor of our brothers and sisters in bondage. The floor is yours."

Mrs. Claprood seated herself as another woman made her way to the front of the room.

"Will that be all, Ma'am?" Meg whispered to her employer after replenishing the tea.

"Are there more tarts? We're running low."

"I'll fetch some, Ma'am."

Meg brought the nearly empty tray back to the kitchen to reload it. Upon returning to the parlor, she found that yet another woman was speaking.

"We must do all we can to oppose the Fugitive Slave Act," the woman announced. "I'm sure we all remember the incident in Boston in May of this year when that blackguard U.S. Marshall Asa Butman captured poor Anthony Burns, returning him to a life of horrors in the South. The good people of Boston showed their contempt by rioting in the streets, but even that was not enough to stop Mr. Butman from carrying out his evil deed. For now, the Fugitive Slave Act is the law of the land, but we are Christians and must answer to a higher law."

A rousing chorus of "Hear! Hear!" erupted from the group.

When the commotion died down, the woman continued, "Should such an occurrence take place in Worcester we must do all we can to protect the defenseless."

"Our Lord forbid such a thing happening here," one woman remarked.

Another stood. "I've heard that some Negroes, born free in the North, have been captured and taken to the South to be enslaved."

"That's outrageous!"

"Abominable!"

"Utterly despicable!"

Exclamations of indignation filled the parlor.

"Ladies! Ladies!" Emily Claprood's voice called the meeting back to order.

Meg slipped from the room, wondering how long before the meeting ended so that she could clean up. They had been meeting in the Claprood's parlor for the past several months. Each session seemed longer than the one previous.

Shortly before Meg was due to prepare the day's final meal, Mrs. Claprood appeared in the kitchen. "The ladies have departed," she announced.

After gathering the remnants of food and drink and depositing them in the kitchen, Meg returned to the parlor to set the chairs back in their rightful places. She stopped to examine the banner still hanging on the wall. It showed an outstretched palm of a man's hand. On the fleshy part beneath the thumb were two strange markings. Meg wondered at its meaning.

"Powerful, isn't it?" asked Mrs. Claprood coming up beside her.

"I'm sorry, Ma'am. I don't understand it."

"It's the hand of Captain Jonathan Walker. In 1844 a group of escaping slaves in Pensacola, Florida begged him to take them to freedom on his ship bound for the British West Indies. The good and brave man did so, but sadly he was apprehended at sea by an American vessel and returned to Pensacola where he was imprisoned. Later he was tried and sentenced to be branded upon the hand. Those two letters," Mrs. Claprood traced the curving symbols on the palm, "stand for Slave Stealer. The brand was meant as a lifelong mark of shame. However, one of our illustrious poets, John Greenleaf Whittier, wrote a most noble poem, 'The Branded Hand', in which he claimed they stood instead for Salvation to the Slave." She turned her gaze from the banner to Meg. "It is a most stirring poem, an ode to the nobleness of Captain Walker and a warning to those who would hold their fellow humans in bondage. The final stanza is my favorite.

'And the masters of the slave-land shall tremble at that sign,
When it points its finger Southward along the Puritan line:

206

Can the craft of State avail them? Can a Christless church withstand,

In the van of freedom's onset, the coming of that hand?'"

Mrs. Claprood's gaze traveled upward, her own hand held aloft as she recited. When finished her raised hand lowered to land upon her heart. "Stirring, isn't it?"

"Aye, Ma'am. Do you want that it should stay here, or shall I take it down until the next meeting?"

Mrs. Claprood sighed. "Take it down but do preserve it carefully. I wish my girls had been here today. They would benefit greatly."

"Aren't they members?"

"Oh, they attend when the mood strikes them, but they are young and busy with amusements."

A knock sounded at the door.

"See who that is, please, Margaret. I'll put away the banner."

Meg opened the door to find Mrs. Pratt. She ushered her into the parlor, then went for Mrs. Claprood.

"Shall I bring tea?" Meg asked after announcing Mrs. Pratt's arrival.

"Wait to see if this will be a quick visit."

Meg followed Mrs. Claprood to the parlor, awaiting instructions.

"Sophronia, my dear, this is not your normal day to call. What brings you by?"

"I hope I haven't caught you at an inconvenient moment," said Mrs. Pratt.

"Your timing is perfect. The ladies left a short time ago."

"Oh, of course, your anti-slavery ladies."

"You really should join us, Sophronia. I believe you'd find the conversation most enlightening."

"Perhaps," she said, pursing her lips. "At the moment, I've a matter of importance about which to speak with you."

"Of course, dear." Mrs. Claprood turned to Meg and nodded. Meg slipped away to the kitchen to fetch tea and a tray of leftover tarts.

On her way back, she stopped when she heard Mrs. Pratt mention Kathleen's name. She stood in the hallway out of sight.

"It's my own fault," said Mrs. Pratt. "I allowed them to spend too much time together when Clara was younger. I thought cooking together could do no harm, even bring mutual improvement. I didn't think what a negative influence an Irish Bridget might have on the child."

"What negative influence?" asked Mrs. Claprood. "When Kathleen was here, I thought her a lovely person. Certainly, Margaret is a fine girl."

"She is not proper company for my Clara. Why, I overheard her telling her friends that she thinks of that maid as an older sister."

"Kathleen must be very good to her if Clara's so fond."

Meg leaned her back against the wall, the tray growing heavy in her arms.

"The girl is a Catholic." Mrs. Pratt uttered the word as though it tasted rancid on her tongue. "Hardly a fit sisterly figure! I've forbidden any further contact. Clara is now fifteen and in dire need of a female model to guide her. That's why I've come to you. Might one of your daughters be willing to take Clara under her wing?"

"I will speak with Pamela and Deborah. Is Clara interested in gardening? My girls enjoy sharing their love of flowers and showing off their conservatory."

"It matters not what interests her. She needs guidance in how to behave in polite society. I teach her, but she must practice with others."

"Does she not have friends her age?"

"Yes, but I'd like her to associate with ones older than herself, to bring her along more rapidly. Clara must make a good marriage, be a paragon in society. The foundry is doing well. We'll be coming up in the world. You do understand."

"I believe I do," said Mrs. Claprood. "I wonder what is keeping Margaret."

"Laziness, no doubt," said Mrs. Pratt.

"Our Margaret is anything but lazy."

"Emily, all Bridgets are lazy. It's only constant vigilance that keeps them in line."

Meg took a deep breath before entering the parlor.

"Very sorry for the wait, Ma'am," she said to Mrs. Claprood. "There was no tea left from earlier so I had to make it fresh." She set the tray on the low table, arranged the cups and saucers, the plate of tarts, and linen napkins, then bobbed a quick curtsy before leaving the room.

"Clara may come as often as she likes. I'm sure my girls will be happy to entertain her," Meg heard Mrs. Claprood say.

"She doesn't want for entertainment, Emily. The girl needs refinement. There is too much male influence in our home. That and the *other*, worse influence."

Meg clenched her fists before storming towards the kitchen. Immersing her hands in hot, sudsy water she scrubbed the afternoon's dishes, glad to keep her hands busy when what she really wanted to do with them was throttle Mrs. Pratt.

Chapter Twenty-Two

"What are you doing here, *a stór*?" Kathleen asked as Clara entered the kitchen from outdoors one day in early October. "I thought you were spending the afternoon with your friend."

"Jane wasn't feeling well. She went right home after school."

"Maybe you should go to the Claproods'."

"I've been there almost every day. Mother insists I go after school and stay until it's time to eat."

"Don't you like it?" Kathleen asked, noting Clara's despondent air.

"Pamela and Deborah are very kind. I do enjoy the conservatory."

"Then why so glum?"

"I miss you, Kathleen."

Kathleen dropped the wet rag she'd been using to wipe down the table and enfolded Clara in her arms. "I've missed you, too, *a stór,* something terrible."

Clara's head now came even with Kathleen's shoulders. How much the girl had grown! Her face had filled out, her hair darkened to a lustrous chestnut brown. Beautiful dark eyes shone up at her through long lashes. Soon the lads would take notice.

"Are you hungry?" Kathleen asked. "Shall I fix you something?"

"No, thank you. Jane and I were eating apples on the way home, but she couldn't manage more than a bite of hers and gave the rest to me."

"I hope she's not very ill."

"She has a sore throat and headache."

210

"Poor lass."

"I'm glad today is Mother's afternoon to make calls. She'll never know if I keep you company."

"Ah, lass there's nothing I'd love more, but it wouldn't be right."

"What's wrong in us talking? Mother said I wasn't to help you with the cooking. If we simply talk and I don't help, I won't be breaking her rule."

Kathleen glanced sideways as the girl seated herself. "Seems a mite cunning."

Clara shrugged. "It's unfair that Mother separated us. We did nothing to deserve it."

"Still, she's your mam and you must obey her."

"Do you want me to leave?"

"No, *a stór*, but neither do I want us in trouble."

"Mother's out. Father, Lemuel, and Harvey are at the foundry. There's no one here but us."

Kathleen smiled and shrugged. She went about her business while Clara told her about school, friends, and the books she'd been reading.

"Did you finish *Uncle Tom's Cabin*?" Clara asked.

"Aye, then I read it again. What a tale! And you were right that it would help me with my English. I'm able to read all the receipts in Mrs. Child's book now."

"Would you like more?" Clara asked.

"I would. It's a joy to read."

"I'll be right back." Clara jumped from her chair and dashed from the kitchen. Upon returning, she lay three books on the table. "My favorites. You may borrow them."

Kathleen picked up each book, read the titles aloud. "*The Old Curiosity Shop, Pride and Prejudice, Jane Eyre.* Hmmm. Which first?"

"*Jane Eyre.*"

"It's long."

"You needn't hurry. Keep them as long as you like."

Kathleen smiled. "You're such a kind lass."

The afternoon passed quickly. Kathleen felt even more keenly how much she'd missed her conversations with Clara. As the girl grew, her mind had sharpened. Though

211

Clara's education had far surpassed Kathleen's she was never condescending, still seeking Kathleen's opinion and approval.

Glancing out the kitchen window, Kathleen noticed the sun's late position in the sky. "Your mother will be home soon. She must not find you in here."

Clara sighed. "Hide the books."

Early one evening of the following week, Kathleen answered the front door.

"I've come to see Mr. Pratt. Is he at home?"

"Indeed, sir. Who may I say is calling?"

"Josiah Orton, Miss."

Kathleen bid the gentleman enter and wait in the front hall while she went to seek Mr. Pratt.

"Sir, you've a caller. A Mister Orton," she said, finding him in his study immersed in account books.

"Josiah Orton?"

"Yes, sir."

Mr. Pratt appeared perplexed. "Did he state his business?"

"No sir."

"Odd. Show him in."

After ushering Mr. Orton into the study, Kathleen returned to the dining room to finish polishing the andirons. It was not long before Mr. Pratt asked her to show Mr. Orton out. Kathleen had just closed the door behind their unexpected guest when Mr. Pratt, standing at the foot of the main staircase yelled, "Harvey! Come down here at once!" He pounded his fist on the curved newel post. Kathleen hurried back to her work.

Mr. Pratt's shout brought forth not only Harvey but Lemuel and Mrs. Pratt as well. They gathered in the parlor where Mr. Pratt continued bellowing.

"How dare you go behind my back?"

"What is this all about?" asked Mrs. Pratt.

"I was just visited by Josiah Orton."

"The jeweler?"

"Indeed. He came to settle terms."

"Terms for what?"

"Apprenticeship. It seems our dear boy asked him for the position. Well, young man?" thundered Mr. Pratt.

"Mr. Orton came here?" Harvey's voice quavered. "I...I...think there must be a mistake."

"You did not go to his shop Tuesday afternoon? The day I sent you on an errand that took you an inordinately long time to complete?"

"Well...I...yes, I did stop in, but..."

"Did you ask to apprentice yourself to him?"

"Mr. Orton is mistaken. I was inquiring for a friend."

Oh, Harvey stand up for yourself, thought Kathleen. He had turned nineteen three months previous, high time he behaved like a man.

"Who is this friend?" asked Mr. Pratt. "Do tell so that I may point Mr. Orton to the proper person."

The andirons gleamed with Kathleen's intense polishing as she willed Harvey the courage to speak his desires.

"Father, I did ask Mr. Orton if I could apprentice to him. I want to be a jeweler. I have wanted it for a long time."

"Harvey, you've never spoken of such an aspiration," said Mrs. Pratt.

"Because he knows better. Or should have," said Mr. Pratt. "Why do you think I've been taking you to the foundry? You are going to be part of my business."

"I'm sorry, Father, I don't care for it."

"Who asked if you care for it? It's the family business. It's what you will do."

"Lemuel will take over after you. Oliver after his father. There's no place for me at the foundry. Even if I earn a position there, once you're gone, Lemuel will be sure to remove me. He's already made that clear."

"I've said no such thing," Lemuel countered.

"You've intimated it."

"You've misunderstood."

Kathleen doubted it. It would be just like Lemuel to force out his own brother.

"Harvey, I'm disappointed," said Mrs. Pratt. "Going behind your father's back, accusing your dear brother of treachery."

Kathleen wanted to gag.

Harvey, with his new found voice spoke next. "Father, I should have spoken to you before going to Mr. Orton. I apologize. Yet at my age I am able to make decisions for myself."

"Obviously, you think you can." Mr. Pratt's tone still held anger, though it was not as strident. Perhaps he was a bit mollified by Harvey's apology.

"Shouldn't you also apologize to poor Lemuel?" asked Mrs. Pratt.

"Oh, he'll be anything but poor once he gets his hooks into the foundry."

"Harvey!" Kathleen twitched at Mrs. Pratt's shrill screech.

"Mother, don't upset yourself on my account," said Lemuel, his voice dripping honey. "Perhaps, Father, you should consider Harvey's wish to apprentice himself to Mr. Orton. He has no aptitude for the foundry business. Mayhap he'll make a nice little life for himself as a jeweler. He'd never succeed in a business that takes true mettle. Why not let him play with the shiny baubles?"

The sound of Lemuel's taunting voice sickened Kathleen.

"He need only apply himself. I'm determined that both my sons follow me. I wish this to be a true family business."

"Father, far better to leave it to Lemuel. He'll have Oliver as a partner. Between them, the business will flourish. Why, even Kathleen has said I should do what makes me happy."

Saints preserve us! Kathleen felt the blood drain from her face. That for once Harvey had used her name instead of calling her Bridget barely registered.

"Kathleen?" Mrs. Pratt uttered her name with incredulity.

"What?" Lemuel, laughed. "You've been taking career advice from the Bridget? Oh, Father, now we know he's not fit for the foundry."

"When did you speak with her?" asked Mrs. Pratt, the word *her* uttered with disdain.

"We were just talking." There was a pleading tone in Harvey's voice.

"She thought to counsel you in your underhanded behavior towards your father? Poisoned your mind against your brother. Where is that chit? I'll turn her out onto the street!"

Kathleen's heart banged in her chest. She detested being run out in such an undeserved manner. Well, she would give them all a piece of her mind before she left.

"You are jumping to conclusions, Sophronia," said Mr. Pratt. "Speak to her. Let her know she's on notice. That should do for now."

"She's an evil influence upon this family. I'll have her out by morning. But before that she'll stand before us all and admit to her shameful behavior."

Oh, I'll stand before you and speak, I will, thought Kathleen, slapping her polishing rag onto the floor.

Kathleen stood, hands on hips, awaiting Mrs. Pratt's summons. But light footsteps sounded on the stairs, followed by the hoarse squeak of Clara's voice. "Mother, I don't feel well."

Alarm replaced anger in Kathleen's heart. She raced for the stairs in time to catch Clara as the girl collapsed into her arms.

"Give her to me, at once," demanded Mrs. Pratt. "Dear Lord, she's burning up."

Mr. Pratt scooped up Clara. As he carried her up the stairs to her room, he called behind him, "Lemuel, go for the doctor."

Grabbing his coat, Lemuel hurried from the house. The rest followed Mr. Pratt up the stairs.

"Bring blankets, a bowl of cool water and some cloths. Quickly!" Mrs. Pratt instructed Kathleen. All her self-righteous anger turned to fear.

215

Upon returning to the bedchamber, Kathleen assisted Mrs. Pratt in undressing Clara. The girl's body was covered in a rash. Her cheeks flamed red as ripe apples.

"This came on suddenly," said Mrs. Pratt. "Clara, where do you hurt?" she asked as Clara's eyes opened.

"My throat," she croaked. "And my head aches terribly."

"The doctor is coming," Mrs. Pratt cooed, stroking Clara's hair.

"We must get her fever down," she said to Kathleen. "Have you any experience in caring for the sick?"

Kathleen's mind flashed to her tiny cottage. She saw the mass of fever-soaked children under a shared blanket, dying one by one. Rory's siblings. She remembered the still form of Aisling before the peat fire as she grew thinner by the day, her rickety body convulsed by endless coughing.

"Aye," she whispered, lost in the nightmare images and slipping into the Irish *aye*. For once, Mrs. Pratt seemed not to notice.

The doctor arrived, declared Clara ill with scarlet fever. He bled her, told them to bathe her forehead with cool cloths, keep the room cool, and give her plenty of liquids. He left them with medicine and instructions for dosage, saying he would return the next day to see how she fared.

That night both Kathleen and Mrs. Pratt sat by Clara's bed, an unspoken temporary truce declared between them. In the darkness of the night, Mrs. Pratt dozed in her chair. Kathleen took advantage of Mrs. Pratt's fatigue to kneel at Clara's bedside. Making the Sign of the Cross, she prayed silently for Clara to get well. She had lost so many she loved. She could not bear to lose Clara too.

Chapter Twenty-Three

By late October, Seamus had taken Nuala to a number of dances, spent all his time with her at the church fairs and picnics, even managed the boat ride he'd promised. Meg and Kathleen found it uproariously funny and teased Nuala mercilessly. Nuala still maintained that she'd never marry, but nothing said she couldn't enjoy herself. Meg and Kathleen made a contest of guessing how long it would be before Seamus proposed.

"And what would you say if he asked?" Meg wanted to know.

"I'd say, he's a grand lad for making merry with, but I'm not one for marrying so if that's on his mind he'd best look elsewhere."

"Does Seamus know how you feel about marriage?" asked Kathleen, one Sunday morning in late October as they left the church.

"We've not discussed it outright. But I have made clear how sorry I am for Irish women who marry and why. I'm sure he's figured it out."

"And yet he continues to court," Meg said. "He must deem himself possessed of great powers of persuasion."

As if summoned by her words, Seamus appeared behind them on the church steps.

"Did you see this?" he asked, showing them a handbill. "They're giving them out all over the city."

"What does it say?" Nuala asked.

"I don't read English very well, but it's a warning, I think. Of a kidnapper who's arrived in Worcester."

"What kidnapper announces his arrival?" Meg demanded.

Seamus laughed. "I don't think he's responsible for creating the handbill. The population is being warned of him."

"May I?" asked Kathleen taking the handbill. "It says that a U.S. Marshal named Asa O. Butman has arrived in Worcester. Seems he's here to catch runaway slaves and send them back to their masters in the South."

"Nothing to do with us, then," said Nuala, straightening her bonnet.

"I'll hear about it from Mrs. Claprood," said Meg. "I'd best get home quickly. She may decide to call an emergency meeting of her anti-slavery ladies. I'll be baking and fetching for them all morning. Never get my work done." Meg shook her head.

"Would you feel safer if I walk you home?" Seamus asked.

All three stared at him.

"I doubt he'd mistake us for runaway slaves," said Meg, then quickly added, "but kind of you to offer."

"Aye. I'll be on my way, then," he said, looking abashed as he hurried away.

"Sorry, Nuala," said Meg. "I didn't mean to run off your lover."

Nuala raised an eyebrow but said nothing which only caused Meg to giggle.

"It would be a horrible thing if this Mr. Butman were to capture fugitives. 'Tis an awful life they have as slaves," said Kathleen, paying no attention to the others.

"They get fed," said Nuala. "That's more than we had in Ireland."

"Aye, but we eat well enough now," Kathleen countered. "We get paid for our work and if we aren't happy we can find another position."

"Then why haven't you done that?" Nuala asked.

"I'm seeing Clara through her illness."

"That lass took to her bed a fortnight ago. She ought to be better by now," said Meg.

"That's what worries me," Kathleen said. "She seemed better for a while, but she's become listless again with her head and throat aching."

"Could be a cold," Nuala said. "Mr. and Mrs. Denton are both sick with them."

"I hope that's all it is," Kathleen said.

"Is Mrs. Pratt still keeping her claws sheathed?" Nuala asked.

"Aye. She's had a terrible fright. There was a moment we didn't think Clara would pull through. Mrs. Pratt actually cried on my shoulder."

"So that's what it takes? Do you think her change of heart permanent?" Meg asked. "You've stayed up more nights than she, done more work of nursing. She owes you that child's life."

Kathleen shrugged. "She isn't as horrible to me as usual. Once Clara's well I suspect she'll go back to her old self, especially with Lemuel to provoke her."

"Then I suggest you leave there and find another position the very minute that girl has recovered," Nuala instructed.

"Nuala's right," Meg agreed. "If Clara hadn't fallen ill just when she did, her mother would have tossed you out on the street. Leave on your own before she can do it, Kathleen."

Meg arrived at the Claprood home, leaving the others heading for Oxford Street. The house was quiet, the family not yet returned from Sunday services. She changed quickly into her uniform and began her chores.

"Of all the insults that could be heaped upon this city, I can think of none worse!"

Meg started. The Claprood family usually arrived from church subdued, but today Mrs. Claprood's voice rang out with indignation from the front hall. "To think that vile man has come to Worcester. How dare he!"

"Now Emily," said Mr. Claprood. "He claims only to be looking for witnesses in the Boston riot. Perhaps that's the truth."

"He's a known liar. Relying upon his word would be perfectly foolish."

"There's an anti-slavery meeting at City Hall tonight," said Oliver. "I plan to attend. I'm certain this will be the main topic."

"Take me with you. I will not stand by while this male-factor kidnaps our city's citizens."

Meg heaved a sigh of relief. If there was to be a meeting at City Hall tonight, there was no reason for Mrs. Claprood's ladies today. Meg could get her work done uninterrupted.

Pamela and Deborah swept through the parlor where Meg was dusting on their way to the conservatory. Pamela had a dreamy, faraway look. Deborah appeared to be enjoying some great secret. Meg wondered at them, appearing so far removed from their mother's agitation.

That evening, Mr. and Mrs. Claprood and Oliver departed for City Hall. Meg, having finished the dishes and put the kitchen to rights, settled in the parlor with some mending.

"Do you suppose he's at the meeting tonight?" Deborah asked as she and Pamela flopped on the parlor sofa.

"I hope so," Pamela said. "Mother would appreciate it if he takes an interest in the cause."

Meg glanced up, wondering of whom they spoke. It was not her place to ask, however, so she returned her attention to her mending.

"Do you believe he was going to seek Father's permission to court you?" Deborah asked.

Pamela sighed. "I really do. If only we hadn't been interrupted with that handbill. After that, no one could speak of anything else."

"Perhaps if he is at the meeting, he will ask Father afterward."

Pamela didn't answer right away. When she did speak, she said, "They'll be all riled up. I hope Edward wouldn't choose a poor time to approach Father."

"I hadn't thought of that. Oh, that awful Mr. Butman! He's causing no end of trouble."

Pamela laughed.

"What's funny?" asked Deborah

"You speak as though Mr. Butman's presence in Worcester causes more distress by delaying Edward Thayer than it does for the poor fugitives he's here to capture."

"I only meant –."

"I know what you meant. It struck me funny, is all."

Meg was nearing the end of her mending when Mr. and Mrs. Claprood returned, Oliver not with them.

"How was the meeting?" Pamela asked as her parents took chairs in the parlor.

"Where is Oliver?" asked Deborah.

"The meeting was tense," replied Mr. Claprood. "Oliver has gone with a host of others assembling outside the American Temperance House where Mr. Butman is staying."

"What are they going to do?" asked Deborah, alarm and excitement both evident on her face.

"It was decided," Mrs. Claprood said, "that the Vigilance Committee should watch the House all night. A group of them spoke with Mr. Bonney earlier today, Mr. Tucker being away. They explained to him what sort of man was residing under his roof and encouraged him to send Mr. Butman away, but he refused. I wish Mr. Tucker had been in residence. Perhaps as senior proprietor he'd have had more sense."

"Oliver is going to stand outside the House all night?" Pamela asked, incredulous.

"I believe they will take shifts," said Mr. Claprood. "They will not allow the man out of their sight the entire time he's in this city. If he's here only to look for witnesses to the Boston riot, as he claims, then he's nothing to fear. If his motives are of a more villainous nature, he may be very sorry he came to Worcester."

Mrs. Claprood sniffed. "To some he says he's here to look for witnesses yet to others he says he's searching for horse thieves. The man is incapable of telling the truth."

As the household was readying to retire, Oliver returned. "I've come to take my rest," he explained, "before returning to the American House at one in the morning for my shift."

"What's happening?" Mrs. Claprood asked.

"The Vigilance Committee has the house surrounded. All's quiet enough that we can't be charged with disturbing the peace, though members ring the bell on occasion. I believe some are attempting to gain entrance to get a good look at the man. We'll be better equipped to follow his movements if we are sure of his looks."

"It is a noble thing you are doing, my darling boy," Mrs. Claprood said, hugging him. "Sleep well."

Once Oliver had disappeared to the second floor, Mrs. Claprood lingered at the foot of the staircase with the rest of the family. Meg stood just outside their little circle.

"We must pray for Oliver's safety and that of all the Vigilance Committee as well as for the protection of whomever Mr. Butman has come to kidnap," announced Mrs. Claprood. "Margaret, please join us before you retire."

Meg bowed her head while the family prayed. She was always ill at ease when in the midst of praying Protestants, but kept a respectful silence. In her mind, she prayed her own silent prayers of an Our Father, a Hail Mary, and a Glory Be for Master Oliver's safety.

Had she known what would happen that night, her prayers would have been for Kathleen.

Chapter Twenty-Four

When the Pratt family returned from Sunday services, Clara went directly to her bedchamber. Kathleen entered her room to find the girl shivering beneath her blankets. She lay a hand on Clara's forehead. Fever. Kathleen cracked the window to let in the brisk autumn air then hurried from the room to gather cloths and a basin of cool water. Why had the illness returned? Last week Clara seemed much better. She had even dressed and taken a meal with the family.

Kathleen rushed from the room, passing Mrs. Pratt in the hallway. "Clara's fever is back. I'm going to get water and cloths," she told her.

Upon returning, Kathleen found Mrs. Pratt kneeling by Clara's bed.

"She's so hot," Mrs. Pratt mumbled. "So very hot."

"Here, Ma'am, let's bathe her with the cool water." Kathleen set the basin on the bedside table then handed a cloth to Mrs. Pratt. They undressed Clara, continually running the wet cloths over her body.

"Should we call for the doctor?" Kathleen asked.

For a moment Kathleen thought she had not understood, such was the blank look in the woman's eyes.

"Yes," she finally said. "Yes, send one of the boys for the doctor or go yourself."

Kathleen left the room, wondering at Mrs. Pratt's demeanor. When Clara had first fallen ill, she'd been galvanized into action. Between the two of them they brought Clara back to some semblance of health. The return of Clara's fever seemed to have the opposite effect on the woman.

Relieved that Harvey was the first of the Pratt males she came upon, Kathleen sent him for the doctor and quickly returned to Clara's bedchamber.

"Harvey has gone," she said.

Though it made her shiver, she opened the window further, trying anything to bring down Clara's fever. Kathleen continued her ministrations, Mrs. Pratt helping, but in such a listless manner, Kathleen wondered if she had taken ill.

"Are you unwell, Ma'am?"

Mrs. Pratt gazed at her. "I thought she was over the worst. And now..." She spread her hands, palms up, in a helpless gesture over her daughter.

When the doctor examined the patient, he declared Clara's condition a relapse, left them with medicine, saying he would return the next day.

"Doctor," said Mrs. Pratt, grabbing at his sleeve. "Will she recover?"

"I cannot answer that. It is in God's hands."

It was not what Mrs. Pratt wanted to hear. "What good is a doctor if he can't cure his patients?" she said as the chamber door closed behind him.

"There is hope," Kathleen reminded her. "The medicine helped before. Let's start her on it right away. I'll go get a spoon and bring your shawl. You're shivering."

When Kathleen returned, Mrs. Pratt was in the chair near Clara's bed, as her daughter slept fitfully. Kathleen wrapped the shawl around Mrs. Pratt's shoulders. Then she sat on the edge of the bed, one arm behind Clara's back to raise her while spooning the medicine into her mouth.

Clara, awake enough only to notice the noxious taste, gagged on the liquid.

"Have some of this," Kathleen coaxed, offering a glass of apple cider. "It will freshen the awful taste in your mouth."

Clara dutifully swallowed a few mouthfuls before falling back to sleep.

Kathleen abandoned the rest of her evening chores to sit the night with Clara. Mrs. Pratt, too, remained in the chair, huddled deeply into her shawl.

As evening moved toward night, Kathleen noticed soft nasal sounds emanating from Mrs. Pratt. Looking up she noted that the woman's head lolled forward, chin resting on her chest, quiet snores announcing that she had fallen asleep.

Kathleen slid noiselessly from her chair to her knees at the side of Clara's bed. Drawing her rosary from her pocket, she began to pray in earnest. The ancient prayers came naturally to her mind in her native Irish. At some point she'd begun speaking them aloud. The soft, chant-like locutions were enough to wake Mrs. Pratt. Kathleen was too engrossed to realize she'd awakened the woman until she heard her scream. She jumped, clutching the rosary to her heart.

"You!" Mrs. Pratt was on her feet, pointing. "It's you. You caused Clara's relapse."

Kathleen stared at her, mouth agape. "Ma'am? Are you all right? Have you had a nightmare?" Mrs. Pratt's face appeared crazed in the flickering candlelight.

"Were it but a nightmare! There is evil in my house."

Kathleen stood. Clara twitched in her sleep.

"That!" she said, pointing to the rosary.

Kathleen opened her hand, looking at the string of beads worn smooth from years of use.

"That and the wicked curse you were muttering over them."

"'I was praying for Clara to recover. I am sorry I woke you."

"Catholic prayers." The words spewed out of Mrs. Pratt like venom. "Idolatrous worship! You're a heathen, a pagan. Your evil has made Clara ill again!"

"I love Clara. I'd never do anything to harm her."

"Those beads. They're..." Mrs. Pratt waved her hands wildly about as if she might pick the right word from the air. "Sorcery. You'll not be doing it in my home to my child! Leave at once."

Kathleen gasped, but before she could say a word, Mrs. Pratt dug her sausage fingers into Kathleen's flesh and dragged her from the bedchamber, down the hall to the

225

back staircase, and finally to the kitchen. There Mrs. Pratt shoved her toward the straw mattress.

"Pack. Take only what is yours. I am watching. Then get out of this house."

Kathleen's face was hot enough to rival Clara's fever as she flung open the cupboard containing her belongings, pulling out the sack she'd brought with her from Ireland.

"Miss Clara is the only reason I've stayed this long." Kathleen kept her tone low, not wishing to bring the whole family down upon her. "I have endured a multitude of insults against my own person as well as my countrymen and my faith." Kathleen jammed her few dresses, bonnet, and cloak into her sack as she spoke.

"I'm evil? Look to your darling Lemuel for evil! You chose to ignore it from the first day he laid hands on me. My mam may be poorer than the poorest person in America, but she's a finer mother than you could ever be. Spoiling one lad, disheartening the other, and ignoring sweet Clara until she fell ill." Kathleen's anger brought out her brogue. "As for me, all ye do is find fault. 'Tis a poor excuse for a mistress ye are!"

Kathleen had finished cramming her belongings into her sack. When she'd first arrived, there'd been little in it. Now it bulged.

"I'll be praying for *a stór* upon me rosary as well as asking all the saints in heaven to intercede on her behalf. Should she recover, you'll be knowing who to thank."

Kathleen grasped the doorknob. Mrs. Pratt slammed a beefy hand against the door, holding it shut. "The uniform," she said, eyes blazing.

Kathleen looked down. She was still wearing her maid's uniform.

"I'll have it sent back to you tomorrow, you miserable excuse for a Christian." Kathleen shoved past Mrs. Pratt, stormed out into the gathering darkness.

She ran all the way to the Claproods'. She pounded on the kitchen door, shivering in the late October air. Dropping the sack at her feet, she rubbed her arms with both hands.

Lamplight glowed in several of the windows, but no one came. She pounded again.

The door cracked slightly, the sliver of a face peering out. Mrs. Claprood. Why would she have come to the servant's entrance? Where was Meg?

Mrs. Claprood pulled the door open.

Seeing her, Kathleen was reminded that the Misters Claprood and Pratt co-owned the foundry. Mrs. Claprood was friendly with Mrs. Pratt.

"Kathleen, what brings you here at this hour? And without a cloak. You're trembling. Come in quickly."

Kathleen nudged the sack aside with her foot. In the darkness it would not be noticed.

"You look stricken, my dear," said Mrs. Claprood. "Is it Clara?"

"Miss Clara's fever has returned. The doctor's been and left medicine for her. I... thought Meg might remember something about treating the many fevers back home. Something, I've forgotten." Kathleen stumbled over her words. She needed a believable excuse for arriving after dark on the Claproods' doorstep.

"Do you think I should go?"

"No, Ma'am. 'Tis only Meg's experience I'm wanting." Not for Mrs. Claprood to obtain an earful of Mrs. Pratt's invective.

"I'll get Margaret. Please have a seat."

Kathleen dropped into a chair near the kitchen table, warming herself by the dying embers of the stove. Soon Meg appeared.

"Miss Clara's worse?" Meg asked. "I'm sure I don't know any more than you do. We relied on Doctor Parker. Where's your cloak?"

"In my sack. I was in a rush to leave."

Meg glanced about the room.

"It's outside. Why didn't you answer the door?"

"Mrs. Claprood's got me making up beds for any runaways that might need sheltering. It's that handbill. Oliver's sleeping now so he can take his turn standing guard at the

American House in the wee hours. Kathleen, what's happened?"

Mrs. Claprood returned to the kitchen.

"Any help for dear Clara?" she asked, looking from Meg to Kathleen.

"Nothing we've not already tried," said Kathleen. "But I thank you for fetching Meg for me. I'd best go."

"But –" Meg began.

"Margaret, we must make up some food for Oliver while he's on duty. Please, let your sister attend to her tasks."

Kathleen backed out the door, grabbed her sack, pulling the cloak from inside. She thought to head for the Dentons'. Nuala would know what to do and the Dentons had no ties to the Pratts. As she turned toward Oxford Street, she remembered Nuala mentioning that Mr. and Mrs. Denton had colds. She dared not impose on that household. Her only option was the Lintons. Loathe as she was to burden them, she couldn't very well spend the night outdoors.

The full moon, a round, orange wheel of cheese, still low in the sky, looked close enough to touch. Clutching her cloak tightly about her, she made her way out of Crown Hill, towards the Meadows.

Since it was a Sunday evening, the streets were mostly deserted. Nonetheless, she hurried along, keeping in the shadows as best she could when walking the few streets lined with gas lights. Upon reaching Main Street, she stopped to catch her breath. Her heart pounded. Legs unsteady, she sat on the front stoop of a shop and watched the moon rise higher in the sky, losing some of its orange glow on the way.   Shivering, she pulled her cloak more tightly around herself. Searching through the muddle of items in her sack, she found a pair of gloves and slipped them on her chapped hands. She dared not rest long. Within a few moments, she headed north.

As Kathleen reached an intersection, she almost collided with a woman who'd just turned the corner from Mechanic Street.

"Pardon, Ma'am," she said, wondering why a well-dressed woman was walking these dark streets alone and hoping not to be questioned herself.

"Going to the American House?" the woman asked.

"No, Ma'am." The question put an idea into Kathleen's mind. She had some money in her sack. Was it enough to get a room for the night? She could withdraw some of her savings from the bank in the morning. Was that enough to keep herself until she found employment? If she could manage, it would spare the Lintons.

"Ma'am, can you tell me the cost of a room at the American House?" she ventured.

The woman lifted her lantern so she could see Kathleen's face.

"Irish, are you?" The lantern moved up and down.

Kathleen stood straight, jutting out her chin. "Aye," she said, placing a hand on her hip.

The woman laughed. "I was not finding fault. As to the American House, you'd not want to stay there tonight."

"Why is that?"

"Are you new in this city?"

"No."

"Then you're the only soul who has not heard! Asa Butman is at the American House right now. The Vigilance Committee has guards outside, watching his every move. That's where I'm headed. Want to see the excitement for myself."

Kathleen remembered Seamus' handbill and Meg's comments about Oliver going to stand guard.

"Oh, aye."

"It's all anyone's speaking of. But you've important matters of a personal nature?" The woman swung her lantern towards Kathleen's sack.

"I...well...will stay with a friend then. Thank you for your advice." The words sounded pathetic even to her own ears. She turned away, but the woman grabbed hold of her arm, causing Kathleen's cloak to swing open.

"You are dressed in a uniform, carrying all you own in the world."

229

Kathleen growled. "And what's it to you?"

"Well, you've got spirit. A quality I admire. Any good at your job? Obviously you've just been fired."

"Very good, especially at cooking. Better than most of you Yanks."

"Why were you fired?"

Kathleen's indignation rose to a new height. "'Tis no business of yours. I don't even know you." She shook her arm free. "I'll be on my way."

"I'm looking to hire help. I run a boarding house and need someone to start straight away."

Kathleen turned back. This woman was odd – out alone after dark, heading for a place no proper lady would go, and forward in her ways of speaking. Yet Kathleen could say the same for herself. Perhaps this was the grandest luck?

"I was fired because I'm Catholic. I dared to pray a rosary over my mistress's sick child, asking Jesus and Our Lady to make her well."

"Is that all?"

"More than enough for my mistress."

"Former mistress, you mean."

"Aye."

"There's much work, but I take in only women and they keep their own rooms tidy so you'll only need to clean the common rooms. And cook our meals. We're full up at present. I'll match and raise your former employer's pay if your cooking is as good as you claim. What do you say?"

Kathleen eyed her. "I'll be allowed time off to attend Mass on Sunday mornings and Holy Days?"

"You'll have the entirety of Sunday as your day off as I will need you on Thursdays, I'm afraid."

Kathleen's heart sank at the thought of only seeing Meg and Nuala on Sunday mornings, but she was hardly in a position to argue.

"Well, what will it be?"

Kathleen took a deep breath. "I'll take it," she said.

"Good. Walk with me and we'll talk about the particulars. What is your name?" she asked as together they continued on Main Street.

"Kathleen O'Connor. And I'll not tolerate being called Bridget!"

The woman laughed. "Not to worry, Kathleen. I am Annie Nichols. You may call me Mrs. Nichols. I'm a widow which is why I run a boarding house."

"I am very sorry. How long has it been?" Despite the darkness, Kathleen could tell that Mrs. Nichols was probably in her thirties.

"Twelve years now." Kathleen caught a note of wistfulness.

"Have you any children?"

"No, thank God!"

Kathleen was startled by the vehement response.

"Life would be even more difficult had I little ones depending on me, don't you see?"

"Oh, of course."

As they neared the American House, they could make out the shapes of a few men standing in the yard. Voices carried on the chill air.

"Ring the bell again, George," one called to another.

The two women drew closer, beyond the border of the House's property. They watched a young man run up the steps to clang the bell. A tired looking older man opened the door.

"Are you planning to do this all night, my boys?" he asked.

"Turn out Butman and the rest of your night will be peaceful," called a man from the bottom of the stairs.

"I've no reason to suspect the gentleman of villainy."

"You mean you'll not turn out a paying customer were he the devil himself," called a fellow posted at the further corner of the house.

"Enough of this foolishness!" said the landlord, slamming the door.

The men laughed. "Wait a while then ring the bell again," one called to his comrades. "He may turn old Butman out to end the nuisance."

"Well, this is far less amusing than I'd hoped," Mrs. Nichols said, turning away from the American House. "We might as well go home."

"What were you expecting?" Kathleen asked.

"A riot, perhaps. Like the one they had in Boston."

"You'd find that amusing?"

Mrs. Nichols stopped walking. She lifted the lantern so the light shone on Kathleen's face. "There are things about me you must not question. My tastes in many things may not be to your liking. My toleration of your religion should be enough to offset them."

Kathleen nodded slightly, wondering what she was getting into.

"The house is on Cherry Street. We aren't far."

As they walked, Mrs. Nichols specified Kathleen's duties. They seemed routine enough. The only odd requirement was that she was to retire to her room for the night promptly at nine o'clock. She was not to leave her room until morning. Mrs. Nichols claimed it was to prevent her from disturbing the paying boarders. Kathleen was sure she'd be tired enough not to have any difficulty meeting this requirement, but the fact that it was a requirement seemed strange. Perhaps life in a boarding house had its own peculiarities. Having a bedchamber to herself was such a delightful prospect that it outweighed her qualms. She followed Mrs. Nichols to the back of a large, old house on Cherry Street and into one of the biggest, best equipped kitchens she'd ever seen.

Chapter Twenty-Five

Meg began her duties as usual before sunrise on Monday morning. Upon lighting the parlor lamps she found Mrs. Claprood asleep in a chair.

At the touch of Meg's hand on her shoulder, Mrs. Claprood jerked awake.

"What time is it?"

"Six of the clock, Ma'am. I'm sorry to have startled you. I did not expect to find you here. Are you all right?"

"Yes. Yes. Thank you, Margaret. I couldn't sleep with Oliver gone. I keep thinking of the riot in Boston."

"Would you like me to make coffee?"

"No, don't disturb your normal routine. I'll await the rest of the family for breakfast. Hopefully, Oliver will be back in time to join us."

Breakfast came and went with no sign of Oliver. The Claprood family partook of the meal in near silence.

"I'm going to the American House," announced Mr. Claprood, rising from the breakfast table.

"Please send back word," said Mrs. Claprood, her face a mask of anxiety.

"You'll know everything as soon as I find out." He patted her shoulder and pecked her cheek.

Within an hour, Meg answered the front door to admit an agitated woman whom she recognized as one of the regulars at Mrs. Claprood's anti-slavery meetings. Meg barely had the woman ushered into the front hallway before Mrs. Claprood appeared.

"Emily, I do apologize for arriving at such an inhospitable hour, but I heard your Oliver was going to the American House. Any news?"

"Nothing, Helen. Oliver has not returned. Chester left right after breakfast." Without taking her eyes from Helen's face, Mrs. Claprood addressed Meg, "Margaret, take Mrs. Whipple's wrap, please, and bring two cups of tea to the parlor."

Meg reached for the cloak she expected Mrs. Whipple to hand her, but instead, the woman said, "I can't stay. I only came to deliver my news. My husband arrived at the American House at the same time as Oliver. He sent word that once an hour someone rang the bell. It seems they'd been doing that all night as a sort of vexation. But the last time, when the landlord opened the door, Mr. Butman appeared in the doorway along with him, brandishing a pistol and threatening death and destruction."

Mrs. Claprood gasped. "A pistol! Was anyone shot?"

"No. The weapon was not fired."

"Thank you, Jesus," Mrs. Claprood whispered. Meg assisted her as she half-slid to sit on the lower part of the main staircase.

"My husband went straight away to Justice Howe and filed a complaint," Mrs. Whipple continued. "A warrant was issued for the arrest of Asa Butman."

"Has he been arrested?"

At this moment Pamela and Deborah appeared in the front hall.

"Who's been arrested?" Pamela asked.

"Mr. Butman," their mother answered. "For threatening the Vigilance Committee with a pistol."

"A pistol?" Deborah's eyes grew big.

Mrs. Whipple cleared her throat. "As I was saying, a warrant was issued. Officer Warren appeared at the American House about four this morning and took Mr. Butman off to await the opening of the courthouse. If you hurry, you may arrive in time for the proceedings. I'm on my way there now."

"Thank you for bringing this news, Helen. Margaret, please show Mrs. Whipple out then help me to change. I will go to the courthouse as well." After bidding Mrs.

Whipple good day, she headed for her chamber with Meg following.

The house seemed oddly quiet all morning. Meg went about her chores while Pamela and Deborah were anything but their usual buoyant selves. They appeared infused with a mix of anticipation, impatience, and fear as they paced the floors, stopping from time to time to look out the windows.

Something else nudged at Meg. Kathleen's visit of last evening struck her as odd. Kathleen knew Meg had no more nursing skill than she, why come to ask for help? Added to that was the fact of her cloak being in her sack which she'd left outside. It made no sense. Questions turned themselves over in Meg's mind all morning. She wished it were Thursday. She decided to go to the Pratts' as soon as she finished work this evening.

As Meg began to wonder who would be home for dinner, Mrs. Claprood returned. Pamela and Deborah flew to the parlor. Meg quickly joined them.

"What's happened?" Pamela asked.

"Girls, sit down. I've much to relate. You as well, Margaret."

Meg took a place by the parlor door while the girls sat near their mother on the sofa.

"Mother, you look shaken," Pamela observed.

"I'm fine, dear," Mrs. Claprood reassured her. "But the dreadfulness of today's events!"

"Tell us everything," Deborah implored. "What happened when you arrived at the courthouse?"

"I got there just as Mr. Butman was being brought in with his lawyer, Mr. Stone. Mr. Thayer and Mr. Rice represented the commonwealth."

"Mr. Thayer?" asked Pamela. "Is he a relation of Edward's? Edward has just gone into law."

"I believe they are somehow related. At any rate, there was but a brief hearing before Justice Green. By the request of Mr. Stone, the case will be continued in a fortnight. Mr.

Butman was held to answer in the sum of one hundred dollars for his appearance."

"Has he left the city to wait out the two weeks?" asked Deborah.

"I daresay he would have could he have gotten away."

"What do you mean?" asked Pamela.

"By the end of the hearing the courtroom was overflowing with people. An even larger crowd had gathered outside. People were yelling 'bring out the kidnapper!' and 'kill the scoundrel!'"

"Kill?" Deborah asked.

"I hoped our good people would never behave in such a beastly manner, but their anger was ungovernable. I dreaded I might witness a murder. Mr. Baker, the city marshal, must have feared the same. He allowed Mr. Butman use of his private room in City Hall as a place of refuge. It was no easy feat getting him there. The crowd – no I must say mob – followed every step yelling insults and hurling rocks. Once Marshal Baker had Mr. Butman safely into his quarters he came out on the steps, beseeching all to disperse, but to no avail. He left, having placed some policemen to guard the entry. That's when I started for home. I couldn't bear any longer to watch our good citizens behave in such a barbaric manner. Besides, I felt unsafe. Being at the courthouse was one thing, but amongst an angry mob was quite another. The few other ladies who had attended the hearing left at the same time."

"Mother?" asked Pamela, her voice quiet. "Did you see Oliver or Father amongst the crowd?"

"It was such a sea of faces I could find no trace of either."

"Do you think they were there?" asked Deborah, her voice almost as subdued as her sister's.

Mrs. Claprood stared at her hands in her lap. Meg had to lean forward in her chair to catch her words. "I suppose they must be, else they'd have returned or sent word."

The trio on the sofa went silent, all looking downcast.

"Father and Oliver may be observing, not taking part," Pamela said, a note of hope in her voice.

"Exactly right, my dear," said Mrs. Claprood, brightening. "I just pray they keep out of harm's way."

Meg cleared her throat. "What shall you have me do about dinner?"

"Dinner! Prepare it as usual, Margaret. If Chester and Oliver are not in attendance, their portions may be set aside for later."

"Very well, Ma'am." Meg rose to leave.

"Oh, I've been terribly remiss," said Mrs. Claprood, rising from the sofa. "Margaret fetch my cloak, please."

"Where are you going, Mother?" asked Pamela.

"In all this commotion, I'd forgotten the visit Margaret's sister paid us last evening. Clara has had a relapse of the fever. I must inquire if I can be of service."

Meg wished she could go, too, or at least ask Mrs. Claprood to find out if all was well with Kathleen. She could not think, though, how she could contrive either. She would have to await Mrs. Claprood's return. Certainly, if anything was seriously amiss, Mrs. Claprood would tell her.

Not long after the woman departed, an urchin of about ten, who said his name was Jonathan, appeared at the kitchen door claiming to have been sent by Mr. Claprood. Meg brought him in, gave him some milk and a biscuit which he devoured while adding more to Mrs. Claprood's story.

Shortly after Mrs. Claprood had left the scene, the door to the office where Mr. Butman had been given refuge was broken open by six or seven colored men who seized him. One of them hit Mr. Butman, knocking him to the ground. Marshal Baker returned. He had the assailant arrested, locking him into another room in City Hall, but the window in that room was not secured. While Marshal Baker stood outside addressing the crowd, a loud noise was heard. Asa Butman's assailant had jumped from the window nearly twelve feet to the sidewalk. No one, it seemed, was interested in recapturing him, and being uninjured, he was able to make his escape.

"Did anything happen after that?" asked Deborah.

"Yes, Miss. You know Mr. Hoar?"

237

"George Hoar, the lawyer?" asked Pamela.

"The very one. Well, he came out of the marshal's office, stood on the steps to talk to the crowd like Marshal Baker had done. He was calling for the people to be peaceful, to not make a ruckus like they did in Boston."

"Mr. Hoar is a strong abolitionist," Pamela observed. "Did they listen to him?"

"Some liked what he said, cheered him on. Others called for tarring and feathering old Butman. Mr. Hoar said he'd promised Mr. Butman he could leave the city unmolested and even that he'd accompany him to the depot so's he could take the very next train. He begged the lot of us not to make a liar of him."

"And?" asked Deborah. "How did they respond?"

"Lots were angry, especially them coloreds. Mr. Hoar, he insisted we be men of our words, though there's some pointed out that the words were his alone. Still, he brought Mr. Butman out onto the steps with him. I never seen a man look so scared. Passing his hat back and forth one hand to the other, then scrunching it up between the two when Mr. Hoar took him by the arm, leading him down the steps. Once they reached the sidewalk, some in the crowd rushed towards Mr. Butman, aiming to do him harm, for sure."

"I'm glad Mother left before any of that," Pamela said. "Did they make it to the train station?"

"Once the crowd started after him, the oddest thing of all happened. The Reverend Mr. Higginson seemed to come out of nowhere. He stepped right up to Mr. Butman and introduced himself. Told Mr. Butman he would stand by him and protect him. Then he took hold of Mr. Butman's other arm and between them they escorted Mr. Butman on his way."

"Reverend Higginson did that?" Deborah asked, confused. "But he was in Boston at the time of the riot. He even took part in it, from what I've heard."

"Two good anti-slavery men were setting an example of peaceful resistance and sound Christian brotherly love," Pamela explained. "I hope the crowd understood their message."

238

"Martin Stowell and Stephen Foster came to assist as well," Jonathan continued. "But that crowd was pretty riled. Didn't like their prey getting away, I suppose. Mr. Butman's protectors took more than a few blows meant for him. They went on toward the depot with five to six hundred men following after, or so I'd guess. There were a few policemen trying to keep them back, but they were no match for that crowd. I saw more than one rotten egg fly through the air. Last I seen of him, Mr. Butman looked like someone mistook him for a frying pan."

"Has he left the city?" asked Pamela. "Did you see him get on the train?"

The boy shrugged. "That's when Mr. Claprood seized me by my collar and offered me this to come give you all the news." Jonathan opened his grimy palm in which he held a few shiny coins. "I was supposed to tell Mrs. Claprood, but since she's not at home, I 'spect you'll give her the message?"

"We will, and thank you," said Pamela. "Margaret will show you out." Meg noticed that Pamela held herself unusually straight. Since Pamela had learned of Edward Thayer's interest in her she'd been occasionally trying the role of mistress of the household on for size.

Meg slipped Jonathan a few extra biscuits and gave little thought to Asa Butman as she focused on what to prepare for dinner and wondering about Kathleen.

Meg was setting the table when the front door opened. The look on Mrs. Claprood's face along with the urgent tone in her voice gave Meg the feeling of having just swallowed a sharp icicle whole.

"Margaret, I must speak with you."

"Mother," said Pamela as she and Deborah rushed into the dining room. "We've so much to tell you. Father sent word about what happened after you left City Hall."

"You won't believe the goings on," Deborah said.

Mrs. Claprood allowed the girls to draw her towards the parlor as she called over her shoulder, "Finish setting the table, Margaret. We'll talk in a few moments."

Meg's hands shook as she completed her task. It seemed forever before Mrs. Claprood reappeared, motioning her towards the kitchen. Meg never took her eyes from her mistress who pulled up a kitchen chair.

"I'm afraid I have some distressing news, Margaret."

Meg nodded.

"Mrs. Pratt has let Kathleen go from her employ."

Meg swallowed hard. "Last night?" she asked. "She threw her out with nowhere to go as it was getting dark?"

Mrs. Claprood cast her eyes down towards her lap. "I'm afraid so. Kathleen must have come here hoping for your help."

"I knew something was wrong. But with so much going on here – and then she left so suddenly."

"I think I know why." There was a look of pain in the woman's eyes. "Because my husband is Mr. Pratt's business partner."

Meg's mind reeled with this information. "She could have told me." Meg shook her head. "What made Mrs. Pratt send her off in such a state?"

"Kathleen knelt by the girl's bed and prayed with those beads."

"Her rosary."

"Yes. It unnerved her. She is especially sensitive to Papist – I'm sorry – Catholic ways. And Kathleen was praying in Irish. Mrs. Pratt was convinced that your sister was performing a pagan ritual over Clara and that it was the cause of Clara's relapse."

"What?" Meg's indignation surged from her belly to the top of her head. "She was praying for the girl to get well."

Mrs. Claprood reached for Meg's hand. "I told her that myself, but there was no reasoning with her. I believe her son, Lemuel, has provoked much of this antagonistic feeling as he seems to have strong nativist leanings." Mrs. Claprood's face and tone grew bitter, surprising Meg with the intensity. "To throw that girl out alone on a chilly night was most unchristian. You can be certain I told her so. Our husbands may be business partners but I will not compromise my own principles when I see a grave injustice."

"Where is Kathleen now?" Meg asked.

"I don't know. How I wish she had felt safe enough to tell us. We would have allowed her to stay the night. Do you have any thoughts as to where she might have gone?"

Meg forced from her mind the unsavory possibilities that could have befallen Kathleen. "Perhaps to the Dentons to see if Nuala could help."

"We'll check there first. Don't you have relatives in the city? The ones whose wedding you attended."

"You mean the O'Sullivans and the Lintons? They are not relations of ours, but I journeyed on the ship from Ireland with Mrs. O'Sullivan and her daughter. They've become good friends. That's likely where she headed."

"Where do they live?"

"The Meadows. At the Arcade."

Mrs. Claprood blanched. "That is not a safe area for anyone to be walking alone at night."

"Ma'am," Meg asked. "May I go there now myself? I'll come back straight away. I promise."

"I shouldn't like you to go alone."

"It's daylight now. The men who have jobs are at the factories. It's mostly women and the wee ones at home. Please, I'm terrible worried about Kathleen."

"There's an angry mob you'd have to cross to get to the Meadows. I can't let you take that chance."

"To the Dentons', then?"

"Yes. Go now. The girls and I will feed ourselves."

Meg grabbed her cloak and ran from the house. Standing outside the Denton home after a fruitless talk with Nuala, Meg glared at the Pratt house down the street. "Ye horrible, evil, villainous, spawn of the devil himself," she whispered, eyes narrowed at the structure that housed those she most loathed. "Excepting Clara, may ya all rot in hell, if anything's happened to Kathleen."

Meg considered defying Mrs. Claprood by heading straight for the Lintons, but changed her mind. Mrs. Claprood was a valuable ally whom she did not want to anger.

As she approached the back door, a thought sprung to mind. *Siobhan.* If Father O'Malley could send Siobhan to watch over her, couldn't she ask Siobhan to watch over Kathleen?

"Siobhan, go with her, please," she whispered. "Ask Jesus to protect and keep her safe." Standing on the back steps, shivering in the cold autumn air, she added an Our Father, Hail Mary, and Glory Be before reentering the house.

"Any luck?" asked Mrs. Claprood who was scooping mashed potatoes into a serving bowl.

"She never went to the Dentons. She must have gone to the Lintons. I wish I could be sure she's safe."

Mrs. Claprood sighed. "We'll hope she made it there without incident."

"Aye, but all that ruckus at the American House. She'd have gone in that direction." Meg placed the roast beef on a platter as she spoke.

"Oh, Margaret, we must believe she arrived safely. When Chester and Oliver return we'll find out what's been happening. I'll have one of them go to the Arcade."

Meg looked into Mrs. Claprood's soft, brown eyes. "Thank you," Meg whispered, her heart full.

Dinner was a quiet affair with only the women present. Meg, her appetite dampened by worry, washed the dishes before Oliver and Mr. Claprood returned. Hurriedly, she warmed their dinners then stood attentively in the dining room while the men told the rest of the afternoon's adventures.

"All the trains had departed by the time Butman's escort managed to get him to the depot," Mr. Claprood explained. "I can't imagine a body could have been more distressed than Butman must have been at that moment. He probably thought he was done for."

Oliver took over. "They'd made it to the corner of Trumbull and Front Streets, when the biggest Negro I've ever seen pushed his way through the crowd, right up to Butman and struck him a hard blow behind the ear that buckled his knees. A melee began that left us all wondering if the crowd or the escort would end up in possession of Mr. Butman or if both would have only pieces."

"How horrible!" Pamela exclaimed.

Oliver nodded, swallowing a mouthful of mashed potatoes. "The escort prevailed, but as Father explained, by the time they got to the depot people were shouting, 'Kill him!' and some suggested riding him out of town on a rail."

"Did he get away?" asked Deborah.

Mr. Claprood and Oliver exchange glances, wry smiles edging their lips.

"Eventually," said Mr. Claprood. "First they needed a hiding place to keep the mob from tearing him apart. They locked him up in the depot's privy."

Oliver's face broke into a full grin. "The perfect place for him, I'd say."

Pamela and Deborah suppressed giggles.

"Stephen Foster stood before the crowd, which had doubled in size," Mr. Claprood continued. "A good thousand. He proclaimed that Butman had solemnly promised to leave Worcester and never return if he could go with no further violence to his person. Foster called the promise a victory won for freedom and admonished the crowd not to mar it with savagery."

Oliver once again took up the tale. "The City Marshal brought a wagon round to the privy's back door, but upon its being opened, a group of Negroes rushed in, one dealing him a terrible blow to the head while others kicked him from behind. The escort managed to drag him out and hoist him up in the wagon, but those in the crowd who were close enough tried to break the wagon wheels. It spooked the horse so that he stomped, snorting and blowing, paying no mind to the driver. Butman was moved into a hack next. How, without anyone tearing him to pieces, I'll never know. But that one's horse was of steadier stuff. He took the man off towards Grafton. He got a stone through the window as a parting gift from the citizens of Worcester."

"So, he's gone at last?" asked Mrs. Claprood.

"He is, my dear. He'd be a perfect fool to return."

"I hope the story spreads far and wide," said Oliver, "so that any others who've a mind to make Worcester their kidnapping grounds will find another place for their filthy business."

"And the crowd?" asked Mrs. Claprood.

"Gone home to dinner or off to work, though I doubt their employers got much use of them after this morning's excitement."

When the gentlemen had finished eating, Meg cleared their plates from the table. Pamela and Deborah went off to discuss the day's adventures.

"Oliver," Mrs. Claprood said. "You should rest."

"I suppose," he consented. "Now that I've eaten, I feel drained."

Mr. Claprood was about to leave as well when Mrs. Claprood placed a hand on his arm. "Chester, I have a great favor to ask of you," Meg heard her say. *Please let him be agreeable*, she prayed, worried that Mr. Claprood might not be as compassionate as his wife.

Meg's fears abated when Mrs. Claprood entered the kitchen to ask directions to the Lintons' dwelling.

A while later, while dusting the parlor, she heard the front door open. Mr. Claprood's heavy footsteps sounded in the hallway. Mrs. Claprood, having heard her husband's return, joined him at the parlor's threshold.

"Chester?"

Mr. Claprood never took his eyes off Meg. "I'm terribly sorry. None of your friends have heard from your sister."

"Oh, Margaret!" Mrs. Claprood took Meg in her arms. "We will go to the police."

"I've already been," Mr. Claprood stated. "They've had no reports of anyone fitting her description."

"They will look for her," Mrs. Claprood insisted.

Will they? Meg wondered.

"Is there anywhere else you think she might have gone?" Mr. Claprood asked.

Meg's mind whirled. "Perhaps Saint John's," she said. "I would like to speak to the priests."

"I will accompany you," said Mr. Claprood.

Meg ran for her cloak and bonnet, forgetting her gloves. Upon arriving at the rectory, she told her story to Father Gilbert and Father Boyce who promised to put out the word to the Irish community. Meg thanked them, having far more faith in their efforts than those of the police.

Meg felt numb during the walk home. The thought of something bad happening to Kathleen turned her blood to ice. She was the older sister. Their mam would expect her to have watched out for Kathleen despite the fact they were both grown women. Her prayers were suffused with pleading urgency. *Siobhan, you prayed me safe all the way to America. Please, I beg you, pray for Kathleen. Please pray she's safe and I will see her soon.*

Chapter Twenty-Six

"Glory be!" Kathleen exclaimed. Even in the dim light of Mrs. Nichols' lantern she could tell that this room was double the size of Mrs. Pratt's kitchen. There were two great work tables in the center and three cupboards against the walls. Pots and pans hung from hooks. A small stove was tucked into a slightly recessed section of the room, a grand one against the opposite wall. One entire cupboard was filled with spices. Herbs hung in long strands from the beams overhead. Against a back wall there was a set of large built-in shelves containing a lovely set of serving dishes, platters, plates, and pitchers, all in the same blue and white pattern.

Kathleen turned towards Mrs. Nichols. "What's this?" she asked, smoothing her hand across the top of a wooden chest with three doors of varying sizes.

"An insulated box with ice in it. It allows food to remain fresh longer. It's called a refrigerator."

Kathleen was astounded. "May I open it?"

"Go right ahead."

Kathleen opened the smallest door. She jumped in surprise at the cold air emanating from the box. The inside was lined with metal. It held several large chunks of ice. She closed the door before opening another. Though not quite as cold as the first chamber, it still held a chill. Inside was a variety of food including a half-eaten pie.

"'Tis a wonder," said Kathleen. "I've never seen anything like it."

"It was a gift," Mrs. Nichols explained. "The ice must be renewed regularly."

"Where do you get it?"

246

"The ice house. That won't be your concern. A boy fetches it when needed."

Kathleen longed for daylight so she could see it all without hindrance. The windows were high, close to the ceiling, ending a few inches above the plate racks rimming the walls. Before entering from the back of the house they had stepped down several stairs. The kitchen was beneath ground level.

"To your room now. I will show you the rest of the house in the morning." Mrs. Nichols pointed to a door at the far end of the kitchen. "That way leads up to the dining room and the main section of the house. This way," she said, turning towards a small alcove Kathleen had not noticed, "is the back staircase. It leads to your quarters."

Mrs. Nichols handed Kathleen a lit chamber candle. Together they climbed three flights of stairs enclosed on all sides. It was a straight ascent to the third floor with no way to emerge upon the second.

Mrs. Nichols opened a door.

"This will be your room."

Kathleen could just make out the room's furniture. Her eyes fell first upon the bed.

"Is this where I'll sleep?" she asked, remembering sharing a bed with Meg and Nuala at the Denton home. She could not believe she would have a bed all to herself every night.

"Yes. The room's small, but I hope it will suit."

She longed to see fully the room's contents, but it hardly mattered. It was hers!

"It more than suits. I can scarcely believe it."

Mrs. Nichols laughed. "I'll leave you to get comfortable. I will come to get you in the morning. Do not leave the room until I come up."

Once Mrs. Nichols had departed, Kathleen sat gingerly on the edge of the bed, smoothing her hands out beside her. "It's not straw," she whispered, pushing her hand against the mattress. Feathers? She stood, picked up the candle for a closer look. "Pillows! Two of them! Meg will never believe this." Upon pulling back the coverlet, a faint scent of lavender arose, causing her to inhale deeply.

Kathleen made quick work of removing her uniform and slipping between the sheets. There was room enough to turn over! She was certain the splendor would prevent any sleep, but early morning sunlight was painting the room with a rosy glow when she next opened her eyes.

Now that she could see better, she was eager to investigate. Arising, she quickly made up the bed. Aye, she could walk from one end to the other in only a few steps. Yet within that space was a bed that could sleep at least two, with a wooden frame, head and foot boards, the four corners topped with carved pineapples. Across from the bed stood a tall chest with three drawers on the bottom, a shelf above them, a set of smaller drawers above that, and another shelf on top. On the other side of the doorway was a washstand. It, too, had a drawer. A bowl and pitcher sat on top. They were of the same blue and white pattern as the serving dishes in the kitchen.

Washcloths and towels hung from the handles with more in a pile on the shelf beneath. A bar of soap, a toothbrush, and tooth powder rested within the drawer. At the foot of the bed was a trunk. Inside were extra bed linens and two quilts. In the wall next to the bed was a tall window with a low seat.

Kathleen stood in the center of the room, turning slowly in each direction. She hardly dared to believe she had a haven all to herself.

Not knowing how soon Mrs. Nichols would come for her, she quickly poured water from the pitcher into the basin, stripped off her shift. The cold water made her shiver.

Once finished, she debated about what to wear. The maid's uniform must be returned. Assuming Mrs. Nichols would provide her with a uniform, she decided on her simple calico as the best choice.

A glance out the window told her that it was past dawn. She wondered what was keeping Mrs. Nichols. At the Pratts she would have had several chores accomplished by now. The boarders must have jobs to get to. Wouldn't they be awaiting breakfast? And what of dinner? Mr. Linton and Ned brought theirs with them to the factory. Would she be expected to pack dinners for all the boarders? If so, she'd need to get started. She considered heading for the kitchen, but remembered Mrs. Nichols stern tone. Perhaps the lady preferred she not rummage the kitchen on her own.

Kathleen removed the contents of her sack, laying everything on her bed. Finding the comb and brush, she returned to the large oval looking glass above the washstand. She'd pulled her hair down from its bun the night before, but never brushed it. Now it was a tangled mess. She unraveled the mats then brushed her long hair until it gleamed. Gathering up the abundant mass, she piled and secured it atop her head.

Next, she decided to put away her few possessions: comb and brush atop the lower shelf of the chest, her bonnets set side-by-side in its deepest drawers, her cloak upon a hook beside the door. Her two fine dresses were carefully laid atop the bed linens in the trunk. Kathleen tucked her rosary into the calico's pocket. The hated uniform hung from one of the carved pineapples topping a bedpost.

She gathered up the three volumes of copied receipts she'd accumulated during her time at the Pratts', eager to put them to use in her new position. Her extra paper and pen and ink pots went into yet other drawers in the chest. That left only the books. Clara had given *Uncle Tom's Cabin* to her as a gift, but the other three were loans. She supposed she'd have to return them with the uniform. Yet she was only part way through *Jane Eyre*. The other two she had yet to begin. She hadn't struck up an acquaintance with their characters yet, but Jane had become a friend and she wanted to finish her story. Taking a sheet of paper, pen and ink from the drawer, she wrote:

Dearest Miss Clara,
Since I am no longer employed by your family, I am returning the books you
loaned to me. I am thankful for your kindness. I hope you won't mind terribly

if I keep Jane Eyre until I have finished. I promise to return it as soon as I

am done. The others I have not begun so I would not miss them as much. I

hope and pray you are well soon.
Ever your loving servant,
Kathleen O'Connor

Kathleen tucked the note inside one of the books, then took *Jane Eyre* to the window seat while she awaited Mrs. Nichols.

The sun's position in the sky told her it was about half past eight when a knock finally sounded on her door.

"Good morning, Kathleen. I trust you slept well."

"Very well, thank you."

"Good. Now let us begin your first day. You are much taller than my last help. I'll have to get new uniforms for you. Meanwhile use these," she said, holding out an apron and cap.

In the light of day, Kathleen could finally get a good look at Mrs. Nichols. She was a handsome woman with dark, curly hair, large dark eyes with long lashes and well-shaped brows. Her upper lip was a nearly straight line with the lower one being quite full, like a tiny half-moon. She had a rounded face, straight nose, and a long, graceful neck. Overall her face gave the appearance of kindness, but something in her black eyes intimated a self-assurance that bordered on dominance. She was only slightly shorter than Kathleen, but broader across the shoulders. She carried herself with a regal bearing.

Mrs. Nichols glanced at the uniform hanging from the bedpost. Following her gaze, Kathleen said, "That belongs to the family I just left. I promised I'd return it today, though I'm not sure how to get it back to them."

"The same boy who obtains the ice also runs errands. He can take it back, if you give me the address." She removed the uniform from the bedpost.

"These books, too, along with this note," said Kathleen, showing the folded paper inside one of the books.

"Fine. Jonah will do it before the day is out. It's time you became familiar with the house."

Seeing the kitchen in the light of day, Kathleen was even more enraptured than she'd been the night before. She longed to rummage through every drawer and cupboard.

"The boarders will be wanting breakfast, but we've still time for a quick tour. Follow me, please," said Mrs. Nichols leading her towards the door at the far end of the kitchen.

"They eat breakfast so late? I'd have thought they'd be to work by now."

Just before opening the door, Mrs. Nichols turned back, her dark eyes boring into Kathleen's. "It is better for you not to ask too many questions."

Kathleen had not thought her puzzlement undue. Mrs. Nichols' visage softened. "Of course, you're perplexed. The ladies who board here have had, shall we say, difficult lives. That is why I take them in. They do not go out to work."

"But how do they earn their living?"

"They work from here. It is their business what they do. That is enough said."

Though more curious than ever, it would not do to pry. Kathleen silently followed her new mistress through the door, down a short hallway, up a flight of stairs, and through another door which opened upon the dining room.

"We are now in the main section of the house. This is where all meals are served. For your convenience I will have a cart placed in the hallway, if I can find out where it's gotten to. That way you can wheel the food down the hall and only have to carry it up the stairs. The table settings are kept in this room."

Two large tables dominated the center of the room with only a narrow aisle between them. The places had already been set for breakfast, one table for four, the other for five.

"I assume it will take you some time to find your way around the kitchen, this being your first morning here, so I set the tables myself, a total of nine settings. There are eight boarders. I eat with them."

"Where are the place settings kept?" asked Kathleen looking about at the dining room's furniture.

"Here," said Mrs. Nichols, leading the way across the wide plank floor toward a large fireplace in which sat a coal stove providing heat. The walls were recessed on either side. In one recess stood a tall hutch. On its three shelves were serving platters, dishes, cups, and a set of pewter tankards with a matching soup tureen. Two doors enclosed the lower end of the hutch. Mrs. Nichols opened them to reveal a well-stocked supply of table linens. Then she took Kathleen to the recess on the other side of the fireplace. In it was a two-tiered wooden cart upon which were stacked plates of varying sizes, coffee and teacups with saucers, and utensils.

To the right of the cart was a large pocket door painted a reddish brown to match the fireplace mantel, the color complimenting the yellow diamond patterned wallpaper. Mrs. Nichols slid open the door to reveal a deep cupboard in which resided a large antique sideboard.

"You will place all the filled serving dishes here," she said patting the top of the sideboard. "You needn't serve nor stay behind while we eat. We are all capable of putting food on our own plates. Once all the food has been brought in, you may return to the kitchen for your own meal."

"My own meal?"

Mrs. Nichols cocked her head. "You do eat?"

"Aye. Whatever is left once the family is done."

Mrs. Nichols raised her eyebrows. "How long were you at your last position?"

"Three years."

"And you survived on the family's remnants?"

"It was enough. I...I came from Ireland."

"Stop." Mrs. Nichols put her hand on Kathleen's arm. "I've heard all about the tragedy in Ireland. Given to the Irish relief fund." The large dark eyes held Kathleen's with such compassion that despite her embarrassment, she could not look away. "You needn't explain. Always make a full meal for yourself. You will not go hungry in my employ, nor will you be relegated to eating anyone's leavings."

Kathleen felt tears prick her eyes. Mrs. Nichols turned away to continue her tour. She led Kathleen to a door opposite the one they had entered, which opened into a parlor. The room's walls had been painted a cream color. Scattered about the wide plank floor were a few soft green carpets. Two side-by-side floor-to-ceiling windows were hung with moss green draperies and topped with cream brocade valances. The room's furniture consisted of one desk, three round tables each with its own oil lamp, and several chairs. An air of calm pervaded the room, lending itself to the pursuit of quiet studies.

"This is our bible parlor. We gather here each Sunday to read and discuss scripture passages. We also pray together and sing hymns. I realize that as a Catholic you may not wish to join us, but please know that if you ever have something you'd like us to pray for, we will be happy to add it to our prayer list."

"Thank you." Kathleen was on the verge of asking if the boarders didn't go to church, but remembering Mrs. Nichols' injunction, changed her mind.

"The doors to this room remain closed," Mrs. Nichols explained. "No one is allowed in here other than the boarders and me. And you of course, as you'll need to clean it. This room is special to us. We keep it private."

"Yes, Ma'am."

Mrs. Nichols closed the door behind her. They were now in the front entry. They crossed before a large staircase opposite the main door to enter another parlor, in which resided the simple furnishings of a comfortable sofa, chairs, side tables, and a large fireplace.

"This is the reception room. If anyone comes to the door wishing to see me this is the room to which you bring them. Nowhere else. They may wait here while you find me."

"Yes, Ma'am."

Next Mrs. Nichols led Kathleen to a door near the back of the room. Before opening it, she stopped. "Before I show you these last two rooms, I want you to understand that we occasionally do some entertaining, all of which takes place

253

in the evening. All preparations for our...events are handled by me. You will not be required to take part in any way. In fact, you will be in your own chamber by the time any entertainment has commenced."

Kathleen noticed that during this speech Mrs. Nichols did not look directly at her, eyes cast somewhere between the wall and the floor. It gave her an odd feeling to which she could not put a name.

Mrs. Nichols drew herself up, returning to her regal bearing before opening the door.

She led Kathleen into the first room of a double parlor. The floor was covered by a large red and gold patterned carpet. The windows were graced by rich red draperies flecked with gold and topped with gold valences. Instead of paint, the walls were covered in a busily patterned paper filled with reds, golds, and forest greens. The riot of patterns and colors made Kathleen dizzy.

The room was filled with sofas, divans, well upholstered chairs, marble topped tables, and a piano. Kathleen had never seen so much furniture in one room. A large alcove lay just beyond, the wallpaper and floor covering carrying through from the larger room. The smaller room contained one table and a few chairs. Behind them stood a mysterious piece of large furniture.

"What is this?" Kathleen asked, stepping up to the tall cabinet against the wall.

It was like nothing she'd ever seen. Ornately carved with the faces of lions nestled amongst a swirling pattern of oak leaves and curlicues, the cabinet seemed of two pieces. The bottom had two carved doors, the top a large glass window. Peering inside, Kathleen saw a multitude of glassware. Upon closer inspection she realized it was not a window, but a glass door with a faceted crystal knob. The oddest thing to Kathleen were the four matching embellishments. All were identical women made of metal. Rather they were half women as the maker had forged not full bodies, but only from the waist up. They were naked and large breasted. Two were on either side of the glass door, the other two beside either of the lower doors.

"That is a spirits cabinet." Mrs. Nichols pulled a small key from her pocket. Unlocking the lower doors, she opened them to reveal an army of bottles.

"I keep the only key to this cabinet," Mrs. Nichols told her. "You'll keep the outside well dusted, the glass door clean, and the glasses sparkling. Oh, and do be cautious when you enter this room. People can be absentminded at times, and glasses get broken. Take care not to cut yourself."

"Yes, Ma'am." Kathleen's earlier sense of relief and delight was beginning to diminish. She had only a rudimentary idea of boarding houses, but she did not believe the average one held such mysterious conventions. Another idea was beginning to surface.

Leaving the double parlors, they returned to the entry hall.

"Follow me and please pay close attention," said Mrs. Nichols as she stood on the lowest step of the wide staircase. "What I am about to show you is of utmost importance."

They climbed the stairs, stopping at the landing where the stairway turned the corner. A small table over which hung a painting of pheasants in an autumnal setting of birch trees and tall grass adorned the landing. Mrs. Nichols stopped before the table, turning towards Kathleen.

"This is as far as your duties will ever take you." She pointed to the shorter flight of stairs that led to the second floor. "Up there are the boarders' rooms. Their privacy is absolute. You are never to go beyond this landing. You may only come this far to dust the table and clean the staircase. The upper floors are cared for by the boarders themselves so your services are not needed. Is that fully understood?"

"Aye, 'tis," Kathleen answered, slipping unawares into her brogue as her mind was busy trying to conjure what really went on in this house.

"Excellent," said Mrs. Nichols. "Let's head back to the kitchen and get on with breakfast."

Chapter Twenty-Seven

Meg slept little Sunday night. Her mind would not stop evoking the worst images of what could have happened to Kathleen. She arose Monday morning feeling as though she'd been trampled by a horse. She went about her morning chores, eyes half shut. The Beast tried her patience more than usual. She scorched the first batch of pancakes, threw them out and began again. What plagued her was the piercing anxiety of being without answers or a way to obtain them. Trembling limbs caused the muscles of her legs to grow so tight they ached. Shaking hands refused their normal functioning, resulting in many dropped items. Distracted thoughts caused mistakes in the simplest of tasks.

As she cleared the breakfast table, she heard Deborah whisper to Mrs. Claprood, "What's wrong with Margaret?"

Meg did not wait to hear Mrs. Claprood's response. She set about preparing to wash the dishes, trying desperately to keep herself busy.

"Would you like to rest, Margaret?" asked Mrs. Claprood entering the kitchen a moment later. "You mustn't have slept well."

"You are very kind to offer, Ma'am, but it's best I keep busy."

"Then let me help you. Being alone with troubled thoughts only magnifies them." Donning an apron, Mrs. Claprood assisted Meg with the dishes, after which she insisted Meg rest.

"Margaret, you've broken three dishes. You must take some rest before we have to purchase an entirely new set of dinnerware." Her voice was stern, but there was such compassion in her eyes that Meg wanted to hug her. Instead she nodded, thanked her, and headed for her attic chamber.

Sleep was not coming. She pulled her rosary from her pocket and knelt to pray for Kathleen. She was deep into the fourth decade, calmed to the point of almost drifting off when she was jolted from her languorous state by a loud rap on her door.

"Margaret? There's news of your sister," Mrs. Claprood called.

Meg flew to the door.

"A boy came by with a note from Kathleen," she said, holding out a piece of folded paper.

In it, Kathleen briefly related how she'd met a woman who owned a boarding house and had hired her on the spot. She would have to work Thursdays, but would see her at Mass on Sunday. Relief flooded through Meg. Kathleen was safe! And already employed! A giddy laugh escaped as she read Kathleen's last sentence. *I've my own room and the kitchen is the grandest I've ever seen.*

"Good news?" asked Mrs. Claprood.

"She's well," Meg said, happy tears sliding down her face. "And working at a boarding house."

"Thank the Lord," said Mrs. Claprood.

"Aye, indeed" Meg answered looking at the rosary beads pressing into her palm.

"Where is the boarding house?"

Meg turned the letter over, but there was no address. "She does not say. I'll find out on Sunday when I see her at Mass."

"Wonderful news!" Mrs. Claprood threw her arms around Meg, rejoicing with her.

"Chester will be relieved. He's been terribly worried. He told me he would go to the police station every day."

"He did?"

Mrs. Claprood nodded. "Margaret, you've become like family to us. I hope you feel the same."

A stab of guilt pierced Meg. She felt affectionate towards the Claproods. Yet she had never told them of her marriage.

"I am so grateful," she said. "I could not have wished for a kinder family to work for."

"I'm glad to hear that. We hope to keep you with us for a very long time."

The arrow of guilt drove deeper into Meg's heart. For a moment she considered telling Mrs. Claprood of Rory, but fear held her back.

She squeezed her mistress' hands. "I'm so relieved about Kathleen, I feel light as a feather. I think I could clean the house from top to bottom while dancing a jig."

Mrs. Claprood laughed. "That would be a sight to see, but I think you'd better forego the dancing, especially if any of my dishes are in close proximity."

* * *

Meg rushed to Saint John's on Sunday, not even stopping for Nuala. She had so many questions to ask. At the church she found the pew she shared with Kathleen and their friends still empty. After genuflecting towards the tabernacle, she knelt, her prayers full of thanksgiving for Kathleen's safety.

A tap on her shoulder brought Father Boyce into view.

"Have you heard anything of your sister, Meg?"

Realization dawned. She'd failed to tell any but Nuala on Thursday.

"Father, I'm so sorry. I should have come to you. She's found a position in a boarding house. I've not seen her since, but she will be here for Mass."

"Praise to our good Lord, but that is wonderful news!"

More parishioners entered the church. Seamus made his way to her. "Any news of Kathleen?" he whispered.

"Aye, she's safe, but how did you know she went missing?"

"Father Gilbert and Father Boyce put the word out. Every Irish man and woman in Worcester's been on the lookout. I'm glad to hear all is well, though I'm surprised no one spotted her."

"She found work right away, but I don't know the details yet."

"Tell her that the next time she runs off to mention it to someone so the parish doesn't have to turn the whole city upside down!" He smiled and winked before heading towards his usual pew.

Chill air hit Meg's back as throngs of parishioners entered in quick succession. She scanned the crowd for her sister's face. Seeing Kathleen she jumped to her feet, nearly knocking the white lace veil from her head. They met in a happy embrace.

"Kathleen, I was so relieved to get your note. Why didn't you tell me what happened that night?"

"Ah, is this the missing lass, then?" asked a man trying to pass them in the narrow aisle.

"Missing no longer," said Meg, grabbing Kathleen's arm to tug her into the pew.

"Saints be praised," said the man before continuing up the aisle.

"What was that about?" asked Kathleen.

"We've all been so frightened for you. Mr. Claprood went looking at the Lintons. When you weren't there, he and Mr. Linton went to the police. Then he brought me here to see if you'd come to the church. The priests spread the word. Seamus says the whole parish has been looking for you."

"They have?"

"Indeed and why has no one seen you in an entire week?"

"This is the first I've left."

"Where is this boarding house? Who is your employer?"

Before Kathleen could answer, the entire Linton family arrived.

"Kathleen!" Mrs. Linton exclaimed. "Where have you been?"

"I sent Meg a note. Didn't anyone tell you?"

Meg and Kathleen scooted down the pew to let in the newcomers.

"We've heard nothing. We've been worried sick."

"I'm so sorry Mrs. Linton," Meg said, leaning forward to look at the others. "I was so relieved when I got Kathleen's note that I forgot everything else. It was thoughtless of me."

Mrs. Linton and Mrs. O'Sullivan fell to hugging Kathleen and thanking God for her safety.

Upon the Lintons' insistence, all gathered in their rooms after Mass to hear Kathleen's story, marveling at her good fortune at finding a new position so quickly.

"It's as though God dropped Mrs. Nichols in your path," Aoife remarked.

"Wish he would put employment in the path of some others," Ned mumbled under his breath. Meg caught the look Aoife flashed him. Others from the Merrifield fire were finding jobs, but as Mrs. O'Sullivan could not stand on her feet for long, her options were limited. She took in laundry, but it paid little. In Mrs. O'Sullivan's downcast face, Meg saw the woman's embarrassment in not being able to do more to assist her daughter's growing family.

"Where is the boarding house located?" Mrs. Linton asked Kathleen.

"On a little side street, not far from the church. I walked to Mass in only a few minutes. Isn't that grand? And I have all day Sunday to myself, though I do have to work on Thursdays."

"What will you do with your Sundays?" asked Nuala.

"I hope you'll spend some with us," said Aoife. "You can be auntie to little Darragh," she said, gently bouncing the infant on her lap.

Smiling, Kathleen held out her arms for the baby, snuggling him close. "Such a good wee lad," she said. "We'll soon become the best of friends."

Meg said little during the visit at the Lintons. It bothered her that Kathleen evaded giving a direct answer about the location of the boarding house. Though she appeared sound and happy, rhapsodized over the grand kitchen, and spoke well of her new mistress, something was not right.

"It's time we got back," Nuala announced. "Some of us have to work of a Sunday," she said, giving Kathleen a playful chuck on the shoulder.

"Kathleen, walk out with us," said Meg as she rose to join Nuala.

Kathleen handed the baby back to Aoife. Once outside, Meg took Kathleen's hands in her own. "What is it you don't want to tell?" she asked, looking hard at Kathleen.

"What do you mean?" The high pitch and darting away of her eyes confirmed Meg's suspicions.

"I understand if you don't want to say in front of the others, but you can tell me."

"Should I walk on?" asked Nuala.

"No," Kathleen answered. "It's naught of consequence."

"So there is something. Tell."

Kathleen sighed. "Things are different at the boarding house."

"Different how?" asked Meg.

"I must go to my room at nine of the clock every evening but Sunday and I'm never to step foot upon the second floor."

"That is a bit odd," Nuala conceded, "but could it be that rules in a boarding house are such that the boarders are not to be bothered at certain times?"

Kathleen shrugged. "That is not all."

"What else?" asked Meg.

Kathleen cast her gaze downward, kicked at a loose stone.

"Kathleen?" asked Meg.

"None of the boarders have outside jobs. I've seen some mending. Two do all the laundry, for which I am grateful. Otherwise, I see nothing that would bring an income. Yet Mrs. Nichols maintains a large house with fine

261

furnishings. She's raised my pay from the Pratts as she says my cooking is far better than she expected. All the ladies praise it." At this Kathleen's smile returned, lighting up her face.

"How do they afford to stay there?" asked Meg.

"I don't know."

"It's their concern," said Nuala. "If Mrs. Nichols is good to you and you are happy, don't question it."

"I wouldn't except that..."

"Except what?" asked Meg.

Kathleen's brow furrowed. "They often entertain in the evening. You should see the rooms they use for it – a jumble of colors and patterns and you never saw so many couches and chairs. You'd think all Worcester was expected to descend upon them. Then there's a strange cabinet full of glasses and bottles of liquor."

"Sounds like Mrs. Nichols is a social bird," said Nuala. "Must you serve at these functions?"

"That's just the thing. I must be in my bed chamber before these entertainments even begin. It's a strict rule. As my chamber is on the other end of the house, I can't hear the goings on. But I see the result the next morning."

"What result?" asked Nuala.

"Empty bottles lined up on the cabinet shelf. Glasses all over the rooms. The smell of liquor and tobacco so thick I open the windows to air it out no matter the chill. I dread the winter. I'll freeze while I work in there."

Unbidden, Meg's thoughts returned to a moment of weakness in Ireland when she'd entered a tavern in hopes of selling her comb for passage money. The tavern was thick with smoke, the smell of ale, and the bawdy talk of men and the women they chose to buy for an hour's entertainment. *But that was a tavern*, she told herself. *This is a boarding house.*

"Open the windows first thing," Nuala counseled Kathleen. "Close the door, then do your other work. When you go back, the rooms should be aired sufficiently. It will still be cold, but at least you can close the windows while you're in there."

"Kathleen, where is this boarding house?" Meg demanded.

"Not too far from the church."

"No. I mean exactly where is it? On what street?"

"I can't remember the name." The words were barely audible.

"That's a lie and you know it. Were you ordered not to tell the location?"

"Meg, I'm happy there. Mrs. Nichols is kind. I can cook in the grandest kitchen. I cannot have guests. It's one of the rules. I so long to show you both the kitchen and the bedchamber that's my very own. But that and not having Thursdays off are the only bad things. Nuala's right. It is not my business what the boarders do nor how Mrs. Nichols entertains her guests."

"Kathleen, where exactly is this house?" Meg demanded. "What if there is an emergency and I need to find you quickly?"

"I can't, Meg. I'm going back to visiting our friends. You'd better get on your way else you'll be late."

Kathleen stalked toward the Arcade. Nuala placed herself in the way.

"Kathleen. What if Meg and I promise not to tell a soul where the house is nor to ever show up there except in the case of the most dire emergency?"

Kathleen looked over Nuala's head at Meg. "Do you promise?"

Meg set her chin. "I promise."

"143 Cherry Street. Not a soul, mind you." Kathleen turned on her heel.

Meg and Nuala watched her disappear into the Arcade.

"Ready to go?" Meg asked.

"Aye," said Nuala. "What do you make of Kathleen's new position?"

"Something's not right about it."

"She likes it, though, despite the odd rules. Certainly Mrs. Nichols treats her a sight better than Mrs. Pratt ever did."

"I don't want Kathleen to get caught up in anything disgraceful."

"Disgraceful?"

"Entertainment evenings leaving spilled spirits and the smell of cigars? No one works to pay their board? I'm thinking it's another kind of house all together."

"A brothel?"

"'Tis my fear."

As they neared Saint John's, Meg stopped a passerby to ask the location of Cherry Street.

"Meg, we promised," Nuala reminded her.

"I only promised I would not tell anyone the location or visit when Kathleen is there. If anyone from the house sees us – "

"Us?" Nuala asked, her head tipped.

"Are you coming?"

Nuala laughed. "Do you need to ask?"

Should anyone have taken note, they'd have seen two well-dressed young ladies strolling down Cherry Street. The morning was mild for early November. They passed on the opposite side of the street, examining the house from various angles. All but the back was visible. It was more massive than the Claprood or Denton homes and well kept. Its large front porch was supported by white pillars in an attempt to resemble a Greek temple, a hallmark of many of the nicer Worcester homes. The unusual aspect was the color. Rather than the murky white of its neighbors, the house was painted red, the window shutters black, the pillars and door frame a crisp, stark white. Two windows sporting elaborate white frames protruded from the third floor, their curved tops and elaborate carvings a contrast with the no-nonsense rectangular windows of the lower two floors. Two brick chimneys rose above the house.

Meg and Nuala walked to the end of the street, crossed, then turned back, appearing to be enjoying the air with a leisurely stroll. Not a soul was in sight. On their return trip, they got a better look at another porch, much smaller than the front's, but echoing its white columns and flat roof.

"The place looks respectable enough," said Nuala.

"Tis quiet."

"Perhaps they're all at church."

"Or still asleep," said Meg.

"Will you tell Kathleen your suspicions?"

"No. I've no proof and she's happy. Kathleen's not stupid. If it is a brothel she'll figure it out."

"Do you think she'll leave even if it's so?"

Meg sighed. "This country, this life. It's changed me. I believe it's changed Kathleen, too."

"So you think she'll stay?"

"If she's to remain a maidservant, then, aye, she might."

"It could get raided by the police. Kathleen could claim she's the maid but most won't believe her. She'd be hard pressed to find another position after that."

Meg stared at the house as if her eyes could penetrate the walls.

"I can't let her be dragged down into such a disgrace. Oh, what Mam would think of us both! If only there was some way to know for sure."

Chapter Twenty-Eight

"Do you celebrate Thanksgiving?" Kathleen asked Mrs. Nichols who had just returned from the market. It was mid-November, yet there had been no mention of the holiday.

"Yes, in fine style," she answered, beaming.

"None of the ladies go to family?"

"We are family to one another."

"Will your family come?"

Mrs. Nichols shook her head. "I've no one." The luster of her smile diminished.

"Might you give me a list of all the food you'll be wanting?"

"Did you do all the work of Thanksgiving in your last position?"

"No. The family went to Mrs. Pratt's relations. Stayed a whole week. I always went to the Claproods to help my sister, Meg. They've a houseful what with Mrs. Claprood's brother and his family descending on them."

"Does Meg know she'll need to do without you this year?"

"I've not said anything, not knowing what was expected of me here. She probably assumes I won't be able to come." A melancholy descended upon Kathleen.

"You relish that time with your sister?"

"Aye. Other than Thursdays and Sunday mornings it was the only time we had. A whole week under the same roof. 'Tis the grandest time of the whole year for us both."

"And you've lost Thursdays." Mrs. Nichols spoke quietly.

"I've nothing to complain of, Ma'am. This kitchen is a dream. And a room to myself? Aye, but that's something I never expected."

"I'm glad you're content, but sorry about the loss of your Thursdays. I will need you for Thanksgiving, but perhaps you can spend a few days to help your sister. The Claproods' company stays on after the day itself?"

"They do. The girls get up sleighing parties, taffy pulls, all sorts of shenanigans! Thanksgiving Day is just the start of festivities."

"It's settled then. If Mrs. Claprood approves you may go on Friday and stay through Sunday."

"Thank you!"

"My pleasure. However, there's much to be done here. I'll make that list. Don't worry that the day will all be on your shoulders. You will have help."

"Who?"

"Us, of course."

Kathleen's brow furrowed. "Us?"

"We are the only family many of us have. We'll all work together, cleaning the house as well as preparing the food. I hope you don't mind a lot of company in your kitchen."

The boarders rarely came into the kitchen. Kathleen mainly saw them when she brought meals into the dining room. She'd only spoken with a few in passing. Other than Tilda and Nessie who did the laundry, she barely knew any of their names.

"They all help?"

"Indeed. I'll gather the girls today to assign them cleaning duties. The household gathers in the kitchen and we bake for hours on end the whole week before Thanksgiving. You never heard so much chatter and laughing. It's everyone's favorite time. And this year, you my dear, will reign as our queen of the kitchen."

Mrs. Nichols was not mistaken in her description of pie baking week. It was a good thing the kitchen was large, what with ten women working in it at once. They could

267

probably have done with half, but no one wanted to be left out. Kathleen set some to paring and coring apples, some to peeling and mashing squash, some to rolling out dough, some to pounding sugar and grating spices, others to mixing ingredients. She, herself, presided over the stove.

The two stoves had specific uses. The smaller one heated irons on wash days or boiled water for tea and coffee. The larger one, the one she'd come to think of as her faithful ally, was for the heavy work. It was like no other. Made of cast iron, it had a built-in tin oven in the front with a removable door for the purpose of allowing the meat to roast as it would over an open fire. There were grates for wood and coal, ash sifters and devices to grade chunks of fuel. Boilers on top of the stove led to a complex system of pipes that carried hot smoke from the fire, heating water along the way. There were also warming closets for heating plates, keeping food warm, and drying fruit. A raised tin lid enclosed the heat radiating from the stove, allowing for more baking space. A variety of flues, insulators, and dampers provided hotter, longer lasting, less smoky fires. Once Kathleen had unraveled the intricacies of the stove, her fascination for all its variations captivated her. She could barely stand to leave it long enough to complete her other tasks.

The house had no planned entertainments the week leading up to Thanksgiving and would remain quiet until the Monday following the holiday. This gave Kathleen a respite from cleaning up the remnants of whatever diversions took place after she was ensconced in her room for the night. That, and the help of the boarders with autumnal cleaning allowed Kathleen to focus all her energies on food preparation.

Glory be to God, who could have ever dreamed this, thought Kathleen, beaming at the coterie of women working at the kitchen tables, looking to her for direction. Even Mrs. Nichols deferred to her judgment. The women chatted endlessly while they worked, giggling as much as the Claprood girls and their cousins.

Buckets piled up with apple peelings and cores, mountains of dough were rolled out to fit the multitude of pie pans, the tables and floor were liberally dusted with cinnamon, mace, sugar, and nutmeg. Stray raisins had to be watched for lest they be squashed underfoot. Smiles, laughter, and a cacophony of voices filled the room along with the scent of baking dough, warm apples, and cloves. Keeping the oven at just the right temperature was an arduous task Kathleen would relinquish to no one.

Kathleen could not remember when she had been so busy, or as happy as she was as Queen of her kitchen, for she had come to think of it as hers. Everyone was in a jolly mood the whole week. She felt that there was more to the cheerfulness of the boarders than mere anticipation of the holiday. Their effervescence, she felt sure, stemmed from something deeper, though she could not place its source. The devastation of her own past and the second chance she'd been miraculously given allowed her to discern in the women a similar experience. It was but a feeling, a knowing without knowing that could come only with a sympathetic kinship.

By the second day of pie baking week, Kathleen had learned the names of all the boarders. She conversed with all, good naturedly bantered with some, and felt the beginnings of a bond that swelled her heart. Kathleen remembered Mrs. Nichols' words about the women having all come from difficult pasts. Though still mystified by many of the workings and rules of the house, she felt sure that Mrs. Nichols was a worthy caretaker. For all her worldly ambition and self-righteousness, Kathleen felt sure, Mrs. Pratt could not hold a candle to the integrity of Mrs. Nichols.

"Would you look at this, Kathleen," called Diana, a young woman with dark hair and eyes who had a way of looking up under her long lashes that suggested a saucy character.

Kathleen left her post at the stove to approach the group of women at one of the tables laughing uproariously.

"Can you tell Amelia likes to talk so much she can't keep her mind on what she's doing?" Diana asked.

Kathleen looked at the dough lined pie pan in front of Amelia.

"I think she's trying to invent a new pie," said Rose.

Kathleen peered into the mixing bowl. Peelings and cores were well stirred with cinnamon, nutmeg, and clove. Far from being embarrassed, Amelia was overcome with laughter.

"What on earth?" asked Kathleen.

"I was talking," said Amelia when she could catch her breath.

By now, the whole kitchen erupted in laughter. Amelia loved to talk. Kathleen could picture her gabbing away while mixing the peelings and cores with the spices, never realizing her mistake until she was ready to pour it into the crust. Diana had noticed just as Amelia was about to lay a lattice work crust atop it.

If pie baking week was a surprise to Kathleen, Thanksgiving Day was astonishing. Up before dawn she boiled, plucked, and roasted the turkey and chickens Mrs. Nichols purchased at the market. She made a light breakfast for everyone, cleaned it up, and returned to preparations for the great feast. Long before dinnertime the kitchen once again bustled with activity. All the boarders and Mrs. Nichols scurried to and fro, setting the table, making sure all platters, dishes and utensils were at the ready. When it finally came time to serve the meal, the boarders helped Kathleen by carrying the many dishes to the dining room.

As the last of the food left the kitchen, Kathleen stopped Mrs. Nichols. Her mistress had always had Kathleen set out the food then leave the boarders to serve themselves. Mrs. Nichols had given no different instructions today, but Kathleen wanted to be sure.

"Would you like me to remain in the dining room throughout dinner, Mrs. Nichols?" she asked.

"Of course," she replied.

Several times Kathleen had seen Meg carry the turkey on its magnificent platter, raising it above her head in triumph as she entered the Claprood's dining room. For the first time, Kathleen would bear the bird to its place of honor. She donned a fresh apron for the occasion.

Kathleen was grateful for the wheeled cart that took the heavy bird along the hallway. Managing the stairs was a bit tricky with the weighty burden, but she did so without mishap. Just before crossing the threshold, she lifted the platter high. A collective utterance of acclaim reverberated through the room. She set the platter before Mrs. Nichols, moved the carving set within the woman's reach. It was then that she noticed Jonah, Mrs. Nichols' errand boy seated at the table. Was he an orphan? How good of Mrs. Nichols to include him.

Once the bird was set down, Kathleen retreated towards the heavily laden tables.

"Where are you going, Kathleen?" Mrs. Nichols asked.

"Here to the serving tables, Ma'am. You did say you wanted me to stay for the meal?"

Mrs. Nichols pushed back her chair. Rising, she faced Kathleen. "Indeed I did, but not as a servant. Please," said Mrs. Nichols, holding her hand out towards a full table setting before an empty seat to her right.

"Ma'am?"

"You will join us, won't you?"

Slowly, she made her way towards the long table.

Kathleen stared at her mistress, bewildered. "I don't understand. Am I not to serve?"

"No. We want you to join us."

Kathleen surveyed the faces of the women at the table. Most were smiling at her, a few had curious expressions as though they could not fathom her resistance.

"You don't have to, of course," said Mrs. Nichols. "But we very much hope you will."

A flushed feeling settled over Kathleen. "I'd like that very much," she said, her voice a husky whisper as she lowered herself into the wooden chair. Feeling awkward, she dared not look up from her place setting.

"Now then, let us join hands," said Mrs. Nichols, reaching out to take Kathleen's. Amelia, seated to the right of Kathleen took up the chain.

Mrs. Nichols began, "Good and gracious God, we give you thanks for keeping us all safe and in good health. We thank you for the bonds of friendship we have formed as we've lived and worked together. We thank you for bringing Kathleen to us. She has been a true blessing."

Kathleen, startled by the words, glanced up, fearing any looks of displeasure, but instead found only placid faces and nodding agreement.

"We also thank you for the bounty placed before us this day as well as the sustenance you provide for us every day. We ask you to bless this food and all of us gathered here to share this joyous feast together. Amen."

Hands disengaged as the women echoed Mrs. Nichols' *amen*. Kathleen involuntarily crossed herself as she uttered "Amen." If anyone noticed, they made no mention of it or gave any sign of disapproval.

Mrs. Nichols proceeded to carve the turkey, laying a slice on each plate as it was passed to her. Then the various dishes circulated, plates piling high with food. Gradually, as she savored the variety of flavors dancing on her tongue, Kathleen was drawn into the conversation. The easy camaraderie of pie baking week returned, melting away her awkwardness. Before the meal was half over, Kathleen was as talkative as anyone, comfortable in the presence of people who accepted her for herself.

Chapter Twenty-Nine

Meg awoke exhausted the day after Thanksgiving. For the past three years she'd had Kathleen. More than ever she appreciated her sister's constantly growing skill at cookery. Somehow she had managed to get through the day with everyone well pleased. Even more than Kathleen's help, Meg missed their private Thanksgiving dinner in the kitchen after duties. It was a lonely meal she ate that year. The one bright spot was the knowledge that Kathleen would arrive soon to remain through Sunday.

Meg had barely finished cleaning up from breakfast when Kathleen knocked at the kitchen door.

Meg had expected her sister to be worn out, too. Instead, she was rosy-cheeked, her broad smile radiating up to her gleaming blue eyes.

That evening after the youngest Amberson children had been put to bed, the rest of the Claprood and Amberson families gathered in the parlor. Deborah and the elder Amberson daughters retreated to the conservatory, but for once, Pamela did not join them. Instead, she seated herself with the adults. A week prior Edward Thayer had requested and received permission from Mr. Claprood to court his eldest daughter. Pamela now inserted herself into the realm of adults, preparing to take her place one day as wife and mother.

Meg and Kathleen sat in a nearby room engaged in mending work, yet ready to jump at the sound of the hand bell Mrs. Claprood kept nearby. In low voices they engaged in their own conversation, Kathleen filling Meg in on pie baking week and the amazing details of Thanksgiving dinner. Meg's mind reeled with the incongruities of the so-called boarding house and the picture Kathleen painted of a benevolent landlady and convivial cluster of women. Suddenly the raised voice of Mr. Amberson caught the attention of both.

"The election of Henry Gardner as Governor will be the downfall of Massachusetts! That rabble-rousing party! And every constitutional state officer, the entire Congressional delegation, all forty state senators, and all but three representatives are Know Nothings. Massachusetts has been taken over. It boggles the mind!"

The hands of both Meg and Kathleen stilled.

"His nomination was a quid pro quo," said Mr. Claprood. "Free Soil votes in exchange for Gardner's promise to back Wilson's bid for the vacant U.S. Senate seat and Burlingame's bid for Congress. Any way you look at it, it's a death blow to the Whigs."

"Gardner's dangerous," offered Mrs. Claprood. "He calls immigrants the greatest threat to Massachusetts. He gives no thought to the horror from which the Irish fled. I can't think what we'd do without our Margaret."

Meg could not help but smile momentarily at Mrs. Claprood's assessment of her.

"I would not worry about losing Margaret, Mother," Oliver stated. "Gardner's full of bluster about nativism, but he was a wool merchant who benefited greatly from cheap foreign labor. He'll focus on his plan to Americanize America, as he calls it, by removing the teaching of all foreign languages and ensure daily readings from the King James Version of the Bible in all public schools."

"He is a former Webster Whig with no love for the abolitionist movement," Mr. Amberson declared. "He even favors the Fugitive Slave Law."

"Outrageous!" Mrs. Claprood's voice went up in pitch. "Such duplicity."

"If he wants to keep the Free Soilers he'll have to make concessions," Oliver asserted.

"It still disturbs me more than I can say that this commonwealth is now ruled by dark lantern politics," said Mr. Amberson.

Seated close, Meg sensed the rigidity in Kathleen's body.

"Do let us change the subject," pleaded Martha Amberson. "This is a jolly time of year."

Meg locked eyes with Kathleen who looked as frightened as Meg felt.

"Meg?" Kathleen asked. "What do they mean by dark lantern?"

"The Know Nothing's opponents use it as a scornful way of describing them. Why?"

"After the first time I heard it I dreamed of Lemuel chasing me with a lantern."

"You are rid of him now."

"I still have that nightmare. It's different each time, but he's always chasing me, always carrying a lantern that casts horrible shadows. They remind me of Mam's dreams."

Their mother had what many called a gift, but what Meg thought of as a curse. Future events revealed themselves to her in a vague form through recurring dreams. A strong feeling accompanied these dreams indicating that they were different from ordinary dreams, that they portended some coming event. Their mam called it having the *feeling*.

"Oh, Kathleen," Meg stated. "If you had the feeling, wouldn't it have begun before now?"

"When did it begin for Mam?"

Meg shrugged. "I never thought to ask."

"What do they mean, these dreams? What's going to happen?"

"Try not to worry," Meg counseled her sister. "More than likely the dreams will go away." Meg wished she could be as sure as she sounded. Their mother's premonitions had never failed.

Saturday afternoon was wet and blustery. The Claprood and Amberson girls remained at home. Working in the parlor, Meg and Kathleen overheard their talk of the Pratt family.

"Is Clara better?" Kathleen asked Meg.

"I believe so, though the Pratts did not go to Concord for Thanksgiving this year, fearing the travel might set her back."

"Could we ask about her?"

"Why not?"

Meg approached the conservatory, Kathleen behind her.

"Miss Deborah, how is Miss Clara faring?"

The five girls clustered around the central table turned their faces towards her.

"She's much better, Margaret. But the Pratts are so concerned they hardly let her out of bed. The poor girl is bored to tears. Come and see the game we're making for her."

Meg and Kathleen peered over their shoulders at the floral books spread on the table. Deborah had divided a large piece of paper with a vertical line down the middle. On one side she was listing the names of various flowers.

"On this side," Deborah said, indicating the blank side of the paper, "I will write the meaning of each, but I won't put them in the same order as the names of the flowers. Clara will have to draw a line from the name of the flower to the correct meaning. And here," she said indicating another paper on which she'd drawn squares with the names of flowers above them, "she can draw a picture of each flower in the box under its name."

"Is Miss Clara interested in the language of flowers, too?" Meg asked.

Deborah giggled. "She is now. We introduced her to the conservatory when she first started visiting. It wasn't long before she became a devotee."

"Her fever is gone?" asked Kathleen.

"Oh, my yes," said Pamela. "Mother's tried telling Mrs. Pratt that the best thing for her is to be up and about as long as she's careful not to overdo. Mrs. Pratt says perhaps next week."

276

"I'd go positively mad if forced to stay in bed while feeling perfectly fine," Deborah lamented.

"Will you go to see her?" Kathleen asked.

"Yes. Aunt and Uncle Amberson are leaving right after church on Sunday. The rest of us are going to visit the Pratts. We'll stay for dinner there. Did mother tell you?" Pamela looked at Meg.

"I'm sure she will." Meg's heart soared at this news. Kathleen did not have to leave until late on Sunday. Once they returned from Mass they would have the house to themselves.

"Would you take something to Clara for me?" Kathleen asked. "She loaned me a book that I've just finished and I'd like to return it to her."

Pamela's eyes widened. Deborah blinked before staring at Kathleen in disbelief. "You can read?" she asked.

"Aye. Miss Clara taught me."

Pamela and Deborah exchanged glances. The Amberson girls, who had been disinterested in the conversation, looked at Kathleen in amazement.

"You were close to Clara, weren't you?" Pamela asked.

Kathleen nodded.

"Is it true you tried to make her into a Catholic?" asked Deborah.

"Deborah!" Pamela exclaimed.

"Well, that's what Mrs. Pratt says."

Kathleen's back stiffened. "I never did any such thing. I prayed my rosary over Miss Clara when she was deep in fever. Prayed for her to get well, I did. Mrs. Pratt threw me out right then and there, thinking I was laying a curse on the lass."

Meg watched the color rise in Kathleen's cheeks. She tugged at her sister's arm.

"Kathleen, fetch the book."

Kathleen clenched her jaw before turning on her heel.

"I didn't mean to upset her," Deborah said. "I shouldn't have asked."

"It's a sore subject," Meg allowed.

277

Returning shortly, Kathleen held out the copy of *Jane Eyre*.

"Oh!" said Deborah. "That's one of my favorites. Did you enjoy it?"

"Very much. Please tell Miss Clara I thank her for the loan."

"I will," said Deborah. "Is there anything else you'd like us to tell her?"

"Only that I miss her and wish her well."

Meg and Kathleen had not been back at their work in the parlor for more than a few minutes when the front door opened. Male voices sounded from the entryway. Kathleen gasped, recognizing one of them as Lemuel's.

"Meg!" she whispered, dropping her dust cloth to grab hold of her sister's arm.

"Go! Through the study and up the back stairs to my chamber."

Once Kathleen left, Meg retrieved the discarded cloth and continued dusting. Inside she was seething. She prayed Lemuel did not enter the parlor as she had the urge to scratch out his eyes. Fortunately, the light-hearted banter between Oliver, Ben, and Lemuel faded away with them. Before they were completely out of earshot, however, Meg heard Lemuel say, "It's a great time to be a citizen of Massachusetts. We'll be rid of the Papist hoard in no time."

Chapter Thirty

By June of 1855 Kathleen's loyalty to her mistress was unshakable. Though Meg had tried to convince her that Mrs. Nichols was not a landlady, but a Madam, the boarding house a brothel, Kathleen refused to believe it. She'd never been so happy in her life. It was not just the joys of the kitchen. It was Mrs. Nichols, with her protective, motherly ways. It was Tilda and Nessie, the live-in laundresses, older than the others, who found joy in taking them under their wings with private chats. It was all the women. They'd become more than boarders for whom she cooked. They'd become friends.

Then there were the Sundays. On a few occasions, instead of going to the Lintons' or to visit Aoife after Mass when illness was rife throughout the Arcade, Kathleen had come back to the boarding house. She spent some time writing letters home, but that could not fill her day completely. So, she would wander into the sections of the house not off limits and catch up on the work she'd had to abandon the prior evening to make her nightly curfew.

One afternoon while polishing the rail of the main staircase outside the closed door of the bible parlor, she could hear Mrs. Nichols' voice as she read the sacred scriptures.

"Which of those two did the will of his Father?"
They said unto him, "The first."

Jesus said unto them, "Verily, I say unto you that the publicans and the harlots go into the Kingdom of God before you."

A murmur of appreciation greeted the end of the scripture passage. Then Mrs. Nichols' asked, "What should we understand from this?"

"Jesus loves us all." This was Amelia's voice.

"Some sinners are worse than prostitutes and tax collectors," came from Rose.

They were studying the scriptures, like good Protestants, Kathleen told herself. Scripture passages Kathleen overheard on other Sundays were about the woman caught in adultery whom Jesus did not condemn, the sinful woman whom Jesus forgave after she bathed his feet with her tears and dried them with her hair. Kathleen stopped cleaning near the bible parlor on Sundays.

It was harder to ignore the daily cleaning in the rooms used for entertaining. The empty liquor bottles, dirty or broken glasses, spills that proper guests didn't make. That and the room bans were the things that she had to close her mind to. Eccentric. Not her place to question. Not her business.

Kathleen deeply suspected the truth. She had been taught that prostitution was a grave sin and prostitutes depraved women. Yet she could not reconcile that with the kindness, warmth, and generosity shown her since the night she'd been wandering the streets of Worcester. She had no real proof and as long as that was true, she could stay. Her mind became agile with excuses to explain away the obvious.

On a warm morning in mid-June, Kathleen stood over the stove preparing breakfast when Amelia, the youngest of the boarders appeared at her elbow.

"You're up early," Kathleen said. The women were usually dragging themselves to the tables as Kathleen brought in their breakfast, some of them still in their dressing gowns.

280

"I wanted to ask you something."

"Oh?"

"Would you teach me to cook?"

Kathleen's mind flew back to pie baking week. Amelia had mixed the spices with the apple peelings and cores.

"Are you sure?"

Amelia blushed. "I'll pay close attention, I promise."

Kathleen, missing Clara's presence in the kitchen, thought how good it would be to have a young assistant.

"Have you asked Mrs. Nichols' leave?"

"Not yet. I wanted to be sure you wouldn't mind first."

"I don't mind a bit. But only with Mrs. Nichols' permission."

A smile spread across Amelia's soft face, lighting up her blue eyes.

Kathleen thought of Clara, now sixteen.

"Amelia, how old are you?" she asked.

"Seventeen."

Just a year older. Kathleen prayed silently that Meg was wrong about this establishment. How could a girl so young be caught up in such a life?

Mrs. Nichols consented. In fact, she seemed happy about the arrangement. Surely Meg was wrong. If Mrs. Nichols was a Madam a pretty young girl like Amelia would be an asset she'd not want to lose. Instead, Mrs. Nichols gave Amelia leave to assist Kathleen all she liked. Amelia rarely got to the kitchen in time to cook breakfast, yet she was always on time to help prepare dinner. As they worked together, Kathleen grew fond of the girl, who was chatty and full of youthful zest yet at the same time had an air about her that indicated she had grown up too fast. Kathleen felt a kindred spirit in her.

"You look tired," Kathleen observed one afternoon as they sat together at the table chopping vegetables.

"It was a long night." Amelia laughed. "Nature of the job, after all."

Kathleen nodded.

"The last gent smelled like wood smoke. I can't abide that smell. After he left, I almost asked Diana if I could change rooms with her, but I wasn't sure if she was done. You can't interrupt, you know."

There it was. Kathleen swallowed the lump in her throat. How could she go on working here while wishing never to leave?

"Do you know if Tilda's done the washing yet?" Amelia asked.

"Aye."

"Not her wash day. She's such a love. She did that for me."

"Why do you hate the smell of wood smoke?" Kathleen asked.

Amelia shrugged. "It reminds me of something bad." She cast her gaze downward. "I've a terrible fear of fire."

"A body would be a fool not to fear it."

Amelia looked up at Kathleen. "It's worse for me."

"Have you been in a fire, then?"

"Yes. It was awful."

"When?"

"A few years ago. It's how I came to be here."

Puzzled, Kathleen asked, "Where did you come from?"

"New York. My mother died giving birth to me. My father put me in an orphanage when I was very young."

Kathleen felt a pang of sorrow. "Your da must have been heartbroken. Hadn't you any brothers or sisters?"

"Just me. And I don't believe my father wanted me anyway."

"Why do you say that?"

"He made his money gambling and robbing people. A baby didn't figure into that way of life."

Kathleen was horrified. "Was it awful to live in an orphanage?"

Amelia shrugged. "I've no memory from before so nothing to compare it to. I had a few good friends. Most of the caretakers were kind. We had food, a roof, and a change of clothes."

"What did they tell you about your parents?"

"That my father cried when he left me there, but said it was for the best."

"He couldn't have been all bad, then. He must have loved you."

"I held onto thinking that my father was out there missing me." Amelia's knife hacked through a head of cabbage. "It was a lie. I wish I was still in the orphanage."

Kathleen reached across the table, placing her hand atop Amelia's. "Careful," she urged gently. "You'll not want to be cutting your fingers off."

"Sorry."

"What do you mean it was a lie?" Kathleen asked.

"When I was fourteen he appeared at the orphanage, told them he was finally in a position to care for me. He wanted me back. Everyone was so excited for me. But I had no memory of this man, yet I was expected to go off with him. He was dressed in his best clothes. Not handsome, but not bad looking, either. But his face was hard, like it was chiseled out of granite. I'll never forget how he acted. 'Amelia! My darling Amelia!' he said and fell to one knee in front of me. 'I've prayed and worked for this day for fourteen years. To have my child back. It's all I've dreamed of.' Oh, he was a smooth one all right. I suppose there was nothing else I could have done even if I had known."

"Known what?" Kathleen asked as Amelia paused.

She sighed. "As we left the orphanage he talked about the lovely home he owned, the beautiful clothes I'd have, the school I could attend. He said we'd have to travel to get there. We took the stage coach, riding all day, stopping at a tavern for the night. When we arrived in New York City he bought me a fine silk dress, bonnet, and shoes. Dressed me up like a doll.

"While eating our evening meal at the city tavern, he told me that a friend was meeting him there that evening. He said he owed a debt, one he couldn't pay. Why could he not pay his debt? Or why not wait until after paying it before he came for me?"

283

Amelia stopped chopping, placed her knife on the table, staring at the pile of cabbage. Kathleen waited. In a moment, Amelia spoke again, softly.

"It was because I was the payment."

Kathleen gasped.

"When his friend arrived, I was to go with him and do whatever he wanted. I'd no idea what he meant. What could I possibly do for some strange man at a tavern? He said after tonight we'd put it all behind us and go on with our lives as though it never happened. It was the most horrible night of my life."

Kathleen's mind reeled. She thought of her own protective, loving da. How he would be spinning in his grave at the thought of a father using his own daughter in such a fashion.

"How could he do it?" she asked.

Amelia shrugged. "Later that night, I realized I had seen him before. At the orphanage we would often go outdoors to take exercise. I noticed a man standing across the street watching, but thought little of it at the time. He decided I was pretty enough to make his scheme work and came for me."

"Are you sure he was really your da?"

Amelia shrugged. "I suppose I'll never know. The people at the orphanage believed he was."

"Did he keep his promise? About putting that one time behind you?"

Amelia snorted. "He'd lied about everything. There was no money, no home. We moved from one unsavory tavern to the next, him showing me off like a prize horse, going to the highest bidder. I thought often of running away, but I had no money, no idea where I was, nor how to get back to the orphanage. I was trapped. Until the fire."

"Fire?"

"One night when I was with a customer, we heard someone scream 'Fire!' I tried to get up meaning to run from the building, but the man grabbed me and pulled me back. 'It ain't here,' he said, 'look'. He pointed out the window. It was the building next door that was ablaze. 'But it

284

could spread," I said. My heart was pounding so fast I thought it would break my chest. 'Probably,' he said, 'but we've time to finish. Get back here.' He'd no sooner rolled off of me than we heard a loud cracking noise. I ran from the bed, grabbed my wrap, and ran out the door. The tavern had caught. The rooms were filled with smoke. I could see flames on the far wall. I ran outside. Others from the tavern were already there. People were running everywhere, screaming, buckets of water doing no good at all. With a great crack, the top floor, where I'd just been caved in.

"I don't remember what happened after that until I was in another tavern, where a kind woman had brought me to her room. She was on her way back to Massachusetts."

"Mrs. Nichols?"

"Yes. She took care of me. In the morning, I told her the whole story. She said I could come with her if I wanted to. The thought of getting away from my father, of staying in one place, not moving every few days, of having a kind woman watch over me, was more than I could resist. We boarded a train that afternoon. I've been here ever since."

Kathleen stared at the girl, the vegetables forgotten. *Poor lass*, she thought. *She never had a chance.*

"You don't want this life, do you? That's why you want to learn to cook."

Amelia looked up at her, surprise on her face. "No one gets out of it. At least not until they become too old. That's why Tilda and Nessie do the laundry. Annie Nichols is a good sort. She won't put anyone out because they've aged. 'We're all going to get old someday,' she says. She's an uncommon one, you can be sure. I've heard the stories. There's many that would throw a girl out on the street the minute customers stopped asking for her. I thought if I started now, I could learn to cook so well that when the time comes I could be the cook. I'd like that so much better than doing the wash."

Amelia blushed. "Not that I'm trying to take your job, Kathleen! It will be years from now. You'll have married or retired by then."

285

"I'm not worried about my job, Amelia. I'm worried about you. You are a lovely young lady. Surely you must yearn for a husband and children? A home of your own?"

"No decent man would have me now. This is my life. I have to make the best of it."

"You could work, be a cook or a maidservant. I can teach you all you need to know about both."

Amelia laughed. "Why do you think we don't go to church?" When Kathleen didn't answer, she continued, "Because there'd be men there who would recognize us."

Kathleen blanched.

"Some of the finest, most upstanding gentlemen of the city are customers. They would not be comfortable seeing us in public. Should one of us slip and make any sign of recognition in front of their wives or daughters? It's why we go nowhere. Annie does all the shopping or sends Jonah to do it. Jonah is Tilda's boy, did you know that?"

Kathleen shook her head. This house held more secrets than she'd ever dreamed.

"He is. A fine little man. He sleeps in the attic."

"Does he know? About his mother?"

"Of course. His father was one of Tilda's best customers. Jonah looks just like him. Dead now. It doesn't matter. The man would never have claimed him. His wealthy widow is respectable, has four spoiled children. But Jonah's lived here since the day he was born."

Jonah's presence at the Thanksgiving table now made sense.

"Tilda's a good mother," Amelia stressed. "She loves that boy. He's a polite child as you might have noticed. That's because Tilda's raised him so. Annie was good not to make her get rid of him. Most madams won't let a girl keep a baby."

"They make them give their own children away?"

"You talk like the child gets to be born. No."

"How?"

"Different ways. Herbs can be tried. Pennyroyal, tansy, or rue tinctures. Look at the advertisements in the newspapers. Pills for female complaints are what they call them. Can be dangerous. I suppose there's no method that isn't."

"How can this be? How could anyone kill a baby?"

"It's not a baby. Not yet. It's nothing until it quickens. After that, it would be a crime and a sin, but before..." Amelia shrugged.

"If you wanted one, you'd think of it as your baby from the moment you realized it was within you. Just because you don't want it doesn't change that."

Amelia blinked. "That's not so. It's nothing until quickening. We're all taught this so that should it happen, we'll know what to do and the sooner the better."

Kathleen was afraid to ask, but she did. "Has it ever happened to you?"

"No, thank God. I hope it never does. It's dangerous. Women die from it all the time. Annie keeps us supplied with pessaries so we don't worry about it."

"Pessaries?"

"You put it inside. It keeps the man's semen from getting to the womb."

Kathleen felt overwhelmed by all she'd heard. But Amelia continued.

"That's one of the things that makes Annie so different. When Tilda told her she wanted the baby, Annie didn't argue. She took her off duty once the child quickened, even delivered the baby herself. She let Tilda nurse Jonah as long as she wanted. That was years before I came, but everyone's heard the story. A good, long break Tilda got before going back to work!" Amelia laughed as though she enjoyed Tilda's getting away with something. "There's no better madam than Annie Nichols."

Kathleen suddenly remembered the meal preparations. "We'd best get going or dinner will be late," she said, wanting desperately for a change of thoughts. It was clear to her now that she had to leave this place. She should go to confession for her association with it.

When Kathleen went to her room for the night, thoughts assailed her. How could she have let herself be so blinded? For the love of a well-appointed kitchen? Sleep

287

did not come easily. She spent much time praying to God for forgiveness. Moments before falling asleep, the thought crept in that she was here for a reason. Amelia had poured her heart out to her. What pain and humiliation she'd endured. Sympathy washed over her. *My child, Amelia needs you. You are here to help her.* These words penetrated her mind just before she fell asleep.

Chapter Thirty-One

"You worry, too much, Darien. The Yanks will never like us, but they need the labor," said Ned's uncle Owen one day after Mass when they were all gathered at the Arcade. Darien Linton had been lamenting the growing anti-Catholic sentiment that accompanied the rising power of the Know Nothing party.

"Our lot will never get better, then?" asked Mrs. O'Sullivan. "As long as we take their low pay, they'll keep us?"

"A fine one to talk, you are," said Ned. "You haven't worked a day since the fire. Low wages are better than no wages, woman."

Meg gasped. Aoife's face turned bright red. Every head in the room turned toward Ned.

Owen scowled at his nephew. "Edward Michael McBrody, how dare ye speak to your mother-in-law that way?"

Mrs. O'Sullivan's chin trembled. "I'm sorry I'm a burden." She bent forward in her chair, her body seeming to cave in on itself.

Maureen Linton went immediately to her sister's side. "It's all right," she said. "It's none of it your fault." She narrowed her eyes at Ned.

Meg had noticed Ned's growing irritability. He was overburdened as the sole provider for his wife, child, and mother-in-law, but she had never before heard such callous, mean-spirited sentiments. She worried for Aoife. If Ned would behave so in front of them what must he be like when they were alone?

"I don't have to take this," said Ned, shoving his chair away as he rose. He slammed the door as he left the room.

"Mam, he doesn't mean it."

Meg wondered who Aoife was trying to convince, her mother or herself.

"I don't know what's gotten into that lad," said Owen. "I'll have a word with him."

"My own fault," said Mrs. O'Sullivan, raising her head. "I've not been able to find work but the laundry. I've become a burden."

"It's not so, Mam," Aoife countered. "You help me with cleaning and tending Darragh. I don't know what I'd do without you. Ned didn't mean it. He'll come 'round and apologize."

"What do you make of that?" Nuala asked Meg once they'd left the Arcade.

"If Rory spoke to my mam that way I'd knock him flat with a frying pan, if Mam didn't do it first."

"Aoife's a different sort. So is Ned. I'd wager your Rory wouldn't dream of speaking to your mam like that with or without the threat of a frying pan."

"Indeed he would not."

"I never thought they should marry. Having Aoife's mother unable to find work adds to the burden." Nuala put up a hand to quell Meg's response. "I'm not siding with Ned. But God help them when another bairn comes along."

Could Rory turn sour as Ned had if they found themselves in similar conditions? *Rory is not Ned*, she reminded herself.

"What of what Mr. Linton said?" asked Nuala. "Do you think they will find a way to send us back? Do you hear any talk about it at the Claprood's?"

"They are more consumed by the anti-slavery issue. Though whenever Lemuel is visiting Master Oliver, he can't help but talk about it. Last time he went on bragging about how much money Governor Gardner's Pauper Removal Law had saved Massachusetts. Said he believes in the governor's advice not to bestow Christian charity on immigrants lest Massachusetts become the receptacle of the vicious, the deranged, and the insane." Meg uttered these

290

last words in a mocking imitation of Lemuel's quoting of the governor.

"So very Christian of him," Nuala said.

* * *

On the sixth day of August, Meg and Nuala set out with a picnic basket, their destination Hope Cemetery. Meg balked when Nuala first proposed the idea. "Ghoulish," she'd called it.

"Hope Cemetery isn't like the burying grounds back home," Nuala explained. "Mrs. Denton's told me all about it. More like a park."

"Park?" Meg could not fathom such an idea.

"Aye. Don't you remember that hilarious story Kathleen told us about Mrs. Pratt wanting to move their plots from Raccoon Plain to Hope?"

"Oh, aye. So laying dead in a park is what the Pratts were after?"

Nuala giggled. "Hope Cemetery's got avenues just like the city. It's how you find your way to the grave you're after. There's shade trees aplenty and more being planted all the time. Mrs. Denton says the monuments are a sight to behold with more going up. 'Tis a bustling place."

A laugh escaped Meg at the irony. "Have the Dentons bought their plots?"

"Mr. Denton says he's not moving from Raccoon Plain. He doesn't want hordes of folks frolicking atop him."

"He's a different perspective from Mrs. Pratt," Meg observed.

"They've all got odd ideas if you ask me. Still, I don't mind having a stroll. We've been looking for something different to do with our Thursdays," she stated.

Meg relented, though if Nuala wanted to picnic in a park she thought they'd be better off with the new one near Elm Street. At Nuala's insistence, Meg wore her finest outfit, her sapphire blue dress, white gloves, and white parasol trimmed with tiny blue flowers. Nuala was fitted out in dusty rose. They blended in remarkably well with the finely-dressed Yankee women who'd come to stroll the tree lined avenues.

The afternoon was mild for August with a light summer breeze. They picked a shady spot under a weeping willow. Spreading their blanket, they laid out their repast of ham and beef slices, cucumbers, tomatoes, bread, and cheese.

"What have you heard of Aoife?" Nuala asked. She'd avoided going to the Lintons' since the row with Ned and Mrs. O'Sullivan.

Meg sighed. "She's with child again."

"How far along?"

"Two months. She's afraid to tell Ned."

"Truly fearful?"

"Kathleen says so. Aoife's told her he sometimes comes home late in a foul mood and smelling of whiskey."

"Thought he took the pledge."

"Not a man of his word, it seems."

"As I feared. He's not harmed her, has he?"

"Not that I know of, but he says cruel things to her and worse to her mam. He never joins us after Mass anymore. Says he'd rather go for a walk than be suffocated by the crowd at the Lintons."

The attention of both was drawn by the conversation of a small group strolling the avenue. Meg and Nuala, effectively hidden by the willow tree's drooping branches, went unnoticed by the Yankee foursome.

"I've no love for the Irishies, mind you, but I still think it was dastardly," said a young lady.

"Softhearted woman," a male voice answered. "You don't see that it made sound fiscal sense. Think. Governor Gardner's Pauper Removal Act netted Massachusetts a savings of one hundred thousand dollars by ridding the state of thirteen hundred charity cases. The fact that most were Irish only proves what a shiftless lot they are."

A different female voice chimed in. "But weren't most of them widows, children, and lunatics from the asylum?"

In the lace curtain shade of the willow's protective branches, Meg and Nuala exchanged fearful looks.

"Don't worry your pretty head, Annabelle," the second man's voice responded. "The commissioners say their main problem is homesickness. They're probably right as rain now."

The voices faded as the group meandered up the avenue. A tightness formed in Meg's chest. "It's happening," she whispered. "They really are sending us back."

Nuala squeezed Meg's hand, swallowing hard before she spoke. "They won't send *us* away as long as we give them what no one else will." The words were typical of Nuala, but rather than announced with her usual assurance, they were uttered in a timorous spirit that gave Meg a shiver.

"Even if you're right, what of the others? What of Mrs. O'Sullivan, Aoife, the Lintons?"

"They're making their own way, not dependent on the state."

How far are any from the poorhouse, thought Meg.

* * *

At home, Meg heard the Claproods revile the Democrat party as evil given that they refused to endorse abolition. Yet they were the only real opposition to the Know Nothings and the closest thing Irish Catholic immigrants had to supporters. Few in the Irish community thought slavery justifiable, yet self-preservation proved a more powerful motivation. People like the Claproods could afford sympathy for the plight of the slaves. Meg often thought that if she were in the same social and economic position as Mrs. Claprood, she too, might feel as strongly about bringing an end to the contemptible institution.

But neither she nor any of the Famine Irish were in that position. They were trying to make their way in a new and hostile land. Trying to hang on to what little they'd been able to achieve. Trying to keep from being tossed out of this new home like so much garbage. To that end, they sided with the Democrats, the only party immune to the wooing of the Know Nothings. The only viable party not trying to fuse themselves with the ever-increasing power of the Know Nothings in order to push through their own agendas. The Know Nothings were as yet unable to disenfranchise immigrant men. As long as they could, they would cast their votes for a democrat. To do otherwise was to vote themselves out of the country.

On September twentieth, a Thursday, Meg and Nuala strolled downtown. The streets were more crowded than usual, especially in the area of City Hall. They quickly learned that an open meeting was being held.

"I'd love to go in," said Nuala, looking up at City Hall.

"Why?" Meg asked. In the midst of a mass of people dedicated to seeing her shipped out of the country was the last place she'd choose to be.

"To learn what they're planning." Nuala looked at Meg, a bemused expression crossing her face. "With any luck, watch them argue themselves out of existence."

"Not likely. Besides we'd stick out like sore thumbs, us amongst all those men."

"Aye." Nuala heaved a great sigh. "I suppose we'll hear the outcome eventually."

They continued their stroll, though unlike most Thursdays, there was a different energy in the air.

"What's going on over there?" Nuala pointed to a large tent set up on the Common.

"Want to go see?"

Nuala winked at Meg. "As if I could resist."

Nearing the tent, it quickly became obvious that this gathering had as much to do with politics as the one at City Hall.

Nuala grabbed Meg's wrist, whispering into her ear, "Don't speak. If anyone hears us they'll know we're Irish."

As they skirted the periphery of the crowd, they overheard the comments of many who had come to observe. Standing directly behind two men engrossed in conversation, they listened.

"Ya think they'll get it straightened out?" the taller man with the brown hat asked his companion.

"If they can agree to adhere to the Springfield Platform."

Oliver and Lemuel spoke this platform. Oliver was in favor of its anti-slavery position. Lemuel saw it as the perfect solution. It would make them so powerful, according to him, they'd have the Papists out in no time.

"That will take a miracle," said the first man. "Sam is mostly ignoring it."

Sam. The code word for the Know Nothing Party. A shiver passed through Meg. If this crowd knew she was an Irish Catholic, heaven knew what they'd do. Only her Yankee clothing and keeping her mouth shut offered any protection. She tugged at Nuala's sleeve, wanting to get away. Before they could extract themselves, a man at the podium called for attention.

"I've received word," bellowed the man, "that a new political party has formed."

A murmur rippled through the crowd.

"This news comes directly from the assembly now in session at City Hall. It's to be called the Republican Party. It has agreed to base itself on the anti-slavery issue alone."

Meg's heart skipped a beat. Another party? One that would not be consumed by hatred of her people?

"What of nativism?" called a voice in the crowd. "Will they do nothing to rid us of the Papist horde?"

When the chorus of *Here! Here's!* died down another voice called out, "Do they forget temperance? Are we to allow drunkenness to run rampant?"

A smattering of vocal agreement was enough for the speaker to call for order.

"No Republican need change his beliefs on other issues," he told the crowd. "Nativist and temperance men are encouraged to join."

The crowd under the tent welcomed this news with thunderous applause.

As the speaker left the podium, the two men in front of Meg and Nuala resumed their conversation.

"What do you make of that?" asked the taller man.

295

"Damned base trickery," answered his companion, then spit a wad of tobacco onto the ground.

"How so?"

As the man turned to look his companion in the eye, Meg caught a glimpse of his profile. Loathing seeped from his countenance. "Don't you see? This could destroy Gardner's plans to commit the fusion party to the nativist principles in the Springfield platform. Wilson's behind it, you can count on it. He's always wanted to ruin Gardner."

"Let's go," Nuala hissed in Meg's ear.

Meg trembled as they walked away. When she thought it safe, she spoke up. "If this new party stays focused solely on anti-slavery –"

"I don't care, as long as they leave us alone."

Nuala had been Meg's rock since the day they'd met. It disconcerted her to see the fear written on her friend's face.

Chapter Thirty-Two

Kathleen sat in her window seat staring out at a blanket of white while waiting for Mrs. Nichols. It was the first Monday of January 1856. Two feet of snow brought the city to a standstill. In the street below, several men huddled against the cold while talking and pointing.

"What are they doing?" Kathleen asked when Mrs. Nichols arrived.

"The new mayor is to be inaugurated this morning. I believe those men are tasked with clearing the roads." She shook her head. "Good luck to them."

"Who is the new mayor?"

"George Richardson," said Mrs. Nichols as they stepped into the hallway.

"Is he a Know Nothing?"

"Sadly, he is. It seems everyone elected these days knows nothing." Mrs. Nichols tittered at her own joke.

"Will he send us back to Ireland?"

Mrs. Nichols stopped halfway down the stairs, turning to look up at Kathleen.

"The mayor hasn't the power to do so. Your greater worry is the governor. More so whoever is elected president."

The seriousness in Mrs. Nichols' face frightened Kathleen. "Could it happen?" She spoke so softly, she barely heard her own words.

Mrs. Nichols looked down before turning to continue her descent. "Pray a Democrat wins."

"Aren't you feeling well?" Amelia asked later that day as they stoked the stove.

"I'm fine," Kathleen said. "Why do you ask?"

"You're quiet. And pale. Is something wrong?"

The political situation had worried Kathleen for some time, but she felt unhinged by the morning's brief exchange with Mrs. Nichols.

"Just thinking about something."

"Can't be good. Will you tell me?"

They sat at the table preparing the beef stew for dinner.

"Politics," Kathleen stated.

"Ugh!"

Kathleen couldn't help chuckling at Amelia's reaction.

"Not your favorite subject?" she asked.

"I'm sick to death of hearing all that Know Nothing talk from the gents that come here. Just last week a fight broke out between two of them. One was a Know Nothing and the other a Free Soiler. The last said something about the Know Nothings not holding up their end of the bargain and before you knew it fists were flying. Thank God Annie won't stand for that nonsense. She tossed 'em both out. Told 'em not to come back until they could hold their liquor and their tempers."

Kathleen thought back to last Wednesday morning. The entertaining rooms had been far messier than usual.

Amelia prattled on. "That's one thing about Annie. She won't abide any foolishness, especially not of the violent sort. They get out of hand, she sets them straight even if it means giving them a kick in the pants right out the door."

Kathleen laughed at the image conjured by Amelia's words.

"There's something I've been meaning to ask you," Amelia said, her voice turning serious.

"Aye?"

"What is it that makes you so devoted to your Catholic faith? Anyone who would rise as early as you do on a Sunday morning to walk to Mass? And those beads you carry, the ones always in your pocket. What do you call them?"

"A rosary."

"Yes, that. They're worn down. You pray with them, don't you?"

"Aye."

298

"I see you reach for them, especially when you seem troubled. They make you feel better?"

"That's true."

"At the orphanage they took us to church every Sunday. The preacher shouted a lot, mostly about hellfire, the devil and staying out of his clutches. I was terrified. Some at the orphanage told us how Jesus loved us. I'd like to go to church again if I could hear about the love part, but I'd not be welcomed in any church now anyway..." Amelia's voice trailed off.

Kathleen put down her paring knife, placed a hand over Amelia's. "My church would welcome you." Her eyes held Amelia's in a steady gaze. "My faith has kept me alive through devastation. It kept me going after Meg left us for America. It saw me through leaving my home and family, through the long journey on a creaky old ship." She sat up straight, jutting out her chin. "My faith's what cost me my last job, the mistress being filled with suspicion of Catholics, suspicion stoked into hatred by her Know Nothing son. Glad I am, that it drove me from that house. God delivered me safely here where I've been happy ever since."

Amelia's eyes widened. "You think *God* brought you to a bawdy house?"

Kathleen drew a deep breath. "At first, I believed Mrs. Nichols when she told me this was a boarding house, despite all the oddities. My sister, Meg, figured it out long before I did. She tried to tell me but I was so happy here, I chose not to believe it. It was you who forced me to accept the truth."

"Me?"

"Aye. The day you began cooking with me, you spoke of what goes on here. After that I couldn't pretend anymore. Not even to myself. I thought to leave the next morning."

"Kathleen, that was last summer."

"I prayed for a long time that night. As I fell asleep, I felt in my heart that Jesus wanted me to stay."

"Why?"

"For you. Because you needed me somehow. I believed he would show me. Now I think he has."

299

"Because I asked you about your faith?"

"What made you ask?"

Amelia was silent, looking down at the table full of vegetables, while gathering her thoughts. When she looked up, her face held a resolute cast. "Annie's been good to me. I'll always be grateful to her. But you were right. I don't want this life. I never did. But I thought there was no way out. I'm still not sure there is. All I know is you've got something I want, though I can't exactly name it. A sort of peace, I suppose."

Kathleen smiled broadly, glad she had listened to that inner voice on the night she'd decided to stay.

"Amelia, what if you learned so well you could get hired as a cook in one of those mansions where they have a whole staff? I hear the cook has one of the best positions in such a home."

"Kathleen, I can't do that. Too many people know what I do. Besides, I'd have to spend a lot more time with you than I do now. I've got to sleep some time."

"Leave that to me. I can't promise, but I'll do my best."

* * *

Kathleen spent the precious few hours after Mass with Meg and Nuala at the Lintons when the weather didn't send them directly home. If the winter storms were bad enough for them to hurry back to Crown Hill, they should also have sent Kathleen straight back to Mrs. Nichols' but Aoife was her reason for braving the walk later on those days. Ever since Aoife had confided in Kathleen that she felt safer with her there, she determined to stay as long as possible.

Kathleen was furious that Ned's continual browbeating had cowed Mrs. O'Sullivan to the point that she spent most of her time huddled in a corner, mending or praying her rosary. Her own mam would never tolerate Ned's abuse. Yet not every woman was Deirdre O'Connor. Kathleen gave thanks every day that she and Meg had inherited their mother's fighting spirit.

As February drew to a close, Aoife neared her time. When Kathleen came to her room after Mass on the twenty-fourth day of the month, she found Aoife pacing the floor, Mrs. O'Sullivan walking beside her, one arm around Aoife's shoulders, the other holding her right hand. Darragh napped on a small pile of blankets. Ned was nowhere to be seen.

"Is it her time?" Kathleen asked, stepping into the barren room.

"'Tis," said Mrs. O'Sullivan. "Her water broke this morning just afore we were to leave for Mass so I stayed."

"How can I help?" Kathleen asked as she took hold of Aoife's left elbow. Aoife's clothes were soaked with perspiration despite the cold room. She winced as Kathleen's strong fingers encircled her arm. An odd puffiness met Kathleen's grip.

"Your arm feels swollen," said Kathleen, gently kneading her fingers above and below Aoife's left elbow.

"'Tis nothing," Aoife gasped before a contraction doubled her over.

Kathleen looked questioningly at Mrs. O'Sullivan. The woman fixed her gaze on Kathleen. "That scoundrel did it."

"Mam, please..." Aoife panted. "Don't speak of it now."

Mrs. O'Sullivan closed her mouth, but her expression told Kathleen there was much more to be said.

"I need to...I need to lay down." Aoife crawled onto the filthy mattress curling up in as much of a ball as her swollen belly allowed.

Since she lay on her right side, Kathleen leaned over, gently coaxing her sleeve above her elbow. Angry purple lumps stood out above and below the joint.

"Don't," Aoife whispered.

"I'm sorry," Kathleen said, her voice soft. Tears streaked Aoife's face.

"That looks fresh," she whispered to Mrs. O'Sullivan as they stepped away from the bed.

"Early this morning," Mrs. O'Sullivan confirmed. "Darragh's crying woke His Highness so he yanked Aoife up by the arm, screaming at her to shut him up. She landed hard on the floor. He left then. Just threw on clothes and walked out the door."

Kathleen realized she had not seen Ned in church.

The two women had moved to Mrs. O'Sullivan's tiny corner of the room, allowing Aoife to rest. The older woman rubbed her face with her hands.

"He wasn't like this while I was working. They were happy then. Now..." her eyes darted upwards to a corner of the room. "Since Darragh's weaned and I've so little to contribute, it's been harder. When Aoife finally told him another bairn was on the way, he said they would have to send me to the poorhouse. That started a terrible row between them."

Bile rose in Kathleen. "How dare he!"

Aoife let out a howl. Darragh awoke, answering with a howl of his own. Both women rushed to the bed where Aoife lay, her tightly balled fists twisting the dingy sheets.

"Mama!" called Darragh as he toddled towards the bed.

"Take him to my sister's and ask her to come," Mrs. O'Sullivan instructed.

Kathleen scooped him up, and carried him down the hallway to the Lintons' rooms.

As Kathleen and Mrs. Linton hurried back to Aoife, they heard the main door to the building bang shut, followed by hurried footsteps. They were barely inside when the door burst open.

"What's going on in here?" Ned demanded.

Kathleen turned to face Ned. In that moment it was as if all the anger she'd ever felt towards Lemuel, Mrs. Pratt, Amelia's father, every Know Nothing in America, and Ned himself swelled inside her. With both hands she shoved against his chest so hard he reeled backwards into the hallway.

"Your wife is bringing your bairn into this world," she hurled at him. "There's no place for you. Be off with ya. Go to your uncle's or Mr. Linton's or to the devil himself, but don't dare to come back until you're called for!"

She slammed the door in his stunned face, half wishing he'd dare to open it so she could throw him out again.

Late afternoon, when the sun hung low in the sky, a squalling infant girl was placed in the arms of her mother for the first time.

"We'll name her Clodagh, after you, Mam," Aoife said.

Mrs. O'Sullivan, stroked Aoife's hair while gazing at her new grandchild. "Ned won't like it."

"He said he didn't care. Said I could name this one. I choose Clodagh."

Mrs. O'Sullivan wiped tears from her eyes.

"Kathleen, you should go before it gets dark," said Mrs. Linton.

As Kathleen descended the stairs towards the main door, she found Ned seated on a step halfway down. "'Tis a lass," she said, as she strode past him, not giving him so much as a parting glance.

Upon entering the boarding house kitchen, Kathleen shook the snow off her cloak and hung it by the door. Amelia was at the table preparing a meal.

"How was your day?" Amelia asked.

"Miraculous," Kathleen answered.

Seeing Amelia's eyes widen, she added, "My friend, Aoife, birthed a baby this afternoon. I've never attended a birth before, except for the pigs we had back home. I could not help but think it was truly a miracle seeing that tiny bairn come into the world. Where is Mrs. Nichols?"

"In the bible parlor. We just finished. She often stays to read until it's time to make supper. I asked if I could try making our meal on my own tonight and she agreed." Amelia's face beamed.

"Good," said Kathleen. "Let me know if you need help."

The same energy that gave her arms the strength to push Ned across the hall, now propelled a purposeful stride from the kitchen into the main section of the house. She knocked on the closed door of the bible parlor.

"Come in," called Mrs. Nichols.

Kathleen entered the room, pulling the door shut behind her. Drawing herself up to her full height, she stood before the reading table.

"Ma'am, I'd have a word with you, if you please," she stated.

Mrs. Nichols raised her eyebrows, but gently closed her book, placing it on the table in front of her. "Please, have a seat. Is something wrong?"

Aye, something is very wrong when a young lass's da sells her body like she's a brood mare. Something is wrong when that lass, at age seventeen, is already thinking how to survive when she's gone past a time when men still wish to buy her body.

This was what she wanted to say, but wouldn't risk angering the one person she needed to placate for Amelia's sake.

"Kathleen?" Mrs. Nichols questioned.

"I'm sorry, Ma'am. I was considering how to put this."

"Just tell me."

Kathleen drew a deep breath while offering a silent prayer. "I've been thinking about Amelia. She told me all that's happened to her and how she came to be here."

"No one here has a happy story. It's why I try to make their lives as bearable as possible."

Kathleen looked Mrs. Nichols in the eye. "You care about them?" It was almost a challenge.

"I should think that would be obvious."

"Were I to propose something that could improve Amelia's life would you agree?"

"I'll have to hear it first. What do you have in mind?"

"Make her my full-time assistant. And make that her *only* job. I'll take less salary, if need be to give her some pay and make up for her loss. She can keep the same hours as me. She can even share my room so as to keep her out of sight of the gents who want to buy her favors."

Mrs. Nichols gasped, her cheeks turning red. It dawned on Kathleen that she still believed her to be ignorant.

"You've no need to pretend, Ma'am. I've known for some time what kind of a house this is. I'd have left if it

304

weren't for Amelia. She's told me she doesn't want this life. If you care about her, then allow me to teach her all I know about cookery. Housework, too, if she's a mind. Then she can find a job and not have to give up her body every night to the highest bidder." Kathleen wished she could bite back the final few words along with their hostility, but they'd escaped.

Mrs. Nichols contemplated the table, running her fingers over the green baize covering. When she finally spoke, it was without looking up.

"I owe you an apology, Kathleen. It's difficult to find help here. I can only pass off this place as a boarding house for so long before help leave in disgust. You've stayed the longest. When I found you on the street, I figured you were in trouble. I knew you'd not been in this country long. I thought that the mix of kindness and intimidation would be enough to keep you a while."

Mrs. Nichols finally looked up at the small huff of a laugh that escaped Kathleen.

"You were right about all, Ma'am," said Kathleen. "My sister, Meg, had it figured out, but I was too happy here. I turned a blind eye until Amelia's story wouldn't allow."

"I've grown very fond of you. We all have. I'm glad to know you've been happy. I hope you're not planning to leave."

"I'm not, because Amelia needs me. Will you – "

"Kathleen, what drove you from that home after dark on a cold night?"

Though annoyed at Mrs. Nichols' attempt to change the subject, Kathleen answered honestly and thoroughly.

"I'm truly sorry you were treated so poorly," Mrs. Nichols said when she finished. "But your tale shows the difference between you and Amelia. You *can* find another job. As far as society is concerned Amelia is a grievous sinner, a depraved woman. She could become the best cook in Worcester, and no one would hire her. Or she wouldn't last. Someone would recognize her. Rumors would fly. She'd be dismissed. The same is true for all the women here. I don't wish to keep anyone in prostitution any more than I wished to be on the job in my younger days. When I had the opportunity to become a Madam, I took it with the conviction that I would protect my girls. Others can condemn me, but I provide my girls with a better life than they'd have anywhere else and I absolutely refuse to take in a virgin. I won't start any girl on this life. I only take in those who've already journeyed on the path. Do you understand this, Kathleen?" There was such pleading in Mrs. Nichols' eyes that Kathleen wished to throw her arms around her. Instead she thought about Amelia and how unfair her life had been.

"I understand that you care and that you're trying your best. I don't believe you're a bad woman. That's why I thought you might be willing to give my idea a try."

"I've already explained why she could not be hired –"

"Remember that you brought her here from New York. When she arrived, no one knew her. If she learned from me then went away from here, she could start fresh. If you let her try."

Mrs. Nichols' brow furrowed and she bit her lip. "Yes," she conceded. "I suppose that could work."

A spark of hope ignited in Kathleen. "We have your permission, then?"

Mrs. Nichols sat up straight, her chin tilted at an authoritative angle. "She can move into your room this very night. If customers ask for her, I'll tell them she's sick. That will work for a time. After a while, I'll come up with something else."

Kathleen jumped up. "Thank you! Thank you!" she exclaimed, throwing herself into Mrs. Nichols' arms, unable to contain her joy.

A knock at the door sent Kathleen back to her seat as Mrs. Nichols' called, "Come in."

Amelia opened the door, poking her head in to announce, "Supper's ready."

"Amelia, let supper wait a few moments," Mrs. Nichols said. "Come in. We have something to tell you."

Chapter Thirty-Three

Meg dusted in the parlor where Mrs. Claprood, her daughters, and Clara Pratt were sewing, Clara having resumed her visits. From overheard conversations Meg knew that Mrs. Pratt had been through three Irish domestics since Kathleen, all of them leaving after short stints. A new girl was starting today, a relief to Clara as it meant she could get away, the majority of the housework and cooking having fallen to her whenever they were bereft of a servant.

Clara always asked Meg about Kathleen. Meg told her that Kathleen was well, working in a boarding house, without saying the location or the landlady's name, but she did agree to pass notes between Clara and Kathleen.

Meg took pity on the girl. The more time Clara spent with the Claproods the more Meg understood why Kathleen was so fond of her. She was an intelligent, polite, articulate young lady of seventeen with a gentle spirit. How could she possibly be related to Mrs. Pratt and Lemuel?

At the moment, the Claprood girls were quizzing Clara on her knowledge of flowers and their meanings while they sewed. A quick learner, Clara had easily amassed a botanical knowledge that nearly rivaled that of Pamela and Deborah.

A knock at the front door sent Meg from the room. She returned with an embossed envelope for Mrs. Claprood.

"Girls, look!" she said, handing the invitation to Pamela. "We've been invited to a spring ball at the Thayers'."

"Mother, we'll need new gowns! May we call upon the dressmaker?" Pamela asked.

"The ball is on June seventh. We haven't much time to prepare," Deborah noted.

"Yes, yes, girls," said Mrs. Claprood. "This is very special. I will call at once upon Mrs. Atkins. We'll need to engage her quickly as I'm sure she has a full schedule."

"How splendid!" Clara exclaimed. "I can't wait to see your new ball gowns."

"May we go now and look for fabrics?" Deborah asked.

"Yes," answered Mrs. Claprood. "Only don't purchase any yardage yet. Get some ideas. Check Godey's Lady's Book to see what's current."

"Come with us, Clara," Pamela invited.

Pamela and Deborah headed for the door, Clara right behind them.

"Please, stop at the post office for mail on your way home," Mrs. Claprood called. Then, turning to Meg she said, "Oh Margaret, this is exciting!" Mrs. Claprood's face glowed.

"I can see that, Ma'am. What can I do to help?"

"'I'll write notice of our acceptance. Please take it round to the Thayers' for me."

Meg waited as Mrs. Claprood went to the desk for her writing paraphernalia. After setting out her ink and paper, she looked up at Meg. "Oh, I didn't mean immediately. Best to deliver our response tomorrow or the day after. Prompt, but not over-eager. Go about your duties for now. After the dressmaker arrives there will be much to do. You'll have to cook for her as well as us. We'll need your help with the sewing once she's left."

"Will she be staying here?" Meg asked, puzzled by the usually unflappable woman appearing so flustered.

"Certainly not. Mrs. Atkins is married. She'll be here much of the day until all three gowns are fashioned and cut. We will take over from there. Oh, I hope she isn't booked. She's the best dressmaker. I believe Edward Thayer will ask for Pamela's hand before long. We must make a good impression on his family for her sake."

Meg nodded, preparing to return to her chores. Before she turned, Mrs. Claprood jumped from her seat. "What am I thinking! I can write our acceptance later," she said recapping the ink. "I must get to Mrs. Atkins right away. I'll be back, soon, Margaret, I hope with good news."

Meg was brought to the front door a week and a half later by an assertive rap. Upon opening it, she was faced with a tall woman, not much older than herself, dressed in a billowing light green skirt and a fitted cloak of darker green the same shade as her bonnet. In one hand she carried a large bag, in the other an armload of books and sketchpads.

"Please inform Mrs. Claprood that Mrs. Atkins has arrived."

Meg stared at the woman whose bright green eyes cut right through her. *This is the dressmaker?* thought Meg. Surely this woman overstepped her bounds. "Servants are received at the back door," she said.

The woman lifted her eyebrows. "I'm sure they are. Does this look like a uniform to you?" she asked, glancing down at her rich garb.

"I'm sorry. There's never been a dressmaker here before. Not since I've been here. Please come in," Meg stammered, opening the door wider and stepping back. "I'll fetch Mrs. Claprood."

Meg found her mistress in the conservatory with her daughters, pouring over fashion plates in the latest issue of Godey's.

"Mrs. Atkins is in the front hall," Meg announced.

"Please show her in, quickly!" said Mrs. Claprood.

"This is so exciting," Deborah clasped her hands.

"Don't act so giddy," Pamela admonished. "Try to behave as if this is a normal occurrence. We don't wish her to think us bumpkins. Come, let's bring the book into the parlor."

Deborah followed her mother and sister into the next room, biting her lip.

"Mrs. Atkins, so wonderful of you to come," said Mrs. Claprood as Meg ushered the esteemed woman into the parlor. "These are my daughters, Pamela and Deborah. We appreciate your making time for us in your busy schedule."

"It was a squeeze, but since it is for a ball at the Thayers', I've made an exception."

"We are truly grateful," said Mrs. Claprood. "Shall we get started? I know your time is valuable."

Earlier in the day, a large table had been placed in the center of the parlor. As the four women gathered around it, Meg thought of Aisling, apprenticed to a dressmaker in Ireland, and wondered if she worked with the same equipment.

"Margaret, the tea and refreshments," Mrs. Claprood instructed.

Meg went to the kitchen to prepare a tray. When she returned, all were deep in conversation about colors, fabrics, and embellishments.

Each day that Mrs. Atkins returned, Meg watched as inconspicuously as possible. She, her mam, and Kathleen had spent countless hours mending the fine clothing of the wealthy British men and ladies in town. She had loved working with the fine fabrics and was eager to help with the Claproods' ball gowns.

Mrs. Atkins finished by the twenty-third of May. When she departed the Claprood home for the last time, she left behind yards of material cut into appropriately sized pieces, along with detailed instructions including drawings of what the final products should look like. Every spare moment was now filled with stitching those pieces together and adding adornments. Meg had never seen skirts with such an abundance of ruffles and flounces. What befuddled her most was a new invention called a cage crinoline. Made of thick wire, it was meant to be worn under the petticoats, giving the skirt a wide bell shape. Such a thing! It was like having half one's body imprisoned. Yet the Claprood women swooned over theirs, agreeing that they were most fortunate to have a dressmaker with access to the latest fashion accoutrements.

Once Mrs. Pratt heard from Clara about the invitation, she began making almost daily visits to the Claproods' on the pretense of walking Clara home. Meg disliked even the sight of her, but it was often not possible to avoid as Meg, along with the Claprood women sewed the ball gowns together. No invitation had been sent to the Pratts. Envy oozed from Mrs. Pratt like slime from a snail.

"I do hope the rains have finally ended," said Mrs. Pratt one afternoon as she fingered the silky blue-green material of Deborah's gown. "It would be a shame if torrential downpours were to ruin this."

Meg watched furtively as Deborah gathered all the fabric, her arms forming a protective circle around it.

"It has been a dreadfully rainy spring," Deborah agreed, returning to her needlework. "It even caused severe damage to the central avenues at Hope Cemetery."

Mrs. Pratt's back stiffened. "Indeed? I'm sure the workers will have everything put in order before the summer's out."

Meg kept her smile hidden. Clara said that Mrs. Pratt had finally badgered her husband into selling their plots in Raccoon Plain and purchasing new ones in the center of Hope Cemetery – the exact location washed out by this spring's downpours.

"I just hope it's done before any of them are needed," said Deborah. "Imagine how frightful it would be were someone to leave this world while their plot was unusable. Although, in a pinch one could be buried in Raccoon Plain. I understand they have plenty of room."

"Deborah!" said Mrs. Claprood. "Such morbid talk. Do speak of something more pleasant."

"I'm sorry, Mother." Deborah lowered her gaze, but Meg caught the slightly upturned corners of her mouth.

On June fifth, two days before the ball, Meg returned from her day off and was making her way up the back staircase when she heard a scream from the other end of the house. She hurried down the hallway towards the chamber shared by the Claprood girls. Deborah stood in the middle of the room, tears streaming down her face. She was wearing her finished ball gown. The blue-green shimmered like ocean waves with the quaking of her body. Four layers of ruffles ringed the bottom of the skirt. A gauzy overlay swept from the bodice to just above the highest ruffle. The only thing marring the gown's beauty was a large, ugly rip from below the waistline to the first layer of ruffles.

"How did that happen?" asked Meg.

"She wanted to practice dancing in her ball gown," Pamela explained. "As she was turning, she caught the waist on the corner of that drawer." Pamela pointed to a chest with one drawer partially open. "She was halfway through her turn when we heard the rip."

"How bad?" Deborah asked, tugging on the skirt to get a better look.

"Stop. You'll make it worse," Pamela admonished.

Mrs. Claprood delivered the bad news. "An entire section is ruined."

"Oh no!" cried Deborah. "Mother we must call on Mrs. Atkins!"

"No, dear. Mrs. Atkins is a dressmaker. She doesn't do mending."

"What will I do? The ball is on Saturday."

"I hate to say this, but I don't think it can be fixed in time. You may have to stay home."

Deborah gasped.

"I'm sorry Deborah. We'll give the Thayers your regrets and tell them you've a cold."

"Are you sure, Mother?" asked Pamela. "I so want Deborah to come."

"It's beyond our abilities and I don't see how we can get someone with skill enough."

Meg crouched in front of Deborah, examining the tear as a surgeon would a deep gash.

"Give it to me. I can mend it," she said.

"You can?" All three asked in unison.

"Aye," said Meg, as she stood. "Kathleen and I mended fancy clothes for the British ladies of Kelegeen. It will take work so I may not be able to get all my chores done, but if you'll give me leave," she said, turning to Mrs. Claprood, "I can have it finished in time for the ball."

"Help me out of this, quickly!" Deborah proclaimed.

"Do you truly believe you can fix it, Margaret?" asked Mrs. Claprood.

"Aye, Ma'am. I do." Meg was not nearly as sure as she sounded. She'd mended some fine clothes at home, but never anything as badly torn as this.

"Take all the time you need. The girls and I will handle all meals and chores until you've finished."

The next day Meg was treated to a breakfast she did not have to cook. Relieved to turn her back on the dirty dishes, she headed straight for the bedchamber, gathered all sewing materials, setting everything out on a table before the sunniest window in the house. All day she worked on the dress, stopping only for meals and to rest her eyes and fingers. It was difficult work, demanding all the skill she possessed, yet how much she enjoyed working with the silky material! Looking over the drawings Mrs. Atkins had left and examining the gown itself, she understood how the clothing went from a picture on paper to a real garment.

The smoothness of the fabric felt good sliding through her hands. She thought of the other gowns. Pamela's was a pale lavender, Mrs. Claprood's dark blue. All had lace trimmings. The bodices were low cut, revealing the neck and shoulders. Large dark lavender bows fell just short of the six rows of flounces on Pamela's skirt. They were all intricate, their colors beautiful, their fabrics luxurious.

As the sun began to set, Meg finished the last stitch. She inspected her work carefully in the waning light. One would have to look closely to detect any hint of mending. Satisfied, she rose to ask Miss Deborah to try on the gown.

"It's beautiful!" Deborah exclaimed as she twirled before the *cheval* mirror in the bedchamber. "Oh, Margaret, how can I ever thank you?" Deborah leaned forward to embrace Meg.

"It was my pleasure," Meg assured her.

"Amazing accomplishment, Margaret," said Mrs. Claprood. "I knew you excelled at mending, but I did not realize by how much."

"It's been a long time since I've worked on so fine a piece."

"You are a treasure," said Mrs. Claprood as she and Meg walked towards the door leaving the two girls to chatter about the coming ball.

"Margaret, wait," Deborah called before Meg reached the hallway. "The day the invitation came, Mother asked us to stop at the post office, remember? I was so excited, I forgot to give you your letter. I found it in my pocket this afternoon."

She handed the letter covered with Rory's handwriting to Meg.

"No harm's done, I'm sure" said Meg.

"Margaret, fix something from the kitchen, then have the evening for yourself and your letter," said Mrs. Claprood.

"Thank you, Ma'am."

Meg threw together a quick repast, then headed for her attic chamber.

My dearest Megeen,

I've the most amazing news to tell you. I've been working all this time for Sir Alfred Stokes. One day while we were in the barn brushing down the horses, I told him all about Brendan, how he was sent to Australia for theft despite he never stole a thing. Sir Alfred's still feeling guilty over all that's happened so without telling anyone until all was in place he called in a favor from a government official he knows in Australia. He got Brendan an early release and paid his passage home! He finally told me once he knew Brendan was on his way. I thought of keeping it a surprise for your mam, but reconsidered, fearing his unexpected appearance might do her in. I needn't have worried. You know your Mam, she'd been having dreams for weeks of waves coming, bringing her something. They left her feeling peaceful, she said. When I told her about Brendan coming home soon, she just smiled and nodded like it was confirmation of her dreams.

It was a different scene the day he walked through the door. She let out a whoop I'm sure they heard all the way to Dublin, threw herself into his arms all the while praising God, crying, laughing, calling out, 'my lad, my lad is home!' all at once. Can you picture it? It was a while afore anyone else could even get much of a look at him.

Best of all was Brigid's reaction. She recognized him immediately. Called his name and ran to him. It stunned us all into silence. She's been better since he's been home. I'm thinking she may come fully around yet.

You'd hardly recognize your brother now, Meg. He's grown tall and strong. He left Ireland a frightened lad of fifteen. Now he's twenty-two, tough as leather, and knowing everything about farming.

The land laws are changing in Ireland. Brendan's working things out with Sir Alfred. He'll be able to farm a good piece of land, keeping more than only potatoes. I've got no words to explain how happy Brendan's return has made everyone. You'll have to picture it for yourself. Imagine being so filled with joy you think you'll burst and maybe you'll know a bit of it.

Brendan was home! Meg dropped to her knees, thanking God for his safe return and for keeping her mam alive long enough to see him. It was some time before she could calm herself enough to return to the letter.

Aisling has finished apprenticing and works full time for Mrs. Fairfax. Everyone says she will be running a dress shop of her own before long. Loreena has taken to helping Brendan with the pigs. You know how she and Brigid always loved those pigs. Brigid even helps with them. Another good sign she will come around. Your mam continues her sewing, though her eyesight is beginning to fail. Loreena makes up what she can't finish. Food is finally in decent supply, praise God and His saints.

That leads me to my best news of all. By the time you read this letter I will already be on a ship headed for America. I used the money I saved from working for Doctor Parker and Sir Alfred. A little extra they both gave me as a go-

ing away present, along with their letters of recommenda-
tion.

I will dock in Boston then take the train into Worcester
just as you and Kathleen did. I have no idea what day I'll
arrive. But don't worry, Meg. I will find you. Think of it. In
only a matter of weeks we will be together. Please look for
a placement for me working with horses. It hardly feels re-
al, but finally we will begin our lives together. Pray for my
safe passage. I love you so much, Megeen and can't wait to
claim you as my wife.

All my love,
Rory

Meg's breath caught in her chest. Rory was on his way.
How long had Deborah had the letter in her pocket? How
long had Rory been on the ship? Dear God, he could arrive
any day!

Meg stood, sat, stood again, paced the small room. A
sensation of unreality washed over her. To think that any
day she could be with Rory again. In his arms. Making a
life with him as they'd been looking forward to since he'd
proposed. How long ago? Over ten years since the moondance. Nine since she'd left Ireland. How much had he
changed? So many thoughts chased each other she became
dizzy. She went to the bed, lying curled up on her side,
hugging her knees. *Rory is coming! Rory is coming! Dear
Lord, please bring him here safely*, she prayed. Anxiety,
joy, disbelief, anticipation – all whirled together within her.

Suddenly, she sat bolt upright. She must tell Mrs. Claprood. What would become of her job? Where would she
and Rory live?

"Dear God, help me," she prayed. "I don't know what
to do."

Chapter Thirty-Four

On the afternoon of Saturday, June 7, 1856, Kathleen and Amelia left Saint John's Church arm-in-arm. Kathleen had brought her to meet with Father Boyce, now the pastor as Father Gilbert had moved to another parish. He began instructing Amelia in the faith right away. He was also working with the Sisters of Mercy to find a respectable position for her as soon as she was fully trained. Today Amelia had been baptized and confirmed with Kathleen as her godmother.

"I'm so excited to attend Mass as a Catholic tomorrow," Amelia said as they meandered back to the boarding house. "I hope no one recognizes me."

"Does the...um...boarding house get many Irish guests?"

"None that I know of. I doubt they've the money for it. They'd likely...um...visit with streetwalkers. I want to leave that life behind. I feel like a new person."

"You are a new person," Kathleen told her. "You've just been baptized. At this moment, there's not a speck of a sin on your soul."

Amelia stopped walking. They'd turned from Green Street to Franklin. "I never dreamed such a thing could be possible."

Kathleen hugged her. Amelia startled Kathleen by abruptly breaking free.

"What is it?" Kathleen asked.

"That man," she whispered, looking down Franklin Street. "The one in the middle."

Kathleen turned to follow her gaze. Three young men sauntered towards them. Kathleen's heart sped up. "Lemuel," she hissed under her breath.

"You know him?" asked Amelia.

She grabbed Amelia's hand hurrying her towards Vine Street. Before turning onto Cherry, Kathleen looked back to see if they'd been followed. She did not see Lemuel, but she still felt uneasy.

"You know Lemuel Pratt?" Amelia asked again as they slowed to a normal pace.

"He's the eldest son of the family I worked for. He hates me. Hates all Catholics."

"Remember I told you about a fight between a Free Soiler and a Know Nothing?" Amelia asked. "Lemuel Pratt was the Know Nothing."

"Does he come often?"

Amelia shrugged. "Not a regular, but more than once. None like him. He's rough."

"With you?"

"No, thank God. He likes Diana best, but sometimes he chooses Rose."

"Do you think he saw us?" Kathleen asked.

"Our eyes met, but we were far enough away that he might not have recognized me. Your back was to him. He'd probably never imagine the two of us together," Amelia said as they descended the steps leading to the kitchen. "This is a special day. Let's not allow Lemuel Pratt to ruin it."

Kathleen smiled. "You're right," she said opening the door.

When they entered Mrs. Nichols and all the women were assembled in the kitchen.

"What's this?" Amelia asked.

"A party," said Mrs. Nichols. "We're celebrating your new life. Come to the dining room. We've made a small feast to celebrate this blessed day."

Kathleen delighted in Amelia's joy and that of the others who seemed to revel in the fact that Amelia had been baptized and was leaving the life of prostitution. Perhaps there was hope for them all. But Kathleen's joy was tinged with anxiety. If Lemuel had recognized her and Amelia, he'd know where to find her.

That night Amelia and Kathleen chatted in the room they now shared while preparing for bed.

"I hope the Sisters find a good place for me," said Amelia. "I don't feel right being here anymore. I will miss you something terrible, though."

"I'll miss you, too. We can write to each other."

"Will you stay on?"

That had been on Kathleen's mind of late. She had confessed to Father Boyce. Though he was happy that she had allowed God to use her as the instrument to bring Amelia to Christ and the Church, he made it clear that she must distance herself from the establishment.

"I'll ask Meg and Nuala if they know of any openings. Truthfully, though, I will miss this place and everyone in it."

They were climbing into bed when startled by a frantic pounding on the door.

Kathleen opened to find Diana looking stricken.

"Kathleen, get dressed. Pack up. Don't waste any time. Hurry!"

"What's happening?" asked Amelia.

"Lemuel Pratt is downstairs. He's demanding she be brought to him."

"What?"

"He's threatening to bring the police down on us if Kathleen isn't turned over to him. Kathleen, move!"

Quickly, she donned her old calico, bonnet and shoes while Amelia raced about, throwing everything else in her sack.

"Why doesn't Annie throw him out?" asked Amelia.

"He's very drunk. Shoved Annie across the room."

"Won't any of the other gents help?"

"He's the only one here. Says he'll tear the place apart. He was storming up the main staircase when Annie sent me."

"Once I'm on the street –" Kathleen started.

319

"Not on the street. We've another way out. Follow me."

The three moved quickly down the back staircase, making as little noise as possible. Once in the kitchen, Diana crossed the room to a massive cupboard.

"Help me. It's heavy," she said, pressing all her weight against its side.

As they pushed, the cupboard slid reluctantly across the floor.

"That's enough," Diana said, grabbing two lanterns. She lit them from her own candle then placed them on the floor.

Kathleen could just discern the outline of a square where the cupboard had stood. Diana reached down, hooking two fingers into a small indentation. Once the trap door was opened, the lantern light revealed a wooden ladder attached to the dirt wall of a hole not much wider than Kathleen herself.

"Is it a root cellar?" Kathleen asked.

"No. It's the entrance to a series of tunnels. They were built well over a hundred years ago, though no one remembers why. Climb down and follow the tunnel. There are a few spots in the city where it comes up. One is the hostelry. Another is where they've just built that new hotel, the Bay State. An entrance to the tunnel was there when it was the Central Hotel. They may have closed it off or they may not even know of it. It's under Exchange Street. There are one or two other places. Just keep going until you find your way out."

Kathleen's heart pounded hard enough to burst.

"What if I can't find my way? I'll be trapped down there forever."

"Follow wherever it leads. It has to come out somewhere."

I can't do this. I can't. The words screamed inside Kathleen's head as she peered into the hole.

The sounds of stomping feet and breaking glass resounded from the main quarters.

"She was with that little blond whore. I'll find her if I have to turn this God forsaken place upside down." Footsteps stormed down the passage towards the kitchen. "That Papist bitch! Too good for me, yet she goes from my father's home to a whorehouse. The Irish slut is due for a comeuppance!"

Lemuel's voice grew louder.

"For God's sake, Kathleen, get down there, now!" Diana threw Kathleen's sack into the hole. It made a soft thud when it hit the packed dirt below.

"What do you want with an Irishie?" Rose's voice sounded near the door to the kitchen. "Don't you like your dear old Rosie anymore?"

Kathleen took a deep breath, hiked up her skirt and swung her legs down the hole until her feet found a rung of the ladder.

"He must not hurt Rose," she said as she felt for the next rung.

"He'll be sorry if he tries," Diana assured her. "*That* Rose has sharp thorns."

"I'll come with you," Amelia said, preparing to follow Kathleen down the ladder.

"No," said Diana. "I'll need you to help push the cupboard back. "Here," she said, handing Kathleen a lantern.

She was halfway down the ladder when the trap door lowered. She heard the cupboard scrape across the floor back into place. Upon stepping off the final rung, Kathleen picked up her sack. She held up the lantern, waiting for her eyes to adjust. A dirt-walled tunnel loomed before her. There appeared to be a change in its shape a yard or so ahead. Muffled voices from above caused her to glance upwards into the pitch darkness. An angry, though unintelligible, male voice revealed how narrow had been her escape. There was no choice now. Forward.

Kathleen uttered a quick prayer before taking her first steps. It was not long before the dirt walls were replaced by brick. The ground underfoot was damp and slightly squishy, reminding her of the bogs back home.

After her first uneasy steps, she quickened her pace, wondering how long it would take to find her way out. As she continued through the long passage, thoughts of her recurring dream of Lemuel chasing her through a dark tunnel assailed her. Perhaps she had her mother's 'gift' after all. As she slogged along, Kathleen had the feeling that she was walking down a gently sloping hill. The air grew warm and moist as she went. How far underground was she?

"Lord Jesus guide me," she pleaded. "Show me the way out."

She dropped the sack long enough to reach into her pocket for her rosary. The prayers uttered in her native Irish, along with the feel of the beads held her rising panic at bay.

A feeling of unreality grew stronger when, on shaking legs, she arrived at another brick archway. Passing underneath, her lantern illuminated a brick wall to her left with two arch-shaped windows side-by-side. The wall turned a corner exposing a third window next to which stood a door frame. The door was open. The tunnel came to a dead end were she to go straight. That left passing through the open door her only choice. She lingered a moment. The brick walls, elegant archways, and windows gave the scene a bizarre feel, like a dream. A scrabbling noise broke the eerie silence. She screamed as something scampered across her foot, a rat hurrying down the passageway from which she'd just emerged.

Her legs ached from walking on uneven, soggy ground. She took a deep breath to steady her nerves. Holding the lantern aloft, she proceeded through the open doorway, stopping a few steps over the threshold.

The lantern light offered only shadows, but it was obvious that the chamber was large and furnished. She placed the lantern and sack upon a table, giving her arms a moment's rest. Dust rose from the surface making her sneeze.

She held her lantern up, turning about, trying to make out anything else in the room. There was something on the wall to her left. A sconce. No candle remained in it.

Turning her lantern, Kathleen could see identical sconces at intervals along the wall. She took a few of the extra candles from her sack, lit them, and stuck them into the sconces for more light.

Several tables, chairs, and a few divans graced the perimeter of the cavernous chamber. But it was the center of the room that claimed her attention. A large space was roped off forming a square. Approaching it, she barely discerned the scuffed outlines of footprints, some facing toe to toe as thought an odd dance had once been performed here.

Kathleen headed toward another table at the back of the room, a large, heavy affair with eight thick legs. The edges were slightly higher than the top which was covered in a fabric like felt or baize. Several numbered balls were corralled in a triangular holder at one end. Long sticks rested against the wall behind the table. This was some sort of game, but unlike any she'd ever seen.

The back wall held two cabinets, one on either side of the row of sticks. Taking her lantern she moved closer, astonished to recognize them as identical to Mrs. Nichols' liquor cabinet. Suddenly, everything made sense. This room was a gaming hall. Even the roped off section in the center now clicked in her brain – a boxing ring, a sport she had never witnessed. But she'd heard many conversations about it between Lemuel and Harvey Pratt. Was the room abandoned or still in use? Would it soon be filled with men ready to gamble and fight?

She searched desperately for a way out and found three tunnels similar to the one that had brought her to this room, one on either side of the cabinets and one through the wall opposite that with the sconces she'd lit. She would have to pick one and pray it would lead to one of the exits Diana had mentioned.

She chose the closest tunnel, the one to the left of the liquor cabinets. It was a much shorter corridor than the one that had brought her to the large chamber. Like that one, though, it had sturdy brick walls and a moist dirt floor. As she moved through the tunnel, Kathleen detected a dripping sound from above. She held the lantern aloft but could see nothing. The further she went, the louder it became. Afraid there was water ahead, she considered turning back, when she noticed a thick pillar ahead on the right. It framed yet another arched doorway. She stopped, peered into the room. It was much smaller than the room with the boxing ring. Taking a tentative step inside, she was brought up short by a rustling noise to her right. Rats was her first thought, but that idea was dismissed when a disembodied female voice whispered in the darkness, "Oscar, is that you?"

Kathleen gasped. "Who's there?"

"It's Sally. I'm here with Phoebe. Who are you?"

"What are you doing here?" Kathleen asked. She shone the lantern light in their direction but could see no one. "Do you have a light? I can't see you." For a moment, Kathleen feared she was either losing her mind or conversing with a ghost.

"Oscar said to wait. He'd come for us. Did he send you?"

"I don't know Oscar."

"Mama, I'm scared." A child's voice.

The woman shushed the child. There was more rustling, then silence.

Kathleen waited. "Sally?" she called. "Are you still here?

"Yessum."

Kathleen detected in Sally's voice an accent different from the Yankees.

"Where are you from?" she asked.

"South Carolina," came the whisper.

Kathleen's mind conjured images from *Uncle Tom's Cabin*. These were escaped slaves waiting to be taken to the next stop on their way to freedom. Relief washed through her. Whoever Oscar was, he would probably come soon and show her the way out.

"My name is Kathleen. I'm lost in these tunnels. May I stay with you to wait for Oscar?"

"Yessum. We're over here." The spark of a candle flame flickered in the darkness. Kathleen walked towards it, nearly tripping when she got close.

"Careful, Missy," said Sally. "It's hard to see."

"What did I trip over?" asked Kathleen.

"The mattress. Sit with us."

Kathleen crouched down onto a thin, rough mattress, filled with corncobs and straw by the feel of it. Now that her lantern and Sally's candle were together there was just enough light for them to see each other.

Sally was a young woman, though thin and haggard. Her hair was caught up in a turban. Her dress looked worn, her dark eyes were large and, Kathleen thought, would have been pretty if they weren't so full of fear. At Sally's elbow sat a little girl, almost her in miniature.

"Is this your daughter?" Kathleen asked.

For a moment Sally's eyes lost their haunted look. "Yessum, my Phoebe."

"She's a darlin'," said Kathleen smiling at the child. "Oscar's taking you on to the next stop then?"

"Yessum. He's to bring us to a Mister Hadwen who will move us on to the next station."

"Do you expect him soon?"

"Don't know. He'll come when it's safe."

"How long have you been here?"

"A few days, I reckon. It's hard to tell how much time's gone by."

"A few days! Have you anything to eat?"

"Phoebe, get that bread now and give it to the nice lady."

"No, no," Kathleen stammered. "I'm not asking for food."

"Oscar gave us a supply. Not much, but the best he could do. We've gone on less. You can get by without much food for longer than you think when you have to."

Those words pierced Kathleen's heart. "I know," she said. "I came from Ireland. We had almost no food for years. Many thousands starved."

"How awful," said Sally. "Where is Ireland?"

"Across the sea. Near England."

"I've heard tell of England. How did you get here?"

Kathleen and Sally shared their stories. In the hours they spent waiting and talking a bond formed between them forged of shared hunger, exploitation, oppression, and fear. Their tears mingled as they leaned their heads together, little Phoebe wrapped protectively between them. Kathleen hadn't realized they'd fallen asleep until she was roused by a gruff male voice urging, "Wake up. It's time to go."

Dazed, it took a moment to remember where she was and why.

"Who's this?" asked the man who must be Oscar.

"This here's Kathleen. She got lost in the tunnels. Can you help her?"

"What's she doing down here?"

"She was escaping a very bad man."

Kathleen, now fully awake, lifted her lantern to see the man to whom Sally spoke. Something about him seemed familiar.

"Your candle's nearly burned down," he said. "Here, take this. I brought extra."

After replacing her dwindling candle with a fresh one she recognized Oscar as one of the Negros who came to pick up the Pratts on Thanksgiving. Then she remembered Diana saying that one of the tunnel's openings was under the hostelry. Quickly she explained her predicament.

"I'm happy to take you out, Miss, but not to the hostelry. That ain't a place to bring a lady at this time of night. Besides, I've got to get these folks to Mr. Hadwen. He's waiting."

They left the room that in the stronger light of two lanterns she could now see held a few mattresses, jugs of water, and chamber pots.

They moved quickly down the tunnel in the same direction Kathleen had been going when she'd stumbled upon the little room. The sound of dripping water grew louder until it was a rushing right above their heads.

"Are we under a river?" asked Kathleen.

"That's the Mill Brook you hear," Oscar explained. "It gets even louder where it connects to the Blackstone Canal. We'll turn off before then, though."

"It sounds right on top of us. Could the water break through?"

"No, Ma'am. You can't see it in the dark, but the tunnel ceilings are made of brick just like the walls. We're forty feet underground. That brook's a lot farther above us than it sounds."

"Forty feet!" Kathleen's skin crawled with the feeling of being buried alive.

"These tunnels have lasted over a hundred years. I doubt they'll give way tonight," Oscar assured her.

"Why were they built?"

"There's some say the land here was too swampy to build on. Not without putting down a strong structure to undergird it. Otherwise any buildings would sink. Could be but that don't account for why they made all them chambers. You saw the big one I suppose, with the boxing ring and all."

"Aye. Is that still in use?"

"Not for a couple of years at least. But they say back in '50 there was a fight like none ever seen. Jem Mace come all the way from England for it. Folks were laying bets. Big money, too. Amounts it would hurt some folks bad to lose. A fifty-round fight, they say. Fifty rounds of bare-knuckle fighting. Can you imagine that?" Oscar shook his head and whistled.

"Did that really happen?" asked Phoebe.

"Maybe. Maybe not. There's lots of stories folks tell. Some have a bit of truth to them, but it's hard to say which part."

"That room has been used for something," Kathleen stated.

"Uh-huh. Still is, though not so much as it once was. You noticed, I'll bet, the three tunnels coming off it? This being one of them. Them tunnels was built as escape routes. Whether Jem Mace was ever here or not, a lot of illegal gambling, pool playing, betting on fights, meeting up with whore...umm... a certain class of ladies, that's all been going on for some time. The police know about it. Every so often they stage a raid. When that happens, folks have to get out quick. Three tunnels sends them in all directions. Harder to round everyone up. These days that room's pretty quiet. Things have their time then fade away. These tunnels get more use now giving folks a resting place while they await a time for Mr. Hadwen to move them on."

"Does everyone in Worcester know about them?"

Oscar let out a hearty laugh. "Wouldn't be much of a secret if the whole city knew, would it? Only certain folk. Ones who have reason to know, and those folk aren't going to blab the word around."

"How did you come to know of them?" Kathleen asked, wondering if Lemuel might be one of those 'certain type of folk.'

"The hostelry workers, we live here."

"You live underground?" Kathleen couldn't believe it. The Pratts may have made her sleep in the kitchen, but at least they hadn't relegated her to the root cellar.

"Us Negroes do," Oscar said. "It's not so bad. We've fixed the rooms up decent, even got us a bathtub down here. Best thing is, no one bothers us. When we're down here, we're our own bosses and that's a good feeling."

Oscar finished speaking just as they arrived at a place where an oblong passage had been built low into the wall.

"That's where you'll go, Miss," said Oscar, indicating the passage.

Kathleen looked at it in dismay. It was narrow, low to the ground.

"You'll have to crawl," Oscar explained, "but only a short while. It opens up within a yard or so. Follow it to the end. You'll come to a ladder attached to the wall. Climb up and you'll come out in the basement of the Arlington Hotel right across from the new Bay State."

Kathleen eyed the hole, which seemed to grow smaller by the minute. "Is this the only way? Can't I go with you?"

"Afraid not, Miss. Mr. Hadwen's putting himself at risk as it is. I show up with someone he don't expect, well...I don't know how he'd take it. This route's been working well so far. Can't take any chances of having it come to an end. I hope you understand."

Kathleen's eyes met Sally's. "I do," she said. Before dropping to the ground, she hugged Sally, careful not to press too hard on the woman's bony frame. She cupped

Phoebe's chin in her hand giving her a wide smile. "God go with ya both," she said.

"And with you as well," said Sally.

Then she turned to Oscar. "I can't thank you enough. I might never have found my way out."

"You take care now. We'll stay 'til you get safely through the hole."

Kathleen squatted. She pushed the sack and lantern in ahead of her. Then she hunched herself as compactly as she could to squeeze through the opening. The hole was not big enough to get onto all fours, so she shimmied along by digging her elbows and toes into the ground, dragging herself forward, pushing the sack and lantern ahead of her. Dirt trickled into the top of her dress, tickling her skin. It was slow going but eventually the tunnel began to widen. Before long she could crawl, then stand. Feeling she was near the end of her journey, she quickened her steps, almost running. The front of her dress, caked with mud, clung heavily. Before long she'd reached the ladder. The climb up was complicated by her sack and lantern, but she made it to the top. Expecting a trap door, she was surprised to find that the ground flattened out. She stood, walked a few steps until coming face-to-face with a door. Supposing it to be locked, she tried the handle anyway. It turned. The door opened into a dark room. She stood directly behind a tall shelf lined with bottles and jars of food. The room was filled with more shelves as well as barrels and crates. She was in the basement of the Arlington Hotel, just as Oscar had said.

The room was empty, but voices and the clanking of crockery could be heard from above. A stairway led to another door, undoubtedly the hotel's kitchen. She looked around, wanting to make a quick escape before anyone appeared in the basement. She skirted past the barrels, wove her way around the crates. Finally, a door. She slid the bolt, opening it as quietly as possible. Fresh air hit her face at once. Stepping outside, she closed the door behind her. Leaning against it, she took in great gulps of air. Dawn was beginning to break. A hint of rosy pink streaked the sky, the crescent moon only a vague outline.

Kathleen looked down at her dress, thoroughly smeared with dirt. It was Sunday. Mass would begin in a few hours. Amelia's first Mass. Exhausted and filthy, she began the long walk towards the Arcade where she would ask the Lintons if she could clean up, borrow a dress from Mrs. Linton or Aoife, confess everything. She would manage, somehow, to get through Mass without falling asleep. Then she would talk to Father Boyce about asking the Sisters of Mercy to find a place for her as they were doing for Amelia. She hated the idea of leaving Meg, but she could not stay in Worcester. She would never be safe until she was free of Lemuel Pratt.

Part Two

Chapter Thirty-Five

The train pulled up to the platform on Foster Street. "I can't believe I'm here." Rory's voice was barely audible as he was speaking more to himself than to his companion who heard him, nonetheless.

"Like dreaming to you, is it?" asked Kevin. "To me as well. And I don't have a wife I'm about to see for the first time in nine years."

"If we can find her," said Rory.

The train station bustled with travelers coming and going. Rory felt even more disoriented than he had when the ship docked in Boston Harbor. From there it hadn't been difficult to find the train headed for Worcester. Now he was standing in Meg's city. Which way to go? He knew the Claproods lived on Crown Street. Where was that? He also knew that Meg had Thursdays off. Today being Wednesday, he should find her home.

The streets were crowded with pedestrians, horses pulling wagons, trains crossing the road. Stores, factories, and houses lined the streets. A cacophony of voices, wagon wheels crunching gravel, the chug-chug-chug, and whistles of trains assailed his ears.

"Excuse me, sir," Rory said, stopping a portly, middle-aged man striding down the sidewalk. "Could you tell me how to get to Crown Street?"

The man looked him up and down, suspicion in his eyes. "What would you want with anyone on Crown Street?

Your kind are in the Meadows. Better head there, laddies."
The last word dripped with hostility.

Rory stared after the man as he walked on.

"Probably best if we ask someone who's dressed like us," Kevin suggested.

A team of four horses pulling a large wagon rounded the corner.

"Look out, there. Watch yer step. Do ya wish to be trampled?" called the driver to a group of youths.

"Did you hear?" asked Rory.

"I did."

Rory waved his hands wildly to get the attention of the driver who had just started moving forward again.

"Aye, what can I do for you?" called the driver.

"Can you tell us how to get to Crown Street?"

"Oh, aye. Head west," he said, twisting in his seat to point behind him. "Then take a left onto Main Street, a right onto Pleasant, then up the hill until you come to Crown on your left."

"Thank you," said Rory.

"Just came in, did you?"

"Aye. We docked in Boston and rode the train to Worcester. I'm Rory Quinn and this is my friend, Kevin Dooley. We've come from Kelegeen."

"Kelegeen, is it?" He looked as though he was searching for a connection then, he shrugged. "I'm Seamus O'Herilhy of Galway."

"Nice to meet you, Seamus. We'll be on our way now," said Rory.

He and Kevin had taken only a few steps when Seamus called to them, "Wait!"

They turned back.

"Kelegeen is where Meg and Kathleen O'Connor are from. It wouldn't be them you're looking for, would it?"

Rory broke out in a broad smile. "Aye, 'tis indeed."

"Their brother?"

"I'm Meg's husband," he announced, puffing out his chest. "How do you know Meg?"

"Hired me out for a sleigh ride once. Her along with her sister and their friend, Nuala. See them at Mass every Sunday, too, at Saint John's. Now I've got to get this load delivered. I'll have to be off. Glad to meet you." With a flick of the reins, the horses moved forward.

Upon reaching their destination, Rory and Kevin stood across from the Claprood's home. Rory stared at the imposing edifice.

"Can you believe Meg lives there? It must seem like a palace to her." A twinge of fear made his chest tingle. He knew he could not give Meg such a grand home.

"Well? Are you going to gawk at it for rest of the day?" Kevin asked.

Rory swallowed. "Do you think she'll recognize me?"

"Get over there."

They crossed the street. Rory hastened up the path to the kitchen door. Kevin hung back at the gate.

"Coming?" Rory turned to ask when he realized he was walking alone.

"Have your first sight of each other in private. Besides, last time Meg clapped eyes on me she'd have just as soon seen me hanged."

"Kathleen and I have both told her how much you've changed."

Kevin gave his friend a lopsided grin. "It takes more than a few words to change Meg O'Connor's mind."

"True enough. Stay where you are. If she doesn't kill me for bringing you along, I'll call for you."

Rory took a deep breath before raising his hand to knock. His emotions were so jumbled he couldn't have named them had he tried.

The door opened. A tall, sturdy, dark haired woman wearing a maid's uniform stood before him.

"Meg," he said.

"Oh, my." Her hands flew to her face, her breathing coming in gasps.

"Meg," he said again.

They stood a moment, searching each other's faces. Then Meg threw herself into his arms, sobbing.

"My God, Rory, you are here," she cried into his neck.

Her voice was the most glorious sound he'd ever heard. He wrapped his arms tightly around her.

"Nothing will ever part us again," Rory said, holding her back enough to look at her face. The face he'd dreamed of, yearned for every day for the past nine years. She was older, twenty-eight now, but the years of regular meals and daily labor had filled her out, given her a healthy glow. She was more beautiful than ever.

"How I've missed you," he said, unable to keep the catch from his voice. He threw off her maid's cap to stroke her bound up hair. Black and glossy, soft as ever to his touch.

"I have it still," she said reaching into her pocket for the comb he'd carved. "I've kept it with me always."

He drew her tightly back into his arms.

"Margaret?"

Meg jumped at the sound of a woman's voice. Rory released her. As Meg turned, she grasped Rory's hand, drawing him into the kitchen.

"Mrs. Claprood," she said, her voice slightly unsteady. "There is something I must tell you."

Rory noticed the astonishment on the face of the woman who must be Meg's employer.

"Who is this man, Margaret?" asked Mrs. Claprood.

The poor woman looked positively scandalized. Hadn't Meg told her he was coming? Had Meg even received his letter?

Rory felt Meg stiffen beside him. "Mrs. Claprood, this is Rory Quinn. He's just arrived from Ireland." Meg looked up at Rory. Unshed tears made the blue of her eyes shimmer. "He is my husband," she said.

"'Tis a pleasure to meet you, Ma'am," Rory said. "Meg's written often of how good you've been to her. I'm grateful to you and your family."

Mrs. Claprood's gaze flickered between Meg and Rory, her face ashen.

"Margaret, why did you never tell me?"

"Please don't be angry, Ma'am. I've wanted to."

Rory could not fathom a reason for Meg to keep their marriage a secret.

The color returned to Mrs. Claprood's face, her cheeks burning red. "You have lived in our home for nine years. We've thought of you as part of the family. But you've been living here under false pretenses. I don't know what to think."

"I hated keeping it from you."

Rory ached at how stricken Meg appeared.

Mrs. Claprood drew in a deep breath. "Let us sit at the table."

Rory placed himself next to Meg, grasping her hand, while Mrs. Claprood drew up a chair.

"When Nuala and I first met at the placement agency," Meg began, "I told her that Rory and I married immediately before I boarded the ship for America and that I planned to work and save money to pay Rory's passage. She warned me never to reveal it to anyone or I would not get a position, as no one hires married women." Meg leaned towards the woman. "I feared I'd lose my position if you found out."

Mrs. Claprood's face softened. "I understand why you didn't say anything at the beginning. But Margaret, have you not come to know us well enough to confide?"

Meg hung her head. "I'd kept it a secret so long that it felt awkward to bring it up."

"You must have known your husband was coming. Why not say something before he got here?"

"That's the thing. Rory's letter telling me he was on his way was the one Deborah forgot to give me until the night I mended her gown. A month had already passed. I knew Rory could arrive any day and I would have to tell you, but everyone has been in such a state of excitement since Saturday night that I didn't know when or how to begin."

"I suppose we have been preoccupied. And it was irresponsible of Deborah to forget about giving you the letter for so long."

Rory sat quietly, taking in their conversation.

"And you, young man, now that you're here what will you do to support your wife? Do you have a job?" Mrs. Claprood demanded.

"Not yet, Ma'am, but I've brought excellent references. I'm trained at working with horses. I'm hoping to find employment as a groom or driver."

Mrs. Claprood frowned. "I see. What of your living arrangements? Where are you staying?"

"I had planned to ask Meg where I could stay until I get settled." A weak plan, he now realized.

"How will you pay for your lodgings?"

At this Rory brightened. "I have money with me. My earnings from home. I can scrape by for the time being."

"Mother!" Deborah popped her head into the kitchen. "There you are. Who is this? And who is that young man sitting by our garden gate?"

"Young man?"

"God Lord, I forgot about Kevin!" Rory exclaimed.

"Kevin?" asked Meg. "You don't mean Kevin Dooley?"

"Aye, 'tis exactly who I mean."

"You didn't mention him coming in your letter."

"Who is Kevin Dooley?" Mrs. Claprood interjected.

"I didn't know he was coming until after I'd posted the letter," Rory told Meg. "Dacey Kilpatrick gave him extra wages when he heard I'd bought passage. He knew how keen Kevin was to get here."

"Mother, what's all this about?" Deborah now stood behind her mother's chair.

"And what is Kevin Dooley going to do here?" Meg demanded. "He'd best not be expecting you to support him, the lazy, shiftless –"

"Meg, he's not like that anymore. I've written that."

"I'll believe it when I've seen it with my own eyes."

"Pardon me!" Mrs. Claprood stood "Who is Kevin Dooley and why is he sitting at our garden gate?"

"Sorry, Ma'am," said Rory. "Kevin is a friend we've know all our lives. He stayed outside so Meg and I could have our reunion privately."

"He's been waiting a good while," said Mrs. Claprood. "Best not leave him out there any longer." She turned to Meg. "Margaret, where do you suggest your husband and this other man lodge for the time being?"

"With the Lintons, I suppose."

"Husband?" gasped Deborah.

* * *

Rory could not help comparing the shabby rooms of the Arcade with the Claproods' home even though he'd been no further than their kitchen. The Lintons' appeared cheery, however. He and Kevin were given a warm welcome. Meg apologized for the extra person, giving Kevin a dark glance as she spoke.

"'Tis no matter," Maureen Linton assured them with a smile. "We always manage to make room."

They were soon joined by Aoife, her mother, and the two babies. Mrs. Linton set out bread, cheese, and a hard-boiled egg for each of the newcomers. Hungry and grateful, they ate as much as they dared. It was obvious the Lintons had little to spare.

"I'm afraid we will be too much of a burden on you," said Rory. "I have some money. We could stay at a lodging if you could tell us of a cheap one."

"And run out of money too soon?" Maureen asked. "You're better off with us."

Rory glanced around. He hated to impose on the kindness of these people who were nearly strangers. All he knew of them were from Meg's letters.

"We won't burden you for long. We're eager to find jobs," Kevin said.

"Best of luck to you with that," said Aoife. "There's many who won't hire Irish."

"Aye, but there are those who will," Mrs. Linton interjected. "My husband and yours both have jobs," she said giving Aoife a pointed look. "They should be home soon," she said turning back to Rory. "We will ask if there are any openings."

Before long, Darien Linton came through the door accompanied by Ned's uncle Owen. Once introductions were made and hearty handshakes exchanged, the conversation turned immediately to opportunities for employment.

"I'm hoping to find work as a groom or driver," Rory explained. "I was taught by two skilled Englishmen."

"What of that lad, Seamus O'Herilhy?" asked Owen. "He was all wound up after Mass talking about starting his new job as a driver for Mr. Archer's Lumber Company. That should mean his job as a groom is vacant." He turned to Rory. "My lad, go there tomorrow and inquire. They hired Seamus so we know they'll take Irish labor."

Seamus O'Herilhy. An odd coincidence, thought Rory, should he replace him.

"I'll explain how to get there in the morning," Owen continued. "Why don't the two of you lads stay with me tonight. I had another nephew who was supposed to come after Ned married Aoife, but he died of typhus before he could board the ship. I've more room than the Lintons."

"That's very kind of you. We'd be glad of it. We can help with the food," Rory said. He planned to replenish the Lintons' larder, as well.

"And you, lad," said Owen, turning to Kevin. "Are you in for the horses as well?"

337

"I've no acquaintance with them at all."

"What can you do, then?"

"Grow some crops. Fish. I learn quickly, though. I'll take whatever work I can get."

"Same as most of us. Darien and I will ask around tomorrow."

"I'd greatly appreciate that," he said.

"Meg, do you have to get back?" asked Mrs. Linton.

"Mrs. Claprood gave me leave to bring Rory and Kevin here, but she said nothing about when I should return."

"Shouldn't be away too long, then."

Meg turned to Rory. He saw longing in her eyes.

"Ah, come together after all these years." The catch in Mrs. Linton's voice betrayed her feelings.

"What will happen to your position?" Mrs. O'Sullivan asked. It was the first time she'd spoken.

"I don't know," said Meg. "The news of my being married shocked Mrs. Claprood." Meg went on to describe the events following Rory's arrival.

"Is she very angry?" asked Aoife. "Do you think she'll let you stay on until Rory has a job and you two can find a place to live?"

"I hope so. She's very kind." Meg sound anything but sure.

"Owen, would you be good enough to take Meg and Rory to your room so they can take leave of each other in private before I walk her home?" asked Mr. Linton.

Alone in the small room, Rory took Meg in his arms. "Meg?" he asked, holding her close.

"Aye?"

"You've been living in a grand house. I never thought about it until I saw it for myself. I can't imagine you'll want to give up that life." The last sentence was so hard for him that he choked on it.

Meg looked deeply into his eyes. "Rory, you deserve the truth." Her voice was rough with emotion. "I've thought about that often. 'Tis true I've grown used to the luxuries around me. I've worried, cried, prayed. I couldn't fathom how I'd react the day you finally arrived. I know now, though. I knew it the moment I saw you."

She swallowed hard. As Rory watched her collect herself, fear shot through him. Had he come this far only to lose her?

338

"Rory, the day we buried your mam, as we walked away from the grave, you told me that one day we would have all the Brits have and more. There was such fire in your eyes."

Rory nodded, remembering.

"At the time I thought it was your anger and hurt talking. But now..."

"Now?"

"Now I believe you. Oh, not that we'll be rich," she shook her head, the ghost of a laugh mixing with her tears. "But look what you've done already. Learning all about caring for horses. Taking care of what's left of our families, waiting all these years until the time was right to come. You didn't even let this stand in your way," she said, holding up his damaged right hand. "What you set your mind to, you do. I know it, because I'm the same way."

He couldn't help laughing. Meg's stubbornness was legendary in Kelegeen.

"Enough of that," she said, teasing him with a playful slap on the arm. Becoming serious again, she explained, "The two of us together, we will make it. I don't know how long it will take or what we'll have to endure on the way, but whatever it is we will do it together. It may not be a life like that of the grand Yankees, but it will be ours. That is what I knew for certain the moment I saw you at the kitchen door."

Rory's mouth stretched into a smile so wide it hurt. He wrapped her tightly in his arms, felt hers encircle him. He was sure now that nothing would stand in their way. They held each other so tightly he swore he could feel Meg's determination fusing with his own.

Chapter Thirty-Six

The rest of June was an eternity to Meg. Rory got the position vacated by Seamus. The pay was low, but better than what Kevin made at the wire works. The Claproods, once they got over their astonishment at Meg's marriage, kept her on until she and Rory could afford a place of their own.

"Think of it. Nine whole years," Deborah had said. "It's so romantic. Like in a novel."

"There's nothing romantic about it," Meg corrected, noting the dreamy look in Deborah's eyes.

"Oh, but there is," Deborah insisted. "Except in a novel you and Rory wouldn't wait for anything as dreary as saving money. You'd run off together and live on love." Deborah finished with a dramatic sigh.

Mrs. Claprood rolled her eyes.

"Good thing we're not in a novel, then," said Meg. "You can't eat love. We'd end up dead."

"Oh!" cried Deborah. "Dying for the sake of love. Even more romantic!"

Meg shook her head. There was no reasoning with a young lady who knew nothing of real poverty.

It was not just the interminable waiting. Kathleen's frightening adventure nagged at her as well. On the Sunday after Meg had belatedly received Rory's letter, she had expected to share it with Kathleen after Mass. But Kathleen had arrived at Mass looking thoroughly exhausted, wearing a borrowed, ill-fitting dress, with dirt embedded in her skin and hair. After Kathleen related the entire story of Lemuel's appearance at the boardinghouse and her escape through the tunnels, they went immediately to Father Boyce for help.

"Gather your possessions and meet me at the rectory in an hour and a half," he had told Kathleen and Amelia who had come for her first Mass. "I'll take you to the Sisters. They'll keep you safe until they can find positions for you."

So it was that Meg spent the rest of June unable to speak with Kathleen. At least she knew she was safe at the convent. She caught a glimpse of her on Sundays when she and Amelia arrived at Saint John's with the Sisters. But as the nuns kept a sort of living shield around them, she could not get near.

If all of that coupled with Rory's sudden arrival had not been enough, there was now the trouble with Aoife, Ned, and Mrs. O'Sullivan. Ned's drinking had increased and with it his bad temper. Too often Meg saw the marks of it on Aoife – a cut lip, a black eye, a slight limp in her walk. She always had an excuse. She'd tripped over something. She'd been so tired from looking after the children she'd walked into a door. Meg believed none of it. If she'd had any doubt, the agonized look on Mrs. O'Sullivan's face dispelled it. On Sunday last, Mrs. O'Sullivan had taken Meg aside.

"If there were to come a time when I wasn't here Ned wouldn't feel so weighed down. His drinking might stop, his temper cool. They'd get on again like at the beginning. Were I gone, I'd not want Aoife or my sister to worry. I'll be fine. Tell them so."

The Thursday following, Meg and Nuala stopped by the Arcade at Meg's insistence. They found Aoife and Mrs. Linton in a state of turmoil. Mrs. O'Sullivan had gone out the previous afternoon to return clean laundry and never come back. Mr. Linton, Rory, Kevin, and Owen MacBrody had searched all night for her. Ned had refused, saying he'd not give up his working man's sleep. Mr. Linton went to the police who promised to look, but their demeanor said one missing Irish woman was worth little of their time.

Meg repeated what Mrs. O'Sullivan had told her on the previous Sunday. "I didn't fully understand," Meg explained. "But now I believe she was planning to go away. She wanted me to tell you not to worry."

"But where would she go?" asked Mrs. Linton.

"Only one place," said Nuala.

Understanding dawned simultaneously in the faces of Aoife and Mrs. Linton.

The poorhouse.

"There's one way to find out," Nuala said. "Up for a walk?" she asked, turning to Meg.

Though the poorhouse in Worcester in no way resembled the one in Kelegeen, for Meg it conjured dreadful memories as a place of last resort. Most who entered left in a shroud. *That was Ireland*, she told herself. *Things are different here.*

As they approached, her fears ebbed. The new brick almshouse was only months old. It sat on acres of farmland and appeared almost welcoming.

"We're looking for Clodagh O'Sullivan," Nuala said to the woman who answered the door.

"She's seeing to the laundry. Are you relatives?"

"Friends," said Meg. "She didn't tell anyone she was coming here. We came to find out. Her daughter and sister are worried."

"Wait here," said the woman. "I'll fetch her."

Mrs. O'Sullivan soon appeared on the front porch, sleeves rolled up above her elbows.

"Thank God we found you," said Meg.

"Did you not tell them I'd be fine? I told you to, remember?"

"Aye, but you didn't tell me you were planning to put yourself in the poorhouse!"

"'Tis not like at home. The Drurys who oversee this place are kindly people. I get decent food and a place to sleep. What else do I need? It will give Aoife and Ned a better chance."

"Ned's good for nothing," Nuala fumed. "Behaving like a madman because things got a bit rough for him."

"That may be," said Mrs. O'Sullivan, speaking in a resigned tone. "But they are married and have bairns. I pray that my getting out of their way will help. It's all I could think to do."

Her eyes pleaded with Meg. "Tell them not to worry. It's for the best."

Meg and Nuala left, relieved to have found Mrs. O'Sullivan safe and well.

"And what if that Know Nothing Gardner decides to send another boatload of Irish off to Liverpool?" said Nuala. "It's from the poorhouses he takes 'em."

* * *

On the last Sunday of June, Meg found the situation at the Arcade worse than ever. Aoife blamed Ned for her mother leaving. She seemed not to care how drunk or abusive he became. By turns she railed at him or refused to speak to him at all. Mrs. Linton was not much better disposed towards him. Ned no longer attended Mass. He spent the morning sleeping off his Saturday night drunk. Meg would have found an excuse not to go after Mass except that it was her only chance to see Rory. Now that Rory knew his way, he'd taken to walking her back to Crown Hill when it was time for her to return.

"I'm learning my way around Worcester," he told her as they climbed the hill towards the Claprood's. "I'm hoping to get requested as a driver. It will be a little extra in my pocket."

As Rory and Kevin were staying with Owen, they both assisted with the rent and food. Owen had offered to have Meg move in, too, so they could be together, but Rory would not hear of it. He refused to take Meg from her comfortable surroundings until he could provide something better for her.

Meg had just said goodbye to Rory when the sound of excited voices reverberated from the parlor.

"Margaret! I thought I heard you come in," said Deborah, bursting into the kitchen. "I've got the most wonderful news! Edward Thayer proposed to Pamela after church this morning. They are to be married in September. Isn't that exciting?"

Not waiting for Meg's answer, she rushed back to the parlor. Meg changed into her uniform then entered the parlor to offer her congratulations to Pamela, seated next to Mr. Thayer on the settee.

"Oh, Margaret, we've so much to do!" said Mrs. Claprood. "You'll stay with us through September, won't you?"

* * *

Edward Thayer made an appearance at the Claprood home most Sundays from that point on often accompanied by his sister, Hyacinth. Pamela, Deborah, and Hyacinth would retire to the conservatory along with Mrs. Claprood where they discussed the wedding, while Edward sat with Mr. Claprood and Oliver in the parlor conversing over politics. Meg made every attempt to work close to the parlor, preferring the men's conversation.

"Gardner!" she heard Edward exclaim late on an afternoon in July. "Now I like him even less. He's managed to turn his Know Nothing party from an instrument of the

343

people into a political machine headed by him and his own ambitions. The man would love nothing more than to be a dictator for the entire country."

"Oliver?" asked Mr. Claprood. "I believe you followed your friend, Lemuel, and voted for Gardner?"

"Father, you and I differed before Lemuel started in on me."

"And I'm grateful you've enough of a mind of your own not to follow him on everything. His recent behavior has been abominable."

"I've been keeping my distance. Our political views have parted ways, too. He is more entrenched than ever in the Know Nothings. I am ready to turn my allegiance over to the new Republican Party."

"What's caused your change of heart?" asked Mr. Claprood.

"Edward's right. Gardner wants only to serve himself. Beyond that, I only joined for the anti-slavery cause. The whole party is splintering. Northern and southern party members can't get along because of the slavery issue. They've nominated Millard Fillmore as their presidential candidate. Fillmore! Can you believe it? He signed the Fugitive Slave Law. And they want that Tennessean slaveholder, Andrew Jackson Donelson for vice president. How could I possibly remain in such a party?"

A measure of hope, Meg thought. Perhaps the Know Nothing party would collapse.

"I've heard that the Republicans are adding nativism and temperance to their platform," said Edward. "Does this bother you?"

"No. No party could remain viable with only one issue. Besides, they need to lure away disillusioned Know Nothings."

"It's a game," said Mr. Claprood. "All of politics is. It just happens to be one with high stakes."

Low chuckles came from Edward and Oliver, but Meg sighed heavily. *The lives of thousands of people. Just a game.*

344

Mrs. Claprood appeared on the threshold, followed by both daughters and Hyacinth Thayer.

"Margaret, we've decided on a dinner served after the ceremony. Do you think Kathleen's employer would let us borrow her for the day? Kathleen's cooking would be perfect."

"I will ask her," was all she could think to say.

Once the Claproods had seen their guests out, Deborah, bubbling over with excitement, returned to the dining room where Meg was ready to take the silver tea service to the kitchen for a polishing.

"The landlady will grant Kathleen leave when she hears the reason, don't you think? Oh, it will be so beautiful! And I do hope they have a baby right away. I can't wait to be an auntie!"

Deborah sailed out of the room. Meg kicked open the door to the kitchen, setting the tea service on the table with a thud. *And I should have my own bairns by now.* She dropped into a chair near the table. The unfairness of life washed over her. Beyond the ache of a nine-year unconsummated marriage, she now had to figure a way to explain why Kathleen could not prepare the wedding feast. She'd lost some of the Claproods' confidence when the truth of her marriage came out. The fact that Kathleen was now hiding out in a convent because of Lemuel Pratt would be even harder for the Claproods to understand.

Chapter Thirty-Seven

"Are you going to talk to Ned today?" Rory asked Kevin.

Ned's drinking was affecting his work. Oily floors, monstrous machines with rapidly moving belts, the possibility of snapping wire that could hit a worker like a whip – all of it was dangerous enough with one's full attention engaged. The reeling effects of a previous night's drinking bout made it potentially deadly. Owen's words of caution proved fruitless, so he'd asked Kevin and Rory to intervene.

"I will, but will it do any good? You remember my da."

"Ned hasn't been at it as long as your da. Remind him he took the pledge."

Rory and Kevin had taken the pledge, too, joining the Father Mathew Society at Saint John's.

"You think that will make a difference?"

"Tell him he's going back on his word to God."

"He's not even going to Mass anymore."

"Then what are you going to say?"

"I was thinking of telling him of my own da. How he nearly destroyed us all with his drinking. The fact that I'm the only one still alive is not entirely due to the starving. My mam and sisters were terrified of him. The lasses lost their minds. I'll ask him does he want to do that to his wife and bairns. Should something happen to him at work, does he want them to remember him with love, or as a no-good drunkard who ruined his family?"

Rory nodded approval. "I wish you luck," he said.

Leaving the Arcade, Rory parted company and headed for the Hendry and Copes Livery Stable. It was mid-July and though the sun hadn't been up long it was already hot.

The stable was a large building on Exchange Street. Every day Rory fed, watered, and groomed the horses, mucked out

346

their stalls, harnessed them when their services were needed, and occasionally acted as driver. He'd become adept at riding while working for Sir Alfred. Exercising the horses by taking them to gallop freely away from the city streets was his favorite duty.

Clyde Hendry had been impressed by his references, but even more by observing Rory's handling of the horses. It did not take long for Mr. Hendry to feel at ease with Rory in the stables. Rory had yet to meet Davison Copes, the silent partner.

Two others worked alongside Rory. Isaiah Burns, an older man, who took care of the conveyances, had been with Hendry and Copes since they began. He was civil enough, but kept to himself. His work was impeccable, every conveyance in perfect condition and sparkling clean whenever called for. The other was a young lad of about seventeen named Breccan Grady. Rory often found himself correcting Breccan's mistakes. One day when Isaiah was looking for Breccan to help hitch up a pair of horses to a wagon, the young man was nowhere to be found.

"He's a lazy one," Isaiah had said to Rory. "Don't know why they keep him on."

Rory stopped his own work to help with the hitching then went to see what had become of Breccan. He found him asleep in the hay loft. Rory shook him, speaking sternly about doing an honest day's work for his pay.

The lad had only smirked.

"You want to lick the Yankee Prods' boots that's your concern. Let me alone."

"What kind of talk is that? Mr. Hendry's a good sort. If you had any honor – "

"Honor? You call the way those Prods treat us honorable?"

"When they see us being shiftless it only gives them fuel for their fire. You want to give the rest of us a bad name?" He nudged the younger lad with the toe of his boot.

"They'll think it anyway. Don't waste your time trying to impress them."

"I don't do my work to impress anyone. I do it because it's right. Besides, it's not just Hendry and Copes, but Isaiah and me in this. You're not holding up your end. Get up and get to work."

"You can't tell me what to do." Breccan rolled over.

Furious, Rory grabbed Breccan by the back of his collar and the waist of his pants. Lifting him in the air, he set him at the ladder. "Get your lazy arse down there and get to work. Either you're proud enough of your people not to embarrass us all or you're a dirty traitor. Which is it?"

Breccan had scowled at Rory, but he'd gone back to work.

In today's unbearable heat, Breccan worked more slowly than ever. By noontime he claimed illness and left the stables. Though irritated, Rory was glad to have him gone.

Sweat poured off him as he cleaned the hooves of one of the horses. Just as he finished Mr. Hendry entered the stable with another gentleman.

"Rory, this is Hiram Archer," he said introducing the other gentleman. "Owner of Archer Lumber. He and his young son Caleb moved here from Maine in the spring. He wants Caleb to learn to ride. I'd like you to show him the gentlest horse in the stable, a good fit for an eight-year-old."

"My pleasure, sir. We've a lovely mare. The perfect little cob she is. I'll take her out so you can have a look."

Rory led out a dun colored Quarter Horse with a dark mane and tail.

"This is Fancy," he said, patting the horse's neck. "She's gentle as a lamb, but sturdy. She'll do right by your lad, Mr. Archer."

Hiram Archer walked slowly around Fancy.

"You know horses, sir?" Rory asked, observing how closely he inspected the animal.

"I do," he said.

"In that case, you'll likely agree. She's a real darlin', she is."

"You've ridden her?" For the first time, Mr. Archer looked at Rory.

"Aye, sir. I like a horse a bit more hotblooded for my own pleasure, but there's nothing I can fault in this lass when it comes to temperament. She's the right horse for a beginner, and no mistake."

Mr. Archer peppered Rory with questions about horses from their care to their quirks. He answered each question with ease.

Mr. Archer smiled. "Where did you learn?"

"Back home in Ireland. I started with a horse named Lily. Best horse in the world. Belongs to a Doctor Parker. He adores her. Taught me all about horses and how to care for them as well as how to ride and drive them. Later I worked for Sir Alfred Stokes, him being the landlord that owned our property. I took care of four creatures that couldn't have been more unalike and glad I was of it. It gave me experience with horses of different temperaments. I learned to deal with each. They're like people, got their own dispositions. Want to get along? Well, understand them and let them be who they are, without losing their respect. It's a give and take, you see."

"You're a wise young man. I'd like to hire you to give my son riding lessons." He turned to Mr. Hendry. "With your permission, Clyde."

"If Rory can do so without losing work time, I've no quarrel with it."

"Do you think you can accommodate?" asked Mr. Archer.

"Aye, sir."

"Excellent. I want Caleb to learn every aspect of keeping a horse. Are you willing to teach him? You'll be compensated well, I assure you."

"If Mr. Hendry's agreeable, your lad can come here to the stable and learn firsthand."

"Clyde?"

"Of course, he's welcome," Mr. Hendry said. Turning to Rory he added, "Just be sure to keep the boy out of harm's way."

"Aye, sir. I'll keep a close eye on him."

"Then it's settled," said Mr. Archer.

Rory couldn't wait to tell Meg his good fortune. Caleb would come to the stables twice a week to spend the days shadowing Rory. On those same days he would take riding lessons after Rory finished his work as well as on Saturday afternoons. All the money he earned from Mr. Archer would be saved for their future. Mr. Archer had even promised a pay increase if he was satisfied with Rory's teaching.

On Tuesday of the following week, Caleb Archer began his training in the stables, with Rory explaining everything he was doing and why as he went about his workday. When they stopped for their afternoon meal, Rory and Caleb sat on bales of hay near the stable entrance.

"How long have you been in Worcester?" Rory asked while slicing a slab of cheese with his pocketknife.

"Since April," Caleb answered, staring at his food.

"Came from Maine, did you?"

"Yes."

"That's east of here, isn't it? Was it a long journey?"

Caleb looked up. "You don't know where Maine is?"

349

"I've only been in America a month. Can't expect me to know this big country already, can you?"

"Oh. Of course. I didn't think."

Rory flashed a smile. "No harm. So, what is Maine like?"

"Cold."

"All the time?"

"No. But often."

Caleb had been quiet all morning. Was the boy not interested in horses or simply shy?

"Ever been on a horse?"

He nodded. "A few times. With my father."

Rory watched as Caleb picked at his food.

"You'll need to eat a mite better than that if you want the strength to be a good horseman."

Caleb dutifully began to eat with more vigor. Rory wondered what kept the child so silent and distant for a boy of eight.

"Your da seems a good man," he tried. "What of the rest of your family? Do you have brothers or sisters?"

A shiver rippled through the small body. "Not anymore," he whispered.

"I'm sorry," said Rory. "I lost most of my brothers and sisters back home in the starving. I miss them every day."

Caleb looked up. "They starved... to death?"

"Aye. Our crops failed several years in a row. Thousands died. That's why I came here. To make a better life."

"That's awful," Caleb said. "Did any but you survive?"

"Two sisters only, Aisling and Loreena. They're still in Ireland. I send some of my pay home to help them. What of yours?"

"They got cholera while Father and I were here in Worcester checking on the building of our new house. When we got home my sister, Elizabeth, was dead. Then Amy died and then Mother a few days after Amy. Mother was to have another baby. I was hoping for a brother."

Rory put a consoling hand on the boy's shoulder. "I'm awfully sorry for you and your da," he said.

The boy nodded, returned to picking at his food.

* * *

"I see you had no luck," said Rory to Kevin the following Saturday, watching Ned leave the Arcade at sundown. They knew he'd head for the nearest pub.

350

"He told me it was none of my business what he did or what his family thought of him. Claimed he worked hard enough to earn a pint or two in an evening."

"If it was only a pint or two," said Rory, brushing away a stone on the Arcade's steps.

"What bothers me most, is how he treats Aoife," said Kevin. "Too like it was between my own mam and da. I remember fearing he might kill her in his drunken rages. Aoife's a good sort. Gives Ned the devil for his drinking, she does. I wish my mam had had some of her spirit. Maybe Da had beaten it out of her."

Rory thought of how much he'd disliked Kevin when they were younger. He'd deemed him a brash, arrogant rotter. He couldn't understand why his brother, Aiden, was friends with him. But Aiden had known more about what Kevin endured at home. If Father O'Malley had not intervened, Kevin would almost certainly have followed the same path as his da. Instead, he was a man who'd built a storehouse of integrity within himself. It was devilishly hard to make Meg see it, but she hadn't been in Ireland over the years in which Kevin's character had been recast. Now Rory would trust Kevin with his life.

Kevin's stare hardened. "I'll not see him do to Aoife what my da did to my mam. I told him if he hurts her again, he'll answer to me."

Rory raised his eyebrows. "I expect Ned had something to say about that."

Kevin snickered. "Said he'd flatten me. I'd like to see that. He's a mean drunk, but a stupid one. I doubt he could get out of his own way."

Rory slapped at a mosquito biting his arm. "Wee devils!"

"We should go in," Kevin suggested.

Inside the door, they were sucked into the building's suffocating humidity.

"Might as well be swimming in a river," said Kevin.

"A river would be refreshing," Rory said. "This is more like a bog on fire. How are your hands?"

"Sore." Slivers of iron had become embedded in Kevin's hands from his work at the wire factory. It was the bane of all the workers. Owen, Darien, and Ned had perpetually swollen fingers and palms. The wire workers spent a good deal of time absentmindedly trying to push out slivers.

That night Rory lay on his mattress reflecting on Ned, a man in his prime wasting his life and destroying his family. He couldn't conceive of treating Meg in such a fashion. Though he'd already taken the Pledge, he vowed again in a silent prayer that he would never take to drink no matter what life threw at him. He asked God to make of him the best husband and da he could be. "I'll give it all my heart, Lord," he prayed, "Please let me be a real husband to Meg and bless us with all the bairns you see fit to send."

Chapter Thirty-Eight

"It's not bad enough they've always got the main streets torn up now they've got to make a mess up here as well," Nuala complained, entering the Claprood's kitchen on a hot Thursday in July.

"They're putting in a crosswalk," Meg told her.

"Are you ready?"

"Aye." Meg tied on her bonnet. "The sooner, the better. All I ever hear is talk of Miss Pamela's wedding. The preparations will be the death of me. You'd think it was the Princess Royal getting married."

"And what of Kathleen doing the cooking?"

Meg growled. "I keep putting them off."

"Our adventure today might help."

"I'm not sure, though I am anxious to see my sister."

Meg and Nuala had made arrangements to visit at the convent on Cedar Street. As they traversed the short distance, skirting debris from ongoing road work, Meg talked about Rory at the stables and his additional job teaching the young Archer lad. "He's saving all the extra income for us."

"Here we are," said Nuala as they reached the imposing brick building, anchored on each end with sharply peaked roofs atop which sat tall, thick chimneys. Four stories high, it had windows of various sizes scattered across its facade. Set into one end were a set of imposing doors. Meg supposed they opened to the chapel. Passing under an arch at the other end, Meg and Nuala followed the walk to the convent's door.

Their knock was answered by an elderly sister dressed in a long black habit, her forehead and chest covered in white cloth, a black veil flowing until it melded with the black of her robes. The woman's face was the color of dough, but her pale blue eyes offered an aura of serenity.

"Yes, my children?"

"Good afternoon, Sister," said Meg. "I'm Margaret Mary O'Connor Quinn and this is my friend Nuala O'Flaherty. Father Boyce made arrangements for us to visit with my sister, Kathleen."

"We've been expecting you. Please come in." Her voice matched her peaceful countenance. "I'm Sister Mary Lawrence," she said as she led them down a long corridor, the lower half of her habit flapping gently as she walked.

"Here we are," said the sister, opening a heavy door. "Kathleen is waiting for you here in one of our common rooms."

The moment Meg entered, Kathleen jumped from her chair. The two rushed into each other's arms as though they'd been parted for years. Nuala hung back until they let go, then joined them.

"Help yourselves," said Sister Mary Lawrence, gesturing towards the tea service on a nearby table. "Please ring the hand bell when you are ready to leave," she instructed before exiting the room.

"Try some of these," said Kathleen handing Meg and Nuala each a small plate of shortbread biscuits topped with lemon curd.

"Mmmm." Nuala's eyes rolled back as she bit into hers. "Did you make them?"

"Aye. The nuns gave me the run of their kitchen. Amelia serves as my assistant. I think they're enjoying our cooking," Kathleen laughed.

"It's probably why you're still here," Nuala joked.

"How long will you stay?" Meg asked as they sat together on the settee.

"Until they find me a placement. I can't stay forever unless I decide to take vows."

"Glory be! Are you considering that?" asked Nuala.

Kathleen laughed again. "No. I love it here, but it's not my calling."

"Any word on where you'll be sent?" Meg asked.

"There were a few possibilities, but they did not work out. They've found a place for Amelia in Rhode Island, though. She'll be leaving in a week." A resigned expression passed over Kathleen's face. "I'll miss her, but it sounds like a good family she'll be going to. There is a Sisters of Mercy convent nearby. They'll help her settle in. She's nervous, but excited to begin a new life. The Sisters there will keep watch over her."

"They found a placement for Amelia more easily than for you?" asked Nuala.

"I think they were trying harder for her. She's no family, poor lass. They wanted to get her settled. I'm safe from Lemuel as long as I'm here. They can take more time."

"And they're not eager to give up the best meals they've ever had," said Nuala.

Kathleen's smile returned.

"Speaking of cooking," Meg began. "Miss Pamela is going to marry Edward Thayer on the fifth of September. The ceremony will be held at the Claprood's home after which they plan to have a dinner. Mrs. Claprood wants you to cook. The Thayers are a prominent family. They want to impress. My cooking will have the opposite effect. Mrs. Claprood's too busy with all the other preparations and no one cooks like you. She still thinks you work at a boarding house. I don't know what to tell her."

"Meg, I can't. The Pratts will be invited. Even if I stayed hidden in the kitchen, even if Lemuel never knew I was there, I wouldn't be able to think straight. I can't do it, Meg. I can't." She gripped her teacup so hard, Meg feared it would shatter.

"I don't expect you to. I simply don't know how to explain."

"Say my employer won't allow it."

"Mrs. Claprood may ask to speak to your employer to plead her case."

"I'm sorry I've put you in such a position, but − oh, wait! Tell her I'm no longer there. That I've moved away. By September it may be true."

Meg thought this over. "I can tell her that I asked you today and you said you'd be leaving your position soon for one in another city."

"What if she asks why Kathleen's leaving?" asked Nuala.

Kathleen shrugged her shoulders. "I got a better offer?"

"That's it! From a relative of one of the boarders," Nuala kept the story going.

"I suppose that's believable," said Meg, uneasy at the idea of once again deceiving Mrs. Claprood.

"What city, if she asks?" Nuala again.

"Boston, I suppose," said Meg.

"It's settled then?" asked Kathleen.

"Aye," said Meg, her head bowed.

"You don't like lying to the Claproods, do you?" asked Nuala later as they walked away from the convent.

"Can you blame me?"

"No. You're an honest soul, Meg." Nuala wrapped her arm around Meg's shoulders as they headed towards the Meadows.

"I'm glad we told Aoife we'd visit," said Meg. "She misses Kathleen more than ever now that her mam's gone."

"As long as Ned's at work, I don't mind visiting. Every time I see him, I've a mind to throw him out a window."

"We share that feeling. Rory says Kevin tried to talk to him about his drinking. Got nowhere."

"You softening on Kevin?" Nuala asked.

"He's still a way to go before I'm convinced. Rory and Kathleen are sure, though. Father O'Malley took him under his wing, and I know well what kind of man he is. I suppose if anyone other than God Himself could set Kevin to rights it would be Father O'Malley."

"Too bad he's not here to work on Ned," said Nuala.

They'd just started down Mechanic Street when Meg noticed two men walking ahead of them. She came to a stop, her eyes narrowing.

"What is it?" Nuala asked.

"Those two. Lemuel Pratt and his da?"

Nuala shrugged. "Can't tell from here. You'd know them better than I."

They continued, keeping their distance. Meg wanted no part of Lemuel Pratt, sure she'd never be able to hold her tongue upon encountering him.

"Looks like they're none too happy with each other," Nuala observed.

One man struck his walking stick on the ground, punctuating his point. The other responded with sweeping arm gestures. The first stopped, turned to face the other. Meg was now sure of their identity. The rumbling of a train chugging down the Albany-Worcester line, drowned out any other sound.

Mr. Pratt wagged his forefinger at Lemuel, almost touching his face as he spoke, in the end jabbing the younger man in the chest. Lemuel pushed his father's hand away, and, throwing his own hands in the air he turned and stalked off.

"Meg, look there," Nuala pointed. "Ned."

Meg glanced in the other direction. A bedraggled young man walked aimlessly alongside the tracks.

356

"Why isn't he at work?" Meg asked.

The words were barely out of her mouth when a train blew its piercing whistle, sending pedestrians scurrying out of the way. A furious Lemuel stalked off in Ned's direction, his head down, lost in his anger. Ned walked on, dangerously close to the tracks. The two men collided. In his fury, Lemuel shoved Ned aside, tossing him directly into the path of the oncoming train.

Ned's legs, the only part of his body Meg could see, rolled like those of a rag doll beneath the wheels. Meg's scream fused with the screeching brakes. Something flew into the air from under the wheels. Ned's shoes, the bloody stumps of his feet still in them. She watched, stunned, as Mr. Pratt, ran towards his son. Lemuel stared at the train, its cars continuing to pass before him. It seemed an eternity before the train stopped. Pedestrians, wagon drivers, road crew workers, all stopped and stared.

Collisions between locomotives and wagons, horses, other trains, and even pedestrians were not uncommon as the tracks crossed the streets at regular intervals. They were still new enough that people were not adept at gauging distances, resulting in frequent tragedies. Meg had heard about them, but this was the first time she had witnessed such a horror.

Meg stared at the train, mouth agape. Nuala tugged her sleeve. "We've got to get to Aoife."

Hurrying, they took a roundabout route, making it to the Arcade before word had time to spread.

"We should go to Mrs. Linton first," Nuala said.

Their knock was answered by one of the children.

"Come in," called Mrs. Linton, looking up from her mending. "What's happened?" she asked, hurrying to meet them, eyes darting from one face to the other.

"There's been a terrible accident," Nuala told her.

Meg and Nuala exchanged glances, then looked at the roomful of children.

"Mary," Mrs. Linton said to her eldest. "Take them all to Aoife's."

"No!" said Meg. "Let's talk in the hallway instead."

Mrs. Linton nodded, following them out the door.

"It's Ned," Nuala began. "He was walking near the tracks, too close to the train."

Mrs. Linton slowly shook her head. "That can't be. Ned's at work."

"We're sure of it," said Nuala. "We were close enough to see him."

"My God! Have you told Aoife?"

"No. We came to you first. Will you come with us when we tell her?," Meg asked, her voice shaky.

"Aye. She'll need us." Mrs. Linton's face crumpled. "She'll need her mam."

Meg, Nuala, and Maureen Linton formed a protective shield around Aoife as they broke the news. At first, she did not believe them. Little by little, Aoife's denial began to crack as Meg and Nuala continually asserted it was him.

At the time the men usually returned home, a knock sounded on Aoife's door. Mrs. Linton opened it to her own husband, Kevin, and Owen.

"Where's Ned?" Aoife asked, her hand clutching Meg's. "Why has he not come home with you as always?"

The men looked at one another as if deciding who should speak. Finally, Owen, toying with his hat, spoke. "Aoife. Ned was fired from his job today," Owen explained. "He was still drunk from last night. He broke one of the machines being careless, just missed maiming another worker. The boss let him go."

"We hoped when he left the wire works, he might have come home," said Kevin. "Should we start making the rounds of the taverns?"

"We know what happened to him," Mrs. Linton told the men. "Meg and Nuala saw it."

Nuala reached for Owen's hand. "I'm so sorry, Mr. MacBrody," she said. "Ned was hit by a train."

The men's faces drained of color.

"That was Ned?" asked Kevin. "We heard about someone getting hit by the train from Albany, but no one knew who it was."

"They'll not know where to bring him," said Owen.

"The train is still stopped," said Darien. "They must be working on getting him out. We'll bring him home."

As the three dashed from the room, Aoife sunk lower. The commotion set Darragh and Clodagh to shrieking. Darragh crawled towards his mother.

"Nuala, take these two to my rooms. Tell Mary. Have her get supper for all the bairns. Meg, help me get Aoife to the bed. Then fetch her a cup of water, please."

All scurried to obey Mrs. Linton. Meg and Maureen sat Aoife on the edge of her bed, one on either side of her. Meg got the water and held the cup for Aoife whose hands shook too violently to hold it herself. Nuala rejoined them, kneeling before Aoife. With hands wiping roughly at her tears Aoife tried to speak.

"Shhh." Mrs. Linton attempted to hush her, but Aoife would not be deterred.

"The last thing...the last thing I said to him this morning..." her face contorted. "I told him if he couldn't come home sober today, then don't come home at all."

Hysterical wailing rose from her belly, emerging in great bursts from her throat. The others held her tightly.

"Mam." The word came quietly from Aoife. Her haunted eyes searched the room as if they would find her. "I want my mam." Spoken just above a whisper, it tore at the hearts of the others.

Darkness settled into the room. Nuala lit a candle. Aoife, worn out, sat limp between Meg and Mrs. Linton, her head on Meg's shoulder.

The door opened. Darien Linton stuck his head in. "He's in Owen's rooms. We thought it best. Owen has gone to Mr. Hurley's to see about a coffin. If one of you will sit with the body, I'll inform Father Boyce."

"Where is Kevin?" asked Meg.

"He went to find Rory."

"Why?" Meg was indignant. "He should have gone with you."

"If it goes as hoped, you'll understand."

"I'll sit with him," said Mrs. Linton rising from the bed. "We'll have to start preparing him for a wake."

A shiver ran up Meg's spine remembering the first time she had helped prepare a body. It was Rory's mam. Her body was smashed and mangled from the cottage being knocked down atop her. Meg knew she would be expected to help prepare Ned's body. She knew also that it would be even worse than Rory's mam. Silently she prayed, *Lord Jesus, give me the strength for it. I cannot do it without your help.*

Owen returned, stating that Mr. Hurley would have a plain pine coffin ready by morning. They could pick it up to save the delivery fee. Mrs. Linton sent Nuala to the apothecary for a small amount of laudanum to see Aoife through the night.

The body was washed and an old bed sheet, sewn by Mary into a vestigial shroud, was laid over Ned's severed legs and feet placed in their rightful positions, his shredded shirt replaced with a clean one. The door to Owen's rooms opened. Rory entered, blanched at the sight of Ned.

"Where have you been?" Meg murmured, exhausted. "It's nearly ten."

"Kevin came for me at the livery. He asked that Fancy be hitched to one of the wagons. Used his last week's pay to rent it. We stopped at Mr. Archer's home to leave off Caleb. When he heard what we were about, Mr. Archer insisted on covering the rental fee. Kevin argued, but Mr. Archer stood firm. Then we went off."

"Off where?" Meg asked.

"Come and see."

The entire group followed Rory across the hall to Aoife's door. It stood ajar. Gasps and stifled cries of "oh!" issued forth as they took in the sight. Aoife lay sound asleep on the bed. In a chair beside it sat Mrs. O'Sullivan, gently stroking her daughter's hair.

"Her face will be the first thing Aoife sees when she wakes up," Kevin whispered.

"You did this? You brought her here?" asked Mrs. Linton.

"I knew Aoife would need her mam. Rory, and I got a wagon, and brought her home. To stay," he told Mrs. Linton. "I've no one in Ireland to send money to. I'll do all I can to see that this family's not parted again."

"With my help, lad," said Owen, his voice husky with emotion. "Ned was my nephew."

Kevin nodded, glancing back at the sleeping Aoife and her mother framed by the glow of candlelight, then turned to the others. "Perhaps we should let them be."

Chapter Thirty-Nine

Meg stood next to Mrs. Claprood's desk. "I've spoken with Kathleen. She will not be able to cook for the wedding."

Pamela, sitting at the parlor table with Deborah, looked up. "She did explain to her mistress that it is *the* Thayers?"

Meg had made up her mind that she simply could not deceive the Claproods a second time. She cleared her throat. "Kathleen is no longer at the boardinghouse," she said. "She is in a convent."

"Kathleen has become a nun?" asked Deborah, eyes wide.

"No. She is cooking for them."

"They do not cook for themselves?" asked Mrs. Claprood. "I don't know much about nuns, but I thought they took a vow of poverty. How is it they hire a cook?"

Meg's hand gripped the rosary in her pocket. "She is not being paid," she said.

Mrs. Claprood eyed Meg suspiciously. "She left a paying job for one without pay? Why?"

Forgive me, Lord. "She's considering becoming a nun. She has to live there a while. To see if she has a true calling."

"Yet she spends her days cooking? How does that allow time for discernment?"

Meg's heart beat faster. "I don't know how it works, Ma'am."

"I see. And the nuns would not let her leave for one day? Not even for a wedding?"

361

"Margaret, please." Pamela begged. "Could you talk to them? Or ask your priest to talk to them? It would mean so much to me."

"I...I can't promise anything."

Meg was relieved by a knock at the door. Clara Pratt entered, looking distressed.

"Everyone is in the parlor, Miss Clara," Meg told her, taking Clara's bonnet.

"Clara, whatever is the matter?" Meg heard Pamela ask.

"I'm not supposed to speak of it," Meg heard as she hung the bonnet on a peg in the front hall.

"You can tell us," said Deborah. "We're like family."

Glancing into the parlor, Meg saw them draw Clara to the sofa. She started down the hallway, but stopped when she heard Clara say, "Father is sending Lemuel to England."

"Will you miss him so much?" Deborah teased.

Meg crept back towards the parlor door.

"It's the reason."

"What is the reason?" asked Mrs. Claprood.

"Lemuel killed a man."

"What?" There was a collective gasp.

"That man who was run over by the train last week."

Meg caught her breath. *Ned.*

The accident replayed itself in Meg's mind. Even she did not believe that Lemuel had purposely tried to kill Ned, but that push had indeed caused his death.

"Father was there. He saw Lemuel bump into the man and push him away. He landed on the tracks right in front of the train." Clara broke down in sobs.

"My dear, it was an accident," said Mrs. Claprood. Though she attempted to sound soothing, Meg detected a note of distress. "I'm certain your brother did not mean for such an awful thing to happen."

"Yes, but he should never have acted that way. Father said if that man had been someone who mattered, Lemuel could have been arrested."

Someone who mattered. In other words, not Irish, thought Meg.

"With Harvey having run off, it's all too much for mother to bear."

Harvey had run off? This was news to Meg.

"Father has had enough of Lemuel's behavior. He'll be sent to Birmingham to learn their new techniques in iron casting. He will be gone for at least a year."

"When will he leave?" asked Pamela.

"Before the end of August."

Meg could hardly wait to get this news to Kathleen. Perhaps she would not have to leave Worcester! She would ask Father Boyce if he could arrange for her to see Kathleen again. This could change everything!

* * *

On the last Thursday of July, Meg met with Kathleen to give her the good news. "If it's for certain he'll be gone, I will cook for the wedding," she told Meg. "I won't enjoy seeing Mrs. Pratt again, but I would dearly love to see Miss Clara."

An idea dawned on Meg. "It will be so busy leading up to the wedding. Do you think the Sisters will let you stay with me at the Claproods for a few days? I'm sure Mrs. Claprood would be happy for the extra help."

"I don't see why not. Once Lemuel is gone, I won't need to stay at all except that I've nowhere to go until I find another job."

"I will let you know the moment he departs. May it be soon!"

Meg's heart was light as she left the convent. Lemuel would soon be gone for at least a year; Kathleen would come days ahead of time to help prepare for the wedding. Once it was over, Kathleen could look for another position in Worcester. Heading back to Crown Hill, Meg felt like skipping.

363

"You look happy," said Nuala when Meg arrived at the Denton's. "Does that mean Kathleen knows the scourge of her existence is to leave for England?"

"Indeed she does."

"And will she cook for the wedding?"

"Aye, she will. And if Mrs. Claprood agrees, she will come a few days early to help."

"Would you like to stop at the Claproods' and ask now?"

"Oh, I would!" said Meg.

Mrs. Claprood, Pamela, and Deborah were delighted at the turn of events. "Yes, please have her come early. Perhaps Monday before the wedding."

Once that was settled, Meg and Nuala strolled out into the bright sunshine. With no specific plans they walked the Crown Hill neighborhood, looking at the new houses going up. Oxford Street, Crown Street, Congress Street, and the Crown Hill sections of Pleasant and Chatham Streets all had new construction.

"Funny how they all want their houses to look the same. Always with the long windows and big pillars," said Nuala. "Mrs. Denton told me the style is called Grecian. They're meant to resemble Greek temples."

"Back in Ireland we had one room," Meg reminisced. "But it was always filled with laughter, singing, and joking, even while we sewed together by the window. Until the starving. We were happy to be together, to be a family. *That's* what I want. The house is just a place to put it."

Nuala sighed. "You're right enough. I wonder if there will ever come a day when being an Irish man doesn't mean you get the lowest of jobs if you can get one at all."

"Rory's job isn't the lowest," said Meg, pride swelling her heart.

"He's the exception."

As they turned onto Congress Street, Nuala pointed to a newly built house. "What do you suppose is the purpose of all that glass?" she asked. The house was fronted with a glassed-in porch. "Must have cost a fortune."

Before Meg could answer, the clop of horse hooves sounded behind them.

"Rory!" Meg called when she turned to see him astride a fine chestnut colored horse. Beside him, on a much smaller one, sat a young lad.

"Megeen, my love!" Rory called, as the horses came to a stop. "And with her the very rose of the O'Flaherty clan! A fine afternoon for a stroll, is it not?"

Meg shaded her eyes as she looked up at him. It was the first time she'd seen him ride. What a dashing figure he cut! "What brings you here?"

"Taking Caleb home," said Rory pointing to the house they'd been discussing.

Caleb tugged on Rory's sleeve, giving him a quizzical look.

"Ah, forgive my ill manners. It must be the sun," he said, grinning ear to ear. "Master Caleb, allow me to introduce to you my darlin' wife, Mrs. Quinn and her dear friend, Miss O'Flaherty. Ladies, this young gentleman is Caleb Archer, son of Mr. Hiram Archer of Archer Lumber."

"Pleased to meet you," said Caleb, doffing his cap and nodding towards each woman in turn.

"Pleased to meet you, as well," said Meg. Hearing Rory speak of her as Mrs. Quinn was as sweet in her ears as the chime of church bells. Watching his manner with the lad she thought what a good da he would be. His confidence with the horses, his air of gentility even if it was only mimicked, assured her he could hold his own with any Yankee gentleman.

"We were admiring your father's house," Nuala told the boy. "But why all those windows?"

"To grow things," Caleb answered. "My mother loved her vegetable garden. As there wouldn't be room for one here, father made a greenhouse of the porch."

As they spoke, a horse and carriage approached from the other direction.

"That's Father now," said Caleb as the driver passed through an open gate. Mr. Archer alighted stepping directly from the carriage through a door onto the porch. The horse and carriage then disappeared behind the house.

Having seen the group, Mr. Archer waved them over.

"How did your lessons go?" he asked his son.

"Very well, Father. Rory is a good teacher."

Mr. Archer smiled. "Glad to hear it. And who have we here?" he asked turning his attention to Meg and Nuala.

"Rory's wife and her friend. Oh, that is to say, Mrs. Quinn and Miss O'Flaherty, may I present my father, Mr. Archer?"

Mr. Archer's brow raised slightly. "Why, Mrs. Quinn, a pleasure to make your acquaintance." He took her white gloved hand, kissing the air just above it. Meg was glad to be meeting Mr. Archer on a Thursday when she and Nuala were dressed like Yankee women.

"And Miss O'Flaherty, a pleasure to meet you as well."

Caleb dismounted from Fancy. Handing the reins to Rory, he turned to his father. "I didn't know Rory was married. Did you, Father?"

"I did not. This is a pleasant surprise. Were you ladies walking in the area?" he asked, looking perplexed.

"It's Thursday," said Nuala. "Our day off. The weather is perfect for a stroll."

"I see. You work nearby then?"

"I work for the Dentons and Meg works for the Claproods."

"I haven't met many of the neighbors yet, I'm afraid. You must work on a live-out basis," he said to Meg. "You are fortunate to find such a position. I'm told most families prefer their help to live in. Or perhaps you have a profession?"

Meg glanced at her feet. "I live with the Claproods."

Mr. Archer turned towards Rory who had dismounted and stood among them.

"Meg and I were married just before her ship sailed from Ireland. We've both worked and waited to be together, going on ten years now. We're saving as much as we can to have a place of our own."

Mr. Archer took a step back, his mouth falling open. "You've been married ten years?"

"Aye," said Rory. "I stayed in Ireland caring for our families while Meg came here. She's been sending back money and a fine job she's done. She brought over her sister, Kathleen. Once Meg's brother reached an age where he could take over, I joined her here." Meg was thankful for Rory's discretion regarding Brendan.

"My Megeen is why I'm so grateful to you for the added job of teaching Caleb. The extra money brings closer the day we can live together."

Mr. Archer's face still held a look of wonder. "I am amazed by your perseverance. I hope your wait won't be much longer."

The driver returned from behind the house. "Horse and carriage are put away, Sir," he said. "Will that be all?"

"Would you ride Fancy back? She belongs at Hendry and Copes. That way you won't have to walk and Rory is freed from leading her back with his own mount." He turned to Rory. "Do you think that would be satisfactory to Mr. Hendry?"

"I don't see why not," Rory answered, handing the reins to the driver.

"Mr. Archer do you keep your own horses, then?" Nuala asked.

"Two of them, Miss O'Flaherty" said Mr. Archer. "In my carriage house on the property. Rory, might you be interested in seeing it?"

"I would," Rory agreed.

"You ladies are welcome, of course."

The house extended a ways back, much larger than it appeared from the street. Meg could not help eyeing the three imposing stories, the long stretch of house that connected to a smaller section with barn style doors and small square windows beside them, placed higher up.

"I've never seen such little windows," said Nuala.

"For the horses," Mr. Archer explained. He opened the doors to reveal the carriage pushed all the way to the back while along the walls hung a variety of horse accouter-

367

ments. Two sleek Arabian geldings stood in stalls, one on either side of the building.

"They're perfect beauties," Rory gushed. "May I?"

"By all means," said Mr. Archer, opening one of the stall doors. "This is Molasses. He's the one you saw pulling my carriage."

Molasses, named for his deep brown color, contentedly munched hay, oblivious to his admirers.

Next Mr. Archer opened the door to the other stall. "This," he said beaming proudly, "is my pride and joy. His name is Eclipse."

Rory gasped. Meg crept closer, awed by the animal. He a was pure black Arabian, gleaming as though he'd been coated in lacquer. His tail was a long plume, his mane thick, voluminous. Even standing still, the well-toned muscles rippled under his sleek skin and hair.

"What he must be like to ride!" Rory said.

"Imagine riding a streak of lightening," said Mr. Archer. "Feisty, too. Still, he's a horse you can trust as long as he trusts you." Eclipse neighed, tossing his mane in a haughty manner.

"You can see why I want Caleb to start with a well-schooled horse," Mr. Archer said to Rory as they exited the carriage house.

"Aye, indeed. Those two are not for beginners."

Mr. Archer chuckled.

"Does that belong to you, Mr. Archer?" asked Nuala, pointing to a half-finished building set back from the house.

"Yes," he said, his voice losing its cheerfulness. "That was supposed to be an art studio for my daughter, Amy. My children were raised to know that because they had been given much, much was expected of them, as is written in the Scriptures. Amy would have worked hard at her art lessons, making the most of the gift God gave her. Now, though..." He lifted his hands then let them drop to his side. "I don't know. Perhaps, I'll just tear it down."

Rory had told Meg the family's story. Her heart ached for this kind man in his terrible sorrow.

"Don't tear it down, sir" she said. "Perhaps you'll think of something that honors Amy's memory."

Mr. Archer looked curiously at Meg. "What a fine idea. I will give it thought."

That night Meg dreamed of Rory atop a fine black stallion. He galloped toward her, bent to scoop her up, never so much as slowing the horse's pace until they came to the door of a large, beautiful house. The front door.

Chapter Forty

On the morning of September first, 1856, Kathleen arrived at the Claproods'. She found the home buzzing with activity despite the early hour. Eager to put her cooking talents to use, she'd brought along her newest receipt books.

"What first?" She asked Meg, noting her sister's tired eyes, wrinkled apron, and cap askew.

"That's a good question. Everything is so topsy-turvy. We've been sewing for two weeks straight making Miss Pamela's *trousseau*. At least that's almost finished."

"Her what?"

"*Trousseau*. A French word for a big trunk to be filled with clothes, bed and table linens. Yank brides must all have one. Everything brand new. We've made dresses and underclothes to last years! There are petticoats, corset covers, nightgowns, nightcaps, dress sleeves, and handkerchiefs aplenty. I've been sewing my fingers to the bone."

"All that yourself?"

"The Claprood ladies have helped. Miss Clara, too. It wasn't so bad until they started shopping. They spent so much time at the dry goods stores, they left the rest of the sewing to me."

"What on earth was left to buy?"

"Armloads of sewing notions, linens, shawls, slippers, hair combs, bonnets. Such extravagance seems a sin to me, but all necessary because Miss Pamela's marrying a Thayer. She'll be receiving guests of high standing. Hosting grand ladies. She doesn't want to embarrass her new husband by not measuring up to expected standards." Meg rolled her eyes. "Lucky I am, all I had to give Rory was my heart."

Kathleen shook her head. "There's so much about these people I'll never understand. Am I to help with the sewing, then?"

"The *trousseau's* nearly finished, thank goodness. The dressmaker has been several times. Wait 'till you see the wedding dress she designed. 'Tis a beauty. Mrs. Claprood, and Miss Deborah got new outfits designed by Mrs. Atkins as well. We'll need you to help finish them tonight. As if that weren't enough, Master Oliver and Mr. Claprood must be properly attired, too."

Kathleen laughed.

"What's funny?"

"Properly attired? You sound like a Yankee!"

Meg shrugged, laughing. "There's no help for it! Miss Pamela's got an embroidered silk waistcoat going for Mr. Thayer. Thank goodness that's a gift from the bride so she's to make it herself."

"I thought you loved sewing."

Meg sighed. "I could do it all day if it was my only duty."

"Well, I'm here now."

"Every room in this house will be put to use" Meg explained. "The master bedchamber is to become a dressing room for guests to fix their hair and adjust their gowns upon arrival. Tea and sandwiches, scones and jams will be set out all around the first floor. Extra tables are arriving today just for that. Oh, and the best china will be used for all of it, even the cucumber sandwiches, with the plates sitting on white doilies, no less."

Kathleen saw the blood rise in her sister's cheeks as she spoke. She put a hand on Meg's shoulder. "Calm yourself. You won't get things done any faster by working yourself into a lather. Let's make a list. We'll put it in order of when each task must be completed and work our way through it. It's not all on your shoulders now."

Meg took a deep breath. "I'm glad you're here."

"I've never seen a Yankee wedding. Sounds like a spectacle to behold!"

371

Every day from sunup to sundown Meg and Kathleen worked, readying the house, finishing the sewing, making sure they had all the ingredients for the wedding supper, going to the market for whatever they lacked.

The parlor and conservatory were to function as the main rooms for the wedding and reception. For days Mrs. Claprood, Pamela, and Deborah changed their minds repeatedly about the arrangement of the rooms. Would the guests stand or be seated for the ceremony? Where would they set out the wedding feast? Which flowers from the conservatory would adorn the rooms? As the ceremony was to begin at eight o'clock in the evening, a new chandelier with four burners was installed in the front parlor. Two recently purchased candelabras holding five candles now stood on either end of the fireplace mantle, the mirror above to reflect their light.

"Do you suppose they go to all this trouble for only the oldest daughter?" asked Kathleen as they climbed into Meg's bed late on Wednesday evening. "Or will you have to go through this again when Miss Deborah gets married?"

Kathleen caught Meg's horrified expression in the candlelight.

"Miss Deborah hasn't got a suitor yet," Meg said. "I'd best not be here by the time she's to marry. I'd like to get on with my own marriage before then." Meg extinguished the candle plunging the room into darkness.

"I'm sorry," Kathleen said as they snuggled under the sheet. "It must be awful to go about this wedding nonsense when you and Rory should have been together long ago."

On Thursday afternoon Mrs. Atkins arrived to make sure everything was ready.

"Bridget, let Mrs. Claprood know I'm here," she said, stepping into the front hall.

Deborah appeared. "Mrs. Atkins, this is Margaret and her sister, Kathleen."

"Oh?"

"Margaret, who fixed my lavender dress."

372

Meg and Kathleen exchanged puzzled looks while Mrs. Atkins stared at Meg with an expression bordering on awe.

"You repaired Miss Deborah's ball gown?" she asked.

"I told Mrs. Atkins about how badly I tore it, Margaret, then showed it to her."

"Oh, aye," said Meg.

"Remarkable work," Mrs. Atkins' tone warmed. "How did you learn to sew like that?"

"From my mam. Then she nodded toward Kathleen, "the three of us did the mending work for the town ladies."

"Your work is impressive, Margaret."

"Thank you, Ma'am."

"As a dressmaker I rarely do mending, but many of my clients ask for it. Would you allow me to refer them to you?"

Meg readily agreed. When they were alone in the kitchen Kathleen noticed a smile on Meg's lips and a dreamy look in her eyes. At last. Something positive from all these wedding shenanigans.

On Friday evening Kathleen bustled about the kitchen with Meg and Nuala, who the Claproods had hired for the big night, at her bidding.

"Is there a room in this house that doesn't have food in it?" Nuala asked, returning from setting out the last tray.

Tables had been set up everywhere, rose petals to match the rose pattern on the fine china scattered over them. Plates of cucumber, watercress, and tuna sandwiches, raisin, current, and cranberry scones along with pots of fresh jam sat atop white lace doilies throughout the first floor of the house, with teapots, cups and saucers close. There was a bowl of punch in the upstairs room where the groom and his groomsmen would gather for a toast prior to the ceremony.

The kitchen was in as much disarray as on Thanksgiving. Oysters, roast pork, beef, and fish were to be served along with plum pudding and mince pie. The supper would not commence before eleven o'clock. Kathleen's fatigue from the relentless work week vanished once she'd begun preparing the festive meal.

"The plates and cutlery," she said, looking up from her work to motion to Meg and Nuala. "Please take them into the conservatory now. We can't be clanging about while the couple is saying their 'I do's'."

As the eight o'clock hour approached guests began to arrive. Meg had to peek out the window to see who was at the door. She was to step aside if it was the minister, for it was the task of the chief groomsman, Edward's brother, Richard, to greet the clergyman.

"Such a nuisance," Meg complained, as her work was interrupted for the fourth time. "I wish the minister would get here soon so I don't have to worry if I'll answer the door when I shouldn't."

Pamela, along with her bridesmaids, Deborah and Clara, were ensconced in an upstairs room for hours preparing for the wedding.

Kathleen, Meg, and Nuala, busy with their work in the kitchen, started when the back staircase door opened. Clara popped her head in long enough to say they were ready. This was Meg's cue to inform the groom and groomsmen that the ceremony was to begin. Shortly after she returned, she, Kathleen, and Nuala peeked from behind the dining room door to watch the ceremony.

The bridal party, walking arm in arm, with the bride and groom bringing up the rear, strode regally down the stairs, into the front parlor where they positioned themselves in a semi-circle facing their guests. It was the first look Kathleen and Nuala had of Pamela's wedding gown, a lovely dove colored silk with a lace over-dress. The bodice molded itself to her waist while the skirt flared out over several layers of petticoats. A long, full veil made of the same lace as the over-dress was held in place with a wreath of orange blossoms. Pamela carried a small, white prayer book in her gloved hands.

The minister began the ceremony. Kathleen thought how different it was from Meg's and Aoife's weddings. The bridal couple exchanged vows after which the groom reached into the pocket of the waistcoat Pamela had spent many hours embroidering for him, and brought forth a plain gold wedding band. Edward gazed adoringly at Pamela as he slipped the ring onto her finger. Several guests wiped tears from their eyes.

Once the ceremony ended, the minister presented Mr. and Mrs. Edward Thayer to all assembled. Meg headed straight for the kitchen. The newlyweds were quickly lost to sight as they became engulfed in a sea of guests offering congratulations.

"We'd best get back to work," Kathleen whispered to Nuala. "Please check all the rooms to see if any tables need to be replenished."

Kathleen entered the kitchen expecting to find Meg busy. Instead she was in a chair, her back to Kathleen, bent over, shoulders heaving, the comb Rory had carved in her lap.

Kathleen knelt before her. "It can't be much longer, Meg. Rory has a good job and extra from the riding lessons. Now you'll have extra from your mending."

Meg lifted her head, but kept her gaze on the comb. "I'm happy for Miss Pamela, I truly am. But knowing that her married life has begun, while mine..." Meg shook her head. "Ten years, Kathleen."

Kathleen took both Meg's hands. "Aye Meg, 'tis terribly unfair. But you're so close. God willing, you and Rory will have far more than a mere ten years wedded to come."

"You are the best sister anyone could ever have."

Nuala breezed into the kitchen. "We need more tea for three of the tables and the cucumber sandwiches are all gone."

Meg and Kathleen had time to disengage before Nuala registered that anything was amiss.

"What's going on out there?" Meg asked Nuala.

"They're still congratulating the bride and groom. The ladies can't seem to stop clucking 'Mrs. Thayer' as if the girl's Christian name disappeared the moment the reverend declared them man and wife. She don't seem to mind. Beaming like a ray of sunshine, she is."

From the kitchen they could hear the tinkling of the pianoforte. The Claproods had hired a player to provide background music for the rest of the evening.

What cooking had not been accomplished ahead of time continued for the next several hours. Meg spent most of the time washing pots, pans, mixing bowls, and all implements to be used and reused. When not up to her elbows in suds, she counted the number of tiny cake boxes lined up on silver serving trays, making sure each had an 'at home' card attached informing the recipient of when the couple would return from their wedding tour, ready to receive guests. Assembled the previous evening, these were to be sent home with each guest so it was important that they not be short any.

"They're lining up in the conservatory," Nuala announced upon returning from one of her forays. "It's only half past ten!"

"Dinner is to be served at eleven and it will be ready at eleven," said Kathleen.

"No surprise," said Meg. "There are so many guests some figure they'd best get in there early if they're to get a seat."

"They assume right," said Nuala. "They won't all fit in that room."

"That's why there are tables all over the house," Kathleen explained. "Speaking of which, would you clear the tea services to make room for supper plates?"

Alone in the kitchen, Kathleen surveyed her night's work. She hoped she'd created an attractive presentation for each offering.

Moments before it was time to transfer all the food to the conservatory, the three hurriedly washed their hands and faces then exchanged their stained aprons for crisp, starched ones.

"We're ready," Kathleen announced.

In a small parade the three women carried huge platters of food from the kitchen to the conservatory, setting them out on the long, pushed together tables covered with matching cream-colored linens. A few more trips and all the food

376

along with great bowls of lemonade and punch and several bottles of wine were out of the kitchen and on the tables. Toasting of the bride and groom began soon after. Meg, Kathleen, and Nuala returned to the kitchen to get the cleaning done while the guests enjoyed supper.

"I wish I hadn't sat," said Meg when they finished. "I don't think I'll be able to rise from this chair."

"We'll all sleep well tonight, that's for certain," said Nuala.

"If we ever get that luxury," said Meg. "Imagine all the cleaning once they've finally cleared out."

"It's nearly one now," said Nuala. "They can't stay much longer, can they? Why don't they do these things in the morning or afternoon like people with some sense in their heads?"

The kitchen door opened. Mrs. Claprood beckoned to Kathleen. "You must come at once," she said.

"Is something wrong?" Kathleen's mind raced. What could have gone awry?

"Quite the opposite. Mr. Nathaniel Thayer, Junior is so impressed with the food, he wants to meet you."

"Is he Mister Edward's father?" Meg asked.

"No, dear, he's Edward's cousin. Quickly, Kathleen. He's an important gentleman."

"Mr. Thayer, this is Kathleen O'Connor," Mrs. Claprood introduced her. "She's the sister of our Margaret. We borrowed her for the evening as we do for every Thanksgiving week. She's the wonder of the kitchen."

Kathleen bobbed a curtsy, then stood straight and tall meeting the gentleman's eyes. He smiled broadly. "I have never had such delectable fare in all my life. You have remarkable talent."

"Thank you very much, sir. 'Tis kind of you to say so."

"Are your services currently engaged?"

"No, sir. I've been staying with the Sisters of Mercy while I...considered joining their order, but I've realized it is not my calling."

"A loss for the Sisters, but a gain for your next employer. I've a very dear friend whose wife is looking for a head cook. They live in Lancaster. I would be delighted to recommend you to them if you are interested."

Kathleen's heart skipped a beat. Head cook – her heart's desire! But where was Lancaster?

"I'm not familiar with that town. Is it far?"

"About thirty-six miles. A few hours by coach."

A few hours from Meg. She didn't know anyone there. What if the family was like the Pratts? How could she bear that without her sister to lean on?

"Sir, are you sure they won't mind that I'm Irish?" she asked. "And Catholic?"

Nathaniel Thayer laughed. "My dear girl, the Beardsley's have several Irish Catholics in their employ. They care not about from whence they come nor what religion they profess. It is a rather grand mansion. You'd be working with a full staff. If what I experienced tonight is any indication, I'd say you're up for it. May I speak to the Beardsley's on your behalf?"

"Aye, sir. You may," she said, head held high. "I thank you kindly for it."

"Very well. How can you be reached?"

Mrs. Claprood beamed. "You are welcome to send word here, Mr. Thayer. Margaret can reach her sister."

Once released from the conversation, Kathleen hurried back to the kitchen to tell the good news. Meg threw her arms around her, nearly lifted her from the floor.

"What a triumph for you!" Nuala chimed in.

"I haven't got the job yet," Kathleen reminded them.

"You will," Meg insisted. "Think of it, Kathleen. You'll spend your days doing what you love best."

"I'm sure they've got a kitchen the likes of which you can't imagine," said Nuala. "And a full staff. You'll be in charge of the kitchen, giving orders to your assistants. You must write often and tell us about it."

Meg lifted a stray hair from her sister's brow. "Wait until Mam hears. She'll be ever so proud!"

Chapter Forty-One

As Rory walked to the livery stable, he turned over in his mind the recent conversations he'd had with Kevin. Through another man at the wire works, Kevin had learned of job openings on the railroads in the west. "There's a vast land out there," Kevin had rhapsodized. "They're building more railroads, pushing further west. You can start from scratch in a place where maybe being Irish isn't such a hindrance."

Rory wasn't interested. He had a good job. Two jobs. Soon he and Meg would make a decent home together. He'd not be dragging her across the country. Meg had waited too long.

Kevin, however, was determined to go. He planned to leave before year's end to work on the railroad, sending money back to Aoife. Meanwhile he'd get to know the land, see if there was a way he could make a go of it. If so, he'd return, marry Aoife and take her, her mam, and her bairns west to a new life.

Rory had sensed the attraction from the beginning. They weren't officially courting with Aoife still in mourning. She'd never say it, not being one to speak ill of the dead, but she was calmer without the threat of abuse hanging over her. She and Kevin had fallen into an easy friendship especially once Owen invited Aoife, her mother, and the wee ones to live with him so as to lift the burden of paying rent for their own rooms. It was a kind gesture, but Owen's rooms were now almost as crowded as those of the Lintons – another reason Rory wanted to find a place as soon as possible.

The tangy scent of late October air leaked through the factory smoke. Rory inhaled deeply whenever he caught a whiff of it. It was faint in this section of Worcester, stronger where Meg lived. How he wished he could give her a home where she could enjoy the earthy smell of rain, the sweet scent of blooming flowers in the spring and the musky sweetness of decaying vegetation in the autumn. For now, he just hoped to find something a step or two above the Arcade.

"Morning," Isaiah mumbled, nodding to Rory as they reached the stables simultaneously, though from opposite directions.

"'Tis bound to be a lovely day, don't you agree?"

Isaiah grunted his assent before heading to the back of the stables where the conveyances were housed.

Rory laughed. He'd grown fond of Isaiah once he'd figured out that the man, though short on words, was made of integrity. His work was impeccable as was his punctuality. Mr. Hendry said that Isaiah had never missed a day since the livery opened over ten years ago. On the rare occasions he offered his opinion, it was because he felt too strongly to hold his tongue. He'd say his piece once and be done. Some thought him irascible, but Rory believed he was simply a quiet man who valued his privacy. He liked knowing Isaiah was in the stable, his presence a solid pillar holding everything in place.

Breccan, however, managed to irritate Rory every day. Lately he had added to his faults by smoking a pipe during dinner break.

"Not a good idea, lad, what with all the hay" Rory admonished the first time Breccan lit up.

"Ain't your business."

Isaiah walked by at that moment. "Take it outside," he'd said, his voice flat as ever.

Breccan had scowled at Isaiah's back, but stepped out the door with his pipe.

As happened often, Breccan sauntered into the stable twenty minutes late today.

"Again?" Rory said.

Breccan shrugged. "I see none of the horses carrying a watch."

"The horses aren't the ones who hire and fire, now are they?"

"Neither are you. Or were you thinking of squealing?" Crossing his arms, he gave Rory a sideways glance.

"Get to work. And finish a job. I'm sick of having to complete what you leave half done."

"Too bad for you," said Breccan, entering one of the stalls.

Rory shook his head wondering what gave the lad such a miserable attitude.

Later in the day, Rory was in one of the stalls when Breccan passed by on his way to the loft. "Little rich boy is here," he said, nodding towards Caleb who had just entered the stable.

Rory poked his head out. "Afternoon Caleb. Go get Fancy ready. We'll work on cantering today."

Caleb made a beeline for Fancy's stall. Rory was pleased with the boy's progress. He'd proven an apt pupil, attentive, good at taking direction, never offended by correction. Eager to learn, he'd grown comfortable with Rory. They'd formed an easy friendship but one which left no doubt that Rory was in charge.

Rory could hear Caleb speaking gently to Fancy while he cleaned each of her hooves of any stones, then brushed her down to rid her of dirt that might irritate her under her saddle.

Finishing his own job, Rory entered Fancy's stall to watch Caleb as he threw a blanket over Fancy's back, making sure the front of it touched right up to her withers as Rory had taught him.

Knowing the saddle was too heavy for him to throw onto Fancy's back, Rory had just reached for it when they were both startled by the sound of footsteps down the ladder. Rory turned to see Breccan half-run, half-fall from the loft.

"What's this?" Rory asked as Breccan landed in a heap.

Without answering, Breccan scrambled to his feet and ran out the door. Rory rolled his eyes. "Rascal," he muttered.

Watching Breccan's hasty departure, Isaiah heaved a heavy sigh. "Might want to check the loft 'fore you leave," he said.

"I'll do that."

Rory placed the saddle atop Fancy's blanket. "Go around to the other side," he instructed Caleb. "Keep your hand on her as you go...because?" he prompted.

"Never walk behind a horse without touching her so she knows where you are, else you're liable to get kicked," Caleb recited as he followed to the letter.

"Good, lad. Now, what's the first thing you're going to do?" Rory asked.

"Throw the stirrup over the saddle," came Caleb's voice from the other side of Fancy.

He pulled a box up near the horse. Rory watched as the small hands settled the stirrup atop the saddle. "What's next?

"Pull the strap down here," said Caleb. Rory could see his face under the horse as he reached for the hanging strap. "And slip it through the buckle."

Rory nodded. He'd make sure everything was pulled snug before they set out so that the saddle wouldn't fall, but wanted the boy to learn by doing.

"Now it goes through the first metal ring," said Caleb. "And now the second one. Pull tight and make sure everything is even." Rory couldn't help smiling as he heard more of his own words repeated back to him.

"Pull it through again, come at the ring from the right, loop it through and pull tight," Caleb continued. "This side is done."

"Now I'm going to reach under and grab the belly strap." Again Caleb's head bobbed beneath the horse. "Next I'm going to –"

"Wait!" Rory cut him off.

"What? Did I miss something?"

"You're doing fine," Rory said. "Stay here. I'll be right back."

A crackling sound had caught Rory's attention. The smell of smoke, different from that which often wafted in from the factories, gained intensity. Quickly Rory made for the ladder, taking every other rung in his hurry. Sparks shot through the hay on the far side, the section almost right over Fancy's stall.

"Caleb! Isaiah!" he yelled. "Get out! The loft is on fire!" The words were barely out of his mouth when the sparks erupted into flames, catching from bale to bale in rapid succession. Rory scurried down the ladder in time to see a floorboard engulfed in flames land in front of Fancy's stall, blocking the entrance.

Isaiah appeared, his face grim. "The boy's in there," he said.

"Caleb, can you hear me?" Rory called.

"Yes," came the timid reply.

"Are you where I left you? You haven't moved?" Rory called as he grabbed a bucket, sloshing water from the closest trough into it.

"I'm here."

"Good. Stay so I know where you are. I'm coming."

The two men threw bucket after bucket of water at the burning floorboard. It was no use. Flames fell through the hole in the hayloft floor. Smoke choked them. Horses whinnied and neighed. The battering of hooves kicking stalls competed with the crash of falling timbers.

Rory upended a bucket of water over his own head, thoroughly drenching himself. Grabbing a shovel, he swung at the burning, upright floorboard knocking it away. Once in the stall, he slipped free Fancy's rope and shoved her. The terrified horse balked. Isaiah then grabbed her mane, pulling her out. Rory found Caleb huddled on the floor. He yanked off his soaked shirt, wrapped it around the boy, and crouching as low to the ground as possible, carried him out of the stable, depositing him on the sidewalk.

Bells clanged as fire engines headed for the stable. Isaiah had taken Fancy out to the street. Good. Rory put the

383

lead rope in Caleb's shaking hands. "Keep her steady. Isaiah and I will get the others out. Will you do that, lad?"

The boy nodded. Good enough.

Rory and Isaiah started from the back of the stable where the worst of the fire raged, setting each horse free, shoving them out onto the street. When the fire engines arrived, the firemen took over. Rory sat with Caleb at a safe distance, Fancy next to them. Isaiah had disappeared. Rory knew all the horses were out, so Isaiah's vanishing unnerved him. He could be lost in the gathering crowd, but something told him otherwise.

"Stay here," he ordered Caleb. "Don't move unless the firemen tell you to," he said, noting that they were hosing down the closest buildings to keep the fire from spreading.

Retrieving his wet shirt from the boy, Rory darted down a nearby alley to cross over behind the stable. As he'd feared, he found Isaiah struggling to pull out the conveyances.

"Leave them be!" Rory called over the crackling frames.

"They're my responsibility," Isaiah called back.

"But not worth your life."

The man was not to be deterred so Rory grabbed hold of one side of a carriage's traces. With Isaiah on the other side, both pulled hard. Rory was astounded that the older man had attempted to undertake it alone. They got out all but three vehicles before the roof collapsed.

Isaiah hung his head. Rory patted the man's shoulder. "You saved most. No one could fault you for the ones that were lost."

"Still, it rankles." They stood together, watching. As the walls caved in on themselves with a mighty groan, Rory felt his ability to provide for Meg caving in with them.

"Move away!" the firemen yelled as more onlookers joined the crowd.

"We should go," said Rory, noticing men dragging pumpers in their direction. "I'd better check on Caleb."

Skirting the firemen, they returned to the street. It appeared that half of Worcester was gathered on Exchange

384

Street. Rory searched the crowd for Caleb. He was not where he'd left him. Looking farther down the street, he noticed all the horses gathered together. Caleb was there with Mr. Archer and Mr. Hendry. "Come on," he said to Isaiah.

"Praise the Almighty!" said Mr. Hendry as Rory and Isaiah approached. Caleb flung his arms around Rory's waist.

"The boy told us what happened, but when we couldn't find you, we feared you'd gone back inside."

Rory ruffled Caleb's hair, then gently disengaged, returning him to his father's arms.

"After getting Caleb and all the horses out, Isaiah went back to try to save the vehicles. I only helped. Three were lost, sir."

"I'm grateful for your quick thinking and bravery, both of you," said Mr. Hendry, pumping Rory's hand and then Isaiah's. "The building is gone, but you saved the horses and most of the conveyances. Most importantly, you rescued Caleb."

Isaiah looked uncomfortable. "Did the best we could. Sorry we couldn't get to them all."

"The building, the vehicles – they can be replaced. Insurance will cover most of it. No one was hurt, that's what's important."

Mr. Archer, who'd been clutching Caleb tightly since Rory returned him, let go of the boy and stepped forward. He put a hand on each of Rory's shoulders. "Caleb said you risked your life to save him. I can never express how grateful I am."

"It took the two of us." He nodded towards Isaiah.

"You, sir, have my everlasting gratitude as well," he said, shaking Isaiah's hand.

"Only did what any decent man would."

"Where is that scoundrel, Breccan?" asked Mr. Hendry. "Caleb thinks he is somehow responsible for the fire."

"Aye," said Rory. "Smoking a pipe in the loft, most likely."

"We told him not to smoke in the building," Isaiah added.

Mr. Hendry nodded, his countenance grim.

"Rory!" He heard his name called over the din of voices and rushing water from the hoses.

"Meg!"

She scrambled towards him, shoving and elbowing aside any gawkers who couldn't be bothered to move.

"Thank God," she cried, throwing herself at him.

Rory wrapped his arms around her. Her maid's cap had been lost in her flight. Locks of black hair, loose from her bun, tumbled down her back. She sobbed in his arms, holding him so tightly he thought his ribs would break. Years of labor had further strengthened a powerful woman.

Isaiah coughed, whether from the smoke or discomfort at her public display, Rory wasn't sure. Meg let go enough to look into Rory's face. Her own was tear-streaked. Wet strands of hair clung to one cheek. She squeezed his arms.

"Megeen. I'm fine. We're all fine," he said, brushing the soaked tresses behind her ear.

She looked from Rory to the collapsed, smoldering stable, then back.

"I know," he whispered. "I'll find another job."

Her brow furrowed. "Is that where you think my mind's at?"

"Well...I...is it not?"

"By all the saints in heaven, Rory Quinn! I was looking at that heap thinking how close you came to being under it. Then I was thanking the good Lord with all my heart that you are not."

"But we've waited so long, worked so hard, and we were so close."

"Ahem."

Rory and Meg turned to Mr. Archer.

"I require a caretaker for my property, one who could also handle my two Arabians. I thought of you, Rory, but was reluctant to lure you away from Mr. Hendry. Given the present circumstances the job is yours if you want it. You'll be well compensated. There are two good sized rooms on the far end of the third floor. You and your lovely bride are welcome to live there. I currently employ a cook who lives out. If Mrs. Quinn would care to take on the duties of running my household, I'd be most obliged. For a proper salary, of course."

Meg and Rory stared at Mr. Archer, then at each other. Caleb took each of their hands. "Oh, would you, please Rory, Mrs. Quinn?" he begged.

"Meg?" Rory asked.

A smile unfurled across her face. "Aye!" she said.

Rory lifted her in his arms, swung her around, oblivious to the curious, perplexed, and horrified stares of the nearby crowd.

Chapter Forty-Two

Early in the morning of the following Thursday, Meg made her way to the Arcade with a proposal for Aoife. Though Mrs. Claprood had been sorry to lose Meg, she wished her much happiness. Meg had asked if Mrs. Claprood would agree to hire help on a live-out basis at least temporarily until she could find a replacement, hoping Aoife would assent. Mrs. O'Sullivan could watch the children while Aoife earned better pay than she could returning to factory work. Mrs. Claprood was reluctant, but when Meg promised to instruct Aoife on all the necessary duties, she consented. Now all Meg had to do was convince Aoife.

"Meg, you darlin'!" Aoife threw herself into Meg's arms. Meg was pleasantly surprised, but life had changed for Aoife. She had taken Meg into her confidence about Kevin. He had been able to secure a position as a railroad worker in Missouri and would leave in the spring and be gone at least a year. He'd send much of his pay to her while watching for any opportunity to make a life for them in the west. Aoife wanted to contribute to their future. Meg's offer was an answer to a prayer she'd never dared to pray.

Mrs. O'Sullivan was delighted at the thought of watching over her grandchildren while Aoife worked.

"Come," said Meg. "I'll introduce you to Mrs. Claprood. The sooner you settle in the position, the sooner Rory and I can be together."

Aoife peered down at her tattered dress.

"Don't worry," said Meg. "We'll go in the kitchen door and straight to my quarters. You can borrow something of mine. With the money you'll earn you'll have much better clothes before you know it. Remember I'll be only a short walk away. You can come for my help anytime."

Once clad in one of Meg's dresses, Aoife was ready to meet Mrs. Claprood.

"What if I say the wrong thing?" Aoife fretted.

"Mrs. Claprood's a love," Meg assured her. "You've nothing to worry over."

They entered the parlor where Mrs. Claprood sat at her desk reading the latest anti-slavery pamphlets.

"Mrs. Claprood, this is my friend, Aoife MacBrody."

Mrs. Claprood looked up, smiling. "Very nice to meet you, Aoife."

She bobbed, her curtsy a graceless dip. "Very nice to meet you too, Mrs. Claprood."

"Tell me, what experience do you have with homemaking?"

"I keep house in our rooms. I cook all our meals, though I'm sure they're not so fancy as what you have here. Meg said she'd teach me everything. I promise to work hard and do my best."

Mrs. Claprood smiled warmly. "I'm sure you will. When can you begin?"

"As soon as you like Ma'am, but..."

"But?" asked Mrs. Claprood.

"I've two bairns."

"Two what?"

"Children," Meg interjected.

"Oh, yes, Meg has told me."

With her next words, Aoife surprised Meg for the second time that morning. "I won't leave them if they're sick. I'm taking work to support them, but I won't be less of a mam to them for all that. I hope I don't seem rude, but I had to make certain there's an understanding between us about it."

Mrs. Claprood rose from her chair. She took Aoife's hands in her own. "That speaks well of you. It is understood. Will you have a way to let me know if you can't come?"

"I'll send Mary, Aunt Maureen's oldest. She's nearing the age to go out to work herself. Perhaps she could take my place if there's a day I can't come."

Turning to Meg, Mrs. Claprood said, "Would you please show Aoife the house and go over her tasks before you begin your afternoon off?"

"You're hiring her?" Meg asked.

"I'm willing to try this arrangement." Turning back to Aoife, she said, "You may return home before dark each day and have every Thursday afternoon and Sunday morning off. Your wages will be the same as those paid to Margaret when she began. Is that satisfactory to you?"

"Aye, Ma'am."

"Very well, then. Welcome to our home, Aoife."

Aoife broke into a broad grin. "Thank you, Ma'am. Thank you so very much."

Meg spent the rest of the morning taking Aoife through every room in the house, showing her where all the cleaning supplies and cooking implements were kept, and explaining all her duties.

By afternoon, Nuala and Kathleen arrived at the kitchen door. They all trooped up the back staircase to Meg's attic chamber. Nuala had brought along an overnight bag borrowed from Mrs. Denton. Over the years, Meg had accumulated more belongings than would fit in the humble sack she'd brought from Ireland. Still, it didn't take long for the four of them to have Meg packed and ready to move to her new home.

Kathleen flopped down on Meg's bed. "You said you'd have a home of your own one day."

"It's not my home," Meg reminded her. "We'll be living in Mr. Archer's house. We've a section of the third floor to ourselves, is all."

"For now," said Kathleen. "But you'll make good money, the two of you. You'll have a house that's really yours before you know it. Has Mrs. Atkins sent anyone to you yet?"

"No," said Meg. "But she did ask Mrs. Claprood where to find me once she heard I was leaving." Meg laughed.

"It's not like I'm going far." Congress Street was adjacent to Crown. It wasn't much further than around the corner, but suddenly it felt a world away.

"What of you, Kathleen?" asked Aoife. "When do you leave?"

"The Beardsley's are sending a carriage for me on the eighth of November."

Aoife sighed. "It's strange how so much has changed."

Meg glanced at Nuala. "How long will you stay on at the Denton's?" she asked.

Nuala shrugged. "They're getting on in years. Mr. Denton is sick more often than not. One of their daughters has mentioned taking them to live with her, so I might be out of a job sooner than I think."

"Maybe you could work here," said Aoife. "I might well be temporary," she added. No one but Meg and Rory knew of her brewing romance with Kevin.

"Possibly," Nuala agreed. "At least I know they're a good family. But I doubt I'll ever find a family as amusing as the Dentons."

* * *

That night, Meg slept for the last time in her attic bed. Aoife would arrive early the next morning and work with her throughout the day. The last meal finished, Meg would join Rory at Mr. Archer's house. She lay in bed thinking of all the years she'd spent with the Claproods. She wouldn't be far away, but leaving was bittersweet. She'd worked hard. She expected to work just as hard for Mr. Archer even once her wee ones began to arrive.

Meg ran a hand over her flat belly. Could it be possible that within a year she might become a mother? Sleep eluded her. The past and the future fought for her attention. By the time morning came she was no longer sure whether she'd slept or not, whether all the images floating in her brain had been waking thoughts or dreams.

* * *

The last dish was returned to the cupboard when a knock sounded at the door. Meg opened it to find Rory and Kevin standing in the moonlight. Kevin planned to come every workday, refusing to let Aoife walk alone to the Arcade after dark. Aoife went off to let Mrs. Claprood know she was done for the day.

Meg and Rory gazed into each other's eyes.

"Are you ready?" he whispered.

She nodded. She had changed from her maid's uniform into the brilliant blue dress that set off her eyes like sapphires.

In the next moment, Mr. and Mrs. Claprood, Oliver and Deborah filed into the kitchen with Aoife in their wake. They surrounded Meg, Mrs. Claprood and Deborah hugging and kissing her, Oliver and Mr. Claprood wishing her well.

"Take good care of our Margaret," Mr. Claprood said, turning to shake hands with Rory. "She's quite dear to us."

"I will, Sir. You've no worries about that."

"Aoife, you did a fine job today. We'll look forward to seeing you in the morning," said Mrs. Claprood as Kevin helped Aoife into her cloak.

"Thank you, Ma'am. I'll be here bright and early."

The two couples left the house, strolled down the back walkway to the sidewalk where they said their good nights, setting off in opposite directions.

When they reached Mr. Archer's home, Rory let Meg in through the kitchen door.

"Would you like a look around?" he asked. "Or wait for morning?"

"I'll wait," said Meg

Rory smiled. "Come, then. I'll show you to our rooms."

Our rooms. How beautiful the sound of those words.

Before they could reach the back staircase, Mr. Archer and Caleb appeared in the kitchen.

"I won't keep you. I just wanted to welcome you both to your new home."

"How grateful we are for your generosity, Sir," Meg said.

"My dear, it is I who am indebted beyond any measure of repayment. If it weren't for Rory, I'd have lost my boy."

He looked down at Caleb, by his side. "He's all I have left. What would I do if I'd lost him, too?" The man's voice was now almost a whisper as though he'd forgotten they were there.

Meg placed her hand on his arm. "Mr. Archer, Rory and I understand what it is to lose family members. Many at once."

"Yes. Of course. That's a bond we'll always have."

Caleb tugged at Rory's sleeve. "You're not going to bed yet, are you, Rory? I've been practicing my knot tying. I want to show you."

"Oh, no you shan't!" said Mr. Archer, trying to contain a laugh. "We shall send Rory and Mrs. Quinn on their way with our good nights. Your rope tricks can wait until morning."

Caleb's pout quickly changed to a grin. "That's right! They live upstairs now. Tomorrow, then?"

"Aye. Tomorrow," said Rory.

Once they reached the second floor, Rory set Meg's bags down inside a room with a sloping ceiling and one window. A rocking chair was tucked under the eaves along with a small writing table with a lamp in the middle. To the left, just inside the door was the bed. It was large enough to hold two with room left over. The rails of a brass frame gleamed in the soft light at its head.

Our bed. Meg's heart beat hard. She had not expected to feel so nervous.

"Meg?" Rory asked, catching her hand in his own and pulling her down on the bed beside him.

"You are so beautiful," he whispered, reaching up to pull out the hairpins that held her bun in place. He ran his fingers through her hair, smiling, his gaze never leaving her face. He took her chin between his thumb and forefinger, lifting her face to his, leaning close.

"Wait," she said, just before their lips touched.

393

Meg reached into her pocket, pulled out the comb he had carved for her. She stood, faced him, slid the comb through her hair, slowly, sensuously, letting the hard tines do their work of stroking the tangles from the thick locks that fell just beyond her hips.

Rory took her waist, pulled her to him. She let the comb fall on the bed and herself into his arms until they lay side-by-side. He traced the lines of her face, kissed her mouth, nibbled at her ear lobes. Meg leaned into his arms, holding tight. Soon they were shed of their clothes, marveling in each other's caresses. It was more wonderful than Meg had imagined. Sensations she could not have guessed at rippled through her, engulfing her in wave after wave of ecstasy.

What pleasure was to be had in the marriage bed! For the rest of her life she could experience such rapture with the man she loved with all her heart. She prayed that soon they'd be blessed with tiny lives they'd make together with their love.

As there was no lady of the house in Mr. Archer's home, Meg was given free rein regarding the housekeeping. Ten years of working for Mrs. Claprood had taught her well. Best of all, she was relieved of cooking!

Mr. Archer's house was larger than the Claproods'. There were three floors plus an attic. The carriage house was Rory's domain, but Meg passed through often as the laundry room opened onto it. After washing a load of laundry in the huge soapstone sink, she carried it down the short flight of steps leading to the second floor of the carriage house then out atop a porch where she hung it to dry. If Rory was in the carriage house, he'd always give her a knowing smile. She'd smile back, a coy game, a promise of nighttime delights to come. It was a new courtship, perhaps a product of having been denied their marital bed for so long.

Meg loved having an entire section of the house to themselves. Across from their room was another, larger, empty room with a pitched ceiling. They had not yet decided what to do with it. Meg sometimes stood in the doorway, imagining a sitting room, a place to which they could invite friends. It could also make a nursery.

Just beyond the laundry was a whitewashed room meant for ironing and sewing. Meg set up all her sewing paraphernalia on one of the large tables placed between two tall windows. She hoped some of Mrs. Atkins' customers would solicit her for mending soon.

Just beyond the sewing room was a door that was a curiosity. It opened onto another back staircase, this one leading to the third floor where presumably the children of guests were to sleep. This same door, when swung in the other direction, closed off Meg's and Rory's section of the house from that of the Archers. She liked to close off the hallway. It helped to make their section of the house feel truly separate and their own.

The rooms meant for family and guests were exquisite. Meg was especially fond of the grand staircase. It curved elegantly from first to second to third floor turning gently around on itself in a wide spiral.

Meg's favorite room in the main part of the house was the parlor. It featured what at first appeared to be floor-to-ceiling windows, three of them in a row. Meg soon found they were not windows at all, but each one a double door fitted with large panes of glass. French doors, Mr. Archer explained. They led out onto the glassed-in porch she and Nuala had admired from the street. *Oh, would Pamela and Deborah love this porch*, thought Meg, as it served as a greenhouse with rows of pots and standing beds filled with vegetables and flowers. A gully ran the length of the porch closest to the street.

"It's for the water," Mr. Archer had explained. "We don't want puddles all over the porch, so we water the plants here and the water slides down." At the end was a small hole in the floor out of which the water ran to the ground below. "It was Sophia's idea," he said, his voice gone quiet. "I imagine what she would have done out here," he said, his gaze traveling over the plants still hanging on despite the early November chill thanks to the heat retained by the glass.

Meg's second favorite was the dining room. She loved the rich crimson wallpaper with its large cream-colored flowers, the blue, rose, and green geometric shapes of the carpet beneath the oval walnut table, and the great white marble fireplace. What intrigued Meg the most was the brass chandelier that hung above the table. Four upward curved arms branched out from its center topped with open white globes. Rather than candles, the chandelier was lit with gas. Mr. Archer showed her how it was done. Fascinated, Meg was also a bit fearful of it. She was unable to picture Mr. Archer's explanation for the use of the extra gas jet on the chandelier.

"When we have guests for a special occasion, you'll attach one end of rubber piping to the jet and the other to a lamp in the center of the table. That way we'll have light from above and at table level. It's the newest thing," he said.

Despite the greater size of the house, Meg did not find it any more difficult to keep up with than she had the Claproods. With only Mr. Archer and Caleb to serve and Janet to do the cooking, it was, in many ways, easier.

Meg received permission from Mr. Archer to host a small gathering on Thursday, November sixth. Kathleen was to leave for her new position at the Beardsley mansion that Saturday. Meg wanted to give her a send-off. She invited the Lintons, Aoife and Mrs. O'Sullivan, Kevin, Owen MacBrody, and Nuala. She wanted Clara Pratt as well, but wasn't sure how to go about it. Clara was seventeen now and had not had any contact with Kathleen since the wedding.

Finally, Meg decided to ask Deborah Claprood for help. Relishing the flirt with danger, Deborah readily agreed to act as messenger, advising Clara of Meg's invitation. She devised a ruse whereby Mrs. Pratt would think Clara was spending an evening with Deborah to practice elocution. Fortunately, the celebration coincided with a large church meeting for the Pratts and Claproods.

Clara and Deborah walked together to the Archer home, knocking on the kitchen door. Heartily welcomed, both made themselves at home.

Well wishes, expressions of happiness over Kathleen's good fortune, and tears at her leaving formed the basis of the festivities.

At one point, a knock sounded at the door between the kitchen to the main section of the house. Meg and Rory exchanged amused glances. Only Mr. Archer would knock on a door in his own home!

"I thought you might be interested in this," he said as he entered brandishing a newspaper. "It's the final results of the presidential election."

All voices stopped. For the Irish, this election was a matter of survival. A Know Nothing victory could mean deportation. A Republican victory might not be as bad, but the Republicans had taken on the nativist agenda as a tactic to lure disillusioned Know Nothings. Only a Democrat win would ensure their security in their adoptive country for the next four years.

"It says here," said Mr. Archer, making a show of snapping the paper taut before continuing, "that the fifteenth president of the United States of America, duly elected by the people of this great nation, and to be inaugurated on March fourth in the year of our Lord, eighteen hundred and fifty seven, is..." he stopped, looked up from the paper to make eye contact with each person in the room, all of whom appeared transfixed, eyes riveted on Mr. Archer, "James. Buchanan, Junior."

A roar went up the likes of which should have blown the windows out of the house. Rory lifted Meg in the air, swung her around, and kissed her soundly in front of everyone.

"Saints be praised!"

"And all his angels!"

"Glory be to Jesus!"

The shouts of thanksgiving continued amid relieved laughter, hugs, and backslapping. Only Deborah and Clara remained calm. A Republican win might have brought the country closer to an end to slavery. Still, both young women hugged their friends when they saw their palpable relief.

"I won't disturb your party any longer," said Mr. Archer. "I just wanted to bring you the news. And I thought perhaps, champagne might be in order."

Mr. Archer reached for the door to reveal Caleb unsteadily balancing a bottle of champagne and several glasses on a silver tray.

Swiftly, Meg took the tray.

Glasses were filled, toasts were made, Mr. Archer and Caleb congratulated the guests *en mass* then wished Kathleen all the best in her new position before leaving the little throng to their revels.

"You've got a corker for an employer," said Mr. Linton.

"He's a darlin' that's for certain," Meg agreed.

As the evening wound down, each took a turn saying goodbye to Kathleen.

Only Aoife and Kevin stayed behind waiting to walk Kathleen back to the convent on their way to the Arcade. While they chatted with Rory, Meg took Kathleen aside.

"I'm so happy," she said. "But I will miss you something awful."

"At least it's not like when a whole ocean was between us. I'll write. You do the same."

"I will."

"And you let me know when," she said, furtively patting Meg's belly.

"Nothing yet," said Meg.

"I want to be the first to know. Well, the first after Rory, of course. Promise."

Meg laughed. "I promise."

"Kathleen?" Aoife called. "I hate to take you from Meg, but we should go."

"I'm ready," said Kathleen.

"I'm not," said Meg. The sisters embraced. "Be the best cook the Beardsley's could ever hope for," she whispered. "Enjoy every minute of it. And never, ever forget how much you're loved."

"Meg, you will always be my inspiration."

As they closed the door on their departing guests, Rory held Meg tight. "Lancaster's not far. You'll see her."

"I know," said Meg. "She's a life to live and so have we."

Chapter Forty-Three

Thanksgiving Day 1859
Worcester, Massachusetts

Meg smoothed one hand over her belly as she set the dining room table. Several weeks late for her courses she was sure another bairn was on the way. She'd yet to tell Rory. She'd want him to know first, but she also wanted to tell Kathleen before she returned to Lancaster. This year the Beardsleys had been invited to spend Thanksgiving with relatives in Connecticut. That left Kathleen free to spend Thanksgiving week with Meg and Rory. This would be the first year they'd have her to cook the Thanksgiving feast. As she placed the last plate on the table, Meg took a deep breath, savoring the scents emanating from the kitchen. In the next moment, a wave of nausea washed over her. Another sign.

This was also the first year Meg and Rory would not spend Thanksgiving with Mr. Archer and Caleb. They had been invited by the sister of Mr. Archer's late wife to spend the holiday week with them in Maine. They were invited every year, but until now, Mr. Archer hadn't the heart to go. This year, however, he'd decided it was time Caleb got to know his mother's relatives better.

Lifting her gaze from the table, Meg took in her surroundings. Even after more than two years of living in the little cottage, it sometimes still didn't feel real. She had to look hard at the rooms, the furnishings, the decoration to remind herself that this home did indeed belong to her and Rory. The building Mr. Archer had intended as an art studio for his daughter had become a small, two-story cottage – a home Meg and Rory could call their own. Mr. Archer worked out a plan whereby Rory did the lion's share of physical labor to finish the building, then had a small amount deducted from his weekly pay until the cost was completely covered.

They'd moved in July of 1857, one month before the birth of their twin girls, Siobhan and Saoirse. Now she was sure another would be joining them in less than a year. The thought caused a fullness in her heart, with tears threatening at the corners of her eyes. Another sign of new life sprouting within. She would tell Rory tonight.

"We're almost ready," said Nuala, popping her head into the dining room.

Once Mrs. Atkins began recommending her and word spread about her superior sewing abilities, Meg had more mending work than she could manage. After the twins were born, she became overwhelmed trying to care for them while running Mr. Archer's house as well as her own. So at the end of 1857, when Mr. Denton passed away and Mrs. Denton sold the house and went to live with her daughter, Nuala was hired as a maid-of-all-work by Mr. Archer. It freed Meg to attend to her other chores. Since Meg and Rory had moved into the cottage, Nuala was given their section of the "big house" as she referred to Mr. Archer's home. During spring of this year, Nuala had married Seamus O'Herilhy who still drove freight for Archer Lumber Company, the two of them occupying the rooms Meg and Rory once used. Meg took great pleasure in teasing Nuala, the confirmed spinster, who had finally succumbed to the handsome driver.

"I'd not have married were it not for the unusual circumstances," Nuala would always insist, referring to her ability to continue working and earning money despite being married. Meg had her doubts having watched them fall ever more deeply in love over the years. Unless she missed her guess, it would have taken an enormous act of will for Nuala to decline his proposal. In any case, Meg was grateful for Nuala's constant presence. Rory and Seamus had become close friends. Meg hoped Nuala would soon bring wee ones into the world. She loved the idea of their children growing up together.

Meg went to the parlor where Rory sat conversing with Seamus and Darien Linton. The Linton children, scattered about the floor played games, the older girls keeping an eye on Meg's napping twins. Only the Lintons' eldest, Mary, was missing. Mary, having taken over for Aoife, now lived with the Claproods. Once Kevin had returned after a year's work on the railroad, he married Aoife and took her along with her bairns, her mam, and Ned's uncle Owen back to Missouri where he and Aoife ran a dry goods store. They all lived in a log cabin he and Owen built together. Their first child had been born this April – a boy they named Brian in honor of Father O'Malley, Kevin's beloved pastor in Ireland.

"Come to the dining room. Dinner is nearly ready," Meg announced, amused at how they all scrambled to get at Kathleen's food.

Too small a room for this crowd, only the adults would eat in the dining room. The children would sit at a borrowed Archer table in the parlor. But all gathered in the dining room first for the initial formalities.

For the first time in her life, Meg presided at her own dining room table for Thanksgiving dinner. Rory led them all in praying the Catholic Grace. Then, just as she'd seen Mrs. Claprood do, Meg stood to carve the turkey Kathleen set before her.

It took a good portion of the afternoon to eat the huge repast Kathleen had prepared.

"I don't think I can get up from this table," said Darien, moaning and rubbing his stomach. "But I don't regret a single bite."

"We'll wait a bit before serving the pies, then," said Nuala.

"Pie! Pie!" The cry came from the parlor as the younger children clamored for dessert.

"Where do they find the room?" Seamus asked, glancing through the open door at the band of youngsters.

Meg grinned. "First carry your plates to the kitchen, all of you."

"I love this holiday," said Maureen as she joined the line-up of women scraping, soaking, scrubbing, drying, and putting away the endless crockery, "but sure it is I'm glad it only comes once a year. This was the finest one ever. I wish my sister could have been here to share it."

"Mrs. O'Sullivan and Aoife are having their own Thanksgiving in Missouri." Meg said.

"I'm sure we'll hear all about it. I'm grateful to Father O'Malley for teaching Kevin to read and write so he can keep us informed. And for teaching you and Rory the same so you can read the letters to us and write back. He's a great man, that Father O'Malley, may the good Lord bless his soul. There aren't many of us can read and write."

"It will be different for our bairns," said Nuala. "Especially now that William Rice is mayor."

Up to her elbows in soapsuds, Meg lifted her head high and recited the new mayor's words from memory. "The next generation, at farthest, will pull down any division walls which the present may build, and it is better therefore, for all good citizens to aid in the process of assimilation and absorption, than by any unwise and partial measures to defer its completion."

"Think of that, Meg," said Nuala. "Our children will be educated right alongside their Yankee neighbors."

"You'd better get starting having them, then," said Meg, handing her a soapy plate.

"Seven more months should do it," she said, rinsing and passing the plate to Mrs. Linton to dry.

Meg dropped her dishrag. "What? Are you?"

"I am," said Nuala.

All dish washing stopped as the women threw their arms around Nuala, hugging and congratulating.

"I'll be right back," Meg said.

She went to the parlor, sought out Rory, and drew him outdoors. The frosty air of late November felt good against her skin, heated from being in the kitchen with its fired up stove.

"I've something to tell you and it can't wait another minute." She took his hand, placed it on her belly.

"Too full for pie?" he asked, grinning.

"Hardly."

"Another one, then?"

She nodded.

He pulled her tightly to him. "I love you, Megeen."

Upon returning to the kitchen, Meg resumed her place. "There. Now that Rory knows, I can tell. Nuala and I will have bairns at about the same time."

Kathleen gasped. "Meg!"

Nuala's head snapped in her direction. "They'll go off to school together!"

"Aye. Walk hand-in-hand."

The dishes done, they all gathered in the parlor. Everyone hushed as Meg unfolded the most recent letter from Ireland, written by Father O'Malley as dictated by her Mam.

To my sweet lasses, Meg and Kathleen, and that darling of a lad, Rory,

Imagine a home of your own with rooms, upstairs and down! I try to think of you in it, but can't quite get it settled in my mind. I wish I could see it. Someday when I'm in heaven, I'll look down on you and then I'll finally know what it looks like.

We were glad to hear from Kathleen that she loves her position. The Beardsleys sound rich as kings. She says they're very good to her so we're grateful. It's another thing I like to picture – Kathleen with a staff of servants taking orders from her. When you were all wee ones hanging round my skirts, your da and I would never have dreamed such things could happen. It should make you wonder what the future holds for your own bairns. May it be good, please God.

Saints be praised that Rory does so well with taking care of the horses and property with no trouble from his hand. He's as fine a lad as ever there was, Meg. Only your own da could equal him.

We were all glad to hear of Kevin's wedding and move west. He's an adventurous spirit, that one. He'll do well. Father O'Malley is especially gratified to learn how far he's come. They write to one another you know, so we keep informed about that family, as well.

Mrs. McDermott's daughter had her likeness taken, not a drawing or painting, mind you, but something that captured her image by some sort of contraption. [Note from Father O'Malley: Your mam means a daguerreotype. I suppose you've heard of them, even seen them in the homes in which you've worked.]

If there's any chance, and it's not too dear, would you have such a thing done of yourselves and send it to me? I'd cherish it forever. It's been so long since I've laid eyes on any of you that I don't know what you look like now and I've never seen my grandchildren. It would do this old heart a wonder of good to have it. But if the cost is too much, I'll understand.

Here Kathleen interrupted. "So that's why you did it? Why didn't you tell me?"

"It was a surprise," Meg answered.

The day following Kathleen's arrival they had all dressed in their best clothing, Rory, Meg, Siobhan and Saoirse, and Kathleen, to have their likeness taken by a photographer. It would be sent with the next letter home.

Meg continued.

Aisling has a dressmaker's shop of her own now. She does a grand business yet still comes by once a week to visit. She looks well, says she's never felt better. The lass is a walking miracle if you ask me.

Brendan's time in Australia taught him more about farming than a lifetime of growing potatoes in Ireland could. Now that the land laws have changed and we've such an improved state with Sir Alfred, Brendan's growing all sorts of crops. He's a small pig farm as well. Loreena and Brigid help a lot with that. God bless those little piggies, they seem to have brought Brigid back to herself. She

405

has an occasional lapse, but for the most part she's the bonny lass she was before the starving. She can do almost as much work as Loreena now and Loreena's as powerful as a Viking.

I'm well enough for an old woman. My dreams are peaceful, praise God.

Doctor Parker sends his best wishes to all. Father O'Malley sends his prayers and blessings. All of us send our love.

Forever in my heart,
Your loving mam

More than one eye was being wiped by the time Meg finished reading.

"I miss them all," said Kathleen.

"I've heard of some who've gone back," said Nuala. "Lasses who didn't marry, but saved their money for a trip home. Some went for a visit. Others went to stay."

"If you save your money, Kathleen, you might be able to visit," said Meg, hoping it for her sister, wishing it for herself.

"Perhaps," said Kathleen. "I've decided to do what Nuala always said she'd do. Stay single, save my money, and have enough to live on with a place of my own once I'm too old to work. A trip home might cut into that a bit, but it would be worth the sacrifice. I just wish I could take you all with me."

"You might want to leave for a while, if war comes," said Darien.

"Do you think it will?" asked Nuala.

"Mr. Brown's raid on Harper's Ferry last month has a lot of folks riled up," said Rory.

"He's going to hang," said Darien. "Not sure if that will make things better or worse."

A shiver ran up Meg's spine. She looked at her twins playing with a set of blocks on the floor. She thought of the new brother or sister who would join them before next summer ended, God willing. The idea of their world being disrupted by war was unbearable.

The sun had set by the time several pies were sliced and plated. As they started on dessert, a knock sounded at the door. Meg opened it to a gentleman who immediately removed his hat and asked, "Is Miss Kathleen O'Connor here?"

Something about him looked familiar.

"I'm Harvey Pratt, Mrs. Quinn," he said. "I'm sorry to intrude, but if I might have a word with your sister, I'd greatly appreciate it."

Meg remembered hearing that Harvey had run off a few years ago. What would he want with Kathleen? She opened the door enough to allow him entrance. "Wait here," she said.

In a moment, she returned with Kathleen, Rory, Nuala, and Seamus.

"Master Harvey?" said Kathleen.

He broke into a wide smile. "I'm so glad I found you. Clara wrote that you'd be here this year. My family has gone to Concord as usual, so I decided to make the trip to Worcester while they're away."

"Oh." Kathleen was obviously puzzled. "Why didn't you go to Concord?"

Harvey looked down, running the rim of his hat through his fingers. "I wanted to speak with you. You're the reason I came home."

"I am?"

"I want to thank you. In person."

"Thank me? For what?"

"You were the one I told how much I wanted to be a jeweler, but my father was adamant about my going into the family business."

"I remember."

"You told me I should be allowed to do what I loved. That I had a right to it."

Kathleen nodded. "Your mam was not at all pleased when she heard."

"I'm sorry for that. But if not for you I would likely be working at the foundry and miserable."

"I never told you to run away from home."

"Nonetheless, I needed to do it. You were the only one who believed in me. And you stood up to my mother, more than once. I came to the conclusion that if you had that much courage, I had better be able to summon some up for myself. You inspired me, Miss Kathleen. I wrote letters to jewelers in New York without anyone knowing. When one of them, Josiah Avery, agreed to take me on as an apprentice, I went. It was exactly the right thing for me. I'm on the road to success and, I hope, happiness. I've never forgotten that I owe a great debt to you for encouraging me especially at a time when I was at my most obnoxious," he said, a blush rising on his cheeks.

"Aye, that you were!" Kathleen laughed, then reached out to give him a hug. "I am happy for you Master Harvey. I hope no lasting harm's been done between you and your parents."

"We've reconciled. Father visited me in New York. He told me that he'd learned that trying to force any of us to his way of thinking only pushed us away. Once he got a look at my work, he even said he was proud of me." Harvey's voice broke as he uttered those last words.

He looked past Kathleen at the others, then back to her. "I won't bother you folks any longer. I only wanted to thank you."

Harvey turned toward the door, but before he could go, Rory stepped forward, introducing himself.

"We were about to enjoy some of Kathleen's pies. You're welcome to join us."

Harvey's eyes lit up. "Are you sure? I don't want to intrude."

Rory glanced at Meg who smiled and nodded her approval.

"We're sure," he said.

When the last of the dessert dishes were put away, Harvey seen off, and the Lintons on their way home, Meg settled her sleepy children into bed. Exhausted, Kathleen returned to Mr. Archer's home with Nuala and Seamus, ready to tumble into the bed in the room across from theirs.

408

The house finally quiet, Meg returned to the kitchen to await Rory who was bedding down Mr. Archer's horses for the night. She sat at the table, watching the chamber candle's flame flicker. Meg would only have candles in the house. Mr. Archer had tried to convince her to let him put in gas fixtures, but she refused. She was never comfortable lighting those in his home. Her mind was set forever on the subject when on New Year's Day a gas explosion destroyed the Pleasant Street firehouse and damaged a nearby school.

The door opened bringing in a blast of chilly air. Rory entered, sat beside her.

"A wonderful day," he said.

Meg tore her gaze from the flame to look at Rory, breathing deeply of the hay and late fall air that clung to him. "The best Thanksgiving ever," she said.

Rory traced the strong cheekbones of Meg's face with his fingertip. "You are the love of my life, Megeen," he said, his voice a husky whisper.

"And you mine," she answered.

"While I was in the barn, I was thinking about the day I proposed to you. It seems a lifetime ago."

Meg nodded. "Aye. It does."

He took her face in his hands. She covered them with her own, then kissed the rough knuckles of both. "It was all worth the wait."

The End

IF YOU ENJOYED THIS BOOK, PLEASE LEAVE THE AUTHOR A REVIEW

Eileen O'Finlan holds a bachelor's degree in history and a master's degree in pastoral ministry. Her debut novel, *Kelegeen* was published in 2017 and in 2018 became a BWL bestseller. She lives in central Massachusetts with her calico Maine coon cat, Autumn Amelia.

Author's Note

Worcester is a real city in central Massachusetts. Some incidents in *Erin's Children* come directly from Worcester's history, particularly the Merrifield fire and the riot that occurred when Federal Marshal Asa O. Butman arrived in Worcester.

The Merrifield fire was believed to have been started by an overheated sewing machine as described in the story. Several adjacent businesses were destroyed in the fire and about five hundred people were put out of work. There were a few injuries, but no deaths.

My depiction of the riot brought about by Marshal Asa O. Butman's appearance in Worcester follows the accounts written in local newspapers of the time. Several people mentioned in the riot scenes were real people who played a role in that incident. Their words and actions are those attributed to them in contemporary accounts. I did not put my own words into the mouths of non-fictional characters.

The Crown Hill area where Meg, Kathleen, and Nuala live and work, is now designated as an historic district. I tried to stay true to the architecture and the continual home building of the time period. According to one of the experts on Worcester's history with whom I consulted, when Worcester's wealthiest citizens began leaving Main Street to build homes in the Elm Street area, they really did sell entire rooms from their Main Street mansions to new homeowners, many in the Crown Hill area who, in turn, had their own houses built around a room or two moved from a Main Street home.

The catacombs under the downtown city streets are also real and according to Charles W. Longeway, Sr., author of *Worcester's Forgotten Catacombs*, have been in existence since the 1700s. They are closed off now, but Mr. Longeway, a former Worcester City engineer, has seen, photographed, and diagrammed them. To the best of my ability, I depicted them in *Erin's Children* as they are described in Longeway's book.

As part of my research for writing *Erin's Children*, I studied the Worcester City Documents for the decade of the 1850s which included all the annual reports of the mayors and the city departments and committees for each year. Whenever possible, I used exact dates and weather conditions. For example, severe early frosts did occur in 1851 causing farmers to lose a good share of their harvest resulting in a shortage of produce and an early halt to all outdoor work. This created a measure of concern to the citizens of Worcester with regards to food shortages.

The hurricane was not real, however, in late summer of 1851 there was a severe storm that spawned a tornado which did take the roof off the Quinsigamond Village School building.

The Hendry and Copes Livery Stable is fictional. There was a livery stable in the Exchange Street area, though to my knowledge it never burned.

The brothel and its occupants are entirely fictional, though according to the City Documents, arrests were occasionally made for "keeping a house of ill-fame" which suggests that, like most cities, Worcester had at least a few.

Constant road construction and improvements were the bane of Worcester's residents in the 1850s as they are to this day. Some things never change!

I enjoyed incorporating some of Worcester's history into *Erin's Children*. However, this book is a work of fiction. While Thayer is the name of a prominent family in Worcester and Lancaster, Massachusetts, the characters of Edward Thayer and his relatives depicted in the story are entirely fictional.

BWL Publishing

bwlpublishing.ca